Louise Candlish studied English at University College London and worked as an editor and copywriter before writing fiction. She lives in London with her partner and daughter.

Visit the author's website at: www.louisecandlish.co.uk.

# THE DOUBLE LIFE OF ANNA DAY

Anna has waited a long time to fall in love, and now that she has she doesn't intend to let the small matter of Charlie's mother stand in her way. Meredith Grainger is well-bred, highly cultured and impossible to impress. Anna hasn't even been allowed to meet her. Then Charlie leaves the country on business for the summer and Anna decides to take matters into her own hands, reinventing herself into the perfect, butter-wouldn't-melt new model. Garden parties, Sunday tennis, little vintage dresses from Laura Ashley — it all seems so easy. Until, that is, she decides to join Meredith on an Art Explorer's trip to Andalucia. There, she begins to wonder if she might be a little out of her depth after all . . .

LOUISE CANDLISH

# THE DOUBLE LIFE OF ANNA DAY

615

*Complete and Unabridged*

# CHARNWOOD
*Leicester*

First published in Great Britain in 2006 by
Sphere, an imprint of
Little, Brown Book Group
London

First Charnwood Edition
published 2007
by arrangement with
Little, Brown Book Group
London

British Library CIP Data

Candlish, Louise
    The double life of Anna Day.—Large print ed.—
    Charnwood library series
    1. Mothers and sons—Fiction
    2. Large type books
    I. Title
    823.9'2 [F]

    ISBN 978–1–84617–725–5

Published by
F. A. Thorpe (Publishing)
Anstey, Leicestershire

Set by Words & Graphics Ltd.
Anstey, Leicestershire
Printed and bound in Great Britain by
T. J. International Ltd., Padstow, Cornwall

This book is printed on acid-free paper

*For J and M*

# Acknowledgements

My thanks to Claire Paterson and to Christelle Chamouton, Molly Beckett, and Rebecca Folland at Janklow & Nesbit, London; Jo Dickinson, Sarah Rustin, Clara Womersley, Louise Davies and the rest of the lovely publishing team; Jane and Michelle; Kate Knowles at Dulwich Picture Gallery; also Heather, Dawn, Joanna, Mikey, Mats 'n' Jo, Roni, Tracey, Chalkie, Mandy, Sharon, Nips and Greta for friendship and kindness during the writing of this book.

# PART 1:

# LONDON

# 1

Strange though it may sound coming from someone who sells for a living, I never expected to find myself deceiving people. As far as I was concerned, my boyfriend was the one who did that. He'd been leading a double life since the day we met, was celebrated for it, defined by it, his methods and motives debated even by those who'd never laid eyes on him.

First, there was the Dulwich Charlie, the well-brought-up boy who lived with his mother in the kind of grand wisteria-wrapped house that never finds its way out of the family — not while someone like Meredith Grainger defends the deeds, at any rate. This was the little prince who raised his breakfast cornflakes to his mouth using the same silver spoon he'd found there at birth, and who saw nothing peculiar in spending whole evenings with sixty-year-olds drinking sherry and discussing the new lecture programme at the Dulwich Picture Gallery.

And then there was the Charlie for everyone else, the one who ate takeaways in front of the TV using only his fork (though he drew the line at eating straight from the carton), and took pains to keep up with the football scores, the album charts and other matters of civilian importance. Citizen Charlie, I thought of him, the Charlie with the common touch, the one who touched me.

But when I pointed all of this out to him some months after we'd fallen in love, for I was busy at work and the full Meredith situation was slow to dawn on me, he said that everyone led different lives to a greater or lesser degree, sometimes *more* than two. There were those out there who were veritable *chameleons*.

'Who do you know who acts exactly the same with everyone?' he asked, reasonably. 'Think how different you are with your colleagues from how you are with me.' He always remembered to say different *from*, never different *to* (Meredith, I was to learn, did the same). We were lying in my bed at the time and a disused ashtray inspired an example. 'What about the other night, when we were out with Caro? You were *smoking* again. And I can't believe how much you swear when you're with your work crowd. You're ten times more cynical.'

All of this was true. While not Charlie's pupil exactly (even I know a Svengali must be older than his protégée and Charlie is my junior by four years), I had certainly cultivated a gentler, more sensitive persona when I was with him. He called it my tender side, which I thought made me sound like a particularly choice cut of beef. Nonetheless, I enjoyed exploring this other me and I enjoyed Charlie exploring her too.

Yes, there were two Annas, one for work and one for him, but that wasn't the same as leading two lives, and it was important to me that he recognised the distinction. I pulled the duvet up and propped myself on one elbow to face him.

4

'Of course we all adopt different behaviours ... ' — the plural seemed to lend my argument a clinical flavour — ' ... depending on who we're with. That's just common sense. No, what's the word ...?'

'Expediency?'

'Exactly. But just because I don't lie naked with my ad director when we're discussing rates doesn't mean I'm doing what *you're* doing. No, you have people in one life who don't even know the ones in the other exist!'

'Well, you know Meredith exists,' he pointed out, refusing to take me seriously.

'Yes, but *she* doesn't know about *me*.' How patient I was then! 'Do you realise that I still don't know your home address, Charlie?'

'Don't you?' He looked genuinely startled. 'Three Park Crescent, Dulwich. Happy now?'

'Hmm. I bet there's no such place. And did you even open that birthday card I gave you? Did you actually put it up in the house? On display?'

His eyes, the colour of clay, widened with amusement. 'On *display*? Yes, it's on my desk. Just for a limited period, mind you, before I donate it to the Tate.'

I tried not to giggle. 'I suppose you've scribbled out all the kisses in case *she* looks inside?'

'I prefer my kisses in physical form, if it's all the same.'

Adept at denial though he was, he was leading a double life all right, there were no two ways about it (actually, there were). I even looked the

5

term up in the dictionary when he'd gone, but reference materials were not especially well represented on my shelves and the only tool available, a pocket dictionary from my college years, listed nothing between 'double knit' and 'double-lock'.

Occasionally, now, I wonder if I shouldn't have been content with what I had. Perhaps I should have sat tight and concentrated my famous charm offensive on *him*. He was still a one-in-a-million catch, even if I was only allowed half of him, and since love magnified his delightfulness at least a hundredfold my stake was surely worth fifty non-Charlies.

He preferred his kisses in physical form. I remember the feeling so well it makes me tremble.

★   ★   ★

Today is the day. It's etched on the inside of my eyelids before I even realise I'm awake and when I pull up the bedroom blind it's scrawled across the sky Red Arrows-style. Over and over and over: 26 June. The last Saturday in June; the day before Charlie leaves for San Francisco; the date I set when I finally lost my patience with him and said, 'Tell her or I will.'

'I *mean it*,' I said next, and then I marched back to the office and wrote a big red M in my daybook, the one that holds every detail of every deal in current negotiation by the sales team. If it's written in there then it's definitely happening. Not that I'd be likely to forget a date of such import, of course, but you never know when you'll be in need of that extra visual prompt. I might suffer some rogue blow to the head, for instance, followed by full-on Hollywood-style amnesia and, lo and behold, Charlie would be free once more to bury his head in the sand — just where he likes to keep it.

Luckily it is Saturday so I don't have to share headspace for this personal crisis with the broader one of managing twelve developmentally arrested newspaper sales reps, or, for that matter, their scarcely more sensible group heads. (Only yesterday my number two, Steve, was found to be the brains behind a Friday afternoon frenzy that led to a waste-paper basket being tipped over Ronnie's head — cold coffee dregs and all.) Nor must I wait six hours for a hangover to lift, because I left the bar after one glass of wine last night expressly to keep a clear head for today. Act with a sober head, repent with a sore one, that's what my father always says. In his office fridge he has champagne for his clients and elderflower pressé for himself — they are almost exactly the same colour.

It is 9.30 a.m. by the time the phone rings. I am up, dressed, drinking coffee and staring at the small triangle of river visible from my living-room window. The water is pale and steely, and if I lean back on the sofa and narrow my eyes it looks like mercury is being slowly funnelled into the room. I don't know whether to be soothed by this or frightened. And it hardly helps matters that I can no longer look at the Thames or any of its bridges, buildings or walkways without thinking of Charlie.

'Is that you, Anna?' It's him, of course, but there is a flatness to his voice that makes me kill the smallest flare of hope that he's calling to say he's done the deed, he's bringing her across town *as we speak*. They're on Tower Bridge right now!

Foolish of me. Even if he had delivered, it would be *I* who must be presented to *her*. Any meeting between us would be on her turf.

'Charlie, hi.'

'That didn't sound like you at all.' He scrapes from the back of his throat that dry little chortle that's as familiar to me as my own voice.

'No? I assure you it is.' I don't chortle.

'You sound weird.'

'Weird?'

'I don't know, *guarded*.' His voice is an absolute heartbreaker in its own right, gruff and tender at the same time, the kind that would make kittens roll on to their backs and submit — were kittens ever in evidence in the kind of bars and restaurants we tend to inhabit. Women, then. I've seen the effect that voice has when he speaks to them for the first time: they sort of swallow and put their fingers to their lips to cover their disarmament. On the phone, disembodied, it is intensified still, filling your head with intimacy before buckling away, leaving you to imagine all kinds of reasons why. Distress? Lust? An adolescence devoted to high-tar cigarettes?

'I'm fine,' I say, trying hard to sound it. 'How come you're up so early?'

'Oh, I still haven't finished this bloody paper. I'll be mailing it off on my way to Heathrow at this rate. I'm seriously busting a gut here.' If I sound guarded then he sounds unusually free, which can only mean that Meredith isn't in the vicinity. He's probably at the top of the house in his studio, where only a sheet of toughened glass separates him from the open sky. I haven't seen his new workspace myself, refitted at Meredith's expense when he enrolled at architecture school, but he tells me the views over Dulwich Park are an inspiration. He says he sometimes feels like he's being cradled by the arms of the trees.

'That's cutting it fine.' But I find it hard to sympathise with deadline junkies as I like to have important documents tweaked to within an inch of their lives at least forty-eight hours before presentation. 'I suppose that means you're calling to cancel lunch?'

'No, not at all!' There's a pause while he considers how to handle this unyielding new me. Is it possible he's been thinking my ultimatum was just another piece of posturing? A bit of busy-body office-Anna sneaking mistakenly into the newly mellowed Charlie's girl who usually speaks for her?

Ever since I told him I'd decided that a year was long enough to sort things out he's been buying time. 'A year from the day we met or a year from now?' That was his first question. 'From the day we met,' I decided. 'Caro's party, end of June.' He didn't argue, just nodded, calculating the damage.

'It's only three months, Anna,' he says, now.

'Not even that. It'll go by in a flash.'

So his strategy *is* denial: no surprise there. OK, I'll play along for a minute or two with the idea that I'm sulking about the San Francisco trip. In reality I think it's an amazing opportunity for him; even I've heard of the architect Tomi Endo, who recently built an office block in the City that the press dubbed The Pinecone. If Charlie were to build up a relationship this summer that might lead to his returning to the Endo practice for the fourth year of his degree course, then his career will be made before it's begun.

'And of course I'm still on for lunch.' He's sounding bruised now and I snap on the TV to avoid succumbing. How can a voice be so seductive, *still* so seductive? Shouldn't my desire have faded a little by now?

Row upon row of frowning faces settle on the screen: Wimbledon.

'What's in store for us on this middle Saturday?' a smiling presenter in pearls is asking John McEnroe. 'Will the skies hold? Will a Brit battle into the second week?'

'What's that?' Charlie asks.

'Just the TV. It's the tennis.'

'Look, I just wondered if we can make it one-thirty?' he says, daring to let his mind get back to work. Two critical deadlines in one day; in any other circumstances he'd have my sympathy.

'Sure.' I should end the conversation there, but instead I can't help adding, 'So where's Mummy today?' I hear the intake of breath, imagine him closing his eyes as he waits for me to finally do it, to call in the debt. I can't believe this is actually happening: how did I get from precious new love who had kisses blown across the river when we parted to *bailiff*?

'Don't know,' he says, finally. 'Out with some friends, I think. We're supposed to be having dinner tonight.'

I can't help but find it significant that she gets the dinner date and I the lesser lunch.

'But what is it that makes that stroke *such* a winner?' a female voice breaks in.

'It's her follow through,' says John McEnroe straight off. 'So many players are let down by their follow through.'

'Where are you going?' I ask Charlie. 'For dinner?'

'She's deciding,' he answers, all casual.

Of course she is.

For the record, the M in my daybook stands for Meredith, or, equally, for Mother. The colour red denotes urgency. Or possibly danger.

★ ★ ★

Only one other person knows about today and it's the same person who introduced me to Charlie in the first place.

**I'm coming over**, Caro announces by text, **before you do anything you'll regret**. If I had binoculars I might just be able to see her out on her balcony across the river, where the tourists move below, predictably, magnetically, towards Tower Bridge — the mother ship, Caro calls it.

11

In fact, she must have been tapping at the keypad en route because the buzzer goes only a couple of minutes later. She enters, as she always does, as though arriving on set fresh from hair-and-make-up, all starry smiles and flouncy dark mane. Caro is very keen on the captivating qualities of hair. I've seen her swing it around her neck like a scarf; I wouldn't be surprised if she uses it to rope men's wrists to bedposts.

'So what's the poor bastard got in store for him, then?' she asks me, heading straight for the coffee pot. 'Bugger, this is cold!'

'I'll make some more,' I say, not moving from the edge of the sofa.

She sloshes cold coffee into a mug. 'No big deal, chum, I'll just bung it in the microwave.'

'But it'll taste awful.'

She laughs. 'Don't forget you're talking to someone who once drank a regurgitated B52 without even noticing.'

'Urgh!'

'Well, at least it was me who chucked it up in the first place!'

Caro is an acquired taste and I was happy to acquire her. She is the paper's promotions manager, my best friend in the office and out. We are like schoolgirls: we spend all day together and then when we get home we're straight on the phone with a whole headful of new thoughts. At thirty-one she's a couple of years younger than I am, her private life a fairly accurate representation of how mine used to be before I met Charlie, back when every night was a hen night.

Hedonistic, hysterical, untethered by commitment (we couldn't even *spell* commitment after the first couple of rounds, much less apply the concept to a member of the opposite sex). We even look similar, though my own long, dark hair will be shorn by Monday lunchtime. I haven't actually made the appointment, but everyone knows the first thing you do after a major trauma is get a haircut.

'So, Anna? Are you going to do it? Are you going to tell the old witch her son's a dirty stop-out or not?'

I nod, but I feel nervous; driving test nervous, smear test nervous, worse than either of those because I know I won't feel any better afterwards. I stare up at her, willing her to come up with something to save the day.

'You're not *really* going to go through with it?' She's resting her hip against the kitchen counter, her voice all grave and grainy, as though she's about to lead a studio audience through the moral maze of euthanasia.

'I have to stick to my guns,' I say and for some reason this makes her giggle. 'Caro! I mean it! My ultimatum was that if he hadn't introduced me to his family by — '

'His *mother*,' she corrects.

'His *mother*, his other life, by today — '

She interrupts again: 'By the *end* of today.'

'OK, by the end of today, then I would do it for him. You know what we said: no ifs, buts or maybes.'

'He's still got time,' she says, mournfully, looking at her watch. 'It's not even midday.' Caro

13

loves Charlie. Everyone loves Charlie. *I* love Charlie, more than ever, it would seem. She sighs. 'He's a fool . . . And to think I was tempted to try him myself!' That's her way of saying that bloody glad though she is to have missed out firsthand on this twisted nightmare, she's desperately sorry she pulled him across her polished parquet floor that day and delivered him to my smoking perch by the balcony doors. The party was crammed with new faces, but she chose him. 'When will you tell her, exactly?'

'I don't know. First, I need to meet him for lunch and find out for sure that *he* hasn't.'

We've discussed *how* to do it, of course, repeatedly, with conferences held at least weekly and any number of guest contributors gathering to put their oar in. (Meredith must be the only person left in London who *doesn't* know Charlie's going out with me.) Mostly we start with a letter full of elegant, winning euphemisms and end with Caro waiting in the car outside the Dulwich house, engine running, while I deliver the news to Meredith's face before being bundled back into the passenger seat and spirited out of the country for ever.

'At least he's going to be out of the way when you tell her,' Caro says. The same thought has crossed my mind; has it Charlie's? Does it make either of us a coward, or both? 'You know what?' Caro says. 'If I were him, I'd just lie. I'd tell you I'd done it and that we're all going to meet up just as soon as I get back. Easy.'

'He'd still have to do it eventually,' I point out. 'That's just playing for time.'

14

'Then give him some! He's a student again, remember? Deadlines mean nothing to these people. They operate purely on appetite.'

'Don't! You sound like Jojo.' My father's wife, Jojo, says I've been too results-orientated in my relationship with Charlie, focusing unduly on the Meredith factor (despite my protests, she continues to refer to the matter as an 'obsession'). The reason I do this, apparently, is fear of the intensity of my own emotions, traditionally — but not exclusively — a male failing. I impose business strategies on the relationship to create a frame of reference to which I can relate, hence all my talk of deadlines and delivery dates. She says I should just let things happen 'organically', especially as I'm in no hurry to marry him. (I have my reasons, not that I've ever let Jojo know them.) I say that's rich coming from someone whose seduction of *her* man resembled nothing better than a fox-hunt.

Caro is pulling strands of silky hair over her pout and sighing. 'God, it's exactly like when Dave wouldn't leave his wife for me.'

'Yes, except you didn't *want* Dave to leave his wife. That was your great *fear*, if memory serves. Anyway, Charlie shouldn't have to choose. He's not *married*. As far as I'm aware, there's no social stigma attached to having a girlfriend *and* a mother.'

Caro slurps more reheated coffee and tries a new angle. 'I spoke to Viv last night. She's been back over a week now, setting up her new practice. I was thinking she might be able to help

15

you work out how to break the news to the Big M.'

'The last thing I need is a life coach, thank you very much.'

'She told me on the phone she's offering 'Definitive Results'. It's on her business card.'

'Define 'definitive',' I laugh.

Caro's not the only one to remind me that our former colleague, Viv, is about to launch herself on the denizens of London as a goal-orientated relationships coach; the rest of the sales team could barely talk about anything else all week. The one thing they dislike more than someone leaving the paper in a bid to better himself is someone leaving the paper in a bid to better other people. I haven't seen Viv for months, not since she went off to do a course with the Dalai Lama or Jerry Springer or whoever it was. No, I don't need Viv. Whatever happens today, I'll be following my instinct, not hers.

'It's all so Victorian,' Caro says for the hundredth time.

'It's so *Edwardian*,' I say for the first. But Charlie is not Edward and I am not Mrs Simpson; this is not a constitutional crisis. I have merely asked my commoner boyfriend to tell his commoner mother that he is in love with commoner me and he has failed to do so, it's as simple as that. I should just walk away, shouldn't I? Instead, apparently, I am paralysed from the waist down. The problem is that my prince will *not* come again. The next man Caro leads across the room is not going to be this gorgeous, this interesting, this perfect a fit; he's not going to be

16

so right for me he must have been born with my name on the little tag around his wrist.

'Would it help if I said there'll be other men?' Caro asks, reading my mind. 'Clever, funny, sexy ones whose mothers have emigrated to Australia and developed a fear of flying . . . '

No, I think, they'll be tired divorcees, fathers of other women's children, self-indulgent bachelors who find me too wilful, too independent, too *much*. And then there'll come the day when their tastes free-fall by twenty years. If the forty-five-year-old men want twenty-five-year-old women, then it surely follows that when I'm forty my natural predators will be sixty, men my *father's* age.

I look at Caro. 'You know how wonderful Charlie is. No one else will do. No one.'

# 2

Before I met Charlie I was convinced I'd missed the gene that makes humans seek out their 'other half'. I called what I had with Paul 'love' but it was fairly obvious that it wasn't the same thing that was making other women arrive in the office raw-lipped or red-eyed, depending on whether it was the beginning of the affair or the end. I envied them their heightened senses, egged them on in their manhunts, but as far as I was concerned, Mr Right was whichever incumbent MD was announcing my latest salary increase. Then Charlie came along and it felt so much like irrational hero-worship I knew I must be in love.

Even his opening gambit was new to me, partly for not being a gambit at all but a perfectly well-intentioned remark made by one still-sober party guest to another.

'Incredible at close quarters, isn't it?' he said, noticing me blowing cigarette smoke through Caro's French doors in the general direction of Tower Bridge.

'Yes,' I said, pleased to be mistaken for someone who might have the capacity to appreciate engineering splendour over the trays of vodka shots that riveted the rest of the room.

'I've just been writing about it, actually,' he said and perched with lean, muscular thighs on a nearby leather armchair. 'Sir Horace Jones's perfect bascule bridge.'

'Bascule?'

'It means 'see-saw' in French.'

I was intrigued. There would not be a single other person here, myself included, who could name the architect of Tower Bridge. Certainly not one as good-looking as this — I'd done well not to gape when I saw his face. He had the kind of fine, patrician jawline and cheekbones that would have casting agents jaywalking across six lanes of traffic to sign up, and the fact that his eyes were the most understated of mid-browns — and not something distracting like matinée-idol blue — seemed only to increase his radiance. His skin, noticeably pale for midsummer, even had cute little freckles here and there, nature's own blusher. Adorable! His personal style would need closer observation, however, for he dressed in that preppy smart-casual continental way that makes clothes hard to date . . . were those khakis distressed by age or design? I couldn't be sure.

But I was making the classic tourist's error of studying the appearance of the helpful native instead of listening to the directions he gave and, just in time, I remembered I was in a conversation with this Supreme Being and it was my turn to speak. 'See-saw?' I chuckled gaily. 'Well, I'm very glad I didn't know that when I was at a party up on those top bits not so long ago.'

'Top bits? Oh, you mean the walkways. Well, there's no chance of those see-sawing, I can assure you.' He grinned, looked at me, and grinned some more. I decided then that I would leave the party when he did.

It turned out that bridges are Charlie's passion, as they are, he tells me, for many architecture students. (No one starts out with dreams of extending their neighbour's kitchen, it seems.) In the year that followed that first meeting of minds he has shared with me many of his views on primitive structures, the extension of cityscapes, atmospheric flexibility and other subjects that engage an undergraduate at the Bartlett Faculty of the Built Environment. But if I've learned anything about architecture in that time it's that a new bridge is the ultimate building. What better idea — and what worthier job — than to create the means for us to get to our previously unreachable destination? To join two sides that wouldn't otherwise have been likely to come together.

There would come a time when I'd find hidden irony in this sort of talk, but in those early days it made Charlie all the more refreshing. A man with ideals — I didn't know many of those.

★  ★  ★

When I see him sitting at the bar in Il Bordello and watch him before he notices me — something I would find creepy if it was done to me — I see that Caro and Jojo might have had a point all along. All ideas of ultimatums and 'really meaning it' just seem nonsensical when you spy a young Clint Eastwood before you, heels crossed on the stool beneath him, eyes

20

fixed on the drink in front of him, and find he's waiting for you. He's *your* hero. To bully Charlie is to bully myself because we are utterly right for each other.

These days I'm less startled by his handsomeness, free as I am to scrutinise those lucky bones on the pillow beside me twice a week (any more frequently and Meredith might become suspicious) and more inclined to appreciate the full-length product. His type is classic manchild: he's solid, well built, always the protector and never the aggressor, and he has a kind of sad, infant sweetness about him that takes you by surprise if you haven't been forewarned. As Caro says, Charlie is the sort who should by rights be a womaniser, but isn't. He is perfect, except for one thing. Except for one person.

'Signorina Anna, your boyfriend is already waiting!' The maître d' has spotted me and I interrupt my thoughts to note, as usual, that I see him more often than I do my own father. Charlie and I are regulars at Il Bordello; it's 'our' restaurant, which means I must be careful not to let memories of our first few meals here get in the way today. Of course in reminding myself not to, I immediately get a technicolour splash of his face that first time — Saturday dinner, the top slot, our first meeting after the party. As I walked through the door he looked up at once, eager, impressed, his thought that he knew we were going to be something special clear for me to see. His hair, the colour of damp volcanic sand, was shorter in those days, the set of his mouth a lot warier. He was still — just — in the workforce

21

then, a management consultant for a big American firm in Covent Garden, serving his notice until college began. He's happier now — girlfriend's pesky mother mission aside — says that he would never have expected to find himself so contented, so liberated, not considering he began the stretch in what he once described to me as a straitjacket of sorrow.

He's standing up to kiss me hello. 'Hi, I was starting to think you weren't coming.'

'Sorry I'm late. Caro was over . . . ' Now it's my voice that buckles. I want to be hugged harder than a ribcage can bear, I want to be buttoned up inside his shirt with him, I want to be told that all of this Meredith business has all been a practical joke and the only thing that matters is us.

'I'm starving,' he says and eyes up a nearby steak. 'Shall we find our table?'

We order pizza and wine and chat about the San Francisco trip. Already the restaurant is as muggy as a boiler room, the waiters' breath like kettle steam, voices bellowing around our heads.

'When are you back, again?' I ask. 'Was it the twenty-fourth of September?' I'm not quite ready to drop the fantasy that we're just a normal couple facing a temporary separation.

'Actually I'm coming back on the seventeenth now.'

'Oh?'

'Yeah, it's my mother's sixtieth birthday on the Saturday . . . '

I let go of the fantasy like a nest of snakes. 'Glad there's someone special to hurry home to.'

He hesitates, then ploughs on anyway, knowing it's the best strategy with me. 'She's decided to celebrate, throw a party.'

'Good God, isn't that a bit frivolous?'

At this he attempts — with debatable success — a cheerful Charlie chortle. 'I must admit I'm a bit surprised. I think she might finally be thinking about having some fun again — she's talking about quite a big do.'

'I'll look out for my invitation.' You could ice water with my tone, even in this hothouse, and he gets the message all right.

'Oh, *Anna*.'

This is typical of what kills me about this situation. He will let me believe we're a team, waiting it out together, joined in our goal, he'll reassure me that my suffering is his suffering, my impatience his, and then he'll just step right back again and play the dutiful son called up to defend *her* against *me*. And he's doing it now, today of all days.

Glistening pizzas, loaded with vegetables and sausage, are delivered to our table.

'Food already? Saved by the bell peppers,' he jokes and I know then that he's feeling as nervous as I am, and — worse — as defeated.

'So have you decided when you might be able to come out to California?' he asks after a while.

I shake my head sadly. 'Possibly the third week in August.' But more likely never. Ask me again in twenty-four hours when Meredith knows about us and has mobilised her forces. What will be the first thing she does? Charlie has hinted at measures beyond my ken. Maybe she'll book every available seat on every commercial flight between London and San Francisco this summer so I can't follow him out there. Lord knows she has the money to do something like that. Or maybe she'll have one of her famous hysterical breakdowns so he doesn't make the trip in the first place, then lock him in the cellar and chuck him the occasional dried crust until he breaks.

Then I notice Charlie's expression has changed. No one can read his face like I can and I know in a heartbeat what this faint narrowing of the eyes and grimacing of the mouth mean. He's wishing he hadn't used this particular diversionary tactic because the third week in August is not going to work and I think I can guess why.

'Don't tell me,' I say, '*she*'s visiting you then?'

He can't even look at me now. 'Sorry. She's trying to keep herself busy. You know, bad memories of last summer. She's booked herself up with travel plans.'

'Can't she do the week after?'

'No, she's going on some trip to Spain over the bank holiday with her Dulwich art brigade. They're staying at the parador in the Alhambra and it's the sort of place where you have to book months in advance. There's no way she can change the date. That third week is literally the only one she can do.'

As he eats, I stew. The only one she can do. Well, that's that then. Of course it's out of the question that she might survive twelve weeks without seeing him at all, as any normal mother of a twenty-nine-year-old would do, as my father would without a qualm if it were me working overseas for the summer. Suddenly I want this over with. I push the remains of my food to the side of my plate and look at him with a determination normally reserved for the boys in the office. 'Has it occurred to you that if you tell your mother about us then we might be able to visit you in San Francisco together? Would that not be the solution to this scheduling problem?'

He finishes chewing and carefully positions his knife and fork on his empty plate, blade facing inwards, the way Mother taught him.

I battle to keep my voice reasonable. 'You must remember what we said about today, Charlie?'

'What *you* said about today,' he points out, miserably.

'Well?' I pause. 'Have you told her about us or not?'

'Anna, you know I can't. It's too soon.' And he gives me that look that says, it's only been fourteen months, she's still *grieving*, have a heart. And if it's only been fourteen months for Meredith without a husband, then it's only been fourteen months for Charlie without a father. He's like an amputee unwrapping his bandages and showing me the stump — in the middle of a *restaurant*. But I won't rise to it; the one thing I'm not prepared to do is engage in a competition about who misses their parent more, he or I.

We bonded over dead parents, Charlie and I, which makes it sort of ironic that it's a parent who comes so close to severing us. His father

25

had died of heart failure just two months before we met, my mother had been gone twenty-eight years, but the difference was by the by. We knew at once how the other felt. That party held by Caro and her brother, David, was Charlie's first social outing since the funeral and, as he confessed on our way across Tower Bridge together afterwards, he'd attended only out of curiosity about their flat. He'd wanted to see inside the original Butler's Wharf building for ages. 'It's an architectural landmark, a triumph in master planning,' he told me, and was very interested when I was able to tell him the current market value of some of those apartments. As we spoke, I found myself slowing my usual route march so I could extend the time I'd spend by his side. Later he admitted he hadn't needed to cross the river to get home at all, but could have walked straight on to London Bridge and caught his train from there.

It's no fun now to see him so crushed, but I have to follow through. 'Come on, Charlie, I know she must still be suffering, but do you not think a woman who's recovered enough to throw herself a big birthday party and travel around the world on a variety of holidays is a woman who's recovered enough to meet her son's girlfriend? His girlfriend of a *year*? You must see how ridiculous this is getting? People think I'm joking when I tell them!'

'You don't know what she's like,' he mutters.

'You won't let me!'

'Just give me a bit longer,' he pleads, 'until

after the summer. I can't do anything now, can I?'

I want to scream, to bury my face in my hands and not move a muscle until he's gone. Then, all at once, I have an idea, a good one. My shoulders relax and my eyes shine. 'You know what?'

'What?' He raps his right index finger on the table in front of him, a sign of advanced wariness.

'I'm just thinking that this birthday party of hers might be the perfect opportunity! Listen, Charlie, you could invite me, we could pretend we've just met, see how she takes me . . . Oh my God, it's perfect!'

But he shakes his head. 'I'm not really in a position to invite anyone, Anna.'

'But I'm not just *anyone*,' I say, horrified that I'm getting that sting behind my nose that means tears are not far away. 'Of course you can invite someone.'

'I can't, really.'

'Oh, this is impossible!'

It's getting noisier and I barely hear his voice when he says, 'You know I love you, don't you?' but it's an easy one to lip-read. I look down at the dessert menu, mobbed by doubts. A year into my job I was voted Negotiator of the Year by *Media Week*, but where are my acclaimed powers now? Even my own voice is arguing against me, first in one ear, then in the other: what's another few months when you've already stuck it out for a year? Apart from the Meredith factor, there's nothing to complain about, not the tiniest quibble. You love each other to distraction, everyone agrees. Even that one-woman counter-romantic movement Caro Harding doesn't wish for the end of Anna and Charlie. Maybe a few months' thinking will move him along. If he doesn't confront her after that then I *definitely* will.

He doesn't order his usual panna cotta, neither of us wants coffee, and before I know it we're out on Wapping High Street. It's so humid that the only thing to signal the move from indoors to out is the remote, sour smell of the river. He suggests I walk with him to London Bridge as it's such a warm afternoon. I dither — a bad sign — and then agree, and when he takes my hand I don't do anything to stop him. It's a longer walk than you'd think, but we talk little. Occasionally he makes a comment about an old church or the bones of some new structure on the water. He loves Millennium Bridge, loathes the mayoral building. Personally, I prefer the walk east from Wapping, past the riverside apartment buildings with their lidless eyes and towards the towers of Canary Wharf, which seem to curve into view like iron giants, but Charlie's never been convinced.

Finally, as we come to a halt at the station doors, we still haven't said another word about the ultimatum since we left the restaurant. If I'm not careful he's going to take it as read that I've given in, given up. 'Charlie, I really am serious about — '

'Oh, I almost forgot! I've got something for you . . . ' He reaches into his bag and hands me something from the pad he always carries. I look down at it. It is a pen-and-ink drawing of a garden, or perhaps a park, a series of rapid lines hinting at a child crouched over a flowerbed and a woman stooped behind her, hands out-stretched. Behind them runs the graceful curve of a pavilion rooftop and the tree line fading into the sky. It is a perfect piece of stillness, the postage to an escape. It feels like a promise.

'It's beautiful,' I say, confused. 'Who are they?'

'That's how I imagine you and your mother together,' he says, looking from the drawing to my face with the gentlest eyes. 'When she told you not to pick the flowers in the park because the dogs liked to smell the perfume on their walks. I'm sorry, I didn't mean to upset you.'

'No, I'm fine, it's lovely.' I pretend to study the drawing to hide the fact that my eyes are wet.

Charlie takes the drawing, rolls it up and tucks it into my bag. Then he kisses me between the eyebrows. I stay completely still and, encouraged, he moves to my lips. 'Will you give me the summer?' he asks.

It's such a beautiful thing, the notion that the brightest, loveliest season could be my gift to him. 'OK.'

'You won't go firing off any letters to her? Or making any mystery phone calls?'

'No.'

'No surprise appearance at Heathrow tomor-row?' He's obviously given the situation some thought after all, been worrying about how and when I'll pop up and carry out my threat.

'No,' I agree.

'Promise?'

'Yes.'

'Thank you.' And then he's gone, shoulder just catching the door before he disappears round the corner for the escalator, and I'm left standing on my own by the flower stall. It is closed at weekends, but the board has been left out and its chalked message is still intact:

**YELLOW ROSES £8. GO ON, CHAPS, SHE DESERVES IT!!**

And I know in that second that I'm not going to give Charlie up. I deserve him. He's my reward for having had other things taken away from me. Meredith will not win. There *has* to be a way to beat her.

When I get home there's just one new message on my home phone and it's from Viv. She just wanted to say that she's free tomorrow, even though it's a Sunday. Life's dilemmas don't go away just because some old man in the sky decreed it a day of rest, do they? I write down her number and start dialling. What I need now are Definitive Results.

# 3

'So your boyfriend *still* won't let you meet his mother? God, has *nothing* changed since I went away?' Nothing except Viv herself, who I barely recognise when she glides through the door so smoothly, so noiselessly, that she might have been delivered by travelator. She is wearing a soft smile, minimal make-up, and a pale-green bandanna around her head, though I can see from the ends of her hair that highlights have slipped through the net of Vanity Purification (no joke, she told me on the phone that this was one of the modules she studied in Seattle).

We were never in the same tribe at work — she's blonde and I'm dark, it's too complicated to explain, but it still means something in the offices of a tabloid newspaper — but now Viv and I look like we're from totally different species. At first it's the paprika cast to her skin that's the most immediately startling, though I suppose it stands to reason that the complexion of someone who's spent the last two months on outdoor yoga platforms in Goa is going to look rather better nourished than that of someone who moves from office to taxi to restaurant without ever raising her eyes to the sky. (I make a mental note to book a fake tan for next week.) As Viv speaks, though, it's the sight of her lips that I find oddest — natural skin-pink and strangely intimate — I don't think I've ever seen them without lashings of blood-red Clinique. As she sips her organic green tea (she sensibly supplied her own) she looks relaxed to the point of medication, unlike me, mainlining espresso, elasticated to the point of snapping.

'He still won't even tell her about me,' I say, joining her on the sofa and warming my bare toes with my hands. The closeness of yesterday's weather has been replaced by a sneaky little chill. 'He says she's unstable and still grieving. It's been a whole year now and he's made no progress whatsoever. I'm still his dirty little secret.'

With a sudden move Viv pops the lid off her pen and we both wait for the many ropes of her bracelets to clatter into place like beads on an abacus. 'You'd view the situation quite differently if you met *my* mother-in-law, I can tell you,' she drawls. 'God, if only she didn't want to see me quite so much.'

I can see I'll need to work harder at promoting my cause. Viv has never actually met Charlie and it's always much harder to explain all of this to people who haven't. They imagine some meek little Ronnie Corbett sitcom character, a stammering wimp not worth fighting for, not a celestial beauty whose existence on Earth occurs once in a blue moon.

I show her his photograph and watch her expression lift. 'I love him,' I declare, as though I've been pulled on to the set of some awful daytime TV programme and have only ten seconds to plead my case before the audience votes. 'Yes, he's good-looking, but that's not it.

He has inner beauty!' That should appeal to her new spiritual leanings. 'He's the man I want to be with, Viv, in a proper, permanent, legitimate way. I've *got* to get rid of the Meredith problem, otherwise we'll be stuck in this, this mistress-style arrangement for ever. Surely we're too old for this nonsense?'

Viv arches an unpruned brow. 'I've handled getting men to choose between wife and girlfriend in my training in the States,' she says. 'Of course, that's quite a common dilemma.'

'Which do they normally go for?' I ask.

She pauses. 'I'll be honest with you: the wife. But don't worry, there's no wife here and Charlie shouldn't feel he needs to choose between you two. He can have you both.'

'That's exactly what I keep saying to him!'

She puts down her tea and writes something in her spiral-bound office pad. It's very kind of her to come over on her first Sunday back in town. It's true I've never been much of a fan of the kind of 'life laundry' she is now certified to sift, but you know what they say about desperate times. Somewhere, just somewhere, between her courses on the Western Seaboard and southern India she may have come across a situation like the one I'm in now.

'OK,' she says, glancing again at the photograph. 'To begin with I need to understand exactly where Charlie's coming from. What, specifically, does he fear will happen if he *does* tell his mother about you?'

I take a breath and for the hundredth time try to explain how I've come to find myself in a situation befitting a Brontë heroine. Much as I rail against Charlie's view of the situation when I'm with him, I often find myself defending it to the outside world. 'Well, for starters, that she'll put an end to our relationship altogether.'

'How would she be able to do that? You're both consenting adults.'

'Apparently she practically hounded his last girlfriend out of town. Kept ringing her and warning her off, turning up at his flat without warning . . . '

One time, when Charlie decided enough was enough, he told his parents over Sunday lunch with neighbours that he was thinking about moving in with Jessica. Meredith promptly shrieked, 'Not with that common little shop girl!' (Jessica worked as a PR assistant at Selfridges) and had to be led away for a lie-down. When the subject was broached again, she said, 'Over my dead body,' this time through pursed lips, and threw a wooden spoon at him.

'She has a history of 'breakdowns',' I tell Viv, 'but I get the feeling that's just the Grainger family word for tantrum. Anyway, Charlie says she made his life a misery over Jessica and he has no intention of repeating the experience. Especially after what happened with Max.'

'Who's Max?' I see her write the letters on her pad and underline them.

As well she might. Max is Charlie's older brother, with whom Meredith cut off all contact when emotional blackmail didn't work and he refused to give up *his* unsatisfactory partner. Poor Max had the temerity to fall in love with someone half-Spanish. 'Sara was actually born in Portsmouth!' I laugh. 'But it was all very *West Side Story*, apparently. Now they live in Valencia.'

It sounds made up, but it's all true. Charlie's brother had to leave the country to escape Meredith, that's how poisonous she is. Charlie has been saying for ages that he'd like to take me to meet them — 'then you'll understand,' he says — but it's been so difficult to get anything planned over the past year that we haven't got round to it. Besides, travelling together has not been without its stresses. I remember with lingering humiliation the trip to Tobago in the New Year. Charlie had to pretend to Meredith he was going on his own and she insisted on driving him to the airport. That meant we had to check in separately and couldn't even sit together on the plane. I couldn't help suspecting he was secretly pleased about that, just in case she was up in the spotters' gallery waiting to see him safely above the clouds. I could just imagine her with her Hubble telescope, checking out the seating configuration inside the taxiing plane, making sure no one was getting their mucky paws on her golden boy. Heaven though it was to have him to myself for ten whole days (and nights), it was soon after our return that I issued my ultimatum.

'But *you're* not Spanish,' Viv is busy musing aloud. No shit, Sherlock. She's going to have to do better than that if we're going to make any headway today. I catch myself grumbling; I'm going to have to be a little more patient if I'm going to make headway.

'That's just one example of what might make a partner unsuitable,' I say, reasonably. 'She wouldn't like you, for example, Viv.'

'Why not?'

'Oh, she'd say you're nothing but a work-shy New Age hippie. See? It's not very nice, she's very judgemental.'

Viv is looking injured, the tactic has worked: she's on side. 'What's wrong with you, then?' she wants to know.

Where to begin? Funny how falling in love has made me so aware of my faults when I'd always been quite content with the way I am. For all the new qualities Charlie has divined within me, the fact that he keeps them a secret from Meredith has always been much more of a blow to the ego than I've let on.

'Well, for one thing, I'm older than him. I know three or four years is nothing to us, but for her it's highly irregular. Also, she's an appalling snob, even Charlie admits that, twice removed from an actual title or something. Whatever it is, it makes her far hotter on social stuff than the bloody Royal Family.' I look down at myself, breasts half-exposed in the low V-top, left ankle slightly streaky with last month's self-tan. 'Let's put it this way, Viv: she collects eighteenth-century art and I sell advertising space. You can sort of understand why Charlie thinks we might not mix.'

'Hmm. Has he considered following Max's lead and defying her? Moving away, if necessary?

If she finds herself cut off from both sons, she might rethink.'

Again my reply has been well honed. 'He doesn't want to rock the boat while she's still missing his father. According to Charlie, since he died last year she's been more difficult than ever. That's partly why he moved back in with her.'

'You mean he *lives* with her?'

'I'm afraid so. His view is that we have to accept that she's stuck in some sort of time warp and wait it out until she's strong enough to take the shock. The *shock*! I mean, for God's sake!'

Viv nods. I can see her making the basic mental adjustments that have become second nature to me. 'So, looking at this from her point of view, she lost her husband soon after a traumatic parting with her eldest son, and Charlie is all she has left?'

'It's not that I'm not sympathetic,' I say, hastily. 'Of course I feel for anyone who's lost a member of the family. I know how heartbreaking it is. I'd just like the chance to show my sympathy in person.'

'Of course you would. We'll find a way, don't worry.' But I can tell Viv is still puzzled about something. 'I understand Charlie doesn't want to distress his mother at a vulnerable time,' she says, carefully. 'But as you say, it's been over a year now and surely he should be getting impatient himself. If you ask me, there's something missing. Are you sure there aren't any other motivations I should know about? Something else making him hold off?'

I pause. 'He says it's not about the money,' I

say, finally, 'but Max was disinherited. Charlie's just gone back to college, so I don't think he wants to risk having the funds pulled.'

'Ah,' says Viv.

Ah, indeed. Funny how the mention of money instantly cheapens the whole thing, and the more money revealed to be involved, the cheaper it all becomes.

'He's got a lot to lose,' I admit, looking down at my empty coffee cup.

'He's got a lot to gain,' Viv corrects me, and smiles. I smile back. She's right. He has me to gain. I start to relax; it's comforting that someone might finally view my life paralysis as a surmountable challenge and not fair game for ridicule, as I'm now used to from most of my colleagues and friends.

On cue she asks, 'OK. Tell me what your friends have suggested you should do?'

I don't name some of the crazier ideas people have put forward, like getting Meredith to the 'Love, Love, Love' art show that's been running at Tate Modern and hope she might undergo some sort of epiphany (my friend Maggie, she believes in the power of art); or getting someone to 'go round there and have a right word with the old bat' (Ronnie at work, he knows some 'faces'); or planting a sex toy in Charlie's overnight bag so Meredith will find it and confront him (Caro, who else?).

'Everyone says I should set him an ultimatum and if he doesn't get his act together either end the whole thing or tell her myself and risk the consequences.'

'Easier said than done,' Viv replies.

'I've tried that,' I say, suddenly close to wailing. 'Yesterday was the day. But I just couldn't do it. That's why I called you with this emergency. You're my last chance, Viv!'

'No pressure then.' She laughs loudly at that and I'm surprised by my own relief. She may look like a gingerbread man in a Ghost dress but she's still the same old Viv. She was a very good sales rep, Viv, one of the best. She always came up with something.

As I turn to make us more drinks she calls out, 'One more question, Anna. You've never had any contact with Meredith yourself? I mean, she's never seen you with Charlie, has she?'

'No.'

'Good.'

When I get back she is scratching away at the page like she's tussling with a maths equation. Then she sits upright and looks directly at me. A surge of purpose flows between us: whatever it is she's been learning to do while she's been away I think she might be ready to do it.

'Right,' she says, turning to a fresh page. 'I think I have a solution.' My eyes and mouth open very wide but she gestures to me to hold my horses. 'First, I need you to run through everything we know about this woman. The established facts only, all right? What's her full name?'

'Meredith Frances Grainger.'

'And she lives where did you say . . . ?'

'Dulwich. Dulwich Village. Apparently the 'village' bit is important.'

'What else?'

I'm surprised how much I know about Meredith now I come to think of it. She cooks well, particularly Austrian dishes thanks to a year spent in Vienna with family friends after university. She worked briefly teaching history of art before her two sons came along. Now she's involved with the Dulwich Picture Gallery and has a soft spot for British portraiture. She also likes Moorish architecture. For exercise she takes long walks and has started playing tennis again — it's the only sport she's ever had a passion for. (She always goes to the tennis at Wimbledon too, but wouldn't dream of handing over the scandalous sum demanded for a couple of strawberries and a splash of cream.) She contributes to various Dulwich societies, the names of which I don't remember.

'She's pretty caught up in the local scene, then,' Viv says. 'What else? Plans for the summer?'

Only yesterday there were snippets: a sister who lives in Cornwall, soon to be paid a visit; a sixtieth birthday party in September — a time to start celebrating again. 'Oh, and a trip with her art group to the Alhambra, wherever that is.'

'I have a feeling you might soon be finding out,' she replies.

I look up.

'Right,' she says, head and shoulders still, sage-mode evidently fully engaged. 'Essentially the issue is that you're not good enough for her son.' Not good enough. The three little words no girl likes to hear. 'In *her* eyes,' she adds, quickly.

I shrug. 'That's about the long and short of it.'

'Of course there's always the possibility that *no one* is going to be good enough, but for now I think we need to assume that somebody out there could be.'

'OK.'

'Now, if you're really serious — '

'I'm serious,' I interrupt. 'What d'you have in mind?'

'Well, what I'm thinking is that if Mohammed won't go to the mountain . . . '

'You mean, I go to her, after all?'

'Yes, but not *you* you, Anna, a different you. A more appropriate you. Not one who's sleeping with her son but one who doesn't even know he exists.'

'Wow.'

'It will mean dramatically reinventing yourself,' Viv goes on. 'I'm talking about everything: the way you dress, the things you're interested in, even what you say. Whatever it takes to become the kind of person she likes.'

I gulp. 'A bit like *My Fair Lady*?'

'Kind of. Think of it more as a charm offensive.'

A charm offensive. I like it. 'But what about work?' I remember, frowning again. 'I can't take time off and I definitely can't look different in the office or anything like that.'

'Don't worry,' Viv says, 'there shouldn't be any overlap — you'll learn to switch on and off, and it's not like it's for ever. Now, will Charlie be willing to help, do you think?'

41

'No,' I say, quickly. 'He's away for the summer, anyway.'

'He could still be involved. In many ways it would be easier if he were. If we had a fuller profile of Meredith, it would help massively with — '

'No, Viv. He can't know anything about this, not *ever*.'

She narrows her eyes. 'If you're sure . . . '

I narrow mine back. 'I'm sure.'

'Well, do you know anyone else who lives in Dulwich?'

'There's his friend Rich, who he used to live with in East Dulwich. But I don't want him to know about this, it would get straight back to Charlie. So no. Oh, hang on a minute, possibly Nigel at work. He's just moved south of the river and I'm sure he said Dulwich.'

'Find out. Any in is going to be useful. These places can be very hard to infiltrate. How is the old goat, anyway?'

I try to remember if Viv ever shared my loathing of the paper's ad director, Nigel, who had only been installed a few months when she left. Probably, most women do. 'Same as ever,' I say.

'He could be useful.'

'Hmm. I suppose cultivating someone as dreadful as him will be good practice for me.'

'That's the spirit. Right, let's get to work. And remember, this isn't going to be an instant fix, Anna. This whole thing could take ages, the rest of the year, possibly.'

'There's a bit of a natural deadline as it

42

happens,' I say. 'Saturday the eighteenth of September.'

'Saturday the eighteenth of September it is.'

An hour later, as she leaves, Viv hands me her business card. It is edged in the same green as her bandanna and reads, **VIVIAN TUFT LIFE SOLUTIONS. DEFINITIVE RESULTS. NO DILEMMA TOO LARGE.**

'Don't you mean 'No dilemma too small'?' I ask.

'God, no,' she says, moving into the shadow of the hallway. 'I don't want to be dealing with any *real* losers.'

★　★　★

Frightened, exhilarated, exultant, I look for a long time at the single sheet of paper Viv has left with me before I find a notebook of my own. The one I choose is the same size and colour as the daybooks we use at work, except it's one of those expensive ones with leaves of handmade paper. I thought I might use it as a photo album but Charlie's always been very shifty about having his photo taken — like I'm going to publish shots in the *Dulwich Times* — and it remains untouched. It is this that will become my master file, a secret trove of all that will power this mission. One thing is certain: I'm not going to use my laptop for any of this — laptops are the way of accidental emails and humiliating bombshells. It's also extraordinarily easy to find out someone's password, as anyone working in an open-plan office will attest. Besides, Meredith is an old-fashioned, pen-and-ink sort of subject, so I'll plot my plan in kind.

Blood pumping into my skull as though I'm standing on my head, I start to transcribe. The first page is headed Project Meredith, followed by my goal: *To become the type of woman Meredith Grainger likes.* Viv says that any goal should be expressible in ten words or fewer, but I haven't been able to resist adding the parenthesis: (*and to charm her into inviting me to her sixtieth birthday party where she will 'introduce' me to Charlie*).

I think that sums it up.

The basics of the offensive (let's call it my Management Summary) are as follows:

1. *Infiltrate Dulwich society.*
   *Possible ways:*
   — *join whichever tennis club Meredith belongs to (get coaching?)*
   — *join do-gooding groups and do lots of good*
   — *befriend Nigel if he lives in Dulwich (if not, continue hating him)*
   — *generally patrol neighbourhood with friendly intent*

2. *Become cultured.*
   *Possible ways:*
   — *join Dulwich Picture Gallery*
   — *sign up for the Art Brigade trip to Granada*
   —*become expert in Moorish art and architecture, with particular reference to Granada, Spain; also eighteenth-century stuff*
   — *enrol on beginners' history of art course.*

It's a shame there's not time to *move* to Dulwich, to rent a flat on Meredith's street for the summer, say, but I have a suspicion that property in Park Crescent may be beyond my fiscal reach. In any case, if I implement all of the above actions, there should be no shortage of opportunities to meet her. Frankly, she sounds like something of a local busybody — if all else fails I'll just single out the harridan who's making life difficult for everyone else and introduce myself. I already feel I would be able to pick her out at an identity parade and I've never even seen a photo of her.

The next bit is the crux: during any contact with Meredith she must have no idea that I already know Charlie, certainly not that I know every crevice of his body, and one or two of his mind too. No, she must come to like me independently, *in my own right*. That way she can have no grounds for disapproval when Charlie and I 'start' dating. Ideally, she will think she has set this in motion herself; she can even take the credit. I never thought I'd say this, but Viv is a genius!

The sixtieth-birthday-party addendum is the icing on the cake. I was right when I told Charlie it would be the perfect opportunity; it was the question of who should invite me that I got wrong. So much better that I be *Meredith*'s guest. I admit Charlie may be momentarily confused by events (if I have my way he will be as innocent of my machinations as Meredith herself), and Viv says we'll need to meet for another session specifically to explore this issue. But I'll be able to explain it to him, I know I will. After all, we want the same thing, don't we?

A charm offensive, Viv called it. I think we can safely assume that Meredith will not easily be charmed. She is no toothless, sun-drugged reptile on some clichéd tourist square, oh no. Which means that between now and then every last cell of me must be devoted to my mission. I'll need a budget, of course, and will firm that up tomorrow after consulting Caro. I've already printed out the schedule, which begins today and ends on Saturday 18 September, the date of the party. What happens after that is in the hands of the gods.

# 4

So crammed are the pathways of my brain with thoughts of my new mission, ideas surfacing like air bubbles every second, that it's hard to get down to business on Monday. I didn't have the chance to go through the papers yesterday, a weekend ritual unmissed for the last ten years — bar a handful of two-week holidays — so I'll need to do it now before the Monday Morning Meeting at nine-thirty. Our paper occupies three floors of One Canada Square, Canary Wharf's famous centrepiece 'scraper with the blinking light at its tip, the one that takes forty minutes to evacuate in the event of a fire drill and forty seconds in that of a leaving drink. I'm the first in on our floor, which houses the sales and marketing teams. Bereft of the reps' heckle, the open-plan space feels different, uneasily expectant, as if people are hiding in cupboards suppressing sniggers.

I walk past my own office, a modest internal space with a desk and chair, two small armchairs and a secret cupboard where I keep my ceramic hair straighteners and other tools of the trade, and linger for a moment in the doorway of Nigel's. Not a day goes by without my coveting the glass corner spot inhabited by our sales director, or, for that matter, his job. In the eight years I've worked here the sales director post has come up twice, and twice I've applied. The first time I wasn't even thirty, had only just been promoted to my current position and struggled in vain to get the MD to take my bid seriously. But the second time, last autumn, internal candidates were thin on the ground, and with a campaign that stopped just short of sexual favours I really thought I'd done it. Then, just as I could almost feel the tickle of champagne on the end of my nose, our MD, Jeremy, got an eleventh-hour call from his old chum Nigel at the *Sun*. I was called up to Jeremy's office and told I should be proud to be the youngest female ad manager in the business and that Nigel was looking forward to working with such a rising star. Yeah, right. If there's anything I know about ad directors it's that the first thing on their to-do list is to shoot down any 'rising stars' within range. I got a pay increase, of course, a few more share options to keep me on side, but it's the view that I want.

Instead, I have a splendid panorama of the team, only one of whom arrives for nine o'clock, the contractual start of office hours. Steve, at thirty-four, is the more senior of my two group heads. One part Beckenham wide boy to two parts Docklands yuppie, he has a brain as razor-sharp as his customary shave. Today, however, there is stubble on show. I don't say anything, of course, as experiments in facial hairdressing are constantly afoot in this office (or should it be 'a-chin'?) and if there is one area where men are surprisingly oversensitive it is this.

'Nice weekend?' I ask.

'Mustn't grumble,' he says before doing so at length, mostly about the pesky cold snap yesterday that prevented him from devoting the entirety of the weekend's daylight hours to his local pub garden. 'You're looking a bit chirpy,' he says. 'Get any?'

'Sadly, no,' I say. 'And I won't for a while either. Charlie's gone to San Francisco for three months. Flew out yesterday.'

'Wanker,' Steve says, cheerfully. 'Don't know why you haven't kicked him into touch by now. Do us all a favour and book the skip, will you?'

'Steve!' Another reason to get this show on the road: people are definitely starting to lose respect for me, as well they might. When news of my unusual romantic plight first broke it was, by virtue of the old-fashioned values involved, likened to a Victorian pot-boiler, something of a contrast to the usual dilemmas bandied about around here (should I sleep with him even though I'm marrying his cousin next week? No. Do big breasts make up for a hook nose? Yes). Yes, my misfortune was once regarded with real sympathy, Meredith's opposition considered worthy of complex psychological debate. Now, of course, tabloid sensibilities have kicked in and she's a mother-in-law from hell in need of a good rogering, I'm a loser in love with a C-cup, and Charlie's just the muppet in the middle. Yes, Steve and co. have become thoroughly bored by the whole thing.

The others dribble in, my assistant, Pippa, bringing up the rear. Though she is just twenty-three, the walk from the lift bank to her desk is far too much for her and she is panting. This is because every last drop of energy has been drained by weekend partying in her home town of Croydon. Eight-hour shifts shaking her ass on some club podium are to her what *Who Wants To Be A Millionaire?* is to most: just something to do on a Saturday night.

True to form, she throws down her bag and announces, 'Got off my face on Sat'day and when I woke up, turned out I had a tattoo on my boob.'

This is met with raucous hoots from all quarters. 'Tat for tit,' Ronnie quips, tongue dangling. 'Gissa butcher's, then, Pip.' Bexleyheath boy, tall, dark and sharp, Ronnie's only been here a few months but already messes and teases with the best of them. If I weren't strictly professional about such things, I'd say Ronnie was my least favourite of the sales execs. With the others it's mostly bluff, but with him you always get the feeling that if you pushed the wrong button he'd turn nasty — or at least know someone who could turn nasty on his behalf. I can only be grateful that at twenty-six and not yet next in line for group head, he is unlikely to be my direct rival for a while.

Pippa, who feels no fear, winks at him. 'Wait till it's healed up, Ron. It's still a bit of a dog's dinner.'

'Pippa,' I say, 'wasn't anyone with you when this took place? You need to look after yourself a bit better. Anything could happen to you on these nights out. What were you drinking, anyway?'

She lists every alcopop currently available in the European Union.

'I'm very worried about you. Promise me there'll be no more self-mutilation?'

'Yeah, Mum.' But tattoo aside, she looks fantastic, and I can see why all the blokes routinely salivate over her. She has far too much eyeliner on, but no amount of make-up can disguise the fact that she doesn't need any at all thanks to her lustrous skin, as smooth and white as a new bar of soap, and real cheerleader-blonde hair, hair that still gleams when she hasn't washed it for three days — even Caro is in awe of that.

She keeps on grinning at me, which makes me worry that the 'Mum' thing might be going to stick. Nicknaming is a power game around here. 'D'ya wanna Starbucks?' she asks.

'Please,' I say. 'I'll have a peppermint tea, grande.'

'Peppermint tea? You jokin' me? What d'ya want that piss for?' She's no poet, Pippa. Steve and his execs nod without humour. Health kicks are much frowned upon in our office.

'I've already had three coffees this morning,' I lie, dutifully. 'All double shots.' Now they brighten up. These are the sort of people who would prefer to hear that their manager has a sore throat from choking on her own vomit than that she might wilfully reject caffeine because she doesn't happen to fancy it. The truth is I've got so much adrenaline flying around my system that the mere sniff of caffeine might have me hallucinating.

I look at my watch. Nine-thirty already. Never before have I been so distracted from the week's work, but luckily I could do my job standing on my head. I could probably do it better standing on my head. Ad manager: advertisement sales manager. The advertisement sales part is straightforward enough. We sell space. The more space we sell, the more money we make, and the more money we make, the bigger our bonuses, the more expensive our clothes, holidays and rounds at the bar. The man-management part of my job is rather more challenging. Spend a morning in my office and you'll see that the adult bustle before your eyes is nothing more than special effects, poor ones at that. This place is a playpen and these people are toddlers. Spoiled, greedy, whining, farting, grabbing what's not theirs and biting when it's withheld — and all without the saving grace of the infant's unformed consciousness. My colleagues will do anything for a laugh, even if it means making someone cry in the process: I've seen phone handsets glued to their cradles; deliveries of S&M underwear (the classified department has a constant supply of all things kinky) to reception in the guise of birthday chocolates; tinned pilchards stashed in the toes of shoes (the victim soon changed her mind about walking around in stockinged feet). It never stops. Afternoons are worse because sales execs are one of the few working demographics that still drink at lunchtime — every lunchtime, *before* lunch if they can swing it. The team's favourite line is that one by Frank Sinatra about feeling sorry for people who don't drink because when they wake up in the morning that's as good as they're going to feel all day. New reps are required to parrot this mantra until they live and breathe it. In this team, Frank is the Messiah, or, as Steve says, higher than Messiah.

Nigel's assistant, Rosie, appears, a skinny, apathetic girl who has, contrary to her name, bluish skin. 'Everyone ready for the Monday Morning Meeting?' she asks in the kind of tone that suggests that she for one won't be able to last its course without nodding off. Another clubber. I wonder if she's had her skin inked over the weekend, too.

'Rosie,' I say, ushering her to one side, 'where is it Nigel moved to again?'

She looks puzzled. 'Again? Why's he moved so soon?'

'No, I mean, remind me where it is that he moved to recently, in the first place.'

She strains gamely but no words emerge. Rosie and Pippa have been dubbed the Goldfish Girls for their famously short-term Monday memories.

'Was it Wimbledon?' she asks, looking around as though this is a pub quiz and there are team-mates to step in and help her. But I'm pretty sure it's not Wimbledon, otherwise Nigel would already have been nicknamed after a Womble, as has the old duffer in classified — Uncle Bulgaria.

'Dulwich, maybe?' I prompt.

She smiles. 'Yeah, *that*'s it.'

'Great, thanks. Come on, everyone,' I say. 'Let's go in.'

Nigel is already seated at the head of the conference table that dominates the boardroom, a pile of the weekend tabloids in front of him with the *Sun* already open on top. In both appearance and manner he is straight out of central casting (think Oliver Reed, towards the end): heavy-set, fleshy-of-neck and disappearing-of-hairline, and spouting the sort of gruff, foul-mouthed chauvinism you'd imagine should have disappeared with the Fleet Street letter-heads. But in one respect he plays right against type: he doesn't drink. Unlike his predecessor, James, who had been known to have reached his fourth double vodka-tonic before the clock struck noon, Nigel is sober. So when he uses his catchphrase 'Moving Forward', picked up somewhere between media marketing forums and (as is rumoured) AA, he doesn't mean to the next bar. 'Anna, I want to rethink team structure Moving Forward' and 'We need to look at the expense budget Moving Forward'. Naturally, within hours of his arrival, this tic was already subject to bawdy lampooning in every watering hole around the Wharf, and as second in command, I became his natural stooge — 'On your knees, Miss Day, Moving Forward'. Perish the thought.

Unlike James, with whom I forged an alliance that I (wrongly) believed would involve the ultimate passing of power from master to pupil, to date Nigel has eluded me in terms of any boss-deputy bonding. Our relationship is workaday at best, hostile at worst. I've never quite recovered from the injustice of his appointment, however much I tell myself it didn't matter anyway because I was too busy falling in love off-site to care. I care *now*.

'Anna, about time! Have you fucking *seen* this?' He shakes a copy of Saturday's *Sun* in my face. Actually I have, only moments ago, and could only rejoice that I hadn't fucking seen it sooner: the *Sun* has got Fiat — *two pages* — and the agency told me on Friday there was no business around this weekend, 'nothing to speak of', their *exact* words.

'We knew about that,' I say, quick-smart.

He looks straight at me and licks his lips. 'You're a liar, Day.'

And so it begins. The Monday Morning Meeting, also known as the Monday Leads Meeting, takes place throughout the industry at about the same time and, depending on the ferocity of the ad director, is approached with degrees of trepidation by all who attend. There've been times on a Saturday when I've barely dared turn the page for fear of what I'll find inside our rival papers, working from back to front sometimes to delay the moment of discovery. And there is *always* something. Like the time I went through hell negotiating with the editor for a right-hand first half for Dixons only to find that none of the others had given them anything like as good a position; or that four-page Woolies special in the *Mirror* that still crops up in anxiety dreams — a hundred grand that should have gone our way. You spend all day

Sunday rehearsing the sneers, the insults, the personal attacks, only to have the whole thing played out publicly on Monday with bells on. Only one thing is consistent: if it's gone wrong it's your doing, if it's gone right it's someone else's. And all the time Nigel turns the pages like he's William-the-bloody-Conqueror with the Domesday Book, pausing in his tirade only for some fascinating tits-and-ass commentary. 'Bigger than yours, eh, Anna?' he'll say. Not as big as yours though, Nigel, I'll say in my head. That's the most annoying thing: he gets to say his mean little comments out loud.

We're soon back to the offending Fiat campaign and Nigel scans the faces around the table, close to eruption-point. It's not just the fact that we lost this to the *Sun*, it's that he lost it to his old boss, the man who he was never quite able to oust.

'Who exactly was negotiating this? Eh? Eh?'

'Gave it to Becky to work on, didn't I,' Steve says quickly, naming the only rep absent this morning.

'Becky? What a cock-up! Only good for magazines!' This is Nigel's stock dismissal of a female rep in error.

'Jeez,' Steve agrees, narrowing his eyes at the double-page spread open on the table, 'She's bin royally fucked this time, that's for sure.'

Nigel turns to me and growls, 'Where were you in all of this?'

I fake a smile — he's my Dulwich mate now. 'I can't be everywhere,' I say, sweetly.

'Obviously fucking not. Tell me something I

*haven't* worked out for myself.'

'I thought Simon had Fiat in the bag, anyway.'

I don't normally do this, the blatant blaming of another; it's fine for the toddlers because it all evens out over time, but it's not strictly appropriate at my level. But I know that Simon, our business development manager, who is not required to submit to this free-for-all, wouldn't hesitate to do the same to me.

'I'll find out what happened,' I say. 'We're meeting this afternoon to talk about RingMe.' I mention the new mobile network that everyone's after at the moment in a desperate attempt at distraction. For once it works.

Nigel looks ominous. 'We *have* to get that. No fuck-ups, OK?'

Finally he wraps up the meeting with a parting shot at me — 'Just sort your team out, will you?' — and is out the door before I can assail him on the matter of Dulwich. I even had my line ready: 'Did I hear someone say you live in Dulwich? I've got friends down there, it's supposed to be lovely . . . ' and so on. Not that his particular brand of charisma is likely to have won him admittance to Meredith's inner circle but, as Viv says, an in's an in, no stone unturned and all that. I'll give him half an hour to calm down and then I'll pop in for a chat. But a minute later I see him heading to reception, jacket over his shoulder. Behind him, head bowed like a geisha, scuttles Rosie.

God, today is even more painful than I expected. I deliberately leave my first email from Charlie unopened as an incentive for getting through the team debrief. This is a thorough catch-up on who's negotiating which business. The talk is all of SCCs (single column centimetres), 25×4s (part-size ads), solus (a campaign that's solely ours) and pop, mid and qual (popular, mid-market and quality papers), and might as well be in Klingon for the sense it would make to a normal human being. Not so the segment where we all put our lunches in the diary; that's more like a restaurant review session as everyone discusses how extravagantly they'll be dining at the paper's expense this week. Moving Forward, I should try and rein this in as it's getting silly, but I'm not in the mood today. What are a few overpriced mango salsas compared to the love-of-my-life crisis I'm dealing with at the moment? Finally, only when I've had a session on the flat-plan with our porn-surfing make-up manager Bernie, I turn to my parallel daybook and get on to the real work on my mind. There's a lot to be done. I'll need help.

'Anyone know where Nigel was going?'

'Nigel?' says Pippa, as though she's never heard of the guy.

'Yeah,' Steve chips in. 'You know, Pipster, big bloke, loud voice, the jowls of a turkey, goes by the name of Our Boss.'

She giggles.

'Could you find out from Rosie, please?' I ask.

'S'pose.'

She's back a minute later. 'He's gone to the tennis — Rosie says he's getting dentures, so maybe he had to go to the dentist on the way.'

Steve cracks up.

'Debentures,' I say. 'Thank you, Pippa, I'll catch him tomorrow.'

'Cool.'

Caro bounces into view from round the corner where she and her advertorials team sit. All male eyes settle on the pale olive top clinging to her every curve.

'Great pair of puppies you've got there,' Steve says, as usual.

'Woof woof,' Caro replies, as usual. She has no complaints about being dismissed as the girl with fantastic breasts who spends all day deciding between Pringles and Twiglets for her latest promotion. After all, she's making more money than most of them and lives in a flat they'll own only in their dreams. Besides, she likes the attention. Her nickname, Miss Spinney (short for spinster), was her own initiative.

She turns to me, where I'm sitting in Pippa's seat, and asks in a stage whisper, 'So how did you get on with Viv?'

'Viv? Viv?' Heads are up, tails wagging, they're all puppies now and I'm suddenly sidetracked into updating them on the Viv situation. No one is interested in her spiritual purification, of course, nor the new skills that I have to confess I was pretty impressed by yesterday. Instead, they want to know in roughly this order: has she stopped shaving her armpits? Did she shag any of those bald Buddha types? Is it true she makes you pay twenty-eight pounds for a bit of old string to wear around your wrist?

'You're thinking of the Kabbalah,' Caro

corrects Ronnie. 'That's not her bag at all.'

''S'all the same,' he says, then turns his attention back to humiliating the trainee about his failure to nail the new girl in classified on Friday night.

'It went very well,' I'm finally able to answer Caro, pulling her away from the pack into my office, where she lounges on the seat opposite mine fingering the silver beads of her bracelet. 'Viv was a lifesaver! We've decided it's time I launched a charm offensive.'

'Babes, you're already charming,' she says. 'Everyone knows you could charm the pants off . . . well, someone with very tight pants. Besides, you've already charmed Charlie's off, haven't you?'

'Not Charlie,' I say, giggling. '*Meredith*.'

'Ooh.' She wasn't expecting that. I enjoy the moment.

'I'm totally restyling myself,' I say. 'I'm going to become the old-fashioned, conservative, art-loving girl of her dreams. I'm going to be *demure*.' I fill her in on the details and watch her eyes get wider and wider.

'Wow,' she breathes. 'Do you think you can pull it off?'

'I've got the whole summer. How hard can it be?'

'*Very* hard with any luck!' She shrieks at this and the hounds look up, rightly suspecting the introduction of innuendo into our confab. I get up and close the door. 'How can I help?' Caro asks, excitedly. 'I could try and think if I've ever slept with anyone who lives in Dulwich? I'm sure

I must have; one of those faceless suits, maybe. What's the postcode?' No joke, she actually starts flicking through her address book.

'It's OK,' I say. 'But there is something you can help me with. Are you free for lunch tomorrow?'

'Sure. Why not today?'

'Oh, I've got a late lunch with an agency and then I'm working from home.'

Caro smirks. 'Bunking off to go and check out Dulwich, you mean?'

'Yep. It's about time.'

# 5

For a long time it didn't bother me that I was 'banned' from Charlie's neighbourhood because he made up for it by showing me so much else of London that I'd never noticed before. A centuries-old pub with troughs for the horses and doorways too low for 'noughties' girls in three-inch heels; a building in west London tiled entirely in cobalt blue; all-but-forgotten museums and near-impenetrable private gardens. He was the companion with the limited-edition insider's guide — sometimes I felt as though I were going out with a professional tourist. We usually met at London Bridge and most of our adventures would involve at least a short stretch of the river. I'm glad to say that we fell short of such cinematic sequences as bounding off the London Eye and racing each other across the twin Hungerford footbridges before collapsing together with breathless glee — but only just.

'Which is your favourite London bridge?' he asked me early on, and became at once still and watchful.

I sensed this might be an important test, rather in the way that other men want to know which football team you support (i.e. a potential deal breaker), and so instantly rejected the truth in favour of something more impressive. It wasn't easy: did I go for Tower Bridge, classic emblem of the Big Smoke and a particular talking point for the two of us (or was it too early to speak of 'our' bridge)? Or how about Millennium Bridge, which I'd walked on, with great pleasure, when it wobbled and I was drunk, but never since for fear of disappointment?

'I like Hammersmith Bridge,' I said, finally. 'It's a very smart green and it reminds me of the boat race.'

'You surprise me,' he said to my satisfaction. 'Girls always say Albert Bridge. *Always.* It's the ice-cream colours and fairy lights.'

I stared at him in amazement for that had been my instinctive choice, too.

'You wouldn't believe how many women want to be proposed to on Albert Bridge,' Charlie went on.

'By you?' I teased.

'Not necessarily,' he said, and grinned very agreeably. For a moment there Everywoman's fantasy was mine, too. 'They almost pulled it down, you know. After the Second World War.' I was learning that almost every famous London structure had diced with demolition at some stage. Nothing was for ever. Today's St Paul's was tomorrow's eyesore, Charlie said.

Passing Westminster he told me about his father, a career civil servant who had fiercely opposed his son's plans to retrain as an architect, and those beautiful soft eyes went all pink and glassy. A second later a tear rolled over his left cheekbone and he made no attempt to brush it away. I'd never seen a grown man cry (unless you counted at the final whistle of any one of

63

those routine Euro and World Cup robbings) and my heart clenched to see him doing that little-boy reflex of wince-smiling bravely through his distress.

'Sudden bereavement is the hardest,' I said, tenderly. 'There's no way you could have been prepared, Charlie. It takes longer to get over it, whatever anyone says.'

Behind him the sky was so moody blue it was turning purple and the water had taken on an unearthly pearlescence. 'Can you bear with me, Anna?' he asked. He meant his grief — at least I thought he did. A few months later and I would have naturally assumed he was talking about Meredith. 'Can you?'

'Yes,' I said. 'Of course I can.'

⋆ ⋆ ⋆

Though Charlie knows the waiters in the St Katharine's Dock cafés by name, I have never set foot in Dulwich Village before, not even pre-Charlie. When I look in the A — Z, I'm surprised to find that it is fairly central, not far from Brixton, though one assumes the inhabitants of each wouldn't be seen dead in the other. (Actually, I suppose it's always on the cards that you might be seen dead in Brixton, but Charlie would say that sort of remark is pure north-of-the-river snobbery and I should take a look a little further east of my own back yard.) It's strange to be following his route from London Bridge to home, especially when I realise I don't even know which is his train stop:

North Dulwich or West? I toss a coin and choose West. Crossing a noisy road for the empty parkland beyond, I can't help guiltily looking over my shoulder as I walk past a Georgian mansion, where people are clinking glasses on the sunlit terrace like something out of a BBC costume drama, and hurry on towards the main street. This, helpfully, is called Dulwich Village.

I look around, frown at my map, and look around some more. This *cannot* be Zone Two of London Town. This is a Hampshire village, surely? This is an American movie set of a Hampshire village. It has its own heritage-style signs and glossy white picket fences; it has smiling slow-moving inhabitants who talk not into mobile phones but *to each other*. It would be hard to imagine a place more sedate; in fact, it's almost sedate*d*. Then I remember that Margaret Thatcher used to live in Dulwich. The Iron Lady, they called her. I mustn't get lulled into a false sense of security; behind these passive brick façades are women who eat world leaders for breakfast — and Meredith is one of them.

I feel confident in approaching the Grainger residence, for Charlie, young innocent that he is, let slip on the phone yesterday that Meredith would be driving straight from Heathrow to Henley-on-Thames where she was to spend a few days with friends during the local arts festival. Even so, the drum roll in my chest cavity is painful as I make my way up Park Crescent, a tree-lined street to the east of the park. What if she's back, waiting for me, flanked by a pair of bobbies (for Dulwich will certainly still have 'bobbies' patrolling its streets, not 'pigs' like the rest of the city)? But the garden gate is closed and the front rooms shuttered. I can relax.

The house is a grand double-fronted three-storey number, Victorian or Edwardian — I can never tell the difference — and as it is at the outer edge of the crescent there is a very long curved pathway leading to the front door (black double doors with scrubbed stained glass). The garden, like its owner, is well established, with cascades of ivy and ferns, lots of mature shrubs and a large leafy tree that might be a magnolia. I resist the temptation to go and peer through the slats of the shutters; Neighbourhood Watch is doubtless alive and twitching in these parts and the last thing I need is someone reporting my particulars to Meredith. Besides, I don't need a tour of the interior to see that it's extremely nice, the sort of place you imagine you might like to live when you're in your forties with two children in school and a garden party to plan every summer. Until you look in an estate agent's window and realise you'd be lucky, not without a hefty inheritance and a couple of City jobs between you. You certainly don't get much bang for your buck in Dulwich. If Nigel does live here, then rumours about his deal-making salary hike must be true.

Noting that it was one of the last to be designed by the Victorians and is now Grade II-listed, I enter the park. The sun is still high above the trees and there are small children flying around everywhere, some in school uniform, some just along for the ride on My First Trike. These are not trendily styled mini-adults in slogan T-shirts like those sighted on occasion in my neighbourhood, but proper traditional children, the type who have pigtails and rosebud lips and Clarks sandals. Many seem to be stopping for tea in the park café, so I do the same.

I have to queue for ages to get served and by the time I reach the counter the only thing the infant locusts haven't inhaled is a slice of Victoria sponge and a fairy cake. I snap up both before they go, too.

'Any idea who I need to speak to to join the Art Brigade?' I ask the girl behind the till.

It occurs to me that 'Art Brigade' may not actually be the name of the society to which Meredith belongs, but it doesn't matter because the girl says she lives in Tulse Hill and wouldn't have a clue. 'You could ask at the bookshop,' she suggests.

I sit observing the clientele for a while and make a note or two in my book alongside the research I downloaded this morning. Dulwich residents: 'ABC1, white, high status, highly educated, affluent, mostly families with children.' No surprise there, then. There's not a blue collar in sight, except on the kids' sailor tops. I find myself fascinated by the sight of so many infants in one place, most stuffing sausages and chips into their mouths and doing that gagging face they do when something is too hot. I feel exactly the same as I did when observing the penguins in Cape Point with Maggie: one hundred per cent tourist. One little boy, who could be anywhere between four and eight (I'm afraid I am no judge), is quite unlike the rest in that he is very self-contained, sitting apart even from his own family as he studies sheet after sheet of stickers and prepares to arrange them on the pages of an exercise book. Was Charlie like this, the boy who creates an aura without meaning to, the one who wins your attention even when he's in his own world?

No, there is very little to break the code of Dulwich family life: the occasional oddity in the form of a mixed-race child, a French couple — not that there are too many men in evidence on a Monday afternoon, most, presumably, occupied in bringing home the bacon. There is, however, one older man (retired?) with a new baby and much younger wife (second or third?) — that makes me think of my own father and at once I jump back to my feet. 'Do your homework,' he always says, though when I was at school and had folders bursting with the stuff he was far too busy building his business to remember to say it. But he's right, I need to be out there working the streets, learning Meredith's home turf, knowing my subject inside out. Only then can I fit in.

I leave the café and hover by the tennis courts, trying not to look like a private detective. I wait for a sweating man to puff to the fencing to pick up the balls and I give him my best smile. 'Is there anywhere around here to play tennis?'

He frowns impatiently. 'I would have thought that was pretty obvious.'

'Sorry, I meant a club, a tennis club. I'm looking for the most exclusive one in Dulwich? Aim high, eh?'

He looks at me oddly. 'There are a few,' he shrugs. 'Why don't you try the one over by the velodrome, that's pretty snooty.'

'Perfect. Thank you.' *Velodrome?* What kind of a 1950s utopia have I found myself in?

I jump out of my skin when my mobile rings and Charlie's name pops up. I feel as though I've been caught breaking into his house and hiding under the bed. Instinctively I look over at the roofs of Park Crescent, trying to work out which is his house. There are a couple with glass roof extensions; his must be the one closest to the park gate. If he were in his studio now and happened to have a pair of binoculars to hand he'd be able to see me down here. What would he do? Rush down with handcuffs and escort me to the station? Close his eyes in the hope that I'd vanish into thin air?

'Slept really well,' he reports. 'Better than I expected, anyway. But it's always easier east to west, isn't it?'

'What's your apartment like? How was the flight? I didn't think your phone worked in the States?' I ask, voice jolly.

'Yep, I switched to triband.' That will be for her benefit, not mine. 'Where are you?' he asks, when he's finished describing the pros (central location and bigger than it would be if it were in New York) and cons (defective air-con and no elevator) of his temporary home.

'Oh, just walking through the park after a

meeting,' I reply truthfully, though I know he'll take that to mean any one of London's green spaces apart from the one I'm actually in. 'It's quite a nice day here.'

'Call or email as soon as you know when you can visit,' he says, sounding lost and far away. 'I'm online at home, as well.'

'Home,' I repeat, almost in a whisper and look once more to the rooftops of Park Crescent.

'Well, if you can call it that. It just sort of *smells* so different, you know?'

I feel confused and guilty at the contrition in his tone. He thinks I'm still aggrieved with him. Just an hour in Dulwich and I've already almost forgotten the circumstances of our parting.

'I love you,' I say, but I'm not sure he hears as I'm partially shielding the mouthpiece for fear he'll pick up the local sounds. 'I mean, *really*,' I add, almost in apology. And when he hangs up, the sadness I feel that he's gone for almost three months is tempered more than I might have expected by relief, relief that he's out of the way. If a funny kind of way it is Charlie's absence that is going to make it possible for us to stay together. I couldn't have done it *with* him, if you see what I mean.

I spend the next hour circuiting the main streets, checking every female face that might match Meredith's, though I know she's safely out of town (grumbling, perhaps, at the quality of the mint in her Henley Pimm's). But I get the idea. Everyone in Dulwich is very well mannered and affable and quite content with slow service. In one shop it takes ten minutes to get someone to take the money for a bottle of water. Patience is something I will need to learn if I'm to blend in like a native. I write it in my book under 'Things I Need' and underline it.

Dulwich Picture Gallery stands opposite the main park entrance so I drop into the shop to pick up a guidebook before detouring to the velodrome just off Turney Road. Not far away is a sign for the club the sweaty man must have been referring to: 'Village Lawn Tennis & Croquet Club, 1906'. At first all I can see is a line of children on a shale court taking it in turns to dash forward for a volley. Then, at the end of an unkempt driveway I glimpse grass courts where fours of white-clad egg-shaped bodies move about around the nets, stretching and turning in painful slo-mo: oldies — much more promising.

I scan the nearby sign: 'Members, please note: no player shall occupy a court after playing one set if other members are waiting to play.' In my opinion, no player shall occupy a court after playing one set because he or she will have staggered aside with heart failure before the end of it. These people must be a hundred years old!

The clubhouse, a wooden structure like something out of the Raj, is clustered with more elderly bodies, but when I approach, a woman whose knees crinkle like elephant skin when she straightens up tells me I must speak directly to the members' secretary, Eric, not usually at the club on Mondays (ladies' night, it emerges). I smile my thanks, trying not to notice the gloopy bubble at the corner of her mouth — spittle?

Some sort of food-stuff? It's going to be strange spending time with old people, plainly rife in these parts and presumably well represented in Meredith's circle. Since my grandparents died, within two years of one another in the nineties, I've had little contact with what our paper calls the 'trailblazers of our dangerously ageing population' (as though they're the first to give grey hair and brittle bones a try and subsequent generations will be able to vote 'yes' or 'no'). In sales, we know them only in terms of the silver pound. They are not our favoured demographic. Too discerning.

I scribble down the details and retreat. Next stop the village bookshop, where the sales assistant thinks my art travel group might be something to do with the gallery. I tut — I should have thought of that before — and am turning to head back that way when I spot the village noticeboard across the road. This tells me and anyone else interested that Dulwich is a place for people who refuse to believe they are within five miles of Charing Cross, so various and plentiful is the local flora and fauna. Waterfowl seem to be of particular note and I write down the contact name for the society that protects them, plus those of a handful of other committees.

And then I see it: a yellow flyer headed 'Art Explorer Group: key dates'. Art Explorer! I peer through the glass at the dates. There is nothing listed between 22 June and 27 August, but it is the latter that makes me catch my breath:

'Departure for Granada, Spain', followed by: '30 August: return to London'. This *has* to be the trip Charlie mentioned, the one Meredith has signed up for. My mind hurdles forward two months, frenzied with adrenaline: three whole days and nights with Meredith Grainger, a triathlon of opportunities! I must sign up without delay. On my mobile, I dial the contact number for Moira Poole, secretary.

'Double eight four two, one two four three,' recites an uncertain male voice as though reading it off a document he's never seen before.

'Oh, good afternoon. I mean evening, is it evening yet?'

Confused silence, then, 'Do you know, I hadn't noticed.'

'Er, OK. I was hoping to speak to Moira Poole.'

'Mrs Poole isn't available at the moment.'

'Oh, what a shame. I wanted to enquire about the Art Explorer Group. I'm new to the area and terribly keen on painting.' I've never said 'terribly' in my life, I realise, at least never to mean 'very', and am delighted with myself for slipping into character so seamlessly.

'I see.'

'I'm passionate about the world's galleries,' I throw in. You'd think I was overdoing it, but it's working: I can sense him nodding away like a slightly slower-than-average child who doesn't quite understand that the person on the other end can't actually see you.

'I see. I'm also a member. Humphrey Poole. Perhaps I can answer your enquiries? Oh, I do beg your pardon, Moira *is* here. Let me hand you over.'

The handover proves unfortunate as Moira despises me straight away. 'Where did you get this number?' she asks, all sharp and Scottish, then makes a funny grinding noise with her mouth. I have a horrible feeling I may have interrupted their dinner (old people eat very early, don't they?).

'From the village noticeboard. I'm new to the area and keen to meet like-minded art-lovers.'

'The group has broken for the summer recess.' She makes it sound like Parliament. The Maggie Thatcher influence is alive and well, clearly.

I try again, adding a little more gush to my tone. 'Not to worry, I was just wondering if there are any places left on your trip?'

'Trip?'

'The one to Granada.'

'*Gra-nah-da*,' she corrects. '*Gre-nay-da* is a Caribbean island.'

'Of course. How silly.' I want to sigh. How silly that I'm standing in the middle of this Godforsaken place sucking up to an old biddy with food in her teeth when I could be lying on a beach in sunny *Gre-nay-da* instead. I try again. Then I remember this is a *charm* offensive. 'Would you be kind enough to tell me if there are any places left?'

'I'm afraid there are not,' she huffs. 'We had to limit them in the end because of hotel availability. You must have seen one of our old leaflets. I believe we have a waiting list, but in any case I'm not sure that a new member would be eligible.'

Eventually, after more puffing, she agrees to give me the number of the specialist travel agent the group has used to book its accommodation and flights. Her farewell is very curt. Jeez, if these are Meredith's henchmen I'll be lucky to meet her by Christmas.

I stuff my phone in my bag and head for the station, back to civilisation, civilisation as *I* know it.

# 6

I spend much of the rest of the week immersed in cyber-Dulwich while Pippa holds my calls and replenishes the peppermint tea. First, an Internet search on Meredith's full name, followed by the usual result (yes, I've done it before): 'Your search matched 0 documents', which is no surprise as she's hardly the type to keep her own blog. Moira Poole and her 'Art Explorers' have nothing online either, so I move on to the Dulwich Picture Gallery website and join their Friends, easily done for a matter of twenty pounds or so. Luck is on my side and there's an event in two weeks' time — a garden party to celebrate the opening of their summer exhibition. I mark the date on my calendar and start thinking about who to take with me. No one from the office, that's for sure — there's not a cultural bone between the eejits. And wonderful though Caro is, she'd probably get done for mooning or licking a painting and have us both thrown out.

Next, I ring up and leave a message on the answerphone of the secretary of the Do-gooders' Society, stressing that I am a very dynamic newcomer who will do whatever is necessary to aid its latest cause. What else? I key in 'Dulwich groups' and speed through the pages of results. Is there any living thing in this place that *doesn't* have a committee dedicated to its preservation?

Kingfishers, rhododendrons, deer, joggers . . . And then there are the statue appeals, the blue-plaque proposals, the million-and-one school initiatives. So many causes, so little time; I suddenly know how Princess Diana felt.

Then I remember the tennis club. A quick check tells me that the Village Lawn option is definitely the one, being the only club in the area to be a hundred years old and requiring of new members the sort of jumping through hoops that would satisfy the superiority complex of a woman like Meredith. I ring up and am at once disabused of the notion that I may actually be permitted to join in this lifetime: 'All prospective members must be proposed by an existing member.'

'I'm sure Nigel Gray will propose me,' I say, breezily, though, bona fide Dulwich resident or not, Nigel doesn't seem any more the type than I am.

Much coughing and shuffling. 'I'm not familiar with anyone of that name, I'm afraid.'

'Oh, all right.' It doesn't matter anyway; even if Nigel miraculously turned out to be a member, he would have no reason to propose me or arrange for me to be seconded by someone else, as I'm now told I must also be. Even if I did get that far I'd have to wait for my name to rise on a waiting list that's as long as your arm . . . with racket attached. At that point it still isn't a shoo-in, but remains at the committee's discretion — at that point a Zimmer frame will be the only thing on the receiving end of my double-handed grip. Damn.

But most vexing of all is the Granada trip. The number Moira Poole gave me is for a tour operator specialising in cultural holidays and the slow-speaking dimwit on the phone takes pleasure in telling me that the trip has long been sold out. 'You won't get a room at the parador for love nor money,' she says when I press her. 'They take August bookings *years* in advance.'

I look around my desk for inspiration and catch sight of today's front page. 'What if I said I was calling from Downing Street?'

'Which town?' the woman answers, mechanically.

I turn the page. 'Or for Angelina Jolie?'

But she knows I'm not booking for Angelina Jolie or the Prime Minister — even a tryst between the two of them wouldn't swing this one. 'We have the same package for next year if you'd like to put your name down?'

'No thanks,' I say.

I decide to get Nick, the only rep in the team who, by virtue of a Spanish grandmother, speaks anything other than estuary, to put in a call direct to the hotel. He shakes his head across the office and I'm on the phone to Maggie before he's even hung up.

'Meeting Maggie?' Caro's in the doorway, ear cocked. Maggie was my closest friend before Caro was and the two of them have since developed the same dynamic you find between ex and current partners: dismissive contempt animated periodically by suspicion.

'Just a quick coffee.' I squeeze past, waving. Sometimes I wonder how I manage to take a pee in this place without everyone else knowing. Talking of which, there's only so much herbal tea a bladder can hold, so on my way out I pop into the loo.

Ronnie, breathing over the receptionist, an on-off playmate of his, spots me coming back out. 'Cystitis again, Anna?' he calls out, loudly enough for all waiting visitors to hear. 'Too much sex, eh? Just as well Mummy's Boy's away for a while, I'd say.' Snigger, chortle, snort.

See what I mean?

★　★　★

Maggie is the lifestyle and interiors editor of the paper's Saturday supplement. Saturday is the new Sunday in newspapers — or so we dailies tell our advertisers. She's become surprisingly down-beat about her job these days as she's getting rather grand in her old age and has decided she should no longer be wasting time writing about wallpaper for a tabloid, but rather about what's hanging on it for a broadsheet. In other words, she wants a bit of respect. She's even adjusted her look in anticipation of the career move: out with the old (chunky highlights and underwired bras) and in with the new (Miss Moneypenny chignon and vintage-style camisoles). We're all at it, it seems, Viv, Maggie and I, changing our ways, our looks, our*selves*, now we've finally identified what it is we want.

'Triple chocolate biscotti?' I offer, joining her at an outside table of our local authentic Piedmontese caffè.

'*Triple* chocolate? What d'you want this time?' she asks. But she's smiling. Since I've been with Charlie, Maggie and I have become closer again. Classic stuff, really: she's married, I'm in a proper couple (albeit a semi-underground one), neither of us have children, and so movie-and-dinner for four is firmly on the agenda.

'You're right, I need to ask a favour.'

She just blinks at me and waits.

'There's a hotel I need to get into.' I tell her the details. 'They say it's fully booked, but I'm sure I'd get a room if I were press.'

'The parador at the Alhambra? August bank holiday? That's going to be *very* hard. And we don't do so many travel pieces now we've launched the new monthly.'

'But don't you sometimes contribute to *The Artist's Palette*, as well?'

She rolls her eyes. '*The Painter's Brush*, Anna. I know it's small fry, but it has a very loyal subscription base.'

'I could give you the notes and you could write it up?' I have no qualms about begging. 'Please, Mags! The Spanish tourist people would be chuffed with a mention in *The Painter's Brush*, wouldn't they?'

'I wouldn't have thought so,' she snorts. 'Believe it or not, it's not a big seller outside of the retirement homes of the south of England.'

'Even better! Everyone's after the silver pound right now. I bet this particular tour company would love to get its mitts on all those WOOFies!'

'What're they when they're at home?'

80

'You know, Well-Off Older Folk. Spending the kids' inheritance and all that. And you said yourself how loyal they are, they'll be going back to the hotel year after year, same room, same drink . . . '

She opens her mouth to protest. I can't blame her if she's going to bring up the time she and her husband, Ian, took Paul and me with them on one of her press junkets. It was a cosy little Cotswolds hotel and the ensuing rampage was a little too tabloid for the proprietor's liking. Paul was the sort of person who didn't need to be in a rock band to feel the urge to tip a piano into a swimming pool. When we finally called it a day you could probably hear the groans of relief from orbit.

'OK,' she says, 'let me find out who the PR is.'

'Thank you! I was beginning to think I might have to just turn up and sleep rough.'

She looks up at this and for the first time inspects me with real attention. 'Why d'you need to go there, anyway?'

'The mother will be there,' I say, simply.

'Three guesses as to whose mother you mean,' she says. But she perks up all right. Editorial types always do. They seem to find my situation fascinating. I've been approached by various features editors a few times to talk about it. 'Meet The New Love Triangulists' was what one piece was going to be called (they actually proposed to get Charlie's and *Meredith*'s side of the story, too); 'His Mother Hates My Guts' another. The women's editor of my own paper even wanted to ghost a piece called 'Why I Don't

81

Exist'. Naturally, I've turned down all proposals.

I'm too wired to work so I pop into the bookshop in Jubilee Place and pick up a coffee-table book about Moorish architecture. There are lots of shots of the Alhambra. Some of those tiles would look lovely if I ever get around to doing that wet room I've been thinking about.

★ ★ ★

I remember as a twelve-year-old reading those teen magazine articles about choosing the right outfit for the right occasion. It hadn't been so long since I'd started buying my own clothes for *any* occasion, as Dad had always tasked Grandma or Dawn, my after-school childminder, with my clothes shopping, so I pored over the features with great seriousness: First Date, University Interview, Pyjama Party (not so difficult, that one), and so on. And there would always be one for Meeting His Mother. I would scrutinise the look as though my life depended on it, even though I'd never even had a sniff of a boyfriend at that point. 'Respectable' was the word they would use, 'girl-next-door' — that's 1980s girl-next-door, you understand, not the current version who could easily be mistaken for a pole dancer. In any case, the advice peddled all those years ago by *Blue Jeans* still holds true today. If I'm going to meet Meredith, I need to dress down.

Like all the other women in my office whose age is closer to thirty (or forty) than twenty, my uniform is low-rise black trousers, snug over the buttocks, smart shirt or top in black, white or a currently fashionable actual colour, snug over the bust. It's a very hot July and there's flesh on display in Jubilee Place. My black shirt is made of an expensively softened sheer cotton that's just this side of decent, and I must admit I've undone a couple of extra buttons in the heat. Meanwhile Caro, who knocks off earlier than me most nights and can usually squeeze in a gym session between work and the bar, is similarly dressed but serving up a healthy dollop of tanned midriff to boot. We both have perfect nails, fake tan, lots of jewellery and 'summer' make-up (i.e. the same weight as any other seasonal make-up but it just looks as though there's less). And heels, of course.

'How exciting! The blue-stocking look is very now,' Caro says, but soon grumbles when I steer her away from our usual haunts and towards the few middle-aged outlets selling the kind of suits and dresses you might consider for the wedding of a Muslim friend. 'This is like *Pretty Woman*,' she says, nose curling at the sight of a long herringbone print I'm inspecting. 'But more *Ugly Woman*.'

'Thanks, mate.'

'When you said demure I thought you meant little floral dresses and cashmere cardies?'

'They don't seem to wear that kind of thing down there,' I say, remembering the loose-cut T-shirts and linen slacks. 'I suppose what I mean is *conservative*.' I spy a pair of brown trousers, not a bad cut for this place, though in a slightly squeaky fabric. 'What d'you think of this, Ca?

Brown is quite conservative, isn't it?'

She wrinkles her nose. 'Perfect — if your plan is to time-travel back to nineteen seventy-seven and get a job in Sainsbury's.'

'OK, fine.' I show her a full-length kaftan with a very pretty beaded neckline. 'This might be good for art gallery stuff.'

'Anna, you're going to be hanging out in Dulwich, not Kabul! You can show a bit of leg, surely? Meredith needs to see you as capable of producing sons and heirs, and that means having sex!'

'Oh no,' I protest, 'you don't understand, she mustn't associate me with anything *erotic*. I'm thinking more Lady Di. You know, when she was still a virgin.'

'Oh, please!' Caro throws up her hands. 'No one will believe that. And what about the Spain weekend — you'll roast in that hideous tent!'

'Hmm, well, I might not be going to Spain after all,' I say, frowning.

'You will. I know you when you're in this mood.'

'What mood?'

'Hell-bent,' she says, sweetly.

I decide to take that as a compliment. 'Well, I need to at least *look* angelic,' I say. '*Please* help me.'

She sighs. 'OK, babe. What's the budget?'

'To be confirmed.'

'The best kind,' she says. 'I'm in the West End tomorrow so I'll pick you up some stuff from Aquascutum, but for now, let's see. We don't want fashion, we want *garments* . . . '

84

She packs me off to the fitting room with a stack of 'garments' and insists I return to model each one for her. I soon crack the code: if Caro is disgusted it's too much fabric, if she is pleased it's too little, but if she is neither then it's just right. My final haul features lots of pressed linen, lightweight jersey tops with cut-off sleeves and pearl buttons and shoes you might choose if you were a lot taller than your boyfriend or worked in a bank.

'I swear I won't recognise you in that stuff,' Caro says in the lift back up to the office.

'It's only for Meredith,' I say. 'I won't be wearing it in the office.'

'Thank the Lord. I mean, can you *imagine* . . . ?' We both ponder the consequences of letting loose a primly dressed female in our office. If she were *very* lucky she might be totally ignored. 'What on earth will you wear when it comes to meeting Charlie and the mother at the same time?' Caro asks. 'He's gonna be freaked out by this celibate new look!'

I think hard. If all goes according to plan, the first time the three of us will be together will be at Meredith's party. That, surely, will require a shopping trip of its own. 'I may have to utilise layers,' I say, finally.

'Good thinking.'

Catching sight of myself in the mirror behind us, I reach up and stroke my hair. 'Now, stay calm, Caro, but I'm seriously considering a haircut. Long and dark like this is just too . . . too *sexy*. I need something more suitable for my Dulwich life.'

'Tie it back,' she says, as the lift doors ping open. 'Believe me, you might need to keep something in reserve.'

★ ★ ★

The same afternoon I get a call from the lady from the Do-gooders' Society. Speaking in an excitable rush, she declares herself overwhelmed by my offer to gather together celebrity memorabilia that 'Sotheby's would kill for' to auction at a duck fund-raiser in a few weeks' time. I'll see if my father can help me with that. I'm sure he used to manage Lionel Blair; that should be the right sort of age group.

The do-gooder asks me for my address and expresses surprise at my E1 postcode. 'You don't actually live down here, then?'

'Just waiting for an exchange date on my flat in the village,' I say, off the top of my head.

'Fingers crossed, then,' she says. Afterwards I turn to the page in my book headed 'Lies to Remember', where I've already written, *Terribly interested in art (museums of the world)*. I now add, *Buying flat in the village*. That was a tip from Viv. 'Keep a track of your lies,' she warned me. 'Sod's law someone will remember something you don't.' (So much for her melting pot of Eastern and Western philosophies; Sod's law is where everything really meets — or, as the case may be, bubbles over.)

I'm just making my regular check of the Wimbledon scoreboard online so I can share a few thrills and spills with Nigel tomorrow

86

morning ('It really looked like the Williams girl was taking an early bath for a minute when that Russian/Chinese/French girl had her on the ropes, eh, Nige?' or similar) when Maggie calls me back.

'Mission accomplished,' she states.

'No!' I'm very, very impressed. 'How did you do it . . . I mean . . . ?'

'There are conditions,' she interrupts, sternly. 'Only the room is complimentary, no meals, no drinks, not a nut from the minibar, understand? I've said you're a photographer. Do you even possess a camera?'

There's the Polaroid in the office cupboard, bought for Michelle's leaving do, which featured not one but two Elvis impersonators, both of whom vowed never to take a booking in Canary Wharf again. Otherwise we just use our phones.

'I'll get one. Dad will have something professional-looking.' Clamping the phone between shoulder and ear, I turn to 'Lies to Remember' and scribble, *Hotel: am a photographer.*

'And the best thing is we've got a view of the Summer Palace. Those rooms are supposed to be easily the nicest.'

'We?'

'I'm coming too,' she says. 'Ian's not back from his rugby tour till the Sunday, and I haven't been to Andalucia for ages. I've said I'll do a piece for *The Painter's Brush* and our travel supplement, too. I can probably get them to squeeze it into the second honeymoons special.'

'Hurrah!' I don't know how to thank her. 'The flights are on me.'

'The flights are on Iberia,' she replies with a superior snigger. 'Even *you* wouldn't be mad enough to pay full price for flights to Spain in the school holidays.'

'Great, thank you so much, Mags.' Sometimes I wonder if journalists have to pay for their own groceries.

'I'm glad you're finally taking the bull by the horns,' she adds, at last allowing herself to sound a little excited.

'The cow, in this case,' I say with a giggle.

'A cow wouldn't have horns,' she says. Maggie can be a touch pedantic, but I don't mind. As I put the phone down I can't help but think that it will be useful to have a pedant by my side in Granada.

Sitting there, hand still on the receiver in its cradle, I allow a tiny, sweet anticipatory note of triumph to ring through my body. This really might work. Viva España! Viva Maggie! Viva Project Meredith!

# 7

Even though I have a whole archive of images of my mother filed in my head, there are also the photos and the Super 8 clips to reassure me that she really was here, once upon a time, in my life, devoted to it, creator of it. Like the sun-drenched footage of me pulling at her legs as she talks in the garden with Grandma: without breaking her flow of chatter, she just reaches down and scoops me up for a kiss on the nose. Or the photo of me sitting on her knee at the kitchen table, trying to post a corner of toast into her mouth like a birthday card that won't quite fit through the letterbox. These are the possessions I'd save first if my flat were on fire. I can't imagine not having access to her face; if I haven't seen it for a while, then it feels like cats' claws scraping at scalded skin. Absence makes the heart bleed, it really does.

On 18 July 1977, soon before one o'clock in the afternoon on a residential road not far from Chesham town centre, my mother's death was instant. We know she must have seen the other car veering into the wrong lane because she braked abruptly, but she could never have predicted that it would hit a pedestrian before it did her, an elderly lady stepping into the lane with one of those shopping bags on wheels. The impact caused that innocent contraption, loaded with a week's worth of tinned provisions, to fly through my mother's windscreen, solid, unstoppable, deadly as a boulder. There was no time and no chance, only the kind of real-life tangle of glass, metal and human tissue that made the first poor wretches to come out into the street bow their heads in horror. The old lady was also killed outright, but the instigator of this tragedy, evidently uninjured, took one look at the carnage he'd set in motion and fled. Witnesses talked of his tyres 'squealing', but none could recall the licence number or even be clear of the model of the vehicle.

'Just imagine if it had been a pram and not a shopping bag,' one officer at the scene was heard to say, apparently not finding the body count high enough.

Summoned to the hospital mortuary where the remains of his wife's body lay, Dad experienced one of those yoyos of emotion that don't happen too often in life: first, the kind of grief that tips you overboard and holds your head underwater, then, when it was discovered that his only child had not been in the car but at home with a neighbour, elation, a return of oxygen to his bloodstream, a reason to go on.

Later, as a teenager obsessed with conspiracy theories, I tracked down that neighbour, June, to get to the bottom of where Mum was going that day, without me (funny how, having called her Mummy for all the time I knew her, I switched to Mum at exactly the same age as my friends did, friends who still had theirs). It had never been satisfactorily explained, as far as I was concerned, and I had come to suspect an extra-marital affair, a drug deal, a suitcase in the boot and a bid for freedom from the shackles of a 1970s marriage. June, who I remembered as being rather foxy but who had not aged well, served up PG Tips with the unremarkable truth: Mum was driving to the chemist's to pick up a prescription and June had offered to keep an eye on me for her because I was taking so long to finish my Cornetto and the chemist closed at one on Wednesdays (half days, 1970s opening hours).

'What was the prescription for?' I wondered, hoping she'd offer me a B&H, for I'd just started smoking. 'Did I have a cold or something?'

'Nothing to do with you, hun-bun,' she said, lighting herself one and then tucking the pack censoriously away. 'We were all on tranks in those days.'

As I wait in my father's house for him to come down from his office, I look at the one photograph of Mum that has remained on public display in the Day residence since Jojo came along. Taken in unfashionable black-and-white on the wet sands of Dorset, it's little more than a silver rectangle with stick people inside it, one in the centre, one at the edge. The stick people are Mum and me. 'She looks like a young Raquel Welch,' Caro said when she saw it, though Jojo can't have heard the remark or the picture wouldn't still be there. In any case, you can hardly see Mum's face as she's brought both hands up to her mouth in a dramatic gasp — I must have surprised her by streaking off towards the water when I was supposed to be having my photo taken. Strange to think that our bodies were close enough to fit together into this neat little square, that they were habitually this close, every day, every hour. I hadn't even started school yet when she died.

'Anna! You're early!' Always Anna now, though he used to call me Annie back in the days of that photo.

I kiss my father hello and turn to assess his appearance and condition. He's looking well, very well. He's not tall, but his shoulders are broad enough to make him appear imposing and his crown is still thickly covered. He's good with people, good with them for a living, excelling as he does as a manager of TV talent (he rejects the term 'celebrity' on the grounds that it's not the same thing). It's his skill to seem like a bumbling buffoon while extracting fat fees for his artists. He grins a lot and sort of bobs from foot to foot when he's excited or nervous about something. I'm aware that I do the same.

He's grinning away right now. He has very good teeth for his age, though such opinions are shared at one's peril — 'You can't *still* believe sixty is ancient? Not in this day and age?' — as if life expectancy has been announced to have doubled in the last decade and he's got another century to go. Maybe he reserves the denial act for me, as though achieving longer life himself might make up for the fact that Mum's was so short. Or perhaps decrepitude just holds special horror if you are going to be approaching eighty when your son leaves home for university.

'Feeleex, say night-night to your seester . . . ' I turn to say hello to Marta, the au pair, who holds the pouting arriviste who will one day trouser half of my inheritance — already he's straining to get his hands on the pendant around my neck. Actually I genuinely adore Felix, this gorgeous nuzzly person, still more of a cub than a human. He smells of vanilla and baby powder and his hair is softer than anything I've ever touched. He is one year old and when he finally pincers the trinket, emitting a little 'Oh!', it's as though he's never seen anything so delightful in the whole wide world. Big kisses are exchanged all round and Marta carries him off to bed.

'Where's Jojo?' I ask.

It's one of those odd pieces of symmetry that when Dad finally succumbed to remarriage it was to a woman the same age as my mother when she died: twenty-five. A twenty-first-century version of the 1970s model with nothing serious in between, at least not that I was ever made aware of. It was no surprise when my little half-brother put in an appearance a few years later — decades since I first started asking for him. He has yet to discover that his mother is younger than his sister, but I don't suppose he'll be the only kid on the block to wrestle with that one.

'She's out tonight,' Dad says. 'She's doing some sort of course in jewellery-making.'

'Everyone's at it,' I exclaim and he looks a little uneasy.

'Evening classes,' I say. 'I'm just about to start one myself. A course called 'Looking at Pictures'.'

'Are you now? You do know it won't be likely

to cover *EastEnders*, don't you?'

'Ha, ha.' I roll my eyes.

'Come on, let's have a drink by the pool,' he says.

My father lives in Hampstead in a private lane just off Frognal and has a pool in his back garden. That's a pair of good reasons to love him or hate him before we even start. It's the discovery of the pool that swings the balance one way or the other, even though building one costs barely more per square metre than your more upscale kitchen worktop (he has plenty of those, too, courtesy of Jojo's refit). But it sounds decadent, glamorous, a little piece of Beverly Hills in north London.

'Global warming is going to get a hell of a lot worse,' Dad said when people questioned the wisdom of an outdoor pool in a city that has about three hot, clear days a year.

'I'm so glad the planet's loss will be your gain,' I laughed. But summers *have* improved and now Felix has swimming lessons — if you can call the alternate dunking and gasping of an infant a 'lesson' — and Jojo's personal trainer is able to incorporate a more expensive adult version into her twice-weekly sessions. Sitting here now, however, iced drinks tinkling away in the glass, the breeze picks up and I wish I'd brought a jacket.

'Come on, then,' Dad says. 'Why the sensitive artist routine? That's not like you.' I'm not offended by this. He's the one who instilled in me the preference for commerce over art, its benefits no more finely demonstrated than by our shared journey from Chesham semi to Hampstead pile. It occurs to me that Charlie's re-education programme, that of the lectures on bridge span and lattes on the Tate Modern members' terrace, has been far too leisurely. The new crash course should remedy that.

'It's all part of a new me I've just launched,' I say, feeling the nerve ends flare just saying the words.

Dad raises an eyebrow. 'Your new ad director a bit of a culture vulture, then? God, they know how to pick 'em at that place, don't they?'

'No, nothing to do with work. This is about Charlie.'

'Oh? I thought he'd taken his protractor and gone off to Frisco?'

*Frisco*, I ask you. The teen-Felix is going to be cringing at this sort of talk. 'He has,' I say. 'This is to do with his mother.'

'Ah. *Meredith*.' Dad knows all about the Meredith situation. Though it's obviously galling for him to hear that someone else's parent might not find his issue as delightful as he does, he's had enough dealings with the female of the showbiz species to consider no stance too unlikely, no demand too preposterous. To Dad, it would be suspicious if a woman were *not* difficult in some way. He does, however, have an irritating habit of pointing out that it is not technically *Meredith* who disapproves of me, but rather Charlie making the call on her behalf. Which is why, as I summarise my plans, his expression gradually settles somewhere between amusement and bemusement. It's not my methods he objects to — it goes against his soul to condemn action — he just thinks Charlie should be putting in some of the legwork too. I fill him in on the Granada plan anyway.

'Tell you what,' he says, when I finish. 'Take me to this gallery thing with you and I'll give you a hand with charming the old bird.'

I laugh. 'No offence, Dad, but I'm not sure you're her type.'

'I'm the same type as you,' he says.

'That's the point. Why do you think I'm reinventing myself?'

He cackles at this and hops up to refill our drinks and hunt down an ashtray from indoors. When he comes back he's bouncing from foot to foot again. He has another idea and I have a feeling I probably won't like it. 'I just thought, love, Sammy Duncan will be down on the Costas around then doing PAs at the clubs. How about I set something up in Granada? He owes us a favour.'

I frown. 'I'm not sure that would help.' Sammy is a cretinous singer who left his boy band last summer and after a stretch of binge drinking and rehab is back on his dancing feet and looking for a second chance.

'What weekend are you down there?'

Reluctantly, I tell him the dates.

'This is *perfect*. I'm pretty sure he's near Malaga that Saturday night. Let me check with Lucy first thing.'

'I don't think so, Dad.'

'Come on, all I'm saying is there'd be no harm if a photographer papped him with a mysterious and beautiful older woman. That's you, by the way. Older women are very fashionable right now.'

'I'm sure they'd be very grateful for your validation,' I laugh, amused by his gall: he's not 'ancient' but I'm 'older'!

He joins in. 'If I remember rightly, it's the most stunning place, the Nasrid palaces . . . '

I look up. 'You've been to Granada? I didn't know that!'

'Yep, I went there with your mother before you were born. We spent quite a bit of time in Spain, I seem to remember. Andalucia was very different then, you know.'

I wouldn't know. Dad was too busy for anything more than a long weekend when I was young, so most of my holidays were taken at the English seaside with Grandma and Grandpa, who refused, after the Tenerife disaster, ever to set foot in a plane again (even after the death of their only child in a road accident, they would argue the greater danger of the air). Then, once installed in the workplace, I leapfrogged the Continent altogether in favour of the superior room service of the Far East and Caribbean.

'She went back to the area again later, actually, to do some sketching.'

'One of her Father Christmas trips?'

'I'd forgotten about that.' Apparently, if they wanted a weekend on their own, or even just a night out, Mum and Dad used to say they were visiting Santa in Lapland to give him a progress report on my behaviour. This was because the first time they made the mistake of telling me they were going away for the weekend on their own for *fun* I cried until my face swelled up and I had to be spoon-fed trifle every hour by Grandma to keep me sweet. So sweet, in fact, that I was sick all over the new white boots she'd bought me. After that, Santa was invoked at the drop of a hat. No child would dare argue with Santa. He was the top man, higher than Messiah, as Steve would say. I simply accepted my parents' transplantation from surburbia to elf workshop as pre-schoolers accept everything — initial devastation followed by full-scale amnesia.

'Are there any photos?' I ask. 'From the Granada trip?'

'You've seen all Helen's albums,' he says, more wearily than I was expecting. It's not that he objects to my keeping her memory alive, it's just that he feels like he's the only medium left now her parents are gone too.

'Can I have another quick look? I won't be long.'

'You know where they are.'

★ ★ ★

Not long ago I said to Charlie, 'My mother would *never* have behaved like Meredith.'

'How do you know?' he said, shoulders sinking an inch or two as he resigned himself to another discussion about The Situation. 'You were an only child, weren't you? She might have turned out to be just as difficult.'

'I was only an only child because she died,' I

98

pointed out, and he stroked my hair in apology. He never suggested that his pain was greater than mine simply for its newness. We were the same: 'demi-orphans', he called us.

Actually, Dad has always been quite candid about the fact that he and Mum were having a lot of ups and downs before her accident. More downs than ups, I believe, hence June's 'tranqs'. That's why they hadn't supplied a sibling for me with the blink-of-an-eye age gap decreed by 1970s child-rearing gurus ('They'll entertain each other, leaving you free to crochet a beret!'). Of course they were never on course for divorce or anything; he just doesn't want me to idealise her to the point of deification. 'She was a normal woman,' he once said. 'She had the same good days and bad days as everyone else.' They don't work, of course, these well-meaning remarks; it's a bit like when people say you should imagine the Queen sitting on the loo. That doesn't stop her being the Queen, does it?

Mum's photo albums and private bits and pieces are kept in a trunk in Dad's home office. It took him years to sort them out, defying even the rigours of three house moves, and it was really only after the installation of Jojo and a second generation of wedding gifts that they were officially consigned to storage. He offered to hand the whole lot over to me to join my own smaller collection, but I wanted his to stay with him: quite apart from the risk of total loss in that hypothetical fire, I like to think my parents are still together at least in a small way, even if he has moved on and remarried.

Jojo doesn't mind — if you hook up with someone thirty years older than you, you have to expect to run into a memento or two of past lives. During the course of her ongoing refurbishment programme (now in its fourth year, Dad likens it to painting Forth Bridge), she keeps finding bits and pieces and adding them to the trunk. Every year, as Dad is required to box up shelves of old books to make way for a fresher aesthetic, there are a couple of new finds. She knows I like to see everything, even recipes cut from magazines and found disintegrating between the pages of paperbacks; they all help flesh out the picture.

I know exactly what I'm looking for this evening: her travel diaries. There are several, mostly factual logs of holidays to Europe with Dad — she hadn't travelled abroad before she met my father, what with her parents' phobia and all. Her writing is curvy and girlish, but then she *was* only a girl, not long out of school when most of this was written. I find the entries for the Granada trip:

*Clive sick in bed, it must have been the eggs; You can see the Alhambra walls from our hotel; The light in the Court of Lions was magical. Irving calls the water 'diamond drops' and he is spot on.*

Who is Irving? I wonder, and remember wondering the same thing during a previous study of them. I've been through everything several times before, but never thought I'd be preparing to follow in her footsteps.

There are a few sketches and postcards too, glued on to the paper or tucked between pages. The sketches — of gardens, hill-tops, a tower or two — are spiky, almost urgent, quite different from Charlie's considered style. Mum always had a flair for drawing and had excelled at school, but it was only when I approached school age that she came to apply to art college. The timing made perfect sense, though I gather family opinion on the matter was divided (who knew what beatnik influences might distract her from her rightful place in the kitchen?). It didn't happen anyway, of course; she never did get to explore whatever marriage and motherhood failed to fulfil. When September came around she didn't join the teenagers at the local art school and I was the only girl at the school gate holding Grandma's hand and not Mummy's. For a while, when asked by teachers, I said drawing and colouring in were my favourite things, eked out the scantiest talent for as long as I could, but ultimately even I had to admit I was more of a sums sort of girl.

I notice a photo that's come loose from the stack of albums: my parents sitting together at an outdoor table, Dad smoking and pulling an expression that's not quite grimace, not quite smile. Mum, on the other hand, beams like the sun. She looks so young, Pippa's age, younger than that even. Too young, Dad once told me; a wife at nineteen, a mother at twenty-one. He wasn't much older himself — twenty-seven when I was born — but then at that age, at that time, it would have been significant. He probably made all the decisions; certainly he earned all the money. (No doubt Meredith would approve. She's the type to insist on traditional age gaps.)

I can't stop staring at my mother's photo. I try to remember what I looked like at that age. You might know from our matching olive colouring that we're mother and daughter, but there's little in the grown-up me of her languid elegance so evident in the easy way she hooks lean arms over the back of the chair, fingers curling over the spindles. I am more like my father, it seems — buzzing, jumpy, quick to sacrifice those gasps of delight to the perfectionist's frown — and we're both glad of the fact. He doesn't want the reminder of the grief he felt, and I don't want to remind him of that grief.

'Anna, the takeaway's here.'

He stands in the doorway, the only person in my life I've known from the beginning to the present, and even though I've never lived in this house for any length of time, I have such a strong sense of déjà vu at the sight of him framed by the doorway that it takes a moment for me to respond.

'Coming.'

'Found anything useful?'

'Nothing in particular.'

As we go back down the stairs I say, 'By the way, Dad, there *is* something you can help me with . . . '

★ ★ ★

By the end of the second week my diary is looking fearsomely full. I have Looking at Pictures classes every Tuesday evening (in my neighbourhood, of course, not hers — I don't want to be spotted in Dulwich doing anything quite so remedial); the Friends' party at the gallery on Friday the sixteenth; I've joined the Dulwich Horticultural Society and received notice of a summer lecture on Mediterranean gardens; I've also kept free the weekend of the Dulwich Country Fair, coming up in early August — vintage Meredith stamping ground if ever there was any — and the Saturday morning of another weekend for a lecture at the gallery. Then there's the Do-gooders' celebrity auction to prepare for — this takes place at a parish church hall in the North Dulwich Triangle, wherever that is. I can't actually remember the last time I set foot in a place of worship, unless you count that weekend I spent with an old college friend in Lincoln when we went to the cathedral café for tea and cake.

That pretty much covers most of the local organisations. I have drawn the line at the Dulwich Players, the best known of all the area's groups, or any other theatrical outfit for that matter. If there's one thing I know about Meredith it's that she prizes creative excellence above all else; am-dram will cut no mustard with the woman who would doubtless find fault with Olivier. Too loud, maybe?

But I don't want to be seen to be discriminating. Maybe I'll donate my new wardrobe to them when all this is over.

# 8

**What have you been up to?** says the message from nine thousand miles away. I imagine Charlie's fingertips tapping the desk, lazily, rhythmically, as he waits for my reply. They're missing me, those fingers, just as mine are missing him.

I think, then type, **Oh, the usual**.

Laughable as it may seem, I've promised myself that I will not lie to him over this. I may omit certain details regarding my activities, but I will not lie, not outright. And it's true, I *have* been up to the usual (work, work, work; chat, chat, chat), it's just that I've found time for a fair amount of the unusual too.

He obviously mistakes brevity for melancholy because his reply, before signing off, is very sweet: **Don't forget, A, true love waits**. Followed by a row of kisses.

In the first month of our relationship Charlie took me to the Globe Theatre. Not having given Shakespeare a second thought since school, I had to half-feign delight when he produced the tickets for *Measure for Measure*. I tried hard to make intelligent conversation over interval wine, but what I'd really spent the first two acts thinking was how scandalous it was that an average-sized human could be expected to sit against a bumpy beam for three hours and not scream out for mercy. How could they have run out of cushions? Obviously, knowing how uncomfortable the place was, others had snapped up one for each buttock.

'It's so amazing how relevant these issues are today,' I said, instead, because people always say that about Shakespeare and it was sure to be correct.

'Do you think?' Charlie asked with a studious frown. 'God, I was just thinking the opposite.'

Bugger. I gave him a look of polite but searching intellectual curiosity.

'I mean, you can tell the audience is really struggling to understand Isabella's dilemma. Virginity means diddly-squat to us, doesn't it?' (For the record, I would never use such down-home Dulwich terms as 'diddly-squat' myself.)

'Maybe in the States?' I said. 'True love waits, and all that.' Our paper was obsessed for a time with the latest generation of abstemious Americans and had been publishing shots of the 'bashful babes', asking readers to phone in and vote for their favourite virgin.

Charlie was taken with the phrase and started joking about it until it became our catchphrase, whispered with ironic satisfaction after sex, used entreatingly to end a row; it even became a code word between the two of us for time out on the subject of Meredith. Always Meredith. What did my mind fill itself with before the Meredith dilemma? It's as though the year since Charlie arrived amounts to about ninety per cent of my thoughts. Otherwise I'm thinking about the four or five before my mother left. The time in between just feels like padding.

*★  ★  ★*

The first time I visited, I hadn't noticed what a beautiful building Dulwich Picture Gallery is. Of course a little knowledge enriches one's appreciation, and I am considerably more knowledgeable about the place today than I was yesterday, having speed-read the gallery visitor's guide in the bath this morning. Key facts: it's the world's first purpose-built gallery; it was designed by Sir John Soane (famous, apparently) to house the collection of his friend Sir Francis Bourgeois (yes, really); its exterior lines are simple and restrained and it is light and tranquil within. Handsome, is what Charlie would call it. He often uses words for buildings that others would assign to faces, yet when it comes to faces he rarely comments at all. 'What does your mother look like?' I asked him once, and then seeing him struggle added, 'I mean, what's her face like?' 'Fine,' he responded. 'Just sort of . . . symmetrical.'

'Garden party this way . . . ' says an old love in head-to-toe ruffled purple. She looks like a Quality Street.

'Thank you.' As I follow the pathway towards the gathering, I make a final check of my own appearance. I've dressed very carefully for this first formal infiltration of Dulwich society for it wouldn't take the editor of *Vogue* to work out that there won't be any tattooed breasts on show here. I'm wearing a sky-blue linen dress — smock, to be exact — and as I peer through the throng I pop on a pair of glasses that pre-date my contact lens-wearing days and so are laughably unfashionable. (The only thing is I have to slide them right down my nose if I want to avoid walking into a wall since the combination of two prescriptions makes every-thing resemble very cloudy pond water.) My hair is pinned back at the nape of my neck and my jewellery and make-up are barely visible to the naked eye. Finally, to complete the ensemble, my bag is made of — no joke — *straw*.

I scan the scene. So this is a Dulwich garden party. There is Pimm's with cucumber and mint or sun-warmed white wine and big platters of vol-au-vents and cocktail sausages (offered, it would seem, in no spirit of retro chic). There is a room in the nearby modern extension (bronze and glass, multi-functional, sympatheti-cally linked to aforementioned main building) where the summer exhibition has been hung, but no one is heading that way for now.

I quickly gather that I'm rather *too* dressed down, though have been correct to eschew the little black dress. Colour is king: there are lots and lots more Quality Street ensembles. In fact, what with the smattering of hats and the heels sinking into turf, the sound of voices rising to a pure summer sky and *birdsong*, if that's what it is, it all feels rather like a wedding — just without anyone of the bride and groom's generation. I am the youngest here by some distance. Looking at this crush of jowls and paunches and inexplicable metallic hair tints makes me realise how used I am in my industry to the smooth, snug beauty of youth. Hell, Nigel would be a young buck in this company.

Then I see a face that, at thirtysomething, shouts ingénue. It's Maggie, in a wraparound print dress I recognise from last month's glossies.

She almost walks straight past me. 'Good Lord, where did you get those specs? You *are* serious about this operation, aren't you?'

I kiss her, grazing her cheek with said eyewear. 'Why else would I be spending a gorgeous summer evening at an *art gallery* when I could be drinking Pinot Grigio at Corney & Barrow?'

'There are worse places,' she says, frowning at the lush gardens. 'This is probably the most beautiful gallery in London. Look at it! I always forget what a philistine you are, Anna, whatever Charlie likes to believe.'

'Shh! Not any more!' I giggle. 'I did my first Looking at Pictures class on Tuesday. Just ask me about the laws of perspective. Go on!'

'I'm not sure that's likely to come up at a Friends' exhibition,' she laughs.

I'm not sure any of the subjects discussed in my first evening class will come up, if I'm honest. The session was held at an 'adult empowerment facility' in Limehouse that I'd always assumed was a derelict school with planning issues preventing it from becoming high-spec apartments for people like me. Of the twelve of us seated in a semicircle around a painting of a horse, several looked as though they might be re-entering the community from another kind of facility and the others were female yuppies looking for love. I alone took notes as we were whisked through two thousand years of painting by a girl training to be a voluntary guide at the National Gallery (and so not yet qualified to work for free!). At the end of the class when she asked us if we had any questions no one spoke. It was very awkward. Finally, I asked, 'What's that picture worth, then?' She said valuation wasn't part of the course, but finally admitted it might go under the hammer at about fifteen thousand pounds. That got them all talking!

Maggie is busy scanning the crowd. 'Are we sure she'll be here, then?'

'Not exactly,' I admit, 'but it seems likely. Charlie's mentioned quite a few gallery events and look at the crowd! This is obviously the place to be around here. She might be here already for all we know.' But how to find her? How to get to speak to her? My heart catches at the thought of what may lie just moments ahead.

'OK,' says Maggie. 'Well, we can't approach everyone individually and hope they might be her. What we need is a trusty guide . . . '

As I hoped, she snaps straight into pushy journo mode and before I know it she's identified some sort of fund-raising officer and they're chinwagging away. Even our new friend, a gallery employee rather than a local resident, is on the mature side, with generous padding between waistband and braline. I suddenly remember something Paul once said: 'I reckon women are like brie. The more mature they get, the more slops out the sides.' He wasn't looking to put Keats out of business, Paul.

'Anna Day.' I hold out my hand to introduce myself, admiring my own French manicure. Not a look I've embraced in the past, admittedly, but once she'd recovered from the shock of the new, Tracey at the nail bar near Toni & Guy did a beautiful job.

'Virginia,' she says. 'What a treat to meet two such glamorous young friends.'

I am taken aback, automatically thinking she must mean a friend of Charlie. Has Maggie let the cat out of the bag already? Then, as she talks on, I see that everyone is referred to as a Something Friend — 'This is our Catering Friend, Iris; Mary is our Visits Friend . . . ' — and I remember that this is a Friends of the Gallery party. Of course! I'm a Friend too. Friends play an invaluable role in the life and work of the gallery. We are its lifeblood. I know because it says so in the literature they sent me.

'So many Friends,' I grin, lamely. I'm going to have to improve on this if I'm to leave an impression of remarkable charm.

'Oh yes.' She moves conspiratorially closer. 'I was just telling Maggie that they're a mixed bunch. They really are. Some are rather grand and some are more *ordinaire*.'

I think we can guess which camp Meredith is going to be in. 'Who's the most grand?' I ask, hopefully. But she starts detailing the social credentials of someone called Olive and I quickly lose interest.

'Excuse me while I pop to the loo,' Maggie says and I send her retreating figure a desperate look. Desperate looks so early in proceedings!

Then Virginia steps out into the throng and flags down a passing male as though he's a taxi. 'Ah, here comes Angus! Who's he looking for, I wonder?'

'Virginia, hello, hello.' Although he's about my age and equipped with perfectly decent raw material — dark curly hair and excellent height — I quickly note that Angus has got that tweedy young-fogey thing going that I've never much liked. Charlie's style may be conservative but at least it suggests conservative with a sex life, whereas this one looks as though he belongs on the wall behind a couple of layers of crusty varnish. I watch as his hand hovers an inch or two from Virginia's back as though he hasn't quite got the hang of physical contact. 'It's been a while, yes, quite a while, hasn't it?' His amiable mumbling reminds me of the guy on the phone, Humphrey Poole.

'Anna Day,' I say to him, nails still looking good.

'Angus Poole.' I look up. Did he actually *say* Poole?

'Any relation to Humphrey and Moira?' I ask, easily, as though I'm chums with absolutely everyone here.

'My parents,' he says, just a little grudgingly. 'You know them?'

'Only by name. We've spoken on the phone.' My mind is whirring. If they're the Granada people, then Meredith will surely touch base with her fellow travellers at some point. If I find them, I find her. Welcome to my world, Angus

111

Poole! 'Are they here this evening?' I ask, keen as mustard now.

'No,' he says, 'sadly they couldn't make it.'

'That's such a shame,' I say, disappointed. 'A rival function?'

'No, no, they just happen to be out of town.'

Just so long as Meredith doesn't happen to be out of town with them. There's a pause. I sense that Angus is the sort to cause pauses. He's *very* dry. Virginia and I both take sips from our drinks and smile at him. How appropriate his name is, I decide, for there's something very bovine about him, the distracted way he rocks his head in the cradle of his neck, the way he chews his food, slowly and deliberately. How amusing it would be if he suddenly threw himself to the ground and began grazing at the lawn beneath our feet . . .

'Anna, Angus . . . ' Virginia thinks she might have found inspiration. 'They say people with 'A' names are most likely to succeed, don't they?'

Not necessarily with one another, I want to reply, wishing I could roll my eyes at her. Instead, like the demure young lady in linen that I am, I simper, 'Really? How flattering. It would be nice to think so, wouldn't it, Angus?'

'Hmm.'

He doesn't seem to like me, this junior Poole, which is fair enough, but I wish he'd just move along and leave me to sort out the grand from the *ordinaire* without his help. Instead, he loiters, still not saying anything, until Maggie reappears and, to my surprise, cries out, 'Angus! I didn't think I'd know anyone down here. Are you from these parts . . . ?'

'I live just around the corner in West Dulwich, actually,' he says, a broad smile transforming his whole demeanour. His teeth are smaller than I would have expected, giving the impression that he has more than the usual allocation.

It turns out Maggie and he know each other from some inner-city art initiative. Smile aching, I search for ways to join in as they catch up on how magical it is that so many deprived youngsters now have ready access to turps.

'So if their usual tipple dries up, they're sorted,' I joke, but judging by Maggie's stiff chuckle I've stepped too far out of character. I shut up again.

'Angus is our Travel Friend,' Virginia tells Maggie. 'Aren't you, Angus?'

'I am, I am.'

'You are?' Maggie asks, sliding a meaningful look my way.

He is? Now that *is* interesting, perhaps he'll know something about his parents' Granada trip after all.

'He'll be leading our local arts group on one of their travel adventures next month,' Virginia explains, bang on cue.

'With the gallery people?' I ask.

'Actually, it's a breakaway group,' he replies, not to me but to Maggie, as though she were the one to have asked. 'The Friends are off to Bilbao, but I'm taking my members south.'

Both Maggie and I are hot on the scent now. While I'm still gasping, she gets in first. 'Then

113

you must be one of the Art Explorers we've heard about?'

'That's right.'

'Whereabouts are you going exactly?'

'Andalucia,' he says. 'Granada. Do you know it?'

'Granada?' Maggie acts surprised so well I forget for a moment she's my accomplice. 'I'm heading off there myself soon on a story. When will you be there?'

'August bank holiday weekend.'

Her mouth is agape. 'But that's when *we're* going!'

'How *extraordinary*.' He says it in two words.

'Amazing! Of all the places . . . '

Virginia is beaming at the unexpected cosiness of it all. 'Well, you'll have to get together for a glass of, remind me of the local poison, Angus . . . ?'

'Champagne?' I say, hopefully.

'Sherry,' Maggie remembers, smoothly.

'Oh, I do like a good fino,' Angus says as though revealing some particularly saucy secret. How *have* they become friends? He is *awful*.

'We're really looking forward to staying in the parador,' I chip in. Finally, he looks my way, obviously puzzled.

'Anna sometimes helps me out with photography,' Maggie tells him. 'She'll be accompanying me on this assignment.'

'Yes, I'm the picture person.' I nod. 'Only when my day job allows, of course. I'm in media sales for my sins.' Maggie and I have rehearsed this for just such an opening. Having decided

114

there's no point in passing me off as a professional photographer, the idea is that I'm a frustrated salesperson with artistic leanings — and genuine talent, of course.

'How very glamorous,' Virginia says. 'I don't think we have many Media Friends.'

But Angus can't seem to get his head around the *extraordinary* coincidence unfolding before him. I almost feel sorry for him. 'Maggie, did I hear you say you were staying at the parador?'

'Yes, that's right.'

'But so is *my* group!'

'Such a small world,' Virginia agrees. 'Though I suppose all art-lovers make the pilgrimage to the Alhambra at some point, don't they?' Now she's pressing him into agreeing to let us join their guided tour. This couldn't be better if I'd slipped her a script in advance.

'*Of course* we must coordinate,' he says. 'I see no harm in you joining our tour, so long as the members don't mind, that is.'

'That would be *wonderful*, Angus.'

Oh, this is progress indeed. Angus's *must* be the same trip Meredith is taking. There couldn't possibly be more than one of these self-important little societies going to the same place at the same time; if I could only ask him directly.

'How many charges will you have with you?' Maggie asks, reading my mind.

'Only a handful, places are limited on these things. It's something of a family affair, actually. Both my parents will be coming, and a good friend of my mother's . . . ' At this, I nudge Maggie's arm. He *has* to be talking about her.

115

'Yes,' Virginia says, 'Meredith said she'd confirmed her place.' And I feel heat spreading down my face and over my collarbone. Even if I don't meet her this evening or any time before the end of the month, I'm guaranteed a meeting in Granada. So far so according to plan.

'We're very pleased she's coming,' Angus agrees, 'though I suspect her knowledge will put me to shame.'

'She is *such* a clever lady.' Virginia turns to Maggie and me. 'Meredith used to be a Very Active Friend, you know, but we haven't seen as much of her since her husband passed away last year.'

Maggie tilts her head in sympathy. 'How sad. Well, I can't think of many more life-affirming sights than the Alhambra. I'm longing for that first glimpse of the old palace.'

I slide my glasses up and down my nose. 'Oh, I agree. Those *extraordinary* tiles!'

Angus fishes a business card out of his breast pocket and hands it to Maggie. 'My mobile usually works OK down there, but let's try and speak before then, anyway.'

'Definitely,' she smiles. 'It's been so nice to see you again, Angus.'

'You too.'

How easy was that? She nudges me, clearly elated. I'm so glad Maggie's on board. She's going to be such an asset on the Spanish trip. Not only is she comfortable talking about art with this crowd but she's also highly professional in her approach to information gathering.

Then Virginia speaks again and it's like someone's blown apart the Hoover Dam inside my head, so sudden and overpowering is the crashing of liquid through my ears. 'Oh look,' she says, 'here's Meredith now.'

# 9

Though I've never actually met Meredith Grainger, I have heard her voice before. Twice, strictly against the rules, I've rung Charlie at home. The first time, I hung up in a panic and sat giggling to myself in disbelief; the second, I brazened it out. 'Is Charlie in? This is Anna from college.'

'One moment, please.' Her voice had a slight dip of disapproval to it, as though I'd betrayed an enthusiasm she found distasteful. At the time I dismissed this as paranoia on my part, but later Charlie told me she'd used me as an example of increasing sloppiness in phone manners among the younger generation. Apparently I should have said, '*May* I speak to Charlie, please?' and waited to be asked who, kindly, was telephoning for him before giving my name.

So you can imagine the sort of uptight, dried-out, mean-eyed old buzzard I've been picturing, all nose and claws, swooping at error, delighting in blunder. Which makes the sight of a slight, smiling figure, answering Virginia's raised hand with a restrained wave of her own, totally disarming. My first impression is of softness. Her steps are light and unhurried, the weight of her hand on the bodies she must negotiate to reach us is gently precise, even the fabric of her pale-grey dress looks light as air: there's not a single sharp angle or heavy line to her. As she comes closer, I see that she's not beautiful, not conventionally so — her eyes too wide-set, her dark hair overtaken with silver and the lines on her face well beyond disguise — but it's clear at once that she has a way of regarding those around her with a candour that makes her alluring, commanding even. I know immediately who she reminds me of: Jackie Kennedy. Only one of the most formidable mother-in-laws of the last century. My nerves sizzle.

'Meredith, I'd like to introduce you to Maggie Bishop,' Virginia says. 'She's an arts correspondent for one of the papers, and, I'm so sorry, what was your friend's name again?'

'Anna,' I whisper. I withhold my surname, just in case. (Just in case *what?*)

'Of course. Anna and Maggie, this is the lady we were just talking about, Meredith Grainger.'

'Pleased to meet you,' she says, evidently not at all curious that she has been the subject of discussion. 'What a beautiful evening you've got, Virginia.' How different voices are when you have the benefit of the face in front of you. Hers is brisk, clipped, higher-pitched than I remembered.

'Meredith is one of our Very Dearest Friends,' Virginia says and the others join me in gaping openly at the newcomer. Angus has even repositioned himself squarely between Maggie and me as though completing a line-up at a Royal premiere. I almost expect Meredith to hold out her hand for a kiss.

'Lovely to meet you,' Maggie says.

'Likewise,' I squeak. *Likewise?* I never say

119

that; *Ronnie* says 'likewise'. What's come over me? Oh God, am I going to screw this up? I decide to shut up until the billion gallons of water stop pounding my skull.

'We were just talking about the Alhambra,' Maggie says, sounding enviably normal.

'It turns out these ladies will be there around the same time as us,' Angus adds, deferentially.

'Oh, quite right,' Meredith replies, with emphasis, as though putting an end once and for all to any doubts raised before her arrival. Then, almost distractedly and with a glance into the mid-distance, she adds, 'It's the most exquisite place.' (It must be a Dulwich thing, this pronunciation of 'ex'. I make a note to try it myself — it's little things like that that will help me blend in.)

I take a sneaky sidestep towards her and scrutinise her face properly. I'm struck by no obvious likeness to Charlie, who, I've previously managed to glean, has his father to thank for *that* bone structure and colouring. Her face is heart-shaped, the skin softened with powder, good-quality powder, I'd say, as it lacks that effect of floured dough you sometimes see in the cheeks of older women. Her eyes, golden in this light so probably hazel in shadow, are deep-lidded as well as wide-set; surely they, the true reflectors of a person's spirit, will betray the evil depths I know to exist? But when, for an instant, they turn my way they express neither kindness nor harm, merely dutiful consideration.

'So are you a great fan of the summer exhibition, Meredith?' Maggie asks her.

She glances towards the modern wing. 'I haven't seen the final selection yet, I must admit, but I'm confident there'll be one or two gems.'

Virginia and Angus beam with matching appreciation at some inside joke, before Virginia remembers us and explains; 'Meredith's son has an entry as it happens.'

As it happens! Insanely, I want to weep, cuddle up to squidgy Virginia and really sob. Charlie has a picture on display here! Why didn't he tell me? Why must I always be excluded, so excluded that I can never even be aware of the extent of my exclusion?

They're all looking at me with amusement and I realise my reaction to the news may have been wildly overplayed.

'It's not quite the achievement you might imagine,' laughs Virginia. 'Though the Hanging Committee *have* been rather tough this year. I shouldn't tell you this, but we're getting a lot of complaints about the number of semi-professionals becoming Friends simply to enter.'

'Bloody cheek,' grumbles Angus, as though he's a hundred years old. 'A twenty-five-pound membership and they get themselves free gallery space!'

'Oh, but isn't that part of the fun?' says Maggie. 'There's always such an eccentric mix at these things. The summer exhibition at the RA is one of my favourite events of the year.'

'Yes, mine too,' Meredith agrees, pleasantly, and I see her look at Maggie as if with new, proper regard. *I* want that regard, too, but I can think of nothing to say to earn it.

'Do *you* paint?' Maggie asks her.

'Not these days, no. I used to. I suppose in a way I've forgotten I can.'

'I know exactly what you mean . . . '

As they chat I shift from one foot to the other, still berating myself. Why am I not the one making these light, charming remarks? Why am I so consumed with self-consciousness? I've been imagining this meeting for a year and it feels just as historic as it should, so historic in fact that it's as if I'm already replaying it as an anecdote before it's even passed. If I don't watch out, I'm going to waste my chance completely.

Maggie, sensitive to my fidgeting, duly directs her next remark at Virginia and Angus to leave me with the longed-for opening. Say something, Anna, say *something*!

'It's a wonderful collection here, isn't it?' I nod towards the main building, even though I've yet to set foot beyond the gift shop. I meant to get here early for a quick whiz around, but bloody Simon wanted to meet about Toys 'Я' Us and I was lucky to get away at all.

Meredith blinks. 'Yes, it is. Actually, it's good to hear you say that because so many young people find that period rather dull.'

I feel like she's stuck a gold star on my chest. I'm up and running! Now what? I try to bring to mind the pages of the visitor's guide, but suddenly all I can remember is how much trouble I had getting the shrink-wrap off with my teeth, and how in the end I had to use the nail scissors that were sitting in a pot by the edge of the bath.

I take a calculated risk: 'I love the portraits.' Then, like a pea hunted out from beneath a thousand mattresses, an image resurfaces: 'That beautiful Rembrandt of the girl . . . '

'We're *very* lucky to have the Rembrandts here,' she agrees.

Again I falter and resort to grinning foolishly, not willing to risk any further art talk before I've submitted myself to deeper study. 'Do you live in Dulwich?' I ask, finally.

'Yes, not far from here.' Then, surprisingly, she adds, 'With my son, the one Virginia just mentioned. Charlie.'

I recognise at once her hunger for him, her eager seizure of the chance to bring him into the conversation, to say his name in his absence, even to a complete stranger. I'm feeling overwhelmed again, but this time by the sheer burden of my knowledge over hers. She's been my conqueror for so long, yet here and now it's me who has the advantage. What on earth would she say if I piped up, 'Really getting into Californian life, isn't he?' (This would be nothing less than the truth; Charlie's early missives have been full of comments along the lines of 'the scale of this place blows my mind' and 'the ocean is awesome'.) I imagine her brow creasing, eyes confused, quizzical. 'Charlie, I mean. Your son. I know him, you know.' What would happen then?

Instead I say, 'Dulwich seems like a lovely place to live. In fact, I was just telling Jill from

123

the . . . from the Whatsit Society that I've been looking at flats here . . . ' *Whatsit* Society? Pathetic! But I career on: 'Which are the best streets, would you say, Meredith?'

I spy an infinitesimal raising of the left eyebrow. 'I really couldn't say.'

Already she's backing off. I've insulted her by treating her like one of those vulgar property boomers who like nothing better than to shout about their equity windfall to anyone who'll listen. People like me. Vulgar little sales reps. All at once Meredith strikes me as impermeable, entirely beyond my mortal reach. I should have prepared better; it will take more than a pair of old specs and a couple of art classes to turn the old me into the spell-binding new one. I should have learned my art from Charlie while I had the chance rather than wasting time admiring the idea of myself as pupil. It doesn't help matters that Meredith is so *all there*: no signs of the early onset of Alzheimer's or minor forgetfulness one might hope for in her age group. Nor does she have that jittery hostility I expected — the type of manner that *can* be subdued by charm — but instead is self-controlled to the point of passivity. It could take a decade to become friends with someone like Meredith.

'Well, friends of mine who live here love the tranquillity,' I say with as much humility as I can salvage. 'And of course the schools are fantastic. I mean, I don't have children myself but — '

'That can't be Lesley and Peter,' Meredith says, almost under her breath as she gazes over my shoulder. 'I haven't seen them for an age. Do excuse me, please ... ' She doesn't add my name, and I decide not to resupply it. It's not too late to back out now and forget I ever started this thing. And then she's gone.

'Incredible,' Angus mutters to Virginia and Maggie after they've all nodded goodbye. 'Absolutely typical of Meredith.'

I turn, looking forward to the dirt-dishing (did they notice that snub?), but it seems they are cooing over her generosity. Virginia explains that Charlie's entry to the show was priced artificially high and bought immediately by Meredith, thus making a healthy donation to the gallery by way of the thirty per cent it pockets of all funds raised.

'So does that mean her son will have to pay tax on the seventy per cent?' Maggie asks, like some kind of undercover Inland Revenue inspector.

'That's a point,' Angus says, as though he for one would be up for calling the police. 'Hang about, though, Charlie's a student again, isn't he? Would he pay tax?'

They're not friends then, Angus and Charlie. They can't have seen each other much in the last year if Angus almost forgot that Charlie is back at college. I feel a surge of solidarity with my absent man. Of course he wouldn't like a crusty old toad like this, no matter how close their parents are. 'What's he like, Meredith's son?' I can't resist asking Virginia.

'Oh, *very* attractive,' she says. 'All the girls adore him.'

There is some comfort in the fact that by

125

'girls' she means podgy matrons between fifty and seventy but, even so, panic rises.

'Is he taken?' Maggie asks, jokingly.

'Not that I know of.' Virginia giggles and I'm surprised at the intensity of my own disappointment. How could I possibly have expected to be anything but the secret that I am? I see Maggie wink at me, indicating with her smile that she thinks we couldn't have hoped for a better start. I'm not so sure. But at least now that Meredith's moved on I can knock back a bit of liquor. I'd guess she's the type to make her obligatory rounds of the guestlist before slipping away to 'turn in' early. 'Excuse me . . . ? Thank you!' I swipe at a passing bottle of white wine.

★   ★   ★

What with the rambling speeches by two past chairmen and the announcement of prizes by the current one (nothing for Charlie), it's a while before I get the chance to sneak into the exhibit and look at the pictures. His drawing is in the corner, hung low with the other smaller pieces, but it seems to glow among the still lifes of Granny Smiths and grapes and the quirky tableaux of hares and squirrels. It's of the same scene as the one he gave me at the station that day, but there is no mother and child and he's added a wash of colour. Already the version that I have is so precious to me that this feels like looking at a page torn from my own diary. And then I see it, the red dot on the label: sold. Sold to Meredith. It seems so symbolic, as though he's worn that little red dot for as long as I've known him. I can't resist picking up a price list. There among the two-hundred-and-fifty-pound offerings is Charlie's: 'Over the Park, £4,000'. Twelve hundred pounds to the gallery just like that — Meredith is a Very Dear Friend indeed. But also a proprietorial one. The message is clear: she's prepared to pay through the nose to keep other people's hands off her son. We can look but we can't touch.

Still just about sober enough to spot my own slide into tabloid melodrama, I move away from Charlie's corner and distract myself by eaves-dropping.

'Absolute scandal,' someone is muttering in the tones of a retired colonel. 'Cheating like that. The man's a professional! Hanging Committee my backside!'

'It's them that need hanging,' a second voice agrees. 'Excuse me, won't you, while I just say hello to Donald.'

'Extraordinary composition,' I mutter to myself. 'Exquisite brushwork. Excuse me.'

'What d'ya say?'

I turn to find a hoary old goat leaning in towards me. 'I was just saying the brushwork is rather fine,' I say. 'On this banana medley.'

'Really?' He leans forward so his ruddy nose is almost touching the glass. 'Looks like something my grandson could do.' He pauses theatrically, then bursts out, 'He's not even a year old!' Then he laughs, squirming in his shirt as though he's being tickled. I laugh too, a little warily in case he turns out to be the village idiot, but I soon realise my mistake when he only turns out to be Eric, the Tennis Friend, the Village Lawn Tennis & Croquet Club Tennis Friend.

'I hear it's harder to get into your club than into the Pope's knickers!' I can't deny I've exceeded planned alcohol-consumption levels by now, but plainly I'm not the only one.

Eric squirms again, quite overtaken with mirth. 'Not at all, not at all. We're still taking registrations for the open,' he says.

'The open?'

'You can't be from around here if you don't know about the open?'

'I don't actually live here, I'm house-hunting,' I say. 'What is it? A party, like this?'

'A tournament, my lovely, a fun mixed-doubles event. Round robin in the morning and knockout in the afternoon. Totally open, everyone gets a chance to play on the club courts.'

'Glad to hear it. Could get a bit messy if you let them loose on the roads.'

More chuckles. 'It's usually a wonderful day. You could play the club champions one minute and chaps from the public courts the next. Everyone will be there.'

Everyone. I like the sound of that. 'You mean this crowd?'

'Oh yes, Bob and Carole, Virginia and Martin, Meredith — '

'Put my name down,' I cry. First thing tomorrow I'll book tennis lessons. I played all the time when I was on that French exchange at school. Françoise, my tanned opposite, was quite

128

obsessed, I seem to remember. (I also remember she was in love with Henri Leconte, had penned a fan letter and wanted to deliver it in person, which meant we had to hang around the players' entrance at Roland Garros for hours on end.) Yes, I'll get one of those big rackets with the extended — what do they call it? — sweet spot. I'll cultivate my sweet spot.

He pulls out a notebook and writes down my name. 'And your partner will be . . . ?'

'I'll need to confirm that,' I say, breezily. Already I'm wondering if it will be possible to hire a coach for the day and pass him off as my tennis buddy.

'The only people not allowed to enter are children and professionals,' Eric says, standing back to have another look at the bananas. 'Should have applied the same rule here, eh?'

'Indeed,' I reply.

★  ★  ★

Maggie and I stop in the pub before heading back into town.

'What did you think?' I want to know as soon as we're settled with our drinks. I'm feeling triumphant now, my earlier doubts washed away with the half-dozen glasses of wine. The important thing is that I know I'll be seeing Meredith again; I'll be able to build on a respectable start. 'Do you think we could be friends?'

'Hard to know,' Maggie says. 'She was nice enough, but actually becoming friends . . . that takes time. I just can't see what you have in common.'

'That's the point,' I say, trying not to slur. 'I'm *finding* things in common. Hence tonight and the tennis and Spain . . . '

'Don't take this the wrong way,' she says, which in my experience is a prelude to stinging criticism, 'but next time I wonder if you shouldn't just be yourself a bit more.'

'How d'you mean?'

She pulls a face. 'It's just that there were a couple of times this evening when, well . . . '

'What, what? Tell me! I need feedback — this was my first performance.'

'That's just it, Anna. It was a *performance*. I thought you sounded a bit sarcastic sometimes. Like you were saying the words some holier-than-thou person would say, but in your normal voice.' She mimics me saying how wonderful I thought the inner-city art initiative was and makes it sound like a Dorothy Parker put-down.

'Oh, that was just to Angus,' I say, relieved. 'Not to Meredith.'

'*Just* Angus?'

'Who cares about him?' I snort.

'Well, don't forget he'll be on the Spanish trip. He'll be *leading* the trip. He could be useful to get on side.'

'Hmm.' She's right, of course. It's not just Meredith I need to charm. They all know each other and each other's business. I'll need good press across the board if I'm going to convince her of my suitability. I open my book and make a note to be nicer to Angus when we next meet.

'Perhaps at the mixed open?' I say to myself, scribbling.

She waits for me to finish and then holds my eye in a determined fashion. There appears to be more. 'Another thing, Anna . . . '

'What?'

'Oh, nothing.'

'Stop doing that! Go on!'

'It's just, well, won't Charlie feel a bit ambushed? I mean, if it all works out and you're suddenly socialising with the mother. Won't you have to come clean about how you planned all of this?'

Why do they all get so hung up on that bit? 'I'll cross that bridge when I come to it.'

'Maybe you should consider whether there'll be any bridge. You may be on one side of the river and never get back over to where you started.'

'What?' I haven't got time for this sort of extended metaphor. 'Charlie's an architect now,' I laugh. 'He'll *build* me a bridge.'

'Architects design. Structural engineers are the ones who build.' She can't help herself correcting me, but I don't grumble because I can see she's genuinely worried.

'Look,' I say, 'when the time comes, all I have to do is say you invited me to a gallery thing down here, I met Meredith, didn't even twig who she was at first. We kept bumping into each other, that kind of thing.'

'And what about Spain?'

'I don't know, I'll play up the element of chance.'

'What element of chance?' she says, picking up my book. 'Let's see what you've just written: 'Height: approx. five-foot-four. Weight: one hundred and twelve pounds (unconfirmed). Friends: Lesley and Peter (surname not known).'' She slaps it back down again. 'Look at what you're wearing. And that old lady's handbag! This is a military campaign, Anna. I'm surprised you're not sticking pins into a map of Europe.'

'Give me time.' I light up a cigarette from the emergency pack of ten in my bag and realise I've finished my drink. 'One for the road?'

She just watches me and I can tell she's fighting the urge to give me a lecture. For a journalist she's hilariously puritanical about drinking and smoking on the job. But what she says next surprises me.

'Don't you sometimes look back to Paul and think how uncomplicated that whole thing was?'

'Not *that* uncomplicated,' I remind her. 'He was hardly the perfect gent, was he? Besides, his idea of social advancement was ordering a drink that didn't come in a pint glass.'

'He could have gone for Pimm's,' she says. 'Then he could still have had a pint.'

'True.'

'What I mean is, well, *he* couldn't wait to get you home to the in-laws, could he? He was chuffed to bits to be with you.'

I puff on the cigarette. 'How many hundreds of times am I going to have to explain this? You can't really believe Paul was right for me and Charlie isn't? For God's sake, the man used to

132

blow his nose on the bath towels!' Is that something you condone?'

Maggie sighs. 'That *is* disgusting. Look, don't get me wrong, I'm pleased you're doing something about all this. I'm just saying, aren't these rather elaborate lengths to go to for something that should be happening quite naturally?'

'Sure, but not everything happens naturally. Sometimes you need to intervene, like . . . '

'Like?'

'Like . . . the divine.'

'Oh my God.'

I laugh. 'That's the one.'

'Anna!' But she's laughing with me. Whatever the misgivings of a naturally cautious person like Maggie, I know that underneath it all she's delighted that I'm finally taking destiny into my own hands.

'Well, if you're sure he's worth it,' she says.

'I'm sure.' I stub out the cigarette. I wasn't enjoying it, anyway.

# 10

My experience with boyfriends' mothers is limited. Generally, I've tended not to encourage clan mixing on the basis that we might never see each other again and it's an awful lot of names for everyone to remember for nothing. But Paul's mother, Yvonne, was an exception. She was so ingrained in his life she was impossible to avoid: twice-weekly phone calls and monthly weekend visits, with postcards and emails in between and messages stockpiling every time a friend or neighbour came within spitting distance of the M25. 'We're more like mates,' Paul said, and I liked that; I was mates with my father, too.

I first met her at a Chinese restaurant in the East End, near where Paul lived in a terrace off the Roman Road. She was much older than I had expected, already in her seventies, with monochromatic mid-brown hair (grey, she told me, could be kept in check with nothing less than weekly colour and she favoured a rinse that came in a packet like instant soup). There was nothing of her squat, rounded physique or flat wide-set facial features in her son and little of her voice. While retaining the occasional blunt vowel of his north-eastern childhood, Paul was otherwise stock London media boy — I'd come to view him as a typical southerner with his Marlboro Lights, lager and love of Chelsea FC

— so Yvonne's broad Geordie accent was a surprise. She used phrases like 'queer as Dick's hatband', 'bobby-dazzler', 'chatty' and 'get wrong', and was known for her fabulous line in malapropisms ('Just wait till he gets here, pet, I'll give him the Three Degrees all right!').

Her passion was for making American-style quilts, which she'd spent many hours since retirement piecing together as gifts for family and friends. Paul had a blue-and-grey one in his bedroom, folded into springy layers and used to raise the seat of an old desk chair. It was incongruously hand-crafted and detailed for a man so, well, crude. Then, one Christmas, Yvonne presented me with my own, a lovely specimen in greens and pinks; she told me she'd been collecting bits of fabric for it since Paul and I first started seeing each other. I was touched that she saw me as a green-and-pink person when I invariably pitched up to meet her in head-to-toe black. I used the quilt as a throw on my bed for a while before replacing it with something satiny and the colour of mushroom soup.

Yvonne was not above giving Paul a slap on the backside when he stepped out of line, which he would do by default, his appetite for bad behaviour being gargantuan. By midnight he would be willing to say or do *anything*, including starting a punch-up with his boss or having sex with other women in the loos of bars where I stood drinking a stud wall or two away.

'Thinks with his trousers, my lad,' Yvonne told me after one such incident. I wasn't as bothered as I might have been, but she was at pains to side with me against the horny infidel and I didn't want to hurt her feelings. I guessed his behaviour aped that of his father, who'd left home long before Paul did — I was in the habit of blaming absent parents for their children's misdeeds. But it was a long time since Yvonne had had any control over her son; by then he'd taken on the status of a celebrity guest, the only one of her children who'd 'made it' down south, the one who lit up her life every time he greeted her with that primate's clutch of his.

I liked Yvonne better than Paul by the end. At least she knew when to call it a night and go to bed. Besides which, no matter how far I get with Meredith, she is never going to pinch me on the cheek and call me 'pet'.

★　★　★

Oh dear, Caro is sulking and I've been so distracted it's taken me too long to notice. As well as suffering from general best-friend neglect, she's miffed that her contribution to the Meredith campaign (wardrobe assistant) is less key than Maggie's (co-star and master fixer). Caro wants a speaking part in all of this and I don't blame her — I'd feel exactly the same if I were her. I try to make amends by sending Pippa over with a special delivery of latte with vanilla syrup and cherry muffin (her favoured combo when the fruit fasts are off) and she drops by my office to make up.

'You're really still serious about this, aren't

you?' she asks me. Despite her pleas for a reprieve for Charlie, a part of her expected us to be swamped by the fallout by now, for Charlie to be history.

'Yes,' I say. 'I just feel that I've waited so long already I'm not going to throw it away on a whim.'

'It's only been a few months, you haven't waited *that* long.'

'No, not waiting for him to tell Meredith, I mean waiting for him to come along in the first place.'

She looks at me in astonishment. 'I didn't know you'd been *waiting*.'

I feel myself blush a little. 'Nor did I. But I think I was. Otherwise it wouldn't feel so critical that I keep hold of him now.'

She nods, then says, '*I*'m not waiting. I really don't want this kind of thing.' She gestures, hands apart, like a signer communicating news of anarchy. She's had it before, love, a nasty, unexpected jab of the stuff, and she now regards that mid-twenties skirmish as welcome early immunisation. Since then she's socialised so much with her brother and the City and media boys that she's become masculinised.

'Do you want to come with me to my art appreciation course?' I suggest. 'There's a class tonight and I'm sure they wouldn't mind extras.'

'No thanks, chum, I'm having a drink with Hartley the Hare.' Nick Hartley is one of the newest reps in the sales team run by Steve's opposite, Martin. He isn't destined to stick around for long but, even so, if it were anyone but Caro I'd say she was very brave indeed to dabble internally. These men are as ruthless as they are indiscreet. I know for a fact that Steve has a 'secret' spreadsheet that lists every female in the department and grades her on how good or bad she is in bed. Those who remain untried are simply marked according to how he and the boys imagine they would perform if called for the privilege. The grading system is no simple A, B, C; oh no, it is based on pints. How many pints would Steve or his cohort need to down in order to submit to sex with X? 'Three pints for a stunner, fifteen pints for a munter,' as Ronnie once charmingly explained. Note, please, the three-pint minimum — no woman is alluring enough for them to miss out the pub stop entirely. Other codes include '2B', the lowest any woman can score. This does not, as you'd be forgiven for imagining, stand for the grade of lead in our hero's pencil, but for 'two-bagger'. To clarify: not only must the girl be wearing a paper bag over her head during the sexual act, but so too must the man — just in case *hers* slips.

Imagine introducing one of these charmers to your mother.

★ ★ ★

I am torn away from my scrutiny of Charlie's digital shots of his new colleagues (without exception they each wear dark eye frames — is the world aware that architecture is so bad for your eyesight, not to mention your personal style?) by an urgent RingMe summit in Nigel's office.

'We've got our slot through for the presentation,' he barks at me before I've even had the chance to sit down. Simon is there, playing with his mobile phone, cocky as ever. He is the sort of man who, in his late thirties, already looks thoroughly middle-aged — flat, pale hair receding from the shore of his forehead in a gentle golden line, jaw melting a little further into the neck with every year that passes — and in a funny kind of way this gives him greater authority. His eyes, pure ocean-blue and surprisingly free of broken veins, are his most attractive feature and rightly famous throughout sales and marketing. In this office, anyone able to lay claim to the moniker Old Blue Eyes is only slightly lower than Messiah.

'When is it?' I ask, daybook out.

'Thursday the twenty-sixth, three-thirty.'

I work very hard at hiding my relief. Thank God, *thank God*, it's not twenty-four hours later; had that been the case my Granada leave would have been cancelled as a matter of course and my whole future with Charlie sacrificed to a mobile-phone network that will probably go bust within two years of start-up.

Nigel suppresses a belch. 'So what do we know Moving Forward?'

I try to get in ahead of Simon. 'Well, we know they're going to go with one qual, one mid and one pop. We know they've got a million *minimum* to spend with the tabloid. We know

139

everyone will be pitching for this. We know — '

'We know I was at King's with Mike Dawson,' Simon interrupts.

'Come again?' Nigel says, rapping his mobile on the glass desktop.

'He's only the new marketing director they've brought in to oversee the launch.' Simon can't help smirking. 'I'm playing five-a-side with him on Sunday. I'll lead the charge on this, don't worry.'

'Good man,' Nigel nods.

I roll my eyes. Simon, whose rise within business development has directly mirrored mine in agency sales, has always worked Nigel better than I have. There's no love lost between our two factions. BD execs call sales reps jumped-up monkeys, we call them irrelevant. Simon thinks I do nothing but lunch agencies, I think he does nothing but lunch clients. So far, so co-dependent. Where the conflict lies is in the credit. Whenever we win anything together, he's straight through the door talking up his part in the triumph and downgrading me to the lovely assistant in a spangled bikini. We once came back in a cab together from a successful pitch, parting only at reception, he for the canteen, I for the loo. But when I got to my desk two minutes later there was already an email from him to director level announcing the win. I was merely cc-ed, alongside group heads and selected senior reps. I got straight on the phone: 'That was a quick bacon sandwich.' 'They were all out,' he said. 'I guess I'll just have to go hungry. Heh, heh, heh . . . ' I could almost hear him lick his finger and mark the air.

At least there'll be no such shenanigans with RingMe. With business of this value the client won't make a decision on the day but will keep us stewing for a week or two. In any case, Nigel will want to make the presentation himself, so Simon and I will *both* be relegated to beachwear, and it will be Nigel who gets the call if and when it comes. Not that there won't be a substantial amount of donkeywork for us in advance of pitch day. It's an inescapable fact that the *Sun* and the *Mirror* have more readers than we do and to win this we'll have to promise more than we've promised anyone before: our best rates and positions, promotions, readers' offers, editorial plugs, launch-day specials, front-page flashes, you name it.

'There is no way we're going to miss out on this one,' Nigel says, chins juddering with conviction.

'We won't,' I say.

I notice Simon looking at him strangely, almost shiftily, which makes me wonder what he knows that I don't. It's better than the Masonic signals between the two of them I usually have to decode but, on the other hand, what causes Simon to be wary is likely to cause me plain fear. I wait till Nigel gets up to take a call, standing in the outer glass right angle of the room as if in a phone booth, and whisper to Simon, 'Why do you keep staring at him like that?'

'Like what?'

'I don't know, like you think he's up to something.'

'You mean . . . ?' He grins. 'Just seeing if this rumour's true, that's all.'

'What rumour?'

'Oh, come on, Anna.' He puts his mouth closer to my ear and I catch the faint whiff of lager. 'You must have heard about his Hampstead Heath situation?'

'What? He's *gay*?'

'No, his Hampstead Heath — *teeth*. He's just been fitted with dentures.'

I roll my eyes. 'Who told you that? Pippa?'

'Don't look white enough if you ask me. They must do them to look natural, y'know, yellow them up a bit. Like fake tits that look all droopy like the real thing, just bigger.'

'Yeah,' I say, 'or a penis enlargement. Where do they take the fat from for that . . . ?'

I watch him wince at the same time as I notice Pippa hovering by the open door; no doubt word will shortly spread that Simon is to undergo excruciating genital reconstruction, or maybe even that I am — no rumour is too sensational in this place. You wait, I'll be a transsexual by end of play today.

'Did you want me, Pip?'

'Yeah.' She has come with unnecessary messages, which means Steve's sent her to find out what is being plotted. If RingMe comes off, they'll all be after a piece of the pie. 'Oh, and Jill just rang again.'

'Who's that?' Simon asks, jumpily.

'Just someone I know.'

Pippa grimaces. 'She's rung three times to say . . . what did she say? Yeah . . . how 'thankful' she is. Sounds like a right happy clapper if you ask me.'

I'm not at all surprised that Jill, the brown-owl type who runs the Do-gooders' Society and its various fund-raising activities, has been calling. At last night's auction my lots were far and away the biggest money-spinners of the event. Michael Caine's handkerchief, in particular, caused near hysteria when the village antiques dealer, our auctioneer for the occasion, brought to the floor's attention a small stain in one corner. It was a dead loss in terms of contact with Meredith, however; she was a no-show thanks to being 'full of cold', though she did donate a set of Edwardian egg cups to the cause. (I never did quite gather what the cause was, but the grave threat to tufted ducks had something to do with it.) The egg cups were quite nice, with gold-leafed rims and sweet little saucers. I was even going to bid for them, but then I thought, No, it's not Meredith's cast-offs I want. Besides, I haven't eaten a boiled egg since about 1979.

I have to admit that the evening wasn't at all the session of pure tedium I'd resigned myself to once Meredith's absence had been confirmed. In a way, I've started to quite enjoy the Dulwich folk and their traditional values. I mean, all those people putting time and effort into raising money that's not for them. It's so *wholesome*. In any case, it's all part of building up the right profile around SE21; somewhere along the line my role in such good works will be brought to the attention of Meredith, I'm sure of it. And disappointing though it was to miss her, at least I know her attendance at the mixed-doubles open in two Sundays' time has been confirmed. Eric, who it transpires is Jill's husband, showed me the round-robin schedule he'd drawn up: Meredith and I are not in the same group, but we will meet in the quarter-final if I win my group and she wins hers. Her partner, like mine, is to be confirmed. 'We're a bit low on men,' Eric confided, when I asked him if he knew of a spare. 'It's the women who run the show around here.' You don't say.

'Did an Angus call me?' I ask Pippa, suddenly.

'Angus from Zenith?' Simon queries straight away.

'Oh yeah,' Pippa says, 'I think he did. I forgot that one.'

I've wasted no time in acting on Maggie's suggestion that I get Angus Poole on side. I got his details from her and sent an email asking if he'd like to be my partner for the tennis. Maggie couldn't actually say whether he plays or not but she agreed that everyone in Dulwich would probably play at least one sport traditionally associated with privilege and elitism. When I didn't hear from him straight away I followed up with a message on his voicemail, aiming for a sportive 1950s sort of tone. 'Maggie says she thinks you might be free for a knock and it would be so splendid to meet up again before Granada.'

'And?' I prompt Pippa. 'What was his message?'

'Whose?'

'Angus's!'

Slowly, dawn breaks across her eyes. 'Oh, I think he said he was sorry, but no. Does that sound right?'

Simon hoots. 'Losing your touch, eh, Day?'

I ignore him. 'Yes,' I say to Pippa. 'I know what that means.' Bugger. I thought I was being so clever killing two birds with one stone, but now I find myself entirely bird-free. I *cannot* miss this tennis thing, no matter what, but I can hardly attempt to play alone.

Nigel is reaching the customary climax of impatient 'Yeah, yeahs' that mean he is winding up his phone conversation. I time my move to perfection. 'Simon, you don't by any chance play tennis, do you?'

'Fuck off!' It's not as much of a risk as you might think, as I know Simon is strictly into his posse sports: football, cricket, binge drinking . . .

'How about you, Nigel?' I ask, casually, just as he hangs up.

'What?'

'You were at Wimbledon a few weeks ago, weren't you?'

He takes his seat again, swivels his fat ass in his chair and grins at me. 'I hate to disillusion a fan, but I was only there as a spectator.'

Big male guffaws all round. I don't point out that reports of his Wimbledon excursion suggest that the scant minutes spent outside the hospitality tent were those required to stroll to and from the car park. Could our esteemed leader have fallen off the wagon?

'Seriously, do you play?'

He shrugs. 'You could say I've been known to scatter a pigeon or two with my one-hundred-mile-an-hour serve.'

'In that case, do you happen to be free on August the eighth?' I nod down at his desk diary. This is a technique I've used before. Ask someone to turn up to something they might not want to when their diary is sitting open in front of them. Lo and behold, he turns the pages and we all see the blank slot. I explain my offer.

'The Village Club?' he says. 'How did you get in with that crowd?'

'I've got friends down there,' I say, smoothly. 'And they've invited me to enter their mixed open.'

He looks suspicious.

'Why do you need to be invited if it's an open?' Simon asks, splitting hairs. He hates it if he thinks I've got an in somewhere he hasn't.

'*You* actually *play*?' Nigel persists, unflatteringly astonished.

'Sure.' They're starting to annoy me now. 'I like nothing better than to slip into a little white dress and feel the breeze between my thighs.'

Two sets of eyes widen at that one, and a snort from the doorway tells me Pippa is still listening in.

'Joke,' I smile. 'Seriously, though, Nigel, you live in that neck of the woods; it would be great if we could team up!'

'It's not one of those fucking handicap things, is it?'

I try to remember if Eric said anything about

146

wheelchair teams. 'I don't think so. There might be some old people, though.'

At first it looks as though Nigel is set to respond as he has done to my previous attempts at Dulwich small talk, cutting me off with a criticism of local folk ('Yeah, they're all right, but a bit *mumsy*.' Mumsy to the likes of Nigel is not a style but a crime. His wife, the mother of three boys and to whom he refers as The Woofer, is much pitied by the women of this department.) Then I see that, despite his scorn, he is genuinely unnerved by my overture; you can almost read his thought processes like a storyboard: . . . couldn't possibly be altruistic . . . rude to refuse . . . keep your enemies closer . . . bare thighs . . . she saw the diary. He probably thinks I intend to maim him on court and slide right into that chestnut leather chair before the sun comes up on the Monday morning. How disappointed he'd be if he knew that he's just the only local I know who might make up the numbers while I set about admiring Meredith's backhand. On the other hand, it would be no bad thing to squeeze in a bit of socialising before the RingMe pitch; better that it's me in the pillion seat than Simon.

'I'm sure I heard that the chief exec of RingMe's just bought a place in Dulwich . . . '

Simon's not going to let that one go. 'They're based in *Exeter*,' he protests. But I can see Nigel's considering the proposal.

'I'll do the picnic and organise everything,' I say, treating him to my most winning smile. 'You just have to turn up and start scattering pigeons. And if we don't get through to the knockout bit you'll be home by two o'clock.'

He frowns. 'Of course we'll get through.'

'So you're in?'

'Yep.'

'You off your rocker?' Pippa asks in genuine accusation as we walk back to my office. Then I see a faint blush cross her face and know the wrong end of the stick has, once again, been well and truly seized.

'No,' I say, with emphasis, 'I'm *not* sleeping with Nigel. The tennis is just a Dulwich thing.'

She nods, happily reassured. 'You keep talking 'bout this Dulwich,' she says. 'Is he in editorial?'

# 11

Ever since this began I've been chastising myself for not listening properly to Charlie when he's talked about Meredith. I was interested at first, of course, but soon grew to regard his drip-feed of domestic detail as insulting, a token attempt to involve me vicariously in this other life of his that he was so determined I shouldn't share. To think, there've been so many clues that would be nothing short of priceless now, but I chose merely to raise a sulky eyebrow and feel sorry for myself. Where does Meredith go for lunch, for instance? Where does she head for those mind-clearing walks the Graingers swear by? The river, like Charlie (presumably not, or he wouldn't have wandered there quite so freely with me)? Sydenham Hill? Offa's Dyke? Does she like to read in cafés, browse in antiques shops, pop into garden centres? I can hardly ask him now. 'Hi, darling, work going well, missing you. By the way, I was wondering if Meredith ever goes to that little patisserie by the bookshop?' Once or twice I've considered an underhand query. 'A friend wants to take her parents out to dinner in Dulwich this weekend — where's a good place to go?' But he'd only direct me to the one place he'd be certain she wouldn't go. He'd have palpitations at the thought of anyone from my camp being in the same restaurant as Mother Superior.

And I know that for a fact. Once, back in the spring, we were meeting friends for Sunday lunch at their flat near Marylebone High Street, but they had to pull out at the last minute and it was just the two of us out in the street looking for somewhere to eat. Charlie was really off-hand about it, sulky almost, which is very unlike him. And then we found the perfect place. It was one of those timings that never happens in London: the sun comes out and just as you realise it's going to be a beautiful day you spot a pavement table that's free, laid for two and miraculously lacking a 'Reserved' sign. But Charlie wouldn't take it, insisted we went inside, wouldn't even sit by the window. I don't know who was more bewildered, the waitress or I, as we took a table in the darkened innards of the place. Then, finally, he admitted it was because Meredith had said she might be going with a friend to the Wallace Collection round the corner. He was terrified she might wander by on the hunt for a Bath bun or whatever olde worlde snack she favours, only to stumble upon her precious one in the company of a slut.

I felt sorry for him, then; he was so dejected, like a little boy confessing to wetting the bed. 'If it did happen, you could just say we're friends,' I said, gamely, 'from college or your old job. I would play along.'

'She'd know,' he said, dismissively. 'She's not stupid.'

I lost my patience then. 'Well, in that case she must know that a red-blooded male like yourself will probably be having sex by the age of thirty.

As far as I'm aware, it's only Victorian daughters who are required to preserve their virginity, not the sons.'

'Sex is one thing,' he muttered. It was impossible to know how to take a remark like this. What was he implying? That I might be acceptable as some sort of oat-sowing vessel but not as a legitimate partner, as an *equal*? Or that we looked too established a couple to fool anyone that this was anything but the real thing? I let it go. I had to, otherwise we'd have spent the entire time arguing about Meredith instead of enjoying being together. But he didn't relax, not until the bill was paid and we were safely in a taxi back to my place. As we passed the Wallace Collection on Manchester Square I suppose I should have been thankful he didn't duck.

★   ★   ★

When it first became apparent that I was besotted with Charlie, Caro wanted to know all about the sex, especially when I said it was better than it had been with Paul, a legendary industry love machine (and, some claimed, the originator of the vile 'performance' spreadsheet).

'Why's it better with Charlie?'

'Well, it's longer . . . '

'The sex or the penis?'

'The sex. And it's sort of rougher and cuddlier at the same time.'

'That's hard to pull off,' she agreed, impressed.

Maybe it was also because we have never been

151

able to spend more than two nights a week together for fear of rousing Meredith's suspicions (I never thought I'd be described as a field trip to Liverpool, but there we are) that it has continued to be pulled off. And maybe it's because there's always been that sense of rationing about our time alone together that missing him while he's in San Francisco is not proving to be quite as excruciating as I might have feared. In fact, in terms of the Meredith deadline and Charlie's return, September is perhaps a little too *looming*. Looking at my schedule, there are now just seven weeks left for me to accomplish my task and Meredith will be unavailable for charming for at least one of those owing to her visit to Charlie in the States. And what about that trip to Cornwall that he mentioned she was planning? Have I got enough time, after all? Three months seemed so generous that Sunday morning when Viv and I hatched our plan; now, with just one meeting with Meredith under my belt, I'm not so sure.

Which is how I come to find myself on Sunday 1 August, for the second day running, in Dulwich Park for the Dulwich Country Fair. I'm on my own, that is to say I arrived on my own; now I'm navigating the swirl of children tipping themselves off giant teacup rides and adults looking for other halves while slopping pints of spiced cider over their shirt fronts. Among the other attractions are goats, Friesian cows and sheep shearers. The smell is not nice.

I fit in a treat with my latest Plain Jane ensemble. Admittedly, my Capri pants are L. K.

Bennett but with my latest charity-shop find, a Laura Ashley blouse from years ago (their recent lines are far too fashionable) and the all-terrain sandals bought originally for a beach trek in the Maldives, the combination is suitably country casual. I've ditched the specs but have accessorised with a sketchbook from my Looking at Pictures class. (The only page not still blank is a quick calculation of my expenses over the top of an unrecognisable outline of *The Haywain*, but I don't suppose anyone's going to ask to look inside.) At Caro's suggestion I've allowed my hair to crinkle at the temples and I've left my lips as nude as Viv's. Yes, my demure look is getting there. I've even changed the ringtone on my phone from Eminem to 'trad' ring. It's all in the details.

I've got no idea if Meredith will take it upon herself to appear today. I skulked around for four hours yesterday eating sugared crêpes and fingering crafts; I must have scanned more faces than the ticket collector at the gate and I still didn't see her. But Sundays are different and she does live right on the park: it would surely be impossible to read one of her art books or listen to *Desert Island Discs* with this racket going on. Besides, I could do with a bit of luck.

And I get it. I see her after an hour, down by the cakes in the competition tent, where prizes appear to have been awarded for the smallest shrub, the flattest cake, the sorriest flower arrangement. I'm so happily in character I don't even feel my pulse quicken at the sight of her; it really is like I'm a local girl spotting someone I think I might know, someone standing head bowed over the cakes, head bowed at exactly the same angle as that of the man next to her, almost as though they're praying together. Now, out of nowhere, my body *does* react, violently, nauseously, as though I've been pushed out of a plane without warning: because the man next to her is *Charlie*. I can't see his face, of course, but the build is his, the shoulders have the precise same squareness I know from a hundred intimate clutches, the shirt is the same, the shoes look familiar, and the mustard cords, well, he *might* have a pair, it's not impossible; *she* probably bought them for him for this very outing. Fear surges like a crowd breaking the safety barriers: what on earth is he doing back here? In London? In *Europe*? Is he here for the weekend? Or did it not work out at the Endo practice and he's back early for good? And then my imagination really detonates: can I be sure he ever went to San Francisco in the first place? The few times we've spoken have been calls dialled by him, not me, and the rest of our contact has been online. As for the images he's attached to his mails, well, he could have got shots of bespectacled geeks at any time in his own faculty in London, and those pictures of Golden Gate Bridge are two a penny on stock photography sites. Let's face it, if he's so adept at hoodwinking Meredith, plainly no fool, then he's certainly got the skills to outwit me.

I look wildly around me. Oh God, if he turns and sees me, too, which would be worse, the fact that he didn't tell me he's back or the fact that

I'm here on his stamping ground, unauthorised, breathing the same air as his mother?

'Oh my God.' I realise I've been gasping this aloud. Stay calm, I tell myself, move out of sight, get away from the cakes. But I can't get my legs to work and someone coming up behind me crashes into my heels.

'I do beg your pardon.' A concerned hand steadies my shoulder; I must have stumbled.

'No problem.' I don't even glance at the face.

Then, in a second, it's over. Charlie straightens up and he isn't Charlie at all. He isn't even with Meredith, he's just some taller, sharper-nosed Charlie lookalike who takes a minute to locate his partner, a freckled creature further up the table, and then leads her off towards the bonsai display. Meredith, meanwhile, turns and speaks to a woman to her left, a stout sort with greying pudding-basin hair and high colour. The word that springs to mind is 'menopausal'.

I regroup. I've completely lost the method flow I felt a moment ago and must draw instead on planned moves. How to play this 'bumping into' episode to best advantage? Meredith may not remember me from the picture gallery, at least not clearly enough to greet me by name across the room; therefore I need to be the one to 'recognise' her. I stroll over to the cakes, sketchpad clutched to my chest, and ease into the space left by the Charlie doppelgänger. I pretend to examine the baking disaster straight ahead of me before turning, deliberately misjudging the distance between us, and

155

allowing my left shoulder to make contact with her right one. There's the soft swish of one natural fibre brushing against another, so faint she hasn't even noticed.

'I do beg your pardon,' I exclaim, loudly, and she looks up. First, I frown a little, as though trying to place her face but despairing of my own memory for names; then, I let realisation transform frown to smile, the sweetest, most melting smile I can produce, the sort I give baby Felix. 'Haven't we ... ? *Hello* again, it's Meredith, isn't it?' I add my own name to save any embarrassment on her part, delicately reminding her, 'Virginia introduced us the other day at the gallery Friends thing.'

'Of course. How have you been?' Her voice is friendlier than her eyes, which remain unengaged. I am taller than her but I already feel as though I'm shrinking. I'm struck again by the serenity of her manner; those histrionics Charlie describes, that rampant will he so fears, they must display themselves strictly behind closed doors for it is hard to imagine anyone more *in* control.

'Are you enjoying the fair?' I ask, looking around the tent as though there's nowhere in the world I'd rather be.

'Yes, it's all very jolly.'

'This is my first time: I think I told you I'm new to the area.' I'm self-conscious again, anxious that my grin is too fake and my voice too eager. I stop grinning and nod towards the cakes. 'Bit of a bun fight in here, though, isn't it?' Very poor. I don't blame her for the thin smile; she's

156

already angling for an escape route, but luckily for me she's prevented from moving straight off again by a sudden crush of new bodies in the cake vicinity. The pudding-basin woman and her mate are among those pressing forward and as they hover at Meredith's shoulder, obviously all together, she sees that introductions can be avoided no longer.

'Have you met Moira and Humphrey Poole?'

I pat my hair and turn on the smile once more. 'I haven't, lovely to meet you both. Anna Day.'

Well, well, well, Moira and Humphrey. He is old fogey to Angus's young, the curls greyer, the waistline bulkier, and the dark eyes bespectacled — all the better to see my Laura Ashley-ed bustline (vintage sizes are evidently smaller), I note. When he does meet my eye, however, he grins quite affably. She, on the other hand, is sour around the mouth and, I would guess, naturally suspicious of strangers. Not at all like Brown Owl Jill and, in fact, much more as I expected Meredith to be.

'Your voice is very familiar,' she frowns. 'Have we met before?'

I make a quick calculation. Do I admit I'm the one who rang to enquire about the Granada trip? If I do it will become clear sooner or later that I'm joining them anyway, which does rather open me up to accusations of — how shall we put it? — *imitation*. Preferably not, then, but didn't I tell Angus I'd spoken to his parents on the phone? God, I need a page in my book called '*Truths* to Remember'.

'We spoke on the phone and you were most helpful about the Art Explorer Group,' I say. 'I was hoping to sneak on to one of your expeditions, but I turned out to be too late, which is *such* a shame.'

Now Moira reacts as though I've demanded an explanation as to why an innocent art-lover should have been so horribly shunned. 'Oh, yes,' she says, tripping over her words. 'I remember you. The Granada trip *is* full, I'm afraid. We had to scale it down in the end and it's really only a small private expedition. There'll be more in the future, I'm sure. I would have put your name on the waiting list but *Humphrey* didn't take it down.' We all look at Humphrey, who acknowledges his incompetence without protest. 'The gallery does very good Friends trips, though,' she adds. 'They're off to Bilbao in September and I'm sure there are places left.'

'I completely understand,' I say. 'No need to explain, Moira, really. I was just looking to touch base with like-minded locals in case I move down here. As it turns out, I'll be down in that part of the world, anyway, this summer . . . ' I try to capture that absent-minded air of someone searching out the vaguest of memories: 'You know, I'm *sure* Maggie and Angus discovered it was the same weekend. There's only one bank holiday in August, isn't there?'

'You know our son?' Moira asks, surprised.

'Yes, we have a mutual friend, Maggie Bishop. I'll be in Granada with her.'

'She was the one you were with at the gallery,' Meredith says, as if it all makes sense now.

All three of them relax visibly. I may not be one of them but I can name-check someone who knows someone who's one of them, therefore I just might be *the right sort*. And that is, after all, what I'm here to achieve.

I allow myself a moment's celebration in the form of an out-of-body glimpse of how this must look to someone entering the tent. Four Dulwich types passing the time of day at the cake stall. But now there's a pause and I'm not yet comfortable enough with my modest new persona to wait for it to be filled by someone else, so I grasp at the nearest topic. 'Some of these entries are hilariously bad, aren't they?'

At this you can actually see Moira's shoulders stiffen and there's no mistaking the disbelieving look Humphrey shoots my way. Clearly it's not the done thing to slag off the baked goods. Then, to my surprise, Meredith laughs out loud, a lovely clear burst of delight.

'Oh, Moira,' she says, 'you have to admit some of them *are* rather forlorn?'

'The standard is very mixed,' Moira sniffs.

'Moira's just been awarded second prize in the marmalade loaf section,' Meredith explains to me, mock-gravely.

Oops. I try to stop my lips twitching. 'Congratulations! Which is yours?'

She nods to one of the sturdier efforts, the battle between injury and pride clear in her face.

I want to ask her if she used the cake bowl for her haircut afterwards, but instead gush, 'Well, that looks delicious. I can just imagine the contrast between the firm crust and the crumbly

159

citrus sponge. Do you make your own marmalade, Moira?'

'I do, but I used Cooper's on this occasion.'

Humphrey is looking around, impatient, I sense, to move on from the cake talk that has doubtless dominated the Poole domestic agenda over the last few days. He turns to me, 'Well, please don't let us keep you from — '

'It's OK,' I interrupt, 'I'm here alone.' I don't know what makes me do it, a bid to accelerate the whole thing, overconfidence at the ease of this bonus encounter, but I add, 'I'm afraid I haven't got a chap in tow at the moment, Humphrey; I'm *on the hunt*.' Serious character malfunction: this time the remark comes out as sounding really quite saucy, almost as though I'm propositioning him. I feel myself colour and, not daring to check Meredith and Moira's reactions, I keep my gaze on Humphrey.

'Right then, right then,' he mumbles, embarrassed.

'So keep your eyes peeled for me, won't you?' That's better, nice and jokey; I'm finally finding my voice.

'Well, very nice to see you again,' Meredith says, back to her distant self.

'You too. Bye, then,' I say. I slide a last look at her before I leave and she is still smiling, not quite warmly but not so meagrely either. I wonder if that outburst of laughter ever really happened.

I walk away slowly, slowly enough to hear Humphrey say, '*Who* did she say she was?'

'Anna,' Meredith tells him. It's the first time

160

I've heard her say my name. It feels historic. It also, in the oddest way, feels right.

I leave the site swiftly. They can keep their ponies and chicks and Bakewell tarts. Caro and her brother, David, are having one of their legendary Sunday parties and, as of now, I'm off duty.

★ ★ ★

Of course I only go and bump into Charlie's friend Rich at Tower Hill. A word about Charlie's friends: there aren't very many of them, not close ones, anyway. He's kept in blokish touch with people like David, for whom he used to work and through whom the two of us met in the first place, but his closest friend is Rich. He met Rich during gap-year travels in Australia and though they went off to different universities they met up again in London and shared a flat for several years.

'Did you get my message?' he asks.

He's a sweetie, Rich, an English teacher at one of Southwark's many poorly performing secondary schools. Short, balding, no head-turner, it would be so easy for him to have slipped into stooge territory next to one of London's handsomest devils, but he somehow manages to be Charlie's equal. The word 'stolid' springs to mind, though I've never really known what that means. If it means he is calm and outwardly unemotional, *straight*, then yes, he is stolid. His stolidness is what is attractive about him.

'What message?' I lie. 'When did you phone?'

161

The Meredith project means I've had to be ruthless with my time this summer, and the harsh truth is that Rich has had to be downgraded for this critical period. His bond with Charlie is, rightly, far stronger than any mutual liking he and I have struck up over the last year, which means any attempt at detective work here, however low key, would be counter-productive. In any case, as he attended a state school and East Anglia University rather than a public school and Oxford, I don't suppose he's ever been welcomed into Meredith's inner sanctum. I'm not even certain if he's met her at all or is aware of The Situation. Charlie and I have an unspoken agreement that we won't bicker about it in front of his friends, and when alone with them he's presumably even less keen to discuss details of his emasculating stalemate with Mother.

We catch up on Charlie news (what on earth was I thinking doubting his whereabouts? It would be impossible to fake the sort of detail Rich and I now discuss) and all the time he's looking at me oddly. Then I realise he's probably never seen me with no-make-up make-up and in florals buttoned up to the throat, not to mention the sketchbook still clutched to my chest like a life jacket and the ponytail swinging at my ears. Thank God I didn't repeat yesterday's Calamity Jane pigtails — they looked cute enough, but news of the styling incongruity would have found its way across the Atlantic faster than you can sing 'Secret Love'.

'You look different,' he says.

'Oh, you know, it's the whole vintage prints thing, my weekend look.'

He accepts this without question. 'D'you want to grab a drink? I'm not in a hurry or anything.'

In the normal course of events I would of course invite Rich along to the party as my guest, but I want to go home and change first, which he would doubtless find odd after my last statement and, in any case, I can't risk Caro asking how I got on at the Dulwich Country Fair ('Any sign of the old crone?') with him in earshot. So I fob him off with work excuses — I haven't been through the papers yet, big presentation coming up — and the promise that we must get together before Charlie gets back.

'No problem,' he says, 'I've got marking to do anyway.'

As we part I want to send love to his girlfriend, whom I've met on frequent occasions, but find I can't remember her name.

★　★　★

Much later, when I get home, I check my emails on the laptop and there are two from Charlie. He's concerned he hasn't been able to get hold of me this weekend.

**Is anything wrong? Work dramas?**

I hook up to Instant Messenger to find he's online right now.

**All fine**, I tap out. **Missing you**.

**Missing you more. Californian girls not up to much**.

**Yeah, right**.

## Wish you were here. What are you wearing . . . ?

This is a very nice side effect: the very fact that I'm concentrating on her and not firing off missives to Charlie every five minutes is keeping his interest aflame. I feel a sudden, alcohol-warmed high. I have a very strong feeling this is all going to work out. The campaign is progressing with textbook ease (not that I've ever seen a textbook for ingratiating yourself with your mother-in-law-to-be while deceiving your boyfriend) and the conversation by the marmalade loaves suddenly seems like a major triumph. I've now enjoyed two conversations with Meredith and there are no signs that she's applied for a restraining order — in fact, I made her laugh. She defended me to Moira! We're practically mates! In a few short months we'll be going to art exhibitions together and discussing ideas for Christmas presents for Charlie.

But that night in bed, clenched in the grip of insomnia, I suffer the kind of crisis of confidence that would never strike during daylight hours. What I'm thinking now is, why am I doing this? Why am I worrying about sucking up to some snooty old cow who doesn't know me from Adam when what I should really be doing is lying entwined with the man I love after a nice lazy weekend together? Why isn't he here with me? Why haven't we just made passionate love? OK, so he's following his dream and everyone deserves a go at that, but the question is, am I a part of his dream or not?

In the end I'm so restless I get up again and go

and have a look at the photo of Charlie on the living-room mantelpiece. It was taken just weeks into our relationship when I wasn't yet aware of the Meredith situation. He looks so sad, the shadow of his father captured on film as tangibly as any bodily figure. Then, suddenly, out of nowhere, I remember a comment Jojo made when she and Dad came for lunch one Sunday last summer. Felix was still tiny, carried in her arms throughout the visit, but that didn't stop her making her customary sweep of my flat for Day heirlooms she might like to reclaim. She came across the photo, then tacked on to the bedroom mirror awaiting the perfect frame, and studied it for some time. They'd been disappointed not to meet Charlie himself that day; I'd invited him, of course, but he was busy with his own 'family' commitments.

'Now *there*'s a man crying out to be mothered,' she said, peering at the picture. 'Is that what you're doing, d'you think, Anna?'

*Me* mothering Charlie! As if there were ever a vacancy.

# 12

No sooner is the next day's Monday Morning Meeting adjourned and my hangover held in abeyance by a bucket of black filter than not one but two crises strike. Inspired by our exchange last night, Charlie emails me with an idea. How would I like to meet him in New York over the holiday weekend? The Granada weekend.

**Sorry, babe**, I type in reply, **I have a big pitch on the Thursday. Also, I told Maggie I would go with her on a press trip thingy, not sure where but have already said yes and I don't like to let her down**.

It's true, I tell myself, as a rule I don't like to let Maggie down because she can be quite scary, and I'm not sure exactly where we're going — where is Granada exactly? Near Madrid? Near Barcelona? I honestly don't know.

But the situation takes a distressing turn when I come back from lunch to find a long message from him on my voicemail saying he is so determined for me to visit that he thinks I should come the week I originally suggested, the third week in August. For a second I think he means I should fly out with Meredith but, listening on, I find he means that I go *instead* of her. It gets worse: what he has done is tell her that her planned visit must be postponed because he has to attend a conference that week and won't be around to play host. And she's agreed! She thinks she may be able to rejig her schedule by finding someone else to take her place on her Spanish trip (there's a waiting list, apparently), freeing her up to visit him when it's more convenient. 'What do you think?' he finishes.

What do I think? I think this is a frigging disaster, that's what I think. Waiting for my veins to defrost, I try his mobile but it's switched off. It takes me a minute or two to find the Endo Associates number in San Francisco and to bash out the digits in the correct order. Moving Forward, Nigel has put a lock on international calls — something to do with Becky and a holiday romance she couldn't forget — so I use my mobile. Finally, I get through.

'Anna!' He sounds so absurdly pleased to hear from me I feel like weeping and confessing the whole thing here and now.

'I feel awful about this mix-up,' I tell him. 'Of course your mother shouldn't change her plans. Sorry if I seemed unsympathetic before you left, but I can't let you force her to reschedule. I actually think it's hugely important for you to spend time together.'

There's a silence at the other end and I worry that I may have gone too far. (Did I even slide into my more girlish and gushing Dulwich voice while I was at it?) If he's stunned by my magnanimity then I can hardly blame him; he'd surely expect me to have been brooding about this visiting rights issue since he left and therefore display rather more enthusiasm for any volte-face in my favour.

I rush on, 'I think you should tell her the

conference has been cancelled and she can come out that week after all.'

'You don't want to come?' His voice catches; he's trying hard not to sound injured.

'I do, of course I do, but the thing is, I can't take holiday in August now, not with this pitch coming up. Even if I'd booked it ages ago Nigel would have cancelled it, you know what he's like. Why don't I try to come and see you in early September instead?'

'OK, if you're sure.' And even in his disappointment, even across a telephone line, I can sense his relief that he has been sanctioned to restore the status quo with Meredith.

'Tell me how the placement's going,' I say, quickly. 'What are you working on?'

I'm so busy pondering my own narrow squeak that I barely concentrate on his answer, something to do with public housing in Oakland. Nor is the irony lost on me that I have just stuck out my leg and deliberately tripped up his first, faltering step towards progress; he was actually prepared to put *my* needs before his mother's, a milestone indeed. There's something else on my mind, though, something harder to face up to: the realisation that I'm reluctant to see Charlie at any time before the Meredith deadline, because time spent seducing him would be better spent seducing *her*. I'm becoming obsessed. The truth is that my ideal would be for *neither* of us to visit him in California, giving me an extra week to track Meredith down for neighbourly chats and pre-Granada bonding. I remind myself that Charlie and I will have the rest of our lives together if this works — *only* if this works. It's going to be worth the short-term agony.

He emails me soon after to report that his mother will revert to her original schedule for August after all: San Francisco, Spain, Cornwall. (So now I know she must be going down to Cornwall some time between the bank holiday weekend and her party on 18 September. I note it on my calendar.) **Thanks for being so good about this,** he writes. **It's not for ever, I promise.**

Crisis over. Until the next one. Now Maggie phones and tells me she is pulling out of the Granada trip. She's got chickenpox and even if she hadn't been banned by her doctor from travelling for the next three weeks she'd be damned if she was going to let anyone besides Ian see her with her grotesque new crust or, indeed, the adolescent pits sure to scar her visage for ever after (her words). She sounds very cross when I tell her that I should be all right because I caught it as a child. 'Unless it comes back as *shingles*,' she says, grumpily. Within an hour she's had her assistant bike over the Alhambra file: tickets and documents, her own cuttings about the site and a couple of business cards. There's also a printout of an email entitled: 'Art Explorer: Provisional Itinerary, Granada'. I scan its contents: **We depart from Park Crescent HQ at 8 a.m. for London Gatwick . . . We join our guide for a tour of the Alcazabar, followed by the world treasure the Nasrid palaces . . . We have free time to explore the Generalife gardens or the city of Granada . . . Our executive people carrier returns us to Malaga for the 15.10 flight to Gatwick . . .**

Something tells me this is going to be *very* useful indeed.

Then I see the sign-off: **It will be great to see you again, Maggie. Best, Angus**. Angus. Will he find it so great to see *me*? Will he still let me tag along on the guided tour? For I'll be there, of course, with or without the journalistic credentials. Maggie's withdrawal makes me realise how I've been depending on her presence to validate mine and, more simply, to *help*. Can I really go it alone? Maggie doesn't think so and has offered to find another travel writer who could step in; alternatively I could find my own replacement and make sure one of us supplies her with draft copy that can then be rewritten. It's my call.

I'm rather less skilful in managing this one. After work I go to Corney & Barrow with Caro and we have three bottles of champagne and a very excitable brainstorm. In the morning my first text of the day is from her, saying how chuffed she is about Spain. Caro is coming to the Alhambra. Her follow-up email, waiting for me when I get to my desk, is more explicit: **Spanish men! Might find some use for those vibrating condoms after all, eh?**

I sit back, aghast. My only hope is that Nigel will block us from both being out of the office at the same time, but we're not technically in the same department and it's only one day, anyway, since the Monday is a bank holiday. Plus he's been much chummier since we've become doubles partners; he's even had Rosie find us a court for a practice session tomorrow lunchtime and book a car to take us there. No, he'll give special dispensation all right. My only options are to pull out altogether — and I'm not about to do that — or coax Caro into modifying some of her more colourful habits while we're with the Dulwich lot. God, she's going to hate them all, Humphrey and Moira, Angus . . .

For the tenth time today I take out my calendar. With Meredith in San Francisco for a week from the fourteenth, there will be limited opportunities to see her before the Granada weekend. It's now more vital than ever that I put in some quality groundwork at the tennis on Sunday. I get Caro on the phone; we need to shop for sports gear. Virgin or not, this time I'll be wearing white.

★ ★ ★

Two months ago, when I still slept like a baby with laudanum in its bottle, I could never have imagined that the following images would soon gore my sleep like great shards of glass: coronation chicken, a paperback called *Win Ugly*, Nigel's thighs, Meredith recoiling, cringing away from me in something close to terror . . . Please let the night pass and let me discover it's Sunday morning all over again and the Village Lawn Tennis & Croquet Club Mixed-Doubles Open has yet to get underway. *Please.*

It starts well enough. The weather is overcast but dry. 'Better than sun, to be honest,' Eric tells me. 'Last year we had a terrible problem with prickly heat.' There's a lovely flutter of goodwill around the club, festive almost, as the players

171

crowd around the noticeboard in the clubhouse to see who they're playing first. Meredith's partner is — guess who? — Angus Poole, and his pride in teaming up with his parents' Very Special Friend is plain from the moment they emerge together from a navy-blue Merc (hers, I assume) and begin unloading picnic hamper, ice box, sports bags and rackets. He proceeds to carry the lot himself, glancing repeatedly at her like some star-struck White House intern filling in as Jackie's partner because Kennedy's been called away to see about the Bay of Pigs. Whatever Maggie says, in an odd way I can't help regarding Angus as my potential rival, not ally; how am I going to get *my* compliments in with him fawning all over her?

They greet me together, white-legged and well bred, cautiously friendly in that way that makes me know that, popping up all over the place though I may be, I'm by no means accepted, not yet. But that's fine. Friendship must be earned, I know that. I just want to hurry up and earn it.

Far more bonhomie is forthcoming from Eric and Jill. The combination of my reputation for fund-raising flair and my tanned gym-trim limbs set off by a wispy little Ralph Lauren tennis dress (I was tired and Caro's insistence on less is more prevailed) seems to have made me something of a VIP around the place. I'm introduced to everyone who'll listen, or at least to those who still have their hearing. I'm youngish, new, relatively glamorous (though a bit shiny-faced): I'm a hit. Jill even suggests Nigel and I join her and Eric for lunch, an honour indeed as their

172

ancient tartan blanket by Court Three represents the top table at this event. Which is where the coronation chicken comes in. In no time at all Nigel and I have romped through our round-robin sets, winning each with ease — those practice sessions have paid off; I even have to hold back on slamming my forehands too hard into the corners, for the pace of the day is strictly genteel — and are now unpacking picnic hampers and discussing Ginny's 1977 Wimbledon triumph. Angus and Meredith are out of sight on the other side of the clubhouse, but I made sure I cooed hello on my way back from the loo.

'It would never have happened if it weren't for the Silver Jubilee,' sighs Jill, whose dress looks as though it may pre-date that happy event. 'Wasn't it magical? Do you remember the street party, Eric? It all got rather hectic, didn't it?'

'Bloody hooligans never brought those deck-chairs back,' he grumbles.

I remember the summer of 1977 only for the death of my mother and its dark, confusing aftermath. Day-to-day differences dominated: I ate odd meals at unusual times; I had stinging eyes after bathtime because my father didn't know how to stop the shampoo suds sliding into my eyes (that improved when Grandma took over); I was allowed cocoa *after* I'd brushed my teeth and television long beyond the early evening news bulletin that signalled the end of children's programmes (sometimes up to and including *Coronation Street,* too); my bedtime changed and the voice that soothed me when I half-woke with bad dreams was a deeper one that I sometimes confused with a monster's if the lamp wasn't turned on straight away. Even the air I woke up to each morning smelled different, for Grandma liked us all to start the day with bacon, eggs and fried bread. It was as though all the elements of my existence had been placed in a giant tombola and revolved at high speed. It was so beyond my grasp that I never stopped expecting my mother to appear again — every time a car crunched into the driveway, or a key clicked in the door, every time the school bell went and I ran out into the playground with the others, waiting to be claimed. But by December Dad had moved us away from Chesham and into London and everything changed once more.

None of which makes appropriate chit-chat on the picnic rug, but I can't bring myself to agree that it was a 'magical' time for Englanders all. Nor can I allow my mood to dip, even by a degree, so I concentrate on keeping the lunch plates heaped. 'Would you like some of this baked halloumi and aubergine, Jill?' Our hamper, courtesy of a fantastic deli I found in Borough Market, is much praised. Nigel feasts with intensity, apparently enjoying himself, though I'd prefer him to sit a little further away as his bare thighs are close enough to mine for me to feel his body heat from them. I'm not surprised he's sweating: he's one of those players who treats tennis like football, never stops moving and dashes about as though he's marking someone, panting all the while.

'You must feel so lucky to have such a lovely young lady in your office,' Jill tells him. 'We all think Anna's energy is absolutely extraordinary!'

'Yes, she has her moments,' he says. Thank the Lord he joined the paper after my conversion to monogamy and early nights — if he blabbed even a tenth of my exploits with Paul to this crowd I'd soon lose my saintly shine. He doesn't seem to have noticed anything different about me (the mouth of my Dulwich persona has been well and truly washed out with soap); hell, he's even accommodated his own bad language. It's all going swimmingly.

'Jill's nice, isn't she?' I say, as we reconvene for our first knockout tie.

'Baggy knees,' he says, nostrils curling.

I notice The Woofer has not been invited to spectate today and can't help hoping she's taking the opportunity to jump into bed with an attractive neighbour.

'Who've we got in the quarter-final, then, Day? Let's have a butcher's at the draw.'

'Let me see . . . Oh yes, Meredith and Angus,' I supply, looking at the photocopied draw like I haven't anticipated this match for weeks and the names mean nothing more to me than any of the others.

'Best of British,' calls Eric. He and Jill have finished a respectable second in their group so can now spend the rest of the day boozing and, in the case of Eric, officiating the final.

'We meet again,' I call gaily to Meredith as we gather at the net for the toss. We're the first quarter to get underway and quite a few people

175

have wandered over to watch, some still munching on sandwiches and sipping wine.

'We haven't had the chance to see any of your games,' Angus says, stiffly, but I suspect it's his attempt at joviality and I smile at him encouragingly. I can't help noting that the body beneath the tennis whites is firm and rangy. 'So we know nothing about your style of play.'

'Oh, we just muddle through, don't we, Nige?'

'If you say so.'

It is soon after this that Nigel changes from man to beast and starts hitting the ball like he's Jack Nicholson in *The Shining*. He does nothing to lessen the power of his serve when he's hitting to Meredith and she struggles to return a single one. Seeing several of the club biddies muttering on the sidelines, I try to have a word with him at the next change of ends.

'It's just a friendly little open, no need to play quite so fiercely.'

He reaches into his sports bag and brandishes a book, exactly like he brandishes the *Sun* in our Monday Morning Meetings. I catch its title: *Win Ugly*. 'These bastards have rejected my application twice now,' he mutters, face glossed with sweat. 'I'll show them what they can do with their full membership.'

Mildly alarmed now, I deliberately fluff my next few volleys to let Meredith and Angus win the point. Nigel responds by running down every ball for himself as though he's playing singles, reaching across me at the net, chasing after lobs with bestial grunts of 'Mine!'. Gone are my fantasies of classic rallies, cries of 'Good shot,

176

Meredith!' and breathless plans for a regular rematch. But it's at set point against us that it happens: my worst moment of the Meredith campaign so far, possibly the worst moment of *adulthood* so far. The Smash. In response to a belting serve from Nigel, Angus has sent up a lob as high as Mount Snowdown and it's so obviously in my court that, short of physically wrestling me to the ground, Nigel can only stand back and let me take it myself. He satisfies himself with back-seat driving: 'Let it bounce, Day, let it bounce. Keep your eye on the ball . . . ' I go through the motions, left hand pointing, racket back as though in preparation to serve; the bounce is almost as high as the original ball and by the time it starts to fall again I feel so dizzy with the wait I actually close my eyes.

'Now give it some welly!' Nigel bellows and I do, for the contact is true, right in the sweet spot of my lovely oversized racket, the one that Eric says would be disallowed in the course of normal club competition but he'll turn a blind eye as this is a fun day. Perfect, except I've leaned too far back and I've hit the smash upwards, like a badminton swat, and it's flying out of court, off the map . . . and worse, the racket's gone as well, hurtling out of my fist and over the net, over Meredith's head, finally landing with a suffocated clatter on the grass inside her baseline.

'Six!' someone shouts and there's a terrific round of titters.

As I look around I see people straightening up, apparently having cringed away from possible injury. There is even a wineglass or two, dropped to the ground in alarm.

'Haven't seen anything like that since 'Buster' Mottram in 'eighty-two,' Humphrey says, to more snickers.

I look across the net. Angus is still staring in the direction that the ball was last seen, over the hills and far away, that is, his mouth slightly agape. As for Meredith, she is crouching low, hands over her nose and mouth, eyes enormous and round, and is looking up at me as though I'm a yeti about to club her with my paw.

Noticing her distress, Angus scurries to her side. 'Are you all right, Meredith? Did you think the racket was going to hit you?'

'No, no, it just came so fast . . . '

'Never let a woman take a smash,' Nigel calls across the net to Angus. 'They always fucking bottle it.' He's ready to shake hands and as Angus moves forward uncertain clapping breaks out. It has almost been forgotten that the set has been won, the game is over.

Somehow I get through the rest of the afternoon, dutifully watch Angus and Meredith lose in their semi-final and hang around until it's clear I'll get no further contact with her today. When I get home and look in the mirror my skin is bright red, like I've just beaten my way out of a burning building with a blanket over my head. It might be the sun, of course; I wasn't nearly as vigilant as I should have been about topping up my sun block at four-hourly intervals. Then again, the clouds didn't break all day.

178

# 13

Such things are relative, of course, but I can at least feel lucky about one thing: Nigel is on holiday for a week and word has yet to spread about The Smash. On occasions of particular misery or humiliation, the boys have been known to mock up a front page, headline (often mispelled) and all. I can just imagine it: 'SMASHED! Tennis babe, 33, left red faces all round at yesterday's Dulwich Open with her FRANTIC strokes. Onlookers were STUNNED as 36C Anna BLASTED the ball a mile out of court . . . '

If it weren't for my innate optimism, I swear I'd be at my LOWEST EBB by now. I'm missing Charlie; I need to be *held*. It really hurts to know that it is Meredith and not me who will be flying to San Francisco this week for that arrivals-gate hug. Will she bring up the tennis incident with him by way of an amusing anecdote and, if she does, will she mention my name? (Why did Nigel have to address me repeatedly by my surname?) Instinct tells me not. Last names are not usually given in such reports and, in any case, surely the focus will be on Charlie's Frisco adventures, not Meredith's Dulwich ones? I decide not to worry; Lord knows I have enough on my mind as it is.

Nevertheless I really don't like the idea that the tennis day might have been our last contact before the Granada trip. Ideally, I would have liked another meeting just to make sure she understands that the violence of the moment was simply that: momentary, a freak, and in no way directed at her. Maybe we could share a laugh at my expense? I'm sure I could manage to drum up a sense of humour about the whole thing — for her.

As the week wears on my anxiety grows rather than fades and I decide to cancel an agency lunch and go down to Dulwich. Surely she must have last-minute travel errands I can intercept? She must need sun lotion, a guidebook, a pile of paperbacks for the long flight? I decide the bookshop is my best bet.

The empty pavements and considerate traffic of Dulwich are a tonic after a morning in the office and I feel immediately more hopeful.

'Quiet today,' I say to the girl in the bookshop. I've eked out my browse as long as is decent and there hasn't been a single other customer in that time.

'Should have been here this morning,' she replies. 'I had a right barney with one customer.' She's obviously still smarting about it, keen to recall the battle.

'What happened?' I ask, politely.

'Oh, this customer came in and went off on one because a book she ordered hasn't come in.' Perhaps finding insufficient sympathy in my expression she elaborates: 'She went *mental*, I tell you, she was veining up and everything.'

'That's not fair,' I tell her. 'It's not your fault. Who was it?'

'This local woman, she's usually so nice. But

you know what they can be like around here.'

I do indeed. I buy a book, some literary bestseller by a South American author that will look the business next to my coffee cup at the parador, but as I leave something makes me turn back and ask the girl, 'What was the book, anyway? The one that caused all the trouble?'

She rolls her eyes anew. 'Oh, it was from the Pan-Academic Press, they're always late with deliveries. Something about modern architecture in San Francisco.'

Meredith. It had to be. So it is still there, then, the temper Charlie has talked about, the hysterical streak that scared off her eldest son and made a passive bystander of her husband. The unmanageable Meredith, the unpredictable Meredith who crouched like a POW when a smash came her way, the Meredith who still stands between Charlie and me.

I decide to go straight back to work.

★ ★ ★

I remember Mum getting angry with me just once. I'm sure it must have happened all the time because children *are* annoying, but I can only remember one specific episode. Her face went all hot and twisty. 'If you do that again you'll have to . . . you'll have to be *adopted*. And you *won't* be coming on holiday.' And I did do it again, that crime, whatever it was. I sat snivelling on the stairs as she set about a huffing charade of bag packing and coat-and-shoes gathering (not hard as I'd been packed for the holiday for days) and placed them all by the front door. So harsh. They really knew how to threaten kids in the seventies.

I was still unsettled when we were on the road the next day, partly delighted to be permitted to come after all and not to be queuing for gruel with the other orphans, but partly fearful that they'd remember (for Dad had been swiftly apprised of my badness and was of course on *her* side) and reinstate the threat. Then I'd have to go to a *French* children's home. Should I tell them I felt sick on the ferry and risk being left aboard when we reached Calais? More importantly, was I going to miss out on the Opal Fruits and Wotsits that were a tradition on any long car journey?

Despite the anxiety, I remember feeling disappointed rather than excited when we arrived at the small stone cottage on the edge of a steep riverbank. There were no other houses for miles. There was no pool. And, worst, there was no sign of Coco, the promised resident cat.

'There's nothing to do,' I whined.

'Yes there is,' said Mum, 'there's *everything* to do.' She was of the 'we'll make our own fun' school of holidaying.

'Like what?' I can't be sure that the teenage attitude is not a retrospective addition; I couldn't have been more than three at the time. Maybe I just waited for an example, as you do at that age, taking what people say at their word, waiting for Mum to show me what 'everything' entailed.

Anyway, this definitely happened: she looked around her, then suddenly lay down on the

182

grass, pushed herself off and rolled straight down the bank. It must have been ten metres and she really picked up speed as she went. I still remember my yelp of delight at seeing the swirl of cotton print as it tangled up between her legs. Then I got down and did exactly the same.

After that she carried me back up to the driveway where Dad was waiting by the cottage door, laughing, kissing my hair, and said, 'There's *always* something to do, my sweet love.' Then Dad called us his silly girls and we opened the big, heavy door to see what was inside.

Adoption was never mentioned again.

★   ★   ★

The papers are full of Dad's client Sammy Duncan, who, for those of us who had retained any doubt, has confirmed suspicions that he's unlikely to be hearing from the producers of *University Challenge* any time soon. Evidently he caused cackles on a Saturday morning TV show when he thought Andalucia was an Italian porn star. A quick *Mirror* poll on the streets of our cities has revealed that two out of three teenagers are no wiser than Sammy. Of those who even know Andalucia is a region and not a person, the majority are unable to say which country it is in. Brazil was a popular suggestion. Cue obligatory shots of Brits vomiting in the gutter in Torremolinos.

After years of working in tabloids, this kind of brouhaha doesn't interest me. It does, however, remind me to drop in to see Dad and Felix before I go to Granada. I've already picked up the digital camera from his office in the West End, but the day before the RingMe presentation I'm up in Camden for a meeting and decide to hop on the Northern Line without calling. I don't know what it is but this whole Meredith thing has taken on the same sense of urgency you feel in December, that sense that you must get together with everyone 'before Christmas' in case you find yourself under house arrest for the rest of your days. It's very unlike me to feel so fatalistic, but suddenly that's exactly what I am.

Dad isn't in, in any case, but Jojo gives me a drink. She's lost all of her pregnancy weight — and then some — and looks better than ever: groomed to the gills, in touch with her very expensive self, proud of her position as a rich man's wife. And barely in her thirties! I like Jojo and have done pretty much from the start. She has aspirations but never pretensions. All right, so the world turns for her benefit, but I have sympathy with that view. How else do you get what you want? In some ways, it's harder to achieve what she has — that old-fashioned woman's double gold of wealthy provider and best house in the street — than it is to achieve my own career-based goals. Maybe it's because her choices involve working *with* men, mine against them.

'I hope Dad's dropped the idea of sending Sammy Duncan to see me,' I say to her. Now I know why I'm really here. Sammy Duncan. What with Caro replacing Maggie, I don't need any more loose cannons in my charge. And after the

184

'hiccup' of the tennis day, Granada is going to have to do more than provide a pretty backdrop for the sealing of a beautiful friendship; it's going to have to inspire it from scratch.

'What?' Jojo says. 'Don't know anything about that. But he's a sweet boy, Sammy, since The Priory. He was round here the other day, absolutely wonderful with Felix.' They do this, new mothers, they'd welcome the FBI's Most Wanted into their home if he knew how to microwave a bottle of formula.

But as I leave she cheers me up when she remembers — casually, as though it might easily have slipped her mind for good — that she's found an old book called *Tales of the Alhambra* with Mum's name in the front. 'I *thought* that's where Clive said you were going.'

'She must have read it when she was there,' I say, clasping it with delight. It's a small hardcover like the children's books I used to have. 'Thank you.' I notice that the author's name is Washington Irving. 'He must be the Irving she mentions in her travel diary . . . ' I don't speak aloud the other thought that occurs, that it will be no bad thing for Meredith to see me in possession of such a dusty old edition — it suggests a bit of culture somewhere in my family history.

'Give me a Caribbean beach any day,' Jojo sighs as we kiss goodbye.

A month or two ago I would have agreed.

★    ★    ★·

185

The evening before Caro and I leave for Spain I have another session with Viv. She says she can't close my file with a clear conscience until we've talked through the Charlie 'issue'.

I prepare her organic green tea and pour myself a red wine. I've already had a few celebratory drinks with Simon after the RingMe pitch; we were both blown away by Nigel's performance and — a rarity — even agreed we couldn't have done it better ourselves.

'I have a file?' I ask, surprised.

'You do indeed,' Viv says. 'But don't worry. I'm not medically qualified so none of the information it contains would ever hold up in court.'

I don't ask her how it is that she thinks I'll end up in court, but tell her instead about the tennis incident. By now I am able to see the funny side of it, or at least am able to present the funny side of it to other people while continuing to cringe with humiliation inside. Thankfully, I've yet to have to trot it out for my colleagues as Nigel has barely mentioned it since his return from holiday, beyond a sore remark or two about us having been 'robbed' by the 'posh bastards', and Caro, after much giggling, has agreed to keep the news of my sports debut to herself.

'I didn't actually injure anyone,' I say to Viv. 'It was just mistiming. When I was at school I threw a javelin into the crowd at sports day.' I still remember how I spotted the urgent parting of the spectators before I realised it was *my* javelin that had caused the alarm. It landed flat next to someone's handbag and a rethrow was ordered

186

owing to the cackling of the competitors. I was known as Zulu for a while.

'Do you think you might have psychotic tendencies?' Viv asks, seriously.

'It wasn't deliberate!' I protest. 'Neither of the incidents were.'

'OK, well what you need to do is put it in a box, close the lid and bury it under a tree.'

'The tennis racket or the javelin?'

'The experience.' Clearly her guru-speak has come on in leaps and bounds since our first meeting.

'I'd rather try cremation,' I say. 'So what did you want to talk about in terms of Charlie?'

She sips her tea. 'Well, I'm sure your positive energy will triumph, but just in case Meredith takes an active dislike to you . . . '

'It wasn't *that* bad,' I say.

'Not the smash,' she says. '*You.* You must have considered that you just might not be to her taste, Pygmalion or no Pygmalion?'

'It was *your* idea,' I point out.

'And I'm not saying it's not a good one,' she comes back, coolly, 'or that it won't be successful. What I *am* saying is that we should at least discuss how you'll feel if it doesn't work out after Spain. Where it might leave you with Charlie when he comes back.'

I shrug. 'Same place as before, I suppose.'

'OK,' says Viv, patiently. 'But what if he then turns round and wants to bring you and Meredith together, after all? How will you handle the fact that she knows you already and isn't your biggest fan? I hate to say it, but it could put you in a more difficult position than

187

the one you were in to begin with.'

I think. I think mostly about the step forward Charlie made when he volunteered to cancel Meredith's visit in favour of mine. Was that actually 'progress' as normal lovers define the word? All he did was lie to his mother about a work conference in order to clear the way for a visitor he wanted to sleep with. He didn't even hint to her that there was someone else involved, someone he cares about.

'Oh, he'll *never* initiate it,' I say to Viv.

And in that moment I see the truth. He won't. He never *was* going to. I've given him the summer, but it won't be enough. He'll always want another season from me. If Meredith doesn't like me by the time she opens her precious doors to her birthday guests, then my chances are lost for ever, Charlie is lost for ever. The thought of being without him is enough to suck the air from my lungs, but this has been the risk all along.

'Well, succeed or fail, at least it will be down to me,' I say, with finality. 'I can't blame anyone else.'

'Call me from Spain any time you need advice,' Viv says, as I walk her down to her taxi.

'OK. Thank you. I appreciate your, you know, everything.'

'Don't mention it,' she says. 'You were my first client and it will be good karma for my practice if it all works out.'

'I'm sure it will,' I tell her.

'By the way, is it true what I've heard about Nigel?'

188

'*Nigel?* What's that?'

'That he wears a set of false teeth over his real ones? That can't be hygienic, can it? Tell him I know a fantastic orthodontist in Fulham, trained in the States, the full works.'

'Will do,' I say.

When she's gone I finish packing and check my emails. There's one from Charlie. So the last thing I see before I get on a plane in a bid to convince his mother that I'm fit for her son is this: **Rich said he saw you the other week and you have a 'new look'. Sounds interesting. But I think it would be hard to improve on the original**.

Don't tell me, Charlie, tell her!

# PART 2:
# GRANADA, SPAIN

# 14

It is only when we get to Gatwick airport that I recognise the magnitude of my situation. Suddenly, a weekend away seems a very slim slice of time indeed to contain the amount of work I'll need to put in to get Meredith to like me — and like me enough to contemplate the idea of Charlie and me together without the need to retch or (how did the bookshop girl put it?) 'vein up'.

All around me women of different ages are barking commands to husbands and boyfriends, to airline personnel, to older and younger versions of themselves. They know their minds, all right. 'I've already told you. Didn't you listen?'; 'I said we should have left twenty minutes earlier, I knew this would happen'; and so on. And these are just women of the *normal* variety!

Standing there, I can't help but reassess last night's conversation with Viv. 'We should at least discuss how you'll feel if it doesn't work out after Spain.' No wonder she was trying to steer me towards damage control: it is now two months since she and I cooked up this little scheme and I appear to be nowhere near doing what I set out to do. Meredith would as soon invite a tramp from the street to her party as she would me. I certainly don't need to look at my own 'Contact Log' to remember each of the three entries:

*9 July: Introduced (at the gallery)*
*1 August: Said hello (at the country fair)*
*8 August: Said hello again (the tennis day)*

And then, of course, I managed to undo all of the above hello-ing with that racket-hurling finale. Has she seen enough to know she wants nothing more to do with me? Will she brook no further persuasion, like the mother in the neighbouring line for Faro who categorically refuses to reopen the family suitcase because her child has changed his mind about which toy to take on the plane? 'You should have thought about that before,' she says with exasperated finality and when she catches my eye it feels like a 'told you so' meant directly for me.

Whatever the answer, the fact is I had counted on being further along the line than this by the Granada weekend. So I'm pulling out all the stops. I've decided that being a relief photographer/journalist and art buff (art bluff, as Caro calls me) without the authentic lead vocals of Maggie is not going to be enough to counterbalance the vulgarity of my full-time job in sales, so I have brought with me a couple of new props: prospectuses for the Slade School and the Royal College of Art. If anyone asks, I am applying to art school, at least I am thinking of applying to art school. First, I'll need to weigh up the relative merits of heart (my passion for painting) and head (my commitment to a solid career) and I see no reason why I shouldn't choose to do this when Meredith is within earshot. If it strikes a chord with her in the same way that Charlie's dilemma did, then so be it. If it occurs to her that he and I have a lot in common, well, that's her opinion, isn't it?

In support of this new campaign, I've got Mum's drawings of the Alhambra tucked into my still sketchless sketchbook (I know she wouldn't mind me passing those off as my own), plus the antique *Tales of the Alhambra*, which I intend to scrutinise on the plane — if we ever board the damn thing. The queue is long and, containing as it does a disproportionate number of older people, slow moving.

'God, look at all these fat fucks,' Caro says. 'Are we the only people on this flight under fifty?'

'Caro!' I lean over our luggage trolley for a pep talk. 'Remember the whole point of this trip?' She listens patiently, though I see her eye wander to the pile of magazines she's just bought, many of which come with a free gift. 'It's to present myself as a cultivated potential companion for the son of a highly sophisticated older lady who is holidaying with similarly cultured friends. No one is fat and no one is a fuck. Understood?'

She cracks up. 'Are you going to be this schoolmistressy all weekend? Aren't we going to have some fun?'

'You can have some fun the moment Charlie moves out of her house and into mine,' I say. 'Then we'll party like it's nineteen ninety-nine.'

'No thanks, Millennium Eve was a bit disappointing, I thought. I can't believe I spent it with that faceless suit — '

'You know what I mean!' I sound exactly like one of the exasperated mums. 'Look, I'm not asking you not to be yourself, but could you consider not being quite so . . . ?'

'Myself?' she supplies, good-naturedly.

'Well, yes. It's just really important that we get our stories straight.'

'OK, blue-stocking babe. Nuff said. Oh goody, they've opened another desk . . . '

We shuffle forward in the queue.

'So remind me, then,' she says. 'What *did* you say to Charlie about this weekend?'

I ignore the remote chafe of guilt in my gut. 'Just that I was going with Maggie on a press trip.'

I've decided that the easiest thing is not to speak to Charlie while I'm in Spain, which shouldn't be too difficult as Rich has stepped in to spend the weekend in New York (there is some comfort in the fact that, while not number one, I at least outrank the best friend) and the last thing either of them will want is girlfriends checking up on them. Besides, our contact has settled comfortably into the realm of flirtatious email so it won't be unnatural for us to go several days without speaking directly.

'I'll fudge something when he's back,' I add, pre-empting Caro's next question, something along the well-rehearsed lines of Maggie dropping out, Caro stepping in, and the two of us meeting some rather interesting people. Serendipity will be the key word; that's if we're serendipitous enough to get together with Angus's group at all. I rang the curly-haired bore

196

earlier in the week to remind him of the extraordinary coincidence that I'll be in Granada at the same time as him.

'Oh, right,' he replied, politely enough. 'Maggie did mail me to say she had to cancel. But you're still going?'

'Wouldn't miss it for the world,' I enthused. 'I'll buzz your room on Saturday, shall I?'

'Yes, do, do,' he agreed, but I could tell it was only because he's been brought up to be a good citizen. (Thank you, Moira!)

Caro is looking sceptical. 'But what if Meredith tells *Charlie* about the new young things *she's* been hanging out with? If you have the effect you're hoping to have this weekend, then won't she want to tell him about *you?*'

I wave this off. 'That's the risk I'll have to take, but I should be all right. I don't think they speak every day or anything like that.'

'If you say so.'

The line of seniors in the queue ahead of us turns out to be travelling as one and once the last trundles off with his boarding pass we've reached the check-in desk.

'Just as well the Big M's already been to see him in San Fran,' says Caro, handing over passports and tickets. 'Otherwise it would be sure to come up, wouldn't it? Hey, babe, maybe we should have used fake names this weekend?'

The airline worker looks up at that and I quickly laugh it off. 'Hardly. Anyway, it's bad enough having to remember to take notes and photos while we're there.'

'God, do you really have to do that? I thought

that was just something journalists say to get the hotel.'

'You'll find I wear many different hats this weekend,' I say.

'That's why her bag is so heavy,' Caro tells the airline man and she beams so gloriously he just about manages a smile.

★   ★   ★

This time last year, over August bank holiday, Charlie and I spent the weekend in a cottage in Whitstable. It was our first trip away together. I didn't know about Meredith then, only that she was a 'bit difficult' and Charlie wanted to wait for the right moment to introduce us. I wonder now if he ever really intended to, if my early sympathy didn't somehow make this situation self-fulfilling. I've seen it happen to other people in other circumstances: girlfriends of married men they just can't let go of, institutionalised workmates too terrified of life on the outside to leave jobs that don't suit them. One year becomes two, then three, and suddenly it's too substantial a stretch to admit the whole thing was a mistake that should have been spotted in the first few weeks.

The cottage was a street away from the pebble beach, and low clouds blotted the sea with great shadows of indigo. We walked for ages, past peeling wooden houses and painted huts with rusting bolts, through a huge damp fishery that made our shoes smell for weeks afterwards. It was unseasonably cold and we hadn't a clue how to get the heating to work in the cottage, so we ˅ retreated to a pub on the beach and drank local beer from plastic cups and ate oysters with Tabasco sauce.

'So, are you like all the others?' he asked me, grinning. 'Are you one of those city girls who hankers after the simple life, living by the sea with a dog and a brood of kiddies?'

I grinned back, lacing my fingers through his. 'You're obviously familiar with the type.'

'Every girl I've ever met. Without exception. They work as lawyers or consultants or something in the media but what they really want to do is bake cakes and run a teashop.'

'Having been proposed to on Albert Bridge, I suppose? Well, that's not me. You can rest assured.'

'Oh, I'm not against it,' he said. 'Everyone's entitled to their escape fantasy. I'm just surprised how similar the fantasies are.'

'I *never* want to leave the city,' I said. 'So it's certainly not mine.'

He lowered his voice in that way I'd come to find was like fingertips exploring bare skin. 'I think you'd better tell me what your fantasies really are, then.'

Later, when the tide was out, we walked down the slipway to see how far the water had been sucked away. I lost my balance in the dark and almost fell.

'Oh, I don't like to be beside the seaside,' Charlie sang, laughing, as I stalked off, cross and embarrassed. He caught up and put his arm around me. 'C'mon, let's go back to the cottage.

199

We can pretend we're on a barge on the Thames and haven't left the Big Smoke at all.'

There was nothing much to do in Whitstable. Luckily we'd brought a travel DVD player and some decent wine with us from London.

★　★　★

High above the Spanish plains I flick through my mother's *Tales of the Alhambra*. I'm no literary critic but old Washington really likes the sound of his own voice; I bet he was a right drone at dinner parties. I soon tire of his progress into Granada, where, conveniently, he gets to check into the palace itself and play sultan for a season, but I persevere; after all, the book is sure to be discussed: it's required reading according to the other one on my lap, *The Art Lover's Andalucia*. Old Angus will probably make everyone listen to him read passages aloud over glasses of mint tea. Perhaps he'll don a turban.

Skimming the index, I come across 'The Legend of the Three Beautiful Princesses' and am soon gripped. This is more like it! The trio of lovelies, whose names all begin with 'Z', are held captive by their father who seeks to protect them from the pitfalls of romance by keeping them captive in one of the Alhambra towers. There, with chattering parrots their only company, they spy three likely cavaliers out of the window and fall in love. At this point in the narrative someone, presumably my mother, has underlined the passage 'for love delights to struggle with difficulties, and thrives the most hardily on the scantiest soil'. Meaning what? That she was having problems with my father, hence the solo trip? Why was the soil so scanty in the first place? And, as Nigel might ask, where was I in all of this?

Anyway, after much wallowing on ottomans, the princesses conspire to deceive their father and elope with the cavaliers. They reason that he has not trusted them and so does not deserve their continued devotion. Also, he is left-handed and therefore by definition a hopeless blunderer. The two elder ones make a dramatic escape and, having braved surging rivers and wild mountain passes, soon settle in the city of Cordoba as happy wives. But the youngest loses her nerve at the last minute and stays behind in the tower, only to spend the rest of her days under the dragon watch of the king.

It is thought that she later came to repent her decision.

# 15

Ridiculous as it may seem, I've barely considered the fact that we'll be somewhere with a different climate. After the wettest August on record in Britain, Spain is breathtakingly dry; as we make the short taxi journey from airport to city, the sun bounces off vast roadside hoardings into the car, and Caro and I dive like kingfishers for hats and sunglasses and lip balm. Despite the smell of overheated petrol tanks and parched soil, in the distance green abounds, with palms and cypresses among those I recognise, and all against a backdrop of snow-capped peaks.

'So these are the Sierra Nevada mountains, then?' Caro asks.

'Yes, the Alhambra is atop Sabika Hill.'

'*Atop?*' she repeats. 'Is this how you speak when you're with this crew?'

I giggle. 'No, I've just memorised the guidebook. What did you think I was doing while you were reading all those magazines? Look at the weather, Caro, it's gorgeous!'

'Bit *too* scorchio, if anything,' she says. 'I hope Factor Twenty is going to be strong enough.'

'I'm sure it will.'

'When will we see the others, d'you think?' she asks me, almost as an afterthought. I try to imagine how it feels to be taking a simple weekend break, mind empty, agenda clear, nothing but sun and fun ahead, my greatest dilemma the factor of my suntan lotion — but I can't.

'They'll already have checked in by now. I suggest we book a table for dinner at the hotel and hope they've done the same.' Irritatingly, Angus's provisional itinerary failed to specify venues for meals, but my hunch is that old folk will opt for safety on the first night.

'If we hang out in the bar first we might bump into them,' Caro says, 'and we could suggest we all hook up for dinner?'

'Good idea.' It's hard to imagine Meredith or any of the three Pooles agreeing to 'hook up' with us, but I appreciate Caro's optimism. It strikes me that we're going to need quite a bit of it this weekend.

'Look, there's the Alhambra!'

The fortress sits, square and forbidding, on a high emerald-green hill, the rest of the city sprawled respectfully below as though keeping its distance from a sleeping ogre. Nerves rumble inside me like hunger. Is my life going to change in that romantic citadel? Will I make my leap from outsider to insider? I don't say this aloud as Caro would only mock, but as the road starts to climb and we pass the crowds of tourists at the site entrance, I'm as frightened as I've ever been. The moment we step through the hotel doors the rules will have changed. This is no coincidental meeting in a nearby borough of London; I've followed a sixty-year-old woman to southern Spain — this is out and out *stalking*. Technically, I may even be committing a crime. What did Viv say about her case notes not holding up in court? When this is over, I must insist she burns them.

'This is like a fairytale setting,' Caro marvels as we zigzag through woodland and pass through an arch in the thickest walls I've ever seen: the Puerta de la Justicía, my guidebook tells me. Is justice too strong a word for what I seek this weekend? Something tells me this place will do nothing to subdue the melodramatic notions of a mind trained by tabloids.

'Lordy, I feel like a princess,' Caro says, rolling her shoulders and stretching back against the seat.

'Don't you mean sultana?' I correct her and we laugh. I'm starting to feel sick; it must be the twisting road.

★   ★   ★

The entrance to the parador is just what we hoped for: gardens manicured to within an inch of their lives, doors whooshing open to bathe our bare arms and legs in icy air, a stylish reception staffed by smiling Spanish faces.

'Good afternoon, ladies . . . '

'Hola!' says Caro, with the elongated vowels of the practised flirt. There are two male staff on reception and both, at first glance, are stock smouldering Spaniards.

'Signora Bishop?'

'Oh no, I'm *Signorina* Harding.'

I'm just explaining our last-minute change in personnel when I notice a circle of guests by the window, silent but emanating cold, indignant

Britishness from every pore. 'It's them,' I hiss to Caro, slightly thrown to encounter my prey so soon. The itinerary states that their flight to Malaga and private transfer to Granada should have brought them to the hotel long before us, what with our change of planes in Madrid. Something is wrong.

'Best behaviour,' Caro whispers, excitedly, and nudges me towards them.

'Hi, there! Checking in? I do hope we haven't pushed ahead of you?' I greet the group with a full-wattage beam and get the usual polite murmurs in return. Cheer up, you're on holiday, I feel like saying, be grateful you're not working like me! My view of Meredith is obscured by Humphrey, though I can see the outline of her dark hair and one powder-blue shoulder. Nearer to me Moira grips a large sunhat and, judging by the lardy sheen to her forehead, is taking no risks with UV rays. She looks over at me, all Scottish and vexed.

'Anna, Anna, hello.' Angus slinks out of the hub and shepherds me away to one side. 'I wondered if you were arriving today.'

'We just got in to Granada airport,' I say. It seems important to point out that we are not tailing them, that we've come a different route. I introduce Caro, but he barely seems to register her presence, an unusual reaction to someone so eye-catching, but he is a dull stick after all. Probably gay, too. In turn, she ignores him and stares openly at the two female faces beyond, obviously avid to know which is Big Bad Meredith.

'Just the four of you?' I ask, puzzled. 'I thought you were bringing a whole group, Angus?'

'No, no. We couldn't do the large-scale tour we initially hoped for . . . ' He looks embarrassed. I see I'm not the only one to have booked under false pretences; he's no doubt been using his 'Art Explorer' credentials to wangle a family holiday with trade discounts. Waiting list, my foot. What would he have done if Meredith *had* pulled out and offered her place to someone like me? Just the Poole family and me atop Sabika Hill — God forbid. But as far as I'm concerned, this is all excellent news: the smaller the group, the fewer rivals for her attention.

'What a lovely hotel,' I gush. 'The location couldn't be better, could it? And those gardens! Is something wrong, Angus?'

'We've got a bit of a problem,' he says, frowning. He's blocking my view of the rest of the group so I have no choice but to stop craning for eye contact with Meredith and address him directly. He speaks in a controlled hush, but it isn't enough to conceal his anxiety. 'It seems my Spanish must have let me down when I booked. I thought I asked for three rooms, but they say it was three *people*. They've only given us *one* room, a double with an extra bed. And of course the place is fully booked. They've been double-checking, but . . . '

One glance at the nearest staff member tells me that, sympathetic though he is, no available rooms are going to materialise for these hapless Brits. 'Oh dear, that *is* a pain.' I ooze sympathy, stopping just short of patting his hand.

'If it were at least a suite, then my parents and Meredith could bunk up more easily . . . but they called the extra bed a *cot*. It must be for a child.' It obviously pains him to reveal such details, but he's desperate for a solution and if there's a state of mind I can identify with then that is it.

'Oops,' says Caro, barely listening. Now she sees introductions are going to have to wait, she's losing patience. 'Shall we go up, Anna? I need a shower.' She stretches her arms high above her head, wiggling her hands, and for a moment I fear she's going to sniff at her armpits. But instead she says, loudly, 'I bet they have good toiletries here. Did Maggie say what they were? Hope it's not some rubbish Spanish brand.'

'Hang on a second, Ca.' I turn back to Angus. 'So what are you going to do?'

'Well, the assistant manager is very kindly ringing around for an alternative. I mean, I'm happy to stay somewhere else myself,' he agonises on, 'but who gets the room here? My mother and father or Meredith?' He lowers his voice: 'Neither has exactly *offered* it to the other so far.'

We turn to see that the three of them have now discovered the visitors' book and are turning the pages together. Angus was right to sense danger: none of them is willing to give up the chance to add his or her comments to those hallowed pages. Lord knows how long they've all been standing here refusing to give ground.

'They're obviously waiting for you to adjudicate,' I say, starting to enjoy this unexpected bonding opportunity. I'm distracted for a second by fantasies of recruiting Angus to my mission. He must have known her for years, I'm thinking; she's sure to trust his opinion. If he could just put in a good word . . .

'I really don't understand how this discrepancy arose; I should have asked for written confirmation.' He's seriously beating himself up about this, which is silly, because it is clear to me what has to be done, clearer still when the receptionist breaks in to announce that he has found two rooms at another hotel. It's the only other one within the Alhambra proper, right next door to the parador, and so a neat solution.

'We'll take them, please,' Angus replies. '*Muchos gracias.*'

The man relays this into the phone, then hangs up, adding, 'It is only family-run, but is quite fine.'

I'm sure it is, but I still want full credit for what I'm about to do, which is to save the day. I turn to the others and search out Meredith's eye, ignoring the brief flashback to our last meeting and her unforgettable posture of recoil, that terror in her face. Now she just looks tired and cross. The elbows of her jacket sleeves are rumpled and her sunglasses are pushed back behind her ears so you can see more silver curling at the hairline.

'Hi, everyone. I'm so sorry to hear about the mix-up . . . '

' . . . very poor,' Humphrey and Moira are muttering together, clearly having taken the view

208

that hotel mismanagement is to blame for the situation.

' . . . but I think I have a solution,' I go on. 'Why don't you take the booked room, Moira and Humphrey? I'm sure they can remove the cot.'

'Oh,' Moira flutters, looking up at Humphrey with disbelief, as though she's just been announced the winner of a talent pageant. To Meredith's credit, her expression of weary irritation does not falter.

I pause, dramatically. 'And you, Meredith, you must take *our* room. Caro and I will move to the other hotel with Angus.'

'Our room?' I hear Caro squeak, but I can't look her in the eye, not yet. I step back as though to give her access to the others. 'Sorry, I'm being rude, aren't I? This is my good friend and colleague Caroline Harding. Caro, this is Humphrey, Moira and Angus Poole, and Meredith Grainger.'

'Pleased to meets you's are murmured all round, more eagerly from the Pooles than from Caro, it has to be said.

'You really don't have to give up your room,' Meredith says to me, levelly. But she takes the sunglasses off her head and slips them into her handbag; her thoughts must already have leaped to a nice refreshing shower, suitcase clicked open on the bed.

'Hang on,' says Angus, 'aren't you supposed to be writing an article — '

'I insist,' I interrupt. 'Caro and I don't mind where we stay, we're so excited just to be at the

Alhambra for the first time. We're just filling in for Maggie, anyway, and I'm sure a tour of the hotel will do just as well for the review. We can still use the bar and restaurant and other facilities, I'm sure.'

That last comment was for Caro's benefit, but of the semicircle of heads now surrounding me, hers is the only one not to nod appreciatively. Nevertheless, I feel totally in charge, delighted to have swooped in and dispensed salvation so ingeniously. What a perfect start! How good do I look? Modesty, generosity, the willingness to prioritise culture over personal comfort, age before beauty and all that: am I dream daughter-in-law material, or what? The unfortunate smash will never be mentioned again.

'This is really very kind of you,' Moira says.

'Not at all. The important thing is that we all have a roof over our heads. Now let me just chat to the guys here so I can reassure them Maggie's review will still go ahead. And then we're all set.'

'Thank you,' the three Pooles chorus.

'Thank you,' Meredith echoes graciously.

The hotel management is far too professional to object to my scheme and a time is duly pencilled in for me to return for a guided tour. And so it is that Caro, Angus and I leave the whooshing doors, exit the immaculate gardens and make our way to the hotel next door. Caro trails pointedly behind and I really can't blame her.

'This is actually rather pretty,' says Angus, looking up. The entrance is cool and welcoming with an old stone drinking fountain and carved

210

dark wood panelling, and ivy snakes its way around the door and between the wrought-iron railings of the first-floor balconies.

'Perfect for weary travellers,' I agree. 'How old are these amazing flagstones, d'you think, Angus?'

'Oh, centuries, I'd say.'

Behind us, Caro stops dead. 'Oh my God. Look!'

'What?' I say, coming back out into the sunlight.

'Above your head, there!' She means the hotel sign. 'One star, Anna! *One* star. This is a disaster! There's no way they'll have room service here. Or a pool.'

'I think they might have a different grading system in Spain,' says Angus, but much too doubtfully.

Caro replies directly to me as though I'm the fool to have dared proffer such nonsense, 'Yeah, like one star here is no stars in the UK? Great. The parador was *four.*'

'There you go,' I say, briskly, 'you were slumming it either way.' I link my arm through hers and pull her forward. 'Come on.'

'But, Anna . . . ?'

'Let's just check in and get upstairs.'

'If we must.'

'Thank you again,' says Angus as we prepare to leave him on the landing outside his door.

'No problem.' I linger for as long as is decent, even though Caro has already stomped off.

'Listen, I'm meeting my parents and Meredith for dinner at the parador later; would you two like to join us? Our treat.'

He can't possibly have had the chance to square that with the others, I think; it's silly, but after a year with Charlie I find Angus's spontaneity almost heroic.

'We'd love to,' I say, and as he unlocks his door, using his shoulder to push it open, I pause for a moment to rejoice. Just as I'd hoped! Dinner with Meredith on the first night and I haven't had to gatecrash or grovel or anything — I couldn't have dreamed of a better start to the weekend.

I'm far too elated to worry about the fact that my own room is technically a single, the bed one of those three-quarter-size affairs, walled in on three sides. An armchair and chest of drawers are crammed into the remaining floor space and I can only deduce that the 'wardrobe' is in the kitchen-cupboard-sized unit next to the door. It is so tiny I now have no choice but to meet Caro's glare.

'This is sweet,' I say, experimentally.

'Sweet? It's fucking *minuscule*!' Her face is flaming with indignation. 'There's not even enough space to open my suitcase.'

I lift it on to the bed and snap it open for her. 'If we unpack straight away and put everything in the wardrobe we can see if reception have somewhere to store our empty bags?'

'Hey, I've got a better idea,' she says. 'Why don't we stack the armchair on top of the drawers so we can both stand up at the same time? Oh, but only if one of us stands on our *head*.'

We both laugh but I can tell her heart's not in it.

I pull open the curtains and unlock the shutters. 'Look at the view, Caro, it's lovely!' And it is: the Alhambra walls tinged pink in the sun, pleats of emerald foliage as far as the eye can see, and that improbable horizon of perfect iced peaks.

We lean out together into the dusk air and I notice that we're at the front of the building overlooking the main tourist walkway. On cue, two passers-by notice us and one even takes a photo.

Caro scowls. 'Great, now we're a tourist attraction!'

'Just think of yourself as Helena Bonham Carter in *A Room With a View*,' I suggest, invoking one of her great hair heroines.

'She had an *enormous* room,' Caro sniffs. She plants herself on the bed and watches a gecko scurry from behind the curtains to safety behind the radiator. 'Did she have lizards on the wall, as well?'

'Come on, Caro,' I say, sitting next to her. 'This will do. We're not here for the luxuries. We're here to win over Meredith and I'd say we've made a fantastic start.'

She throws herself back on to the mattress and pouts. 'God, I've just realised, not only are we sharing a single bed in a one-star hotel but it's not even a *freebie*! *She's* got *our* free room.'

'I'll pay for everything,' I say, quickly. 'You just concentrate on having a good time. We'll hardly spend any time inside, anyway.'

'S'pose.'

Satisfied enough, I can wait no longer. 'So tell me, what did you think of Meredith?'

Caro shrugs. 'Was she the one with the shiny face or the Lady Penelope hairdo?'

'The Lady Penelope hairdo. Shiny face is Moira.'

'She looked all right.'

'Was she how you imagined?'

'S'pose.'

I give up for now. I can only pray that the sulk will sink with the evening sun; Caro tends to be at her best after the arrival of cocktail hour.

'Will you sleep against the wall tonight?' she asks. 'I'll get claustrophobic if I have to.'

'Sure. I'm happy either way.'

'I think I'll have a nap now, actually, if that's OK.' She sighs tragically and closes her eyes, fingers still gripping the parador hotel guide.

'I'll wake you for dinner,' I say.

She doesn't answer. I wonder if she'll ever speak to me again.

# 16

My first thought on returning to join the others for dinner is that it's just as well Caro has decided to get an early night after all. Her dissatisfaction with our own hotel would not have been improved by the sight of the parador terrace, which of course turns out to inhabit exactly the magical clifftop position you'd expect from your fairytale. It's the most perfect balmy Spanish evening, the sky settling into night like pools of spilled blue ink, and across the valley just one building stands spotlit amid the darkening green.

'The Summer Palace in the famous Generalife gardens,' Angus supplies before I can ask, adding that I really must make it my business to explore that part of the site before I can even think of leaving.

'It looks like a nunnery,' I say.

'A nunnery? Quite the opposite, if some of the legends are to be believed.'

'Really?' I can't help sneaking a second glance his way. With his hair curling loosely around his neck and his few extra inches of height — I'm in modest flats so as not to strike the slighter Meredith as a giantess — he seems to have been transformed into someone rather more attractive than I know him to be. Either my eyes haven't yet adjusted to the twilight or it must be·the allure of the setting, but, whichever, I hope it has

215

the same effect on the way Meredith perceives *me*.

'Shall we sit down?' he suggests.

'Of course.'

The table is formally laid, silverware twinkling in the light of a single Moroccan lantern. All the tables are occupied, most by couples, and even among the groups the conversation is pitched at an intimate purr. This is a place for lovers and special occasions, which makes me wonder how the other Art Explorers reacted when Angus announced that he'd extended the dinner invitation to two outsiders — exactly the kind of invasion of privacy most Brits would pay good money to avoid. 'I suppose we must,' Meredith will have said with a brisk little sigh. 'It's only right,' Moira might have agreed, 'they *have* helped us out.' And they have certainly taken pains to incorporate us properly, leaving free a seat on either side of the table, one between Humphrey and Moira, the other between Angus and Meredith. Naturally, I choose the latter.

'Is Caroline not joining us?' Moira asks at once. 'She's not well? Oh, I do hope the new hotel is comfortable enough . . . ?' She shoots a sidelong glance at Humphrey as though the two of them have just been discussing the health risks implicit in such a downgrade. Anyone would think they were expecting fatalities this weekend.

'It's lovely,' I reassure them. 'I'm sure Caro will be full of beans tomorrow, she was just tired from the travelling. Well, how nice everyone looks tonight.'

Both women have made considerable efforts

with their appearance. Moira, whose palette, I am learning, is more puritan than Meredith's, is bedecked in a soft sage-coloured shawl, with a delicate golden rope necklace at her throat, while Meredith favours flame-orange cashmere and jewellery that might be opals. Lipstick is heavily in evidence, Moira's smeared slightly from her attack on the large platter of nibbles in front of us.

'Hors d'oeuvres, Anne?' Humphrey offers. 'They're quite splendid.'

All three oldies munch with relish: none is vegetarian or anything-intolerant and if, like my father, they've switched to low-cholesterol spreads at home then they've relaxed the rules here. Bread is buttered generously, and Meredith even sprinkles extra salt on hers, the original content not quite to her taste.

Though friendly, she strikes me as aloof this evening, not only from me but from the others, too, as though she deliberately seeks to separate herself from the rest of us. It's nothing so plain as superiority, but rather a reserve, a glaze, a mind distracted by more tempting thoughts. I notice from the menu that the hotel's full name is the Parador de Francisco and wonder if it makes her think of Charlie in his temporary city on the other side of the world. It certainly makes me think of him; in an ideal world I'd be lunging for the last croquette with *him*, not with Angus and three lip-smacking pensioners.

Orders are taken before I get the chance to ask Meredith's advice about Andalusian cuisine (at least I know to avoid the *tortilla de Sacromonte,*

217

which I've been warned by my guidebook is made of brains and bull's testicles) and so I order directly after her, aping her choice of gazpacho and baked cod. I'm sure I read in the paper recently that mirroring your companion's actions makes them subconsciously like you more. She gives no impression of having noticed, however. Meanwhile, Moira changes her mind twice and needs on both occasions to locate spectacles in pockets before she can confirm her revisions. Then it is time for Humphrey to approve the wine, which he does with a single, deeply drawn sniff and an authoritative glance in Angus's direction — wine selection, it seems, is men's work. Finally, the waiters can retreat and we can get back to that subject all travellers love, Art Explorers included: whether or not one's hotel lives up to expectations.

'Did you say your room is just off that beautiful courtyard?' Moira asks Meredith.

'Yes,' Meredith nods serenely, 'on the first floor. It's very pleasant.'

Here we have hit on another point in my favour: while the Pooles must make do with a room in the twentieth-century extension of the hotel, Meredith, thanks to me, resides in the older part of the building, the portion that contains a celebrated courtyard and the chapel where Queen Isabel herself was originally interred.

'I overlook the *Generalife*,' she adds. She pronounces Spanish vocabulary scrupulously and it takes me a while to relate this to the word Angus used a minute or two ago.

'The classic vista,' he tells her, smiling. 'I'm so glad.'

I can see that no one dares ask what the view from his room might be, or mine, for that matter. Bins, they suspect, or perhaps some noisy air-conditioning unit.

'I must say, it's incredible to think that this was the first sacred place built by the Christians in Granada,' Humphrey says, his face registering due disbelief.

'What's really amazing is all the different uses this place has been put to over the years,' says Angus, earnestly. 'It's been a palace, obviously, but also a convent, a barracks, a poorhouse, a residence for landscape painters . . . '

'Did you know Dali painted Gala here?' Meredith asks them. 'I read it just now in the hotel pamphlet.'

Though I have no idea who or what Gala may have been, I know a good art 'in' when I see one and turn to Meredith with eager eyes. 'Is that true, Meredith? How *very* inspiring. I hope *I'll* have some time to do some drawing while I'm here.'

'I thought Angus said you were a photographer?' Moira says, stickler-quick. 'Is sketching a hobby?'

'Aren't you here to write a review?' Humphrey asks. 'I thought you were a travel writer or some such.'

They all turn to await my answer. Even Angus looks at a loss; after all, Maggie introduced me to him as her photographer collaborator when we first met ('Lies to Remember', I checked last

219

night). I decide to clear this up while I'm still the golden girl.

'Well, I'm neither, technically,' I smile, modestly, 'though my day job is in newspapers; I work as an agency sales manager. Maggie — who *is* a journalist — invited me to stand in for her regular photographer because she knew how long I've been wanting to come here, and taking pictures is a hobby of mine. Of course I offered to help her out with the words, too, when I heard about her chickenpox. It's terrible in adults, you know, it goes on for ever.'

'Nasty business,' Humphrey agrees. 'Badly pocked, is she?'

But Moira is still unclear of my precise credentials and the Scots frown remains intact. 'Why didn't she just send another journalist?'

'It was all very last minute, Moira, and being bank holiday weekend I suppose people are booked up. Of course, I can't claim any *literary* talent: I'll just give her notes. My photographs will probably be fine, but I'm sure they could use agency shots if they're not quite right.' I wiggle my feet under the table, chuffed with this modest new Anna. I don't add that my 'notes' consist so far of 'Walls red, trees green, parador expensive'.

'I see,' Moira says.

'But what I really want,' I add, reaching the crucial propaganda, 'is to be able to paint full time.'

'I had no idea you were so multitalented!' Angus exclaims.

'Oh, I'm absolutely not, not at all,' I protest weakly. 'Just interested in lots of things, I suppose.'

At last Meredith decides to join in. 'What kind of painting do you do, Anna?' She sips at her mineral water and I immediately do the same.

'Oh, I'm still finding my personal style,' I say. 'It's so difficult to define one's own technique, isn't it? It's probably easier if I tell you who my influences are.'

They wait politely.

Thank God I've rehearsed this. 'I love Goya, he would be my favourite.' The fact that I wouldn't know a Goya if a canvas of his fell on my head is neither here nor there; I know the *names* of some of his paintings, having remembered Charlie citing him as a Meredith favourite and looked him up on the National Gallery website. 'Oh, and I'm just rediscovering Murillo.' 'Rediscover' is an ideal word for bluffing, I've found, and Murillo is a useful painter to name-drop to Dulwich Gallery-goers as I found him in the visitor's guide.

'How interesting,' says Meredith. 'I must admit I share your soft spot for the Spaniards, especially while we're here. Art makes so much more sense when you see it in its native context, don't you think?'

'Oh, yes, absolutely, Meredith.'

'You must know the picture by Pradilla of the surrender of Boabdil?'

'I love that one,' I say, gushing, 'it's just so *evocative*.' I've never heard of Pradilla, though I think Boabdil may be something to do with the

221

Alhambra; the name rings a bell from my cramming on the plane.

'So you do figurative stuff, then, Anna?' Angus asks, returning to the original question.

I nod, hoping food will arrive soon and save me from anything too intellectual. This is supposed to be one of Caro's duties, rescuing me when things get technical. Clearly a quick refresher is in order before start of play tomorrow.

'I must admit I found that the most difficult at A level,' Angus says. 'I could never master flesh tones.'

'Oh, your portrait of Uncle John is *very* lifelike,' Moira protests.

'It's rubbish,' he says, but gives her an affectionate smile.

'It is not! You could have taken your art further, I'm sure . . . '

'Mum, I really don't think so.'

'Painting is so emotionally consuming,' Meredith says, crinkling her eyes at Angus. 'I can quite understand why students get frustrated.'

'Do you have studio space?' Moira asks me.

'Not yet. I'm really just a beginner.'

'Well, that certainly sounds like an awful lot to take on, I mean on top of a full-time career. Goodness, I used to think going to a weekly cookery class was all I could fit in around the children.'

'Ah, but children are harder work than any job or hobby,' I say, quick to seize the change of subject. 'Where are you from originally, Moira? Is Angus your only child?'

The starters have arrived and I slurp at gazpacho while listening to her talk about her youth in Edinburgh (as I'd suspected, she and Meredith met at university there), her relocation to London on marrying tax accountant Humphrey, and the daughter they have who is evidently rather less keen than Angus to accompany her parents on cultural jaunts. 'She's one of those with-it girls,' Moira says, which is hard to imagine if Angus is anything to go by. Helpful though he has turned out to be, he still strikes me as distinctly without-it. Clara, meanwhile, is plainly just a normal girl in her twenties, going to a lot of parties, reluctant to commit to any particular career path, probably no stranger to Class A drugs — but I don't say that in this company, of course.

'The boyfriend is an absolute wastrel,' Humphrey says, pausing for some wine. He has a habit of sloshing it into his mouth and holding it there before swallowing, as though preparing to gargle his nightly mouthwash. 'Never wears proper footwear, you know, only sports shoes.'

'We don't really know him,' Moira admits. 'Clara never seems to want to bring him home.'

'Oh, why not?' I put my spoon down. Now this *is* starting to get interesting.

'He lives in *Shepherd's Bush*,' Humphrey says, like it's the South Bronx. 'But anyone would think Dulwich is Land's End the way they talk.'

'Still, I'm sure if Clara likes him he must have some redeeming qualities,' Moira argues. 'He's her choice, not ours.'

'Exactly,' I say, impressed. Perhaps Moira's

not going to be the troublesome sidekick I feared, after all. It occurs to me that she must be fully conversant with Meredith's situation with Max, in which case that last remark was either tactless or pointed.

'Oh, Ed's just finding his way,' Angus says. 'And so is she. You should just leave them to it and not worry about it.'

There is a pause and I can't believe I'm the only one who's keen to hear Meredith's contribution to this debate. At last, lips dabbed with her napkin, she offers it. 'You know, you assume that when your children grow up you'll be equals, but it can never be so.'

'That's very true,' Moira says.

'Well, thank you very much, ladies,' Angus jokes. He really does handle this age group very well.

'What do you mean, Meredith?' I ask.

She looks at me gravely, like a soothsayer about to say one. 'Just that you can't stop worrying, even if you want to, ever. The age of the child — or indeed the parent — is irrelevant.'

'But there must come a time . . . ' I begin, but Humphrey is speaking at the same time, more loudly than me, and I have no choice but to give up and listen to him.

'Where do your parents live, Anne?'

'It's Anna . . . ' I smile.

'Humphrey!' Moira admonishes. 'That's the second time! You *know* her name.'

'It's OK,' I say. Call me whatever you want to, Humphrey dear, so long as you tell Meredith how wonderful you think I am. 'My father's in

224

London. My mother died when I was younger.'

They all look up at this. 'I'm sorry,' Humphrey says.

'Were you *very* young?' Meredith asks.

'Almost five.'

There are compassionate mumbles all round.

'How did she die?' Moira asks. 'If you don't mind me asking.'

'Not at all.' If there's one thing I've learned about old folk it's that they like to know exactly how people have met their maker. They have the same appetite for detail as new mothers exchanging tales of childbirth. 'It was a car accident,' I tell her.

'Oh my goodness, that must have been terrible!'

'I wasn't actually there, myself,' I say. 'But it was all over very quickly, which is something, I suppose.'

'Our neighbour's son had a terrible accident at the Elephant and Castle,' Moira says.

'Oh dear.'

'He survived, but barely, didn't he, Humphrey?'

'Hanging by a thread,' her husband confirms. 'Severe head injuries.'

I watch as Angus sends his parents the sort of 'that's enough' look one might more traditionally expect them to need to give him.

'Aha, what do we have here?' he cries, as main courses arrive. 'The food here looks great, doesn't it?' It's a clear attempt to change the subject, but when I smile gratefully in his direction he is not looking.

Puddings follow soon after and when Meredith grumbles about the courses being served too closely together it is once again Angus who steps in to placate and pacify. He is quite the diplomat, it seems, though at the sight of a vast platter of Andalucian cakes even Meredith isn't complaining for long. I choose the same one as she does so I can have another stab at conversation.

'This is the first time I've had this,' I say to her. 'What's it called?'

'*Piononos*. It is wonderful and creamy, isn't it?' she agrees.

'Nothing compares with Austrian pastries,' I go on, shamelessly, for I know for a fact that fewer foods stir the same passion in her as them. 'There's a fantastic place in Hampstead where my father used to take me when I was little. You choose a cake from a big tray.'

'I know it,' she says. 'On Heath Street? It's Hungarian-run, I believe.'

'That's right,' I beam. 'I was once allowed to eat three cakes in a row as a special treat. I was sick, though.'

'Meredith makes an exquisite Sachertorte,' Moira says. 'Now that *is* a treat.'

Everyone looks at Meredith with due admiration.

'I have to admit I perfected that particular recipe for my own benefit,' she sighs. 'I do have a sweet tooth. I suppose it's one of my last indulgences.'

What does she mean by 'last'? I wonder. Not that I hope to discover news of a terminal illness, you understand, but it is a curious phrase for a

226

fifty-nine-year-old to use. But no one else seems to have found it odd; if anything, the atmosphere gets jollier when Angus asks her, 'What are the others, Meredith? Are they equally as wicked?'

She puts down her fork and considers. 'Oh, novels, I suppose, would be another. I now have to force myself to read biographies and non-fiction; I only allow myself novels every other time.'

'I do the same!' Moira exclaims.

'Such degenerate urges,' Angus teases them.

I have no idea what they can mean; until my recent culture-cramming began, I'd read little but tabloids and women's magazines for years.

'Why on earth don't you just read what you want?' Humphrey asks. 'It seems to me you women *like* making things difficult for yourselves.'

Now there's a good point. I check Meredith's reaction for huffing and puffing, but she appears to be pleasantly tickled by the remark. I wonder what the story is behind Meredith and Humphrey. Has he ever held her attention long enough for a flirtation, a kiss, a full-blown 'assignation'? Even taking into account my own very singular interest in Meredith, it's hard to imagine Moira emerging in any comparison between the two of them as anything but the lesser. Meredith just has that enigmatic quality, that self-assurance that holds your attention for longer.

I remember asking Charlie once if he thought his mother had ever had an affair. Maggie had been talking about his Madonna complex and I was keen to test her theory.

'God no,' he said, looking at me as though I were mad.

'Why not? People do.'

'I don't know, I just think it's highly unlikely.' And he chuckled away at the absurdity of the idea.

But the woman sitting next to me is undeniably attractive, sexual almost, with her flame wrap and dark-orange lipstick; to an older man the hot colours must contrast tantalisingly with her cool manner. Not for the first time I'm struck by the difference between the Meredith I'd conjured in my mind and the one I've met. Yes, there was a sharp word about dessert arriving too early, but all that shrieking and spoon throwing Charlie reports must surely be the work of a completely different person.

'I suppose what I mean,' Meredith says, when the chortles die down, 'is that fiction seems such a frivolous indulgence as you get older and time is more precious. Not something a man would consider, perhaps?'

'Ah,' Humphrey laughs, 'the forthcoming birthday. I wouldn't let it affect your reading matter, my dear.'

I wait, eyes wide, nerves tingling. Is success as ridiculously easy as it's looking to be? Will they explain the party to me? Will Meredith get carried away by the pastry-bonding banter and say, 'You must come, too, Anna, you seem like such an old friend already.' But all she says is 'I'll try to remember that, Humphrey,' and pats her lips with her napkin.

'Has everyone read *Tales of the Alhambra*?' Angus asks, like a tutor on a field trip obliged to bring the conversation back to topics of cultural value.

I snap back to business. 'I've borrowed an old family copy for this weekend. I read it years ago, but I've started it again. Very charming.'

'It really is the most delightful companion,' Meredith agrees. '*Extra*ordinary how in those days one could just pitch up and take rooms in the palace.'

'If I remember rightly,' I say, as though delving into fifteen-year-old memories and not those of only a few hours ago, 'most of the stories involve princes and princesses being kept under house arrest by their parents.' Again, I'm fishing for a comment from Meredith on the subject of mothers and sons, but Angus gets in first.

'A stock fairytale theme,' he says. 'Where would we be without our incarcerated heroes?'

I decide to be brave — we're on coffees now and who knows if I'll get as clear a run again this weekend — and say, playfully, 'Well, from the perspective of a grown-up child — '

'We're *all* grown-up children,' Moira interrupts. A good point, but I ignore it.

'I'm just not so sure I approve of parents interfering so much, do you, Angus? Sometimes it stops us from making our own choices.' Out of the corner of my eye I think I see Angus react with a cautious frown and Moira with a warning one, but I can't be sure because it's Meredith I'm watching.

She sips at her coffee, lips barely parting. 'I'm

229

not sure the parents always see it that way, Anna. They tend to think they're protecting their children, guiding them away from terrible errors when they're too young to realise that's what they are. Like the prince in the tower.'

'But are they errors?' I ask. 'Don't the three princesses escape and become happy wives?'

'Do you mean Zaida, Zoraiada and Zorahaida?' Angus asks, unnecessarily.

'You do have a wonderful memory for names,' Moira tells him, proudly.

'You know, the tower they were supposed to have been kept in is just down there.' He gestures into the darkness. 'The Torre de las Infantas. It's right by this hotel. A shame we can't see it in the dark.'

'They never see their father again,' I persist, not taking my eyes off Meredith.

'Of course, I remember that story,' she says, musing. Then she turns and looks straight at me. 'But one of them stays with him, doesn't she?'

'That's right,' I whisper and, finally, look down. I decide to leave it at that. In any case, the bill is here and Angus has turned the conversation to arrangements for tomorrow.

Where should they have lunch? Moira wants to know. 'We don't want to eat lunch *and* dinner here, do we?'

One senses that mealtime planning will be no simple matter for this group.

'It's probably not worth going into the town,' Angus says, patiently. 'It's quite a climb.'

'We could walk down and get a taxi back up?'

'There are a few other places inside the city

walls,' he says. 'I'll ask the concierge for recommendations.'

Humphrey insists on signing for dinner.

'You're very kind,' I say, thanking him.

'You're the one who's been kind,' he replies. 'One can only imagine what anarchy might have broken out if you hadn't solved the code-red crisis over the rooms.'

I'm starting to like Humphrey.

'If there's anything else we can do . . . ' Angus says.

'Well, actually,' I say. 'There *is* something, but of course you must say no if you don't want to . . . '

'What?'

'Well, it's just that Caro and I will be a bit lost without Maggie, she's so knowledgeable. I was wondering if we could tag along with you for your tour tomorrow?'

He blinks. 'Yes, we talked about that before, didn't we? I'm sure no one would mind that.'

'Of course not,' Humphrey and Moira chorus.

Meredith is digging in her handbag for something and it's impossible to judge her reaction.

'You do realise I'm the guide?' Angus says. 'And this will be my inaugural Alhambra address? You'll all be guinea pigs, in effect.' What a shame he talks like an undertaker, I think. He's so very *dry*.

'Looking forward to being a guinea pig already,' I say, rising.

'But what about the tickets?' Moira asks, and she and Angus turn matching knotted brows to one another.

'They have two-hour slots for the visit to the palace to try to regulate the queues,' he explains to me. 'We may not be able to do that bit together.'

'They can be very stern about such things,' Moira adds.

'Our tickets are at the hotel,' I say. 'I'll check the time when we get back and let you know at breakfast.' There's no need, of course; Maggie booked our tickets expressly to coincide with the time stated on Angus's itinerary.

Before she leaves, Meredith stands for a minute at the terrace railings, looking over at the Summer Palace in silent commune, still as a statue.

'Night, Meredith,' I call, politely. 'Thank you for including me in such a lovely dinner.'

She turns to wish me good night, but it's impossible in the dark to tell if our eyes have met.

# 17

Years ago, in my first term at college, I shared a room in halls with a Swiss girl called Heike whose first language was German, second French and third English. She had a very charming turn of phrase, at times mixing metaphors — 'All this study! I can't keep my head ticking above water!' — at others comically misjudging her tone or that of other speakers. I remember we were sitting around in someone's room near the end of term bemoaning Christmas arrangements. Almost everyone's parents were divorced and remarried, and holiday arrangements, involving borrowed cars, once-a-day bank holiday trains and oversensitive step-parents, were getting more complicated by the hour.

'What about you, Anna? What are you doing over the holidays?' someone asked.

There was no Jojo then, just my father, and for as long as I could remember he and I had gone to my maternal grandparents in St Albans for Christmas Day.

'Oh, I only have one parent to worry about,' I said. 'So it's always easy.'

Then Heike turned round and sighed, 'Luckily both my parents are dead.'

She didn't mean it like that, of course, and we all giggled at the unintended callousness; all she meant was that she was glad to be spared the family politics that came with the full head count. Luckily they were dead.

I think of what she said now and then, that particular word selection. Is it possible that there is an element of plain old bad luck about my current situation? What if it had been *Mrs* Grainger and not Mr who developed that undetected heart condition and perished without warning? From what Charlie says, his father was a reasonable — if overruled — parent to Max and him, distressed both by the fractures Meredith had caused to the family and by his own powerlessness to repair them.

Even so, Charlie's sympathies seem to have settled with his mother long before their bereavement. 'I suppose I've always been closer to her,' he said, a week or two after we'd met. I was so busy sneaking peeks at the love god by my side, marvelling at the ripples his voice sent through my stomach and groin, I didn't hear the mother remark properly, or at least didn't have the early-warning system in place to alert me to the danger. Had I known that this 'closeness' between mother and son would mean that a year down the line I'd be compartmentalised, that he'd be moving back into his childhood home at the age of twenty-nine, that if any progress were to be made I'd have to pursue it myself, would I still have gone ahead with falling in love with him?

Yes, of course I would. You can't choose who you fall for. People who say you can aren't really falling.

★ ★ ★

Whether Caro is still sleeping or, as I fear, reduced to a vegetative state by the trauma of finding her head on a one-star pillow, I can't be sure, but in the morning she's still under the covers as I shower and dress. I decide to go down to breakfast alone. If I bring her up a coffee and croissant maybe she'll feel like she's getting room service after all.

I didn't notice the hotel courtyard properly last night, but it is delightfully cool and shaded, with herringbone cobbles underfoot and a fluttering canopy of foliage overhead. A higgledy-piggledy collection of plates, pots and fans fills every last nook and there's not a matching set of terrace furniture in sight. So what if it's never housed the bones of some Inquisition queen or inspired Dali over his cornflakes? It's good enough for me.

Too early for the mainstream tourists, Angus is one of just a few guests already there, breakfast plate empty and books spread out on the tiled tabletop. He's freshly shaved and has put on a smart shirt, presumably to lend formality to his day's tour-guiding. A little crack of sympathy breaks my total absorption in my own task. Yes, I may have been up since six-thirty rereading the guidebooks and hunting for references to other obscure Spanish painters who, like Signor Pradilla, might pop up to test me, but poor Angus looks as if he's about to be thrown to the lionesses.

'Do you mind if I join you?'

235

'Of course not.' He leaps up and pulls back a chair for me. 'How did you sleep?'

'Fine,' I lie. No need for Angus to know that sleep will be a privilege and not a right for me this weekend.

'And how's Caroline this morning?'

'Tired, I think. We couldn't work the air-con at first and she had trouble getting to sleep. She was still in bed when I came down.' I look around. 'You know what? I think I prefer this place to the parador. It's so pretty.' 'Pretty' is a Charlie word; before Charlie I ranked it alongside 'nice' as a word that damned with faint praise, preferring 'fabulous' or 'gorgeous', but in this circle effusive stands for insincere.

'If you think this is pretty, you've got a treat in store,' Angus says. 'The Nasrid palaces are considered an eighth wonder. That reminds me, did you find out your ticket time?'

I go through the motions of comparing the two tickets and checking the times. 'Here we are, 'Hora de entrada' . . . Oh, fantastic, you're eleven-thirty, we're only fifteen minutes apart.'

'Excellent. There should be no problem going in together, then. I was just preparing for the tour now. I hope you'll enjoy it.'

'I'm sure I will,' I gush. But for now I want to keep the conversation away from the culture. We'll have all day for that, but I might not get Angus, obviously still pliant with gratitude, alone again. 'I hope they're all settling in OK at the parador.'

'I'm sure they will be. Thanks again for your incredible gesture. My parents have been looking forward to staying there for months, I don't know what I would have done . . . '

'Don't mention it, really. It makes no difference to me. I thought Meredith seemed to take the mix-up very well.'

'Yes, she . . . ' He pauses, choosing his words. 'Meredith has a sense of perspective. She'd probably have hunkered down here OK. As you say, it's really very pretty.'

The waiter pours hot frothy milk into my coffee and I drink. It's delicious. Warm toasted rolls and butter follow. For a second I dream that I'm going to sit here all morning, away from them all, just drinking coffee and staring into space. But there is an interrogation to complete.

'Do you know her sons?' I ask between crunches.

'Yes, in fact I was at school with the younger one, Charlie.'

I look up in surprise. I wasn't expecting to be thrown quite so sturdy a rope so soon. What an unexpected gem Angus is turning out to be.

'A shame for Meredith he couldn't be here,' he goes on. 'He was originally going to come, but he's doing a placement in the States for his architecture degree.'

Originally going to come? 'You planned this trip a long time ago, then?'

'Oh yes, before Christmas.' Angus grimaces. 'That's why this business over the rooms is so embarrassing. I couldn't have been more organised if I tried. Everyone knows how hard it is to book the parador.'

While he agonises afresh, I smile in sympathy

and do the maths. Before *Christmas*? It was back in about April that the Endo placement was confirmed and Charlie knew for certain he'd be off to California. December to April: in four months he didn't once mention any commitment to a trip to Granada. The first I heard of it was in June, on ultimatum day, in fact, and in relation to Meredith keeping herself busy over the summer. I can't blame him for not telling me, of course; he probably thought he'd leave it till the last minute to minimise the extent of the resulting sulk. I was not amused when I once found Eurostar tickets to Paris in his jacket pocket — first class and he a student — only to be told he was going for the weekend with *her*.

'We've always done it,' Charlie said at the time. 'It's a family tradition. Every winter, the Louvre, the d'Orsay, the Rodin. My mother forced us; she used to promise us a hot chocolate after every museum. She even carried a bag of marshmallows like the ones we had in our cocoa at home.'

I had to admit that that was quite sweet. By then, Charlie had taken me to a number of London galleries and there'd been times when I would have welcomed a marshmallow break myself. But I didn't care for the idea of the two of them reliving that childhood ritual, doing the circuit of beautiful nudes and then sitting opposite one another in one of those cramped little cafés, *chocolats chauds* steaming away between them. It was too romantic and I was jealous.

'What d'you mean, you were 'forced'? Did she hurt you?'

'Of course not! I just mean museums can be a bit of a bore when you're eight. I remember she and Max had a big argument once when she found him trying to buy a train ticket for Parc Astérix. Of course, Max hasn't come along for years now.'

'Then why do *you* have to?' It felt churlish to protest at this annual weekend with a widowed mother, but I'd become touchier by then, trickier to satisfy. I didn't want Charlie *not* to go, nor to go with me instead of her; what I wanted was the suggestion that I might join them, that I might pull up a third stool at that café table.

'As soon as I'm back we'll book *our* tickets for Paris,' he said, guessing my thoughts. 'You'd love the hotel, it's right by the Sorbonne . . . '

'Charlie! I don't want to be taken to the same hotel as your *mother!*'

Who would have thought six months later I'd be going to any lengths to do exactly that? I turn my attention back to Angus.

'It must be weird for him to become a student again at our age, this Charlie guy.'

'Oh, he's the sort to get right back into it straight away,' Angus says. 'It's important to him to be one of the crowd, if you know what I mean.'

'Is it?' God, he's way off the mark there. We could be talking about different people. I've come to think of Charlie almost as a loner.

'Yeah,' Angus goes on, 'from what I've heard he hardly sees any of his old friends and just sees the new college ones all the time.'

Ah, now I see what's happened. He must mean *me*, I think, glowing with pride. They've noticed Charlie hasn't been around as much, but it's not his college friends he's busy with, it's me.

'Anyway,' Angus says, 'with Charlie, it almost doesn't matter which crowd it is, so long as he's a part of it.'

'That's very harsh,' I say, sharply, before I can stop myself. He looks ashamed, if a little taken aback, and I remember to smile. 'I mean, if someone's just changed career it stands to reason they would want to concentrate on that. I think it takes enormous courage to start at the bottom again when everyone else is getting promoted and moving up.'

'Oh yes, though I have to say the feeling is that it's very much Meredith's idea, the architecture thing.'

'What do you mean?'

'Just that she put a lot of pressure on him to apply in the first place. Leo was still alive then and totally against the idea, but Charlie always sided with her . . . ' This, at least, is not news to me — Charlie has even gone so far as to worry that his parents' feuding over his career change might have hastened his father's death.

What *is* surprising, however, is the note of bitterness, even antagonism, in Angus's voice when he talks about Charlie. It seems to me he may have accumulated some jealousy over the years. Having neither Charlie's looks nor charisma, he has doubtless suffered, year by year, from the comparisons: his portrait of Uncle John

240

is admired by Moira alone, while Charlie shows work at the world's first purpose-built art gallery; Charlie is about to become a top-flight architect with an international client list, while Angus's Art Explorer venture has so far amounted to little more than a family jolly with a cock-up over the booking. What's more, I don't remember Charlie ever mentioning *his* name, so they can't run into each other that much. It must be one of those situations in which children the same age are forced by their parents to be friends and can't wait to go their separate ways. He doesn't *know* Charlie at all.

'Anyway,' he says, 'I don't know why I'm boring you with this: you don't even know the bloke . . . '

I can't bear him to turn the conversation back to the silly old Moorish princes, so I say quickly, 'What about the brother, the one here in Spain?'

'You know about Max?' He's obviously recalling last night's conversation when, unlike his own mother, Meredith was conspicuously silent on the subject of her offspring.

'Yes, Meredith mentioned him before. At the picture gallery.' Or did she? I've spent so much time reading about art I haven't consulted my daybook once since we arrived.

'Well, they had a bit of a falling out,' Angus says.

'Why?'

He laughs now. 'Has Maggie been training you up? I feel like I'm being interviewed!'

'Sorry, I'm just being nosy. Other people's family politics always seem so much more

241

interesting. Go on . . . '

He's less willing to be drawn now, but obviously remembers he owes me and decides that a bit of harmless gossip is a small price to repay for harmony among the oldies. 'I don't know the details but I gather Meredith wasn't keen on Max's wife, Sara.'

'Why not?'

'We didn't meet her, but I think it was the usual stuff mothers disapprove of.'

'Oh, what's that?' If only I could take notes!

Angus grins. 'They hadn't known each other for very long before they got engaged. It was all a bit spontaneous — you know what that generation can be like, they like a respectable courtship. Also, Sara seemed a bit wild . . . '

'Like your sister?' I ask, with a glint.

'Exactly. God forbid she should abandon her needlepoint for a vodka and tonic.'

I laugh. He can be quite funny when he remembers he's young. 'It doesn't sound enough for a falling-out, though?'

'I know, I think she was just worried about the cultural differences. There was a meeting with Sara's parents; her mother is Spanish and they didn't hit it off. Parents are just not so flexible about that kind of thing, are they?'

Meredith clearly isn't flexible about any kind of thing, I think; otherwise I wouldn't be here now. Is he right, though, are all our parents' generation the same? Political correctness is about as effective in my father's industry as it is in my own. In any case, when he refers to Sammy Duncan as having an 'Eyetie' look about

242

him, I can't help considering it a compliment, Italians being hands down more attractive than Brits.

'All of this stuff with the brother must make it hard for Charlie?' I say. 'Or is he already married, too?'

'No, no. I don't think he's seeing anyone at the moment, but he's always been her favourite, so he shouldn't have the same difficulties.'

'If he's the favourite, it might make it *more* difficult?'

'No,' Angus says, with certainty. 'He knows how to handle Meredith. Anyway, it's always harder for the eldest, isn't it?'

The last thing I need is his side of the story on the matter of the ingrate sister, so I press on boldly. 'You make it sound as though Meredith is hard to handle. She seems the most charming woman.'

'Oh, she is, she is.'

'So wise and kind . . . '

Feel free to pass my opinions on to her, I think. But he has picked up his *Blue Guide* and is thumbing his way around the index, mind already elsewhere. The grilling is over.

'What time are we meeting the others?' I ask.

He looks at his watch. 'Half an hour. Should we check on Caroline?' It doesn't pass me by that this is the second time he's mentioned her in the space of two cups of coffee.

'I'll take her a coffee now,' I say. 'Where will she be able to find us in an hour or so?'

'I'll write it down for her,' he says.

We begin our tour at the Alcazabar, which Angus explains was built to a triangular plan as a military fortress and is a self-contained town in its own right. 'We are now standing on the western edge of Sabika Hill. These walls date from the eleventh century, back when the Zirids ruled Granada . . . '

Back when I last had any decent sleep, I think. The sun is pounding my head — I'm the only one in sight without a hat — and it feels like we're walking around a giant domed kiln. I dab bottled water on my wrists and neck but it doesn't make any difference.

'Look at the crowds!' I whisper to Humphrey, who, despite having continued to address me as Anne, is my instinctive choice for partner in illicit chit-chat. The two of us are standing slightly apart from Moira and Meredith, who are practically backing Angus into a nearby dungeon in their eagerness to hear him.

'Hordes of the blighters,' Humphrey agrees. He wears those clip-on shades over his glasses, snapping them up every time he speaks and down when he listens, an effect that takes a minute or two to get used to. 'The limit is supposed to be eight thousand or something.'

'They must all be following the same schedule as us,' I say. Most of the other tourists are in huge groups and together have the appearance of being the world's largest film crew, most operating cameras the size of small televisions.

'Can you hear all right?' Meredith asks us,

suddenly, in the tone of a teacher dealing with the delinquents in the back row. Her face is half-hidden under a pair of oversized sunglasses — she must be doing this Jackie O thing deliberately; in fact, today her 1960s style stops just short of the pillbox hat.

'I'm catching most of it,' I say, edging forward with my best prefect's smile, 'but I must confess I keep getting distracted by the view. Isn't it extraordinary, Meredith?'

'There are some terrific wood engravings of the Alhambra,' she notes, when Angus next pauses for breath. 'You must have seen them, Anna?'

'I don't think I have. What sort of era?'

'The ones I've come across are from the early nineteenth century. So *powerful* in the most clean, precise way. I always think engraving is a medium that could transform the most ordinary scene into an idyll.'

'I always think' is a catchphrase of Meredith's.

'Perhaps there'll be some in the museum,' I suggest. 'Will we be going there today, Angus?'

He looks up. 'I hadn't planned to, but both museums are open tomorrow if anyone wants to have a look at their leisure. Shall we move on?'

We edge through the crowds on a circuit of the site, instinctively drawn to shade and careful to wait for anyone who gets entangled in another group. Every so often Angus gathers us all around him and delivers a little speech about the nearby tower/well/steps. 'There are three dungeons in the Alcazabar . . . We can't get down there, but just imagine a kind of upside-down

245

funnel'; 'This tower has been known by several different names over the years . . . ' and so on. He has a surprisingly engaging manner. I watch the faces in profile: Humphrey, squinting through the snap-ons as though using his eyes for ears; Moira, basking in the near rapture of her maternal pride; Meredith, still and attentive, nodding as Angus urges us to 'Imagine you're a soldier being drilled in this heat' and other hardships that don't seem to me so very far from our own experience. It's impossible to tell what's going on behind her sunglasses, but there are moments when her face looks to me to take on a kind of primeval intensity, as though she is *feeling* Angus's every exhortation. Is this what has brought her to this stalemate with her sons: an overactive imagination? Anticipating worst-case scenarios with the same force as reality: they'll sully the bloodline; they'll embarrass her socially; they'll send her grandsons to state schools; they'll *leave* her?

I find that I'm so busy with thoughts of this kind that I miss most of what Angus is saying, so I cover myself by scribbling notes for Maggie and snapping photos. Caro was right: the photography *is* a bore. Even though I listened properly to the demonstration by Dad's assistant, Lucy ('You really can't go wrong' — famous last words if ever I heard them), it's still far more fiddly than I imagined, especially as Angus keeps pointing out fascinating bumps and dents for me to capture. I can only hope that the thing is recording *something*.

Eventually we climb up to the terrace of the

Torre de la Vela, the tallest of the towers and the point at which the world and his wife seem most determined to gather, thanks, presumably, to the vertiginous views and a photogenic old bell. As I get 'proper' shots of the bell, the others take their own snaps and Meredith starts to tell us of a local custom: on 2 January, the day of the Christian conquest of the city, anybody is free to ring the bell, and it is said that if any single girl of marriageable age does so she will be engaged within the year.

'Before you say anything, I'm not sure I'm considered of marriageable age any longer,' she jokes. But the thought is in her head, obviously, otherwise she wouldn't have said it.

That would help my cause, I think to myself, the entry of a sanguine new partner to show her that life's too short to waste what remains of it overprotecting your children, to keep them prisoners in the tower . . .

'What about Anne?' Humphrey says, interrupting my thoughts.

'Sorry?' I say.

'*Anna*, Humphrey,' Moira corrects. 'But yes, perhaps *she* should come back in January, eh . . . ?'

Spying an excellent opportunity for a formal mission statement, I decide to abandon photography for now. 'Oh, I'm not sure marriage is my goal,' I say, sweetly, hand shading my eyes as I look from one face to the next. 'But I'd certainly be happy to meet someone who loves being here as much as I do, so maybe I *will* be coming back!'

I catch a glance between Humphrey and Moira that makes me fear that they might be planning a little matchmaking of their own. I haven't thought to ask if Angus is single, having assumed as much by the absence of any reference to a girlfriend, but either way I'm pleased that he doesn't seem to have been listening to that cheesy Miss World declaration. What's he looking at, anyway? He's found a space at the crowded edge, near the corner that overlooks the quarter of town built on the steep hillside across the valley. The cypresses stick up like paintbrushes slotted in jam jars between the low, flat-roofed houses, and the palms flutter in the breeze like paper sunshades. It is breathtaking; no wonder the other visitors are responding like frantic paparazzi, and when I call Angus's name he doesn't hear me through the clamour.

'Angus, what's that area over there? It's so lovely, with all the white-washed houses?'

I'm standing right by his side, but he hasn't even registered my arrival, so mesmerised is he by the view. Then I see what he's actually staring at: not the quaint old neighbourhood opposite or the snaking river below, but the viewing platform of a smaller tower fifteen metres below, where the tourists and their stunted shadows are moving from stairwell to battlement and back again. One tourist in particular: a woman. She's leaning over the edge, gazing down at the steep drop below, and her hair tumbles forward like a black-haired Rapunzel. Hurrah! He's human, after all. He's got his eye on some hot-blooded Andalucian beauty when he's supposed to be

248

telling us about rusty old bells. Good for him. Then the dress, a pink-and-yellow daisy print, registers as familiar and I realise that the woman he's looking at is Caro.

'It's the Albaicín,' he stutters, finally, only half-turning. 'It used to be the Arab silk market and is considered the most beautiful quarter of the city, probably the closest to what we think of as al-Andalus.' His eyes don't move from Caro, who is upright again and shading her face from the dazzle of the sun. Perhaps he *did* notice her yesterday and the seed was sown then; well, judging by the dazed look in his eyes, it's grown into a sunflower overnight. 'There's skiing in the Sierra Nevada,' he adds, robotically, 'the highest peak is the Mulhacen . . . '

'Hey, there's Caro,' I say, casually. 'Shall we go and collect her? I'm so relieved she's out and about, I was getting a bit worried.'

We make the descent together, and before we can work out which is the gateway to Caro's tower she bounces up, hair bobbing like inky snakes around her shoulders. 'Hi, chum, I was just looking for you!' She turns her head to the thirty-metre-high watchtower, just as the others emerge from its doorway into the sunlight, and announces at the top of her voice, 'Now *that's* what I call a phallic symbol!'

Meredith and Moira have both removed their sunglasses but the brims of their sunhats remain low over their brows and it's impossible to catch either's eye. I can see from their mouths, however, that they are frowning.

Don't say it, Caro, I pray, just leave it at that, but she has opened her mouth, committed herself. 'How funny, look! It even has a bell on it!'

# 18

We sit in the square and buy drinks from a funny little octagonal hut that has two trees growing through it.

'Quite right, too, keeping up the tradition of offering liquid refreshment to those who pass through,' says Humphrey.

Angus has already told me how free wine was doled out at the nearby Puerta del Vino for all who required it; a singularly dangerous idea, if you ask me. I, for one, am intent on sobriety this weekend (or Meredith's version of it, at least). In any case, this morning most visitors are content with coffees, some eating ice creams or tearing at stiff sandwiches, the slices of Serrano hanging out of the sides of the bread like skinny sun-dried tongues.

I catch Caro alone at the bar, where she's smoking a cigarette and eyeing the bartenders, one of whom has the kind of well-muscled upper body she is known to favour.

'Sleep well?'

'Yeah, once we got some cool air in there it was OK, wasn't it? Thanks for the coffee; I must have just missed you 'cos it was still warm.'

'I'm really sorry about the room,' I say, touching her arm. 'I should have consulted you before I offered it to Meredith. I got a bit carried away.'

'Forget it, it's no big deal,' she says.

'What do you think of the place?'

'It's cool. I love this cute little bar and Alcatraz was fun, wasn't it?'

I don't correct her, but instead watch her cigarette with longing. Glancing over my shoulder, I see the others settling themselves in a line under the shade of a tree. 'The problem with being in Spain is it really makes me want to smoke,' I grumble.

'Smoke, then,' Caro says, offering me the pack.

'I can't, not in front of Meredith.'

'God, does she disapprove of that, as well? Well, I hope you don't expect me to abstain.'

'Of course not.' I want to ask her to abstain not only from smoking but also from drinking, swearing, flirting, making any more remarks about phalluses (or should that be 'phalli'? Angus would know), but I no longer dare. '*Gracias.*' I pay for the coffees. 'Shall we join the others?'

As Caro beams in all directions and helps distribute drinks, Angus and Humphrey eye her as though a film star has choppered in for a red-carpet walkabout and favoured them with the first round of autographs. As for Meredith and Moira, it's still hard to gauge, but their mouths are softer now.

Angus leaps up to make room. 'Come and sit in the shade, girls.'

'First thoughts?' Moira asks.

Caro settles down on the wall beside her. 'Truthfully? I'm amazed by the power of the Magnum.'

'The *Magnum*?'

'Yes, everyone's eating them. I thought it was just a British thing.'

'Caro is a promotions manager on the paper,' I say, quickly. 'Ice creams are on her mind.'

Moira chuckles, gamely. 'What glamorous jobs you girls have.'

'I wouldn't say that,' Caro answers. 'But it's handy for freebies.' She looks surprised by my fake hoot of laughter at this before finally noticing that there's someone who can't keep his eyes off her. 'What about you, Angus?' she asks. 'What do you do when you're not playing at tour-repping?'

I wait for his — and Moira's — protests about the Art Explorers being no mere game, but instead he says, quite simply, 'I'm in insurance at the moment, in sales.'

An insurance salesman! I can't believe it. He sells insurance and Meredith adores him. This is crazy, wonderful news. What I do is practically ethical compared to that.

'But I aim to leave in the New Year to get this travel business off the ground. This weekend is something of a dry run; if it works out, I'd like to bring several groups next summer.'

'Well, your tour so far has been very thorough,' I say, with an ingratiating smile for Meredith. 'I'm really enjoying it, Angus. It's not easy bringing ancient history so vibrantly to life.'

'Well, it's not strictly ancient,' he protests, but is flattered, I can tell, and Moira nods away, pleased as Punch.

'Hey,' Caro says, 'I've got a few financial

questions my brother won't answer. I might pick your brains later if that's OK.' The innuendo in her tone is very, very faint, but it's there all right.

'I'd love to help,' Angus says.

As Moira's smile shrinks, his expands. The words 'hook', 'line' and 'sinker' spring to mind.

★   ★   ★

A part of Angus is lost to the rest of us from that moment on. Granted, he continues his narrative as professionally as ever, leading us to the Royal Palace as soon as our time slot comes around and evoking centuries of history in a bit of scene-setting so passionate that several other visitors try to film it, much to Meredith's irritation. 'Don't let us block your way,' she says, coldly, and they get the message and move off.

But as one glorious room leads to another, it is clear that his own bedazzlement owes rather less to the 'ornate decorative feast', as he describes it, and more to the presence of an attractive new heckler.

'This is what people always think of when they think of the Alhambra,' he says, and we all nod, even though I, for one, have until recently always thought of a restaurant my father used to take me to just off the Edgware Road. 'It was, without doubt, the Nasrids' finest hour.'

'The *Nasrids*?' Caro giggles, elbowing him in the side as though he has told a joke. 'Sounds like something out of *Dr Who*.'

'There's the Zirids, as well,' he says, eagerly.

'What hilarious names! They can't be for real!'

254

I'm as lost as she is by the lists of rulers and dynasties Angus details, but I have to admit to being blown away by the place itself. Somehow the books didn't prepare me for the spectacle of ornate plasterwork, for the way the star-shaped tiles make familiar colours blaze like nothing I've seen before, or for the soaring ceilings with their dizzying patternwork.

'This is incredible!' I say, amazed.

'Wow,' Caro agrees. 'It's all so perfectly intact it looks like it's been computer-generated, don't you think?'

Meredith raises an eyebrow at this, I note.

Angus tries to steer us onward. 'As you can see as we make our way through the site, water is as important an element of the architecture as the tiles and the walls and the stone beneath our feet . . . '

I wonder if the others have noticed his new tendency to address most of his commentary to Caro.

'All this trickling water is making me want to pee,' Caro says and, catching his eye, treats him to a comedy wink.

If she's interested, he's got no chance, I think to myself, and sure enough, taking advantage of the next bottleneck between rooms, Caro grabs my arm and pulls me into the sunlit courtyard ahead.

'Tell you what, I quite fancy old Angus-Pangus.'

'You do?'

'Yeah, he's quite foxy in a strait-laced sort of way. You should have warned me!'

'But . . .'

'Watch out, chum! You've stepped in a fountain!'

She's right, my foot is suddenly icy cold to the ankle. 'Bloody pesky fountains hidden everywhere. How was I supposed to see that?'

Caro laughs, removes her heels and steps in too. 'This is *bliss*.'

Oh my God, another hair-tossing *Dolce Vita* moment. And of course Angus emerges into the light just in time to witness this latest romantic vision; he rushes to offer his hand and help her out, leaving me to shake my leg like a grumpy dog after a good hosing. Caro continues around the palace barefoot, which is probably a crime against Allah, but no one seems to mind, least of all our tour guide.

After that first physical contact, the attraction between the two of them is apparently not to be extinguished by all the fountains of al-Andalus. It's like watching a courtship montage in a slushy movie: first Caro, twirling her shoes in her hand as she moves in close to look at his map; now Angus, dashing forward to steady her as she leans giddily off balance, mid-gasp at the beauty of the wooden ceilings above; then Caro, fingering a column as Angus explains the genius involved in its construction.

'Sublime really is the only word,' I hear him say at one point.

'Ridiculous' is the one I'd go for. Intrigued though I am by this development, I decide to take advantage of the newly vacant spot by Meredith's side and encourage her to share her knowledge with the rest of us.

'Meredith, am I right in thinking they didn't use an awful lot of furniture, the Nasrid kings?'

'They lived relatively modestly,' she says. 'Just a few carpets and basic furniture, some wooden screens. But that's not to say there weren't some tremendously hedonistic times.'

'Ooh, was there carousing?' I ask, playfully.

'There certainly was, and not just the men.'

'I thought all the women were locked away in towers?'

'Only the daughters.' At once I think of that subtle sense of subtext to last night's conversation and, meeting her eye, I wonder if she has too.

'There are some of us who might welcome a return to the harem system,' says Humphrey, bawdily. I don't dare glance at Moira but see that Meredith has broadened her smile somewhat and, apparently on a roll, he adds, 'You'd be hard pushed to get a plasterer this good in London, eh?'

'Don't be ridiculous, Humphrey,' Moira tuts.

By now we've reached the apparently world-famous Patio de los Leones, the kings' residence and highlight of the Alhambra, a decorative frenzy that has the crowds gasping afresh.

'I always think they went a little too far with the fountain,' says Meredith as we turn to face a dozen lions spitting water. 'And it would probably have been gilded originally. Can you imagine?'

'Very ostentatious,' I agree. 'The colonnades are lovely though, aren't they, Meredith?'

'Yes, they're almost rhythmic.'

'That's exactly the right word,' I agree.

'This place really does appeal to all the senses, doesn't it?' she asks, slipping on her sunglasses as we stand in the full blaze of the sun.

'Oh, yes, Meredith.'

We seem to have lost Angus and Caro, but she makes no mention of their absence, absorbed, as earlier, in the past. 'You know this room was named after a family who Boabdil had massacred here during the civil wars before the fall,' she says, as I dutifully find the Sala de los Abencerrajes in my guidebook.

'Goodness,' I say, face serious.

'It's hard, isn't it, to imagine what it feels like to be under threat?' she goes on.

'We have no worries at all, do we?' Moira says, shaking her head with commendable count-your-blessings humility. 'Not in the grand scheme of things.'

This strikes me as another choice opportunity for my own mission. 'Oh, I think we all feel under threat at times, in our own way. Work, relationships, family, we feel threatened by the loss of a job, a house, someone we're close to . . .'

Do I imagine it or does Moira's eye stray over my shoulder at this in search of her son. Poor thing, she wasn't expecting this: first her daughter with a wastrel, now her son with a siren.

'Oh, you never really lose people,' Meredith says to me in that sagelike way of hers and Moira's shoulders relax again. 'You just separate

258

and come back together.'

I don't know who Meredith might be thinking of — her late husband reincarnated? Her eldest son reunited? Or her youngest returned? — but I'm staggered by the dispassion of her delivery considering her family history of conflict and acrimony. True, she doesn't know that I'm familiar with it, but surely it must be common knowledge to her two great friends who stand listening nearby? What must they think of these messages of forbearance and peace? For my part, her profundities are getting frustrating. Time is running out; am I ever going to get beneath that surface serenity?

'I agree,' I say, improvising. 'Losing is just learning to let go, isn't it?' Of course, when I try to say something profound it just sounds like a line from one of those old Peanuts cartoons. I add, 'It can be a good thing, can't it, a healthy thing?'

Moira still thinks I'm talking about the Moors. 'Yes, but the Moors faced the loss of their whole identity. No one should have to 'let go' of that. There's nothing healthy about *slaughter*.'

'Of course not.'

'I do hope this isn't leading to a discussion of the Middle East, ladies,' Humphrey jokes and, as I ponder Meredith's comment about separation, the conversation is soon forgotten by the others in the excitement of our reunion with Angus and Caro in the vast Sala de los Reyes. Here, with help from Meredith, Angus explains to the group the technique used for the vivid ceiling paintings: sheepskin and wood for the surface, with

259

fishbone glue, plaster and pigments mixed with egg yolk.

'And you probably thought oils were tricky enough,' he says to me.

'I certainly wouldn't like to try this,' I say in all honesty. I wouldn't be able to reproduce a square millimetre of it if my life depended on it. Well out of my depth, I decide to slink off to a nearby corner before I make a fool of myself.

Caro tails me, cackling to herself. 'You know what? I've only just realised Angus hasn't been saying 'dildo' at all; he's been saying 'dado' this whole time. What's that, like a dado rail in Britain?'

'Yes, it's the lower part of the walls,' I say. 'You know, where all the colourful Andalusian tiles are.'

'You really are quite the acolyte,' she says, admiringly.

'Sycophant,' I say, drily.

'No, she likes you, you know, I can tell. You're making amazing progress, babe.'

At this I suddenly register my own exhaustion. Caro's right: in the last half-hour I *have* broken through and established a chumminess of sorts with Meredith, but it's taken every last drop of adrenaline to get me here. It's not even lunchtime on the first day and I'm already drooping.

'Shall we skip the last bit and sneak a fag outside?' Caro suggests. 'Come on, it's just going to be more of the same.'

'How can you say that?' I exclaim, in case

Meredith is within earshot, before strolling after Caro to the exit.

In the gardens outside, the heat is more ferocious than ever, but the sight of immaculate garden terraces and lots of flat, cool water is soothing. In fact, the topiary and the ivy pergola that leads to a waterlily pond gives the gardens a formal, English atmosphere, which is comforting.

We find a seat and each smoke three cigarettes in a row. I listen, drowsy and as relaxed as I'm going to be here, as Caro chatters on.

'Here you are!'

Surprise, surprise, it's Angus who is first out to join us.

'Hi,' Caro beams. 'Come and grab a seat. I was just telling Anna how much better I feel about the hotel situation now I know the parador hasn't got a swimming pool.'

She was saying no such thing, having been sharing with me her intuition about his sexual experience (limited in terms of 'covers', extensive in terms of potential), but the information partly explains her sunnier mood and I loyally parrot, 'Yes, no swimming pool, shame.'

'Who needs a pool when you're on the site of Moorish princes?' Angus asks, eagerly.

This is exactly the sort of thing Charlie would say and I feel a sudden, physical yearning for him. If only it were he and not Angus leading this little adventure.

'You'd think they'd fancy a dip occasionally in this heat,' Caro smoulders. 'All those heavy cloaks and turbans and things, and they probably

261

hadn't invented antiperspirants.'

He grins at her, besotted. Does Charlie look at me this way? He must do, I suppose.

'That's why they built so many fountains. They give the illusion of coolness,' he says.

'I need more than illusion, mate. How about a beer? Are we going for lunch now? I'm starving!'

He consults his itinerary.

'Angus! You don't need to look at your notes to know if you're hungry,' she says, but is teasing him, not mocking, a distinction worth noting with Caro. 'God, don't you sometimes feel like you're just going through the motions until you can have a drink . . . ?'

This is getting weird. Not only is Angus saying the sorts of things Charlie might, but Caro is also saying all the things I feel but could never admit to in my culture-vulture guise.

' . . . I mean, it's obviously beautiful and all that, but . . . '

'Ah,' Angus says, fixing her with imploring eyes, 'but that's because of the way we troop around with the other tour groups, our route dictated. But imagine if you were allowed to set up a table in there, back in the private rooms, burn some incense, have someone bring in a few Moorish nibbles, maybe a bit of hashish. Have your beer in there. No tours, no officials . . . '

Yep, he is Charlie all over. The only two straight men in England to use the word 'nibbles'. And he has the same way of filtering public experiences into a very private fantasy, of

262

finding something familiar or intimate in the most monumental building. He probably says 'diddly-squat', too.

' . . . that wouldn't be going through the motions, would it?' he asks Caro, and I find myself waiting for her answer as though for a sign of the outcome of my own situation.

'Yes,' she says, sweetly, and my heart jumps just a little. Then she adds, 'But let's face it, it ain't never gonna happen, is it?'

She uses a double negative; does that count?

# 19

There are so many things about Meredith that
remind me of Charlie that I'm starting to
wonder if he might not be a bit of a snob
himself. The way she winces when Caro
price-checks admired items or uses 'grand' or 'K'
instead of 'thousand', I've seen him do that; the
way she unfailingly remembers her pleases and
thank yous for the smallest thing and frowns
when others don't; the way she blinks with
distaste when a word is mispronounced. What
seems to be her own, however, is her scorn for
tourist traps, with neither trapper nor entrapped
spared her disapproval. An example: on the main
drag not far from our hotel is an attraction that
allows people to dress in Moorish costume and
have photos of themselves taken in front of a
mock-Alhambra backdrop. There is quite a
queue outside the shop and a lot of laughter
coming from within. It looks fun. Not to
Meredith, it doesn't.

'Can you think of *anything* more appalling?'
she says to Moira and me as we pass.

'Cynical money-grabbing,' Moira agrees, as if
we haven't all been charged entrance fees and
premium hotel rates to be here ourselves.

For a moment I dislike them for their sneering
and myself for my simpering agreement. Who
does Meredith think she is? That's what I should
be asking, not falling into line like some frilly

little lady-in-waiting. At the same time I can't help admiring her air of command. It really is a thing of beauty. She sweeps through the site like a dignitary visiting incognito: she doesn't want a fuss to be made of her but she doesn't want to get down and dirty with the proletariat either. Angus may have talked of her hunkering down in the lesser finery of our hotel but it seems to me that Meredith expects the highest quality available wherever she goes. She likes things to be authentic and, where possible, formal. A mid-morning coffee under a tree in the square is one thing; a sandwich on the run is quite another. No, when it comes to mealtimes she wants white linen and wine lists (Humphrey's choice, of course) and coffees and siestas, which is how we come to be sitting in the only Alhambra restaurant besides the parador that could reasonably be considered stuffy.

'What a lovely quiet place for lunch. Good choice, Meredith,' I say, overcompensating for my new-found irritation with a false tinkle of laughter.

She sighs. 'I'm not so sure after all, but I suppose now we've ordered . . . ' The problem is that the terrace is flanked on one side by the main route from site entrance to palace and coachloads of noisy lower orders *will* keep trooping past. Some scoff sandwiches and call to one another with their mouths full; others squawk into mobile phones, a particular Meredith bugbear, it seems (not to mention an explanation of why Charlie's is always mysteriously turned off when he's in Dulwich). 'I often wonder when I see these groups trailing around how many of them have any idea why they're actually here.'

'I know exactly what you mean.' Resentment still prickling away, I find myself willing Caro to butt in and cheek her, even though I've spent the last few hours dreading that very possibility. Caro does the next best thing: she swears like a trooper while praising mobile phones.

'These things are so fucking cool, aren't they?' she says, waving hers about. 'I mean, what did we do before mobiles? We were, like, *Neanderthals*.' She turns to click her phone's camera at the offending tourists. 'Just getting them back for all those photos they keep taking of us at the hotel window.'

'Don't you sometimes wonder how many photo albums you're in around the world?' Angus asks her, for once oblivious to Meredith's disapproval.

'Yeah, like that Woody Allen character,' Caro says.

'You mean Zelig?'

'Was he a Moorish king, too?' she laughs. 'Tell you what, though, it makes me wish I'd dropped a few pounds before we came.'

'Oh, you have absolutely nothing to worry about on that score,' Angus says, allowing himself a wolfish glance at her breasts. The plunge-necked daisy dress seems to have lost its top button.

'You think?' With which she actually feeds him a little dumpling of bread.

And all of this in front of Moira and

Humphrey! I feel a surge of solidarity at the impropriety of it all.

Not to be distracted, Meredith turns to glare at a brace of Italian teens rampaging by. 'I'm going to ask them to find us another table,' she grumbles, eyes searching for the waiter.

'Good idea,' says Moira, as two girls squeal over a text message. 'I *do* wish they'd pipe down. Where do they think they are? Disneyland?'

'Well, that particular group are probably here under duress,' I say, remembering Max and the ticket to Parc Astérix. 'They're *children*. They'd probably prefer to be at a water park.' At the sight of Moira's best raised-eyebrow/pursed-lips combo and safe in the knowledge that she is not Meredith, I can't help ranting on: 'You know, Moira, I always think it might be an advantage to *not* know every last detail of what's ahead. All you need is a pair of eyes to get something out of this place, not a bloody great history lesson!'

There's silence around the table and I immediately regret my contrariness. Moira looks astonished, darting a glance at Angus as though I've slighted him personally. But he continues to inspect the menu with a smile on his lips, doubtless hunting out aphrodisiacs to share with Caro, who, equally engrossed, doesn't seem to have noticed my mini-rebellion either. Meredith, meanwhile, just nods away thoughtfully before delivering her verdict: 'Yes, that reminds me of something Emerson said, 'The eye is the best of artists.''

'I beg your pardon?'

'Don't you see, Anna? We're privileged

because we have that eye.' Though none the wiser as to her point, I bask for a moment in the glory of that precious plural, but snap out of it as her voice rises: 'Of course, *you* can see shape and colour and form everywhere you look. *You* can calculate the sheer back-breaking, painstaking craftsmanship of it all. You're an artist yourself. It's not about the dates for you.'

'Oh, I don't know about that,' I say, uncertainly, for I'm no more artistic than the young mute distributing glasses of iced water, less so, probably.

'But how many of these . . . ' — she breaks off to look once more at the offending mob on the other side of the railings — ' . . . how many of these *creatures* are painters? You can take my word for it that they *need* the history lesson to appreciate the achievement of this place. The fact that it's still here at all.'

'That's true,' I say, frightened. For the first time she's raised her tone to something close to the forcefulness Charlie has described. Thank God she was speaking in *praise* of me and now meets my eye with a laser beam of kindred passion. Could it be that we are really *bonding* over this? Plainly a little independent opinion goes a long way.

'I didn't mean to be rude,' I say to Moira, remembering to be sorry. 'I just remember being that age — '

'Oh, who cares about a bunch of kids?' Caro interrupts. 'Can we please have some vino before I faint?'

'You just don't like being here with the

crowds,' Angus says to Meredith with exactly the required blend of amusement and respect.

She leans back in her seat and sighs her acknowledgement. 'Yes, it was out of season and midweek the last time I was here. But I suppose it's appropriate we must share with the multitudes, given the history.'

With this, her eye lingers on Caro and I just know that from now on, whenever Meredith is out of range, Caro will refer to herself — and probably me too — as The Multitudes.

Humphrey returns from the loo just as a course of sweaty cheese and pâté arrives. Talk of changing tables is forgotten in deference to his thoughts on the restaurant's plumbing idiosyn-crasies and, as we all dig into the food, conversation turns to safer ground still: the green, green grass of Dulwich Picture Gallery.

'You haven't scaled down your involvement, then?' Meredith asks Humphrey. She spreads her pâté very daintily but takes proper hearty bites, never replying to a direct question until her chewing is quite taken care of.

'No, no.'

'He's *such* a good egg,' nods Moira. 'Aren't you, Humphrey?'

I wonder if I will ever think of Charlie as an egg.

'Humphrey is terribly involved with the gallery,' she explains to Caro and me. 'He gives at least twenty hours a week.'

'Only because he's got nothing better to do,' Angus says, playfully. 'Have you, Dad?'

'I suppose it justifies all the golf and tennis,

heh, heh, heh,' Humphrey replies.

Anxious to prevent the conversation straying towards tennis, I chip in, 'Retirement looks rather fun if you guys are anything to go by.'

'I can't wait,' Caro exclaims. 'But I'm going to spend my time playing poker with the *bad eggs*.'

'They'll need two or three men to take his place when he's gone,' Moira insists, indignant again, as though Caro has dared question Humphrey's commitment to the cause.

'Glad to know you're planning ahead, my dear,' Humphrey chuckles.

'Oh, but I am.'

'Always wise.'

Maybe it's because I haven't had the opportunity to watch my own parents together at this age — and the Dad — Jojo alternative is hardly comparable — but I can't always judge the tone of the banter between Humphrey and Moira. It's hard to know if it's good-humoured or plain mean. Either way, Angus is perfectly relaxed in their company, even with new distractions to hand, and seems to know exactly how to steer the conversation to their satisfaction. Exactly which mutual Dulwich acquaintances are '1811'? he wants to know. *That* gets them excited.

''Eighteen eleven'? Is that, like, LAPD code for something?' Caro asks and we both giggle. Geriatric on the rampage, perhaps? But no, they explain, 1811 is just a chic-er class of Friend.

'I don't understand,' I say.

'It just means that there are different levels of

270

Friends depending on how much you pay,' says Angus.

'Ah.' I don't like the sound of this. When I joined the gallery it didn't occur to me I might need to be a better class of Friend to be Meredith's friend. I immediately resolve to upgrade to 1811 as soon as we get back, unless of course it requires being nominated and seconded and all of that nonsense.

'You're eighteen eleven, aren't you, Meredith?' Angus queries on cue.

She pauses to take a sip of wine. 'Actually, I just took the plunge and became a donor.'

A hush descends over the Poole end of the table and Caro and I look at each other in confusion. 'I assume you're not talking about kidneys?' Caro says, finally.

'What's the difference?' I ask, horrified that I may actually turn out to be *two* divisions down from Meredith.

'Donors get extra little treats,' Angus explains.

'Ooh, I like treats,' says Caro. 'Do you mean like goodie bags every time you visit the gallery?'

'Not quite,' says Meredith, amused. She sips at her wine and I sip at mine.

'What then?'

'Let me think. Well, you get to visit public collections outside normal hours, and private collections not normally open to the general public. We're about to visit the conservation studio at the National Gallery, actually — that will be rather nice, I haven't been there for years.'

'Will there be champagne?'

271

'I imagine so.'

'Are *you* a donor?' Caro asks Moira.

'No.' Moira smiles weakly and I get a sudden insight into the dynamic between these two women. Close friends and neighbours they may be, but Meredith undoubtedly has the upper hand in this relationship as, it would appear, in all. Moira must lack a titled relative, a private art collection, the clout to become a donor. I try to think of equivalent imbalances between Caro and me, but there is nothing. Only my wish to make Charlie my permanent partner and her preference for impermanence separates us, but it makes neither of us the superior. Poor Moira.

'Not yet,' Caro says, kind-heartedly, and applies herself to the last piece of cheese, now almost liquid in the heat. 'So tell me about your new travel business?' she asks Angus. 'Will you take the punters to other Spanish cities, too?'

At this I look up. Caro is not usually interested in the details of what her men do during daylight hours; could it be that she is considering 'Angus-Pangus' for something more than a holiday fling?

'I find it very inspiring to hear of your career change,' I say to him, when he finishes his discussion of at least half a dozen other cities I'm not going to visit. 'And your son's, too, Meredith. I think he's very brave to go back to college.'

'Why, are you thinking of returning to education, too, Anna?' Moira asks. 'For your art?'

'Oh, I keep telling her she must,' Caro says,

272

with credible sincerity. 'She's *so* talented.' Talented at painting her toenails, I imagine her thinking.

'Well, I've got prospectuses,' I say, praying they don't ask after A levels and foundation courses or, indeed, about the 'pluralistic' nature of the courses that I've read about in said prospectuses. 'I wouldn't want to leave London, but I like the look of the Slade . . . '

'Charlie is at University College,' Meredith says on cue.

'Oh, is he at the Bartlett?' I make it sound like a household name, though I'd never heard of the place before Charlie told me he'd enrolled there.

'Yes, that's right.'

'What a coincidence,' I say. This is precisely the opening I'd contrived and I continue word-perfect, 'Well, if I do ever find myself back at school maybe I'll bump into him . . . '

There is a pause. 'You're sure to,' Caro chips in, supportively. 'London colleges are such a small world, aren't they? My brother went to the LSE and he knows *everyone*.'

I wait for Meredith to recall my poignant little 'would like to meet' speech on the watchtower, to turn to me and say, 'Well, why don't I put you in touch with each other? It seems to me you have so much in common.'

But she doesn't.

⋆  ⋆  ⋆

After a full day with the others Caro and I are relieved to retreat to our single room to rest and get ready for dinner together. While I dress in the doorway, she sits by the open window in our only chair, hair in a towel, and does her make-up.

'Dull or what?' she says. 'God, considering we're thousands of miles away, they go on about Dulwich a lot, don't they? And that bloody gallery.'

'It is a very nice one,' I protest, wondering where this loyalty has sprung from. 'I'll take you there when we get back.'

'Don't hold your breath, chum. You know what I think? I think the name originated as Dull-wich and they dropped an 'l'.'

'I think you might be right, in point of fact,' I laugh.

''In point of fact'? You know you're starting to sound like one of them, don't you?'

'They're not so bad,' I say and, again, I find that I mean it.

'I like Meredith,' she says unexpectedly. 'I mean, she's an absolute pain-in-the-arse control freak but I prefer her to Moira, anyway.'

'Really? I was just thinking Moira's taking your, er, emerging closeness with Angus very well.'

'She's OK,' Caro says. 'But I don't think she should go barelegged, do you? Her calves are like pork-and-herb sausages with those veins.'

I look at her own perfect polished brown pins and get a sudden sense of how tough it must be for a mother to hand over her treasured prince to a young challenger, especially one as glamorous as Caro; of course you would worry that an

274

enchantress like this wouldn't care for him as you've always done.

'We'll be like that,' I say. 'Sausage legs. In another thirty years.'

'We'll *never* be like that,' she says. 'Or will you still be dressing down when you're sixty?'

I try to smooth out the creases in my dress, one of the ones we bought in Jubilee Place when I first hatched my plan. It's sleeveless brown linen with square wooden buttons and I don't need a full-length mirror to know that the shift cut and unflattering mid-calf skirt length help me resemble a salami wrapped in hessian.

'Of course not,' I say. 'This is purely for the charm offensive.'

Caro sighs. 'It's so *charmless*, that's the problem. You look totally flat-chested. Now if we were in the parador, at least you could have got them to press it and it wouldn't be so scrunched. Maybe a belt would help?'

'*Nothing* will help.'

I sit on the bed opposite her as she rattles through her makeup, her eyes getting wider, her lashes glossier, her lips fuller, as if I can't remember the last time I wore proper make-up. (Thursday's RingMe presentation, as it happens, but that seems like a lifetime ago.) I watch her as I imagine a tiny daughter might watch her mother preparing herself to enter that mysterious after-bedtime world beyond her imagination. Maggie once told me how she used to like seeing her mother put on eyeliner and mascara from those old-fashioned cakes. I've strained to remember magical moments of my own, but I can't, only the application of Lipsyl when lips were chapped and a dab of Germolene if someone had a graze.

'Did you use to watch your mum put her make-up on?' I ask Caro.

She hunts for her powder brush, a utensil virtually the size of a duster. 'Yes, if she was going out and I wasn't already in bed. I'd go and sit on the edge of her bed and brush my hair while she sat at the dressing table. She used to twirl around on the stool and tickle me with the powder puff.'

Caro darts forward and dabs my nose with the brush. I turn my head away, wanting to cry.

'They should bring back those powder puffs,' she goes on, 'in the jars with the heavy silver lids. I bet Meredith and Moira have them, don't you? And proper dressing tables with the triple mirrors.'

She zips up her make-up bag and turns to look at me. It's impossible in a room this size not to feel another person's dip in mood as though feeling it yourself.

'Why don't you dress in my clothes tonight?' she says, gently. 'Be yourself. It wouldn't do any harm to glam it up a bit.'

I shake my head.

'I don't think Meredith would disapprove, you know she wears quite a dramatic shade of lippy herself. I bet her make-up is Chanel or Christian Dior, don't you? She's just that sort of era.'

'Yes, or maybe Guerlain, perfectly pronounced, of course.' I pick up her lipstick and smear a bit on the back of my hand.

'Besides,' Caro giggles, 'next to me, you're hardly going to look like a trollop, are you?'

'You don't look like a trollop.'

'You haven't seen my dress yet.'

She goes to the wardrobe and holds it up. I gasp. I have no idea where she bought her dress, or costume as it may technically be termed, but it is straight out of the wardrobe department of a new, no-holds-barred production of *Carmen*: dark-red satin, plunging neckline fringed with beads, skirt cut into a revealing flounce so the mere act of putting one foot in front of the other gives the world a generous glimpse of brown thigh. I'm amazed there aren't castanets and a black lace fan to go with it.

'Maybe you should save that for tomorrow night when there'll be flamenco?' I say. Humphrey has already indicated that he'll be extending the Pooles' reservation for the parador's 'Especial Sunday Evening of Spanish Music' to include his son's new best friends. Naturally, I'd already taken the precaution of booking through the manager, as well.

'You know I don't believe in *saving* anything,' Caro says, winking. She pulls on the dress and the effect is as jaw-droppingly sexy as it was always going to be. Next to this vision of throbbing femininity, I feel freeze-dried, lifeless.

'Does this mean you'll be spending the night chez Angus-Pangus?' I ask, trying to cheer up. 'I hope you're not considering bringing him back here? That really would be a squeeze.'

'I'm not considering bringing him back anywhere for now,' she says, mysteriously.

277

'This is a first,' I laugh. 'You've known him, what? Twenty-four hours?'

'Less than that, really, we didn't meet properly till this morning. You know, I don't think I noticed him when we checked in. He is *gorgeous*, though. I saw his stomach when he stretched to point at that crumbly carving thingy and it was really quite defined. It's driving me nuts.'

She's right, he *is* attractive. I try to remember that first meeting at the picture gallery. 'He just seemed so tweedy when I met him before.'

'Appearances can be deceptive,' she giggles. 'Just look at you! Anyway, you're too caught up in Mr Perfect Charlie to notice other men. It's not healthy.'

'Tell me about it,' I say. 'Why d'you think I've stalked a pensioner to Spain? It's hardly the act of a sane individual.'

We fall back on to the mattress with laughter and for the first time it feels like a holiday.

'So come on, what about Angus? Why not go for it?' I have never in all my days known Caro to rein in her appetites, nor have I known her to be refused, so that can't be the issue. 'Your tongues were hanging out so far at lunch I was worried you'd both dehydrate!'

'Oh, you know,' Caro shrugs. 'What is it you and Charlie say? True love waits.'

'Yeah, right. What's the real reason?'

I expect her to say she's got her period (got the painters in, as Steve puts it) or can't get hold of any condoms inside these ancient walls, but instead she looks mildly sheepish and mumbles, 'You'll laugh.'

'No, I won't.'

She starts strapping on her heels. 'I suppose I don't want old Moira making me feel all weird and guilty. It would be a bit creepy doing it under her nose with her son and then meeting up with her for dinner or breakfast or whatever.'

My eyes widen. 'Finally, *finally*, you can understand *my* situation!'

She laughs. 'Oh, Anna, it's not the same at all.'

# 20

There's nothing quite like being alone for finding yourself suddenly with the time to contemplate loneliness. Perhaps because I have been an only child for most of my life, I now tend, even when left utterly to my own devices, always to keep another human being somewhere in sight — if only for the diversion of speculating on *his* solitude rather than my own. I remember once visiting a friend in a small village in Devon and, abandoned unexpectedly while she collected a relative from the train station, being drawn to the local church in a way I have never been in the city. There was a service in progress but I had no wish to go inside, only to wait for those inside to come out. I sat for some time, feeling less alone, staring at the stone. Years later, when I told Charlie about it, I found I could remember every detail.

'It was all mottled with white stuff — '

'Lichen,' he interrupted. 'It can look quite pretty sometimes.'

'And I just watched as the audience came out — '

'Congregation,' he corrected me.

'Of course, yes, *congregation*. The thing is, when they came out they all looked so peaceful and ready to face the world, so content with their quiet lives in this tiny village where nothing can possibly happen from one year to the next. And I just thought, I could never be like this, so quiet and content.'

I don't recall where we were when we had this conversation but I remember very clearly the tenderness in Charlie's eyes. 'How old were they?' he asked. 'These people you saw?'

'I don't know, very old, I suppose.'

'Well, wait till you're that age: you might feel differently about peace and quiet.'

I remembered the silent, untroubled faces as they passed me in the churchyard, some two by two, others one by one. 'Some of them were on their own, but they didn't look at all lonely.'

He looked at me as though sensing this was the crux of the tale. 'Maybe they weren't alone, maybe they had family at home?'

'Maybe.'

Then I told him about a dog I'd met on my way to the church, a black Labrador that had come panting over to me. I'd stopped to stroke her and her owner, who had a beard and a wart on the side of his left nostril, said the dog had lung cancer and had only a 'quarter' to go.

'But he wasn't sad or anything; he was very matter of fact, almost cheery. He didn't mind telling a total stranger all the details.'

'Maybe he had no one else to tell?'

'Charlie! You said he had family at home!'

'I said some of the others might have.'

I looked away then, trying to control a spasm around my upper lip. 'I don't know why I'm upset,' I said.

'You don't have to have a reason,' Charlie said.

I lit a cigarette and he didn't pull a face like a

disappointed GP as he often did.

'The dog's name was Smudge,' I said after a while. 'She'd been named that because when she was a puppy she looked like a smudge of black paint on the carpet.'

'That's nice,' Charlie said. 'If we ever have a dog we'll call it that.'

I checked his face then. He seemed to mean it.

★   ★   ★

When Caro emerges on to the parador terrace for the first time there isn't a single other diner who doesn't follow her flouncing scarlet progress to our table. Humphrey even gets to his feet as if to lead a standing ovation. Behind her right ear she has pinned a red rose, procured from a vase at our hotel with the full cooperation of the elderly worker manning reception. Seeing Angus's eye rest on the flower makes me think of the latest of the tales I've read from my book, the one entitled 'The Legend of the Rose of the Alhambra', and I wonder if he's reminded of the same thing. It's the usual fairy story, this time concerning a modest young damsel whose role is to sit winding silk in the garden, freshly plucked rose in her hair. One day the queen's page dashes impetuously forward and snatches the rose and, with that, she is smitten.

Will Angus dare to take the rose? Yes, with his *teeth*, if the amorous look in his eyes is anything to go by.

'Did you know Grace Kelly and Prince Rainier

stayed here on their honeymoon?' he asks her in the candlelight.

'Really?' Caro says. 'I would have thought they would have wanted a pool.'

'I can see I'm going to have to build one for you,' he says, and as she outperforms all other light sources with the voltage of her smile I don't know whether to weep or gag.

Of the others at the table, Meredith seems to benefit most from Caro's dazzle, her dark-grey dress, smoky eye make-up and blood-red lipstick of the same palette as the centrepiece flamenco extravaganza. Moira, like me, is less lucky; in shades of cocoa we look like we're here by mistake, unfit to dine with the Rose of the Alhambra.

Of course, Caro is no modest young maid winding silk but an indefatigable Type A smoking a fag and grilling the queen. I listen eagerly as she picks up where Maggie left off that night at the gallery; though I hate to say it, I seem to work better as a sidekick.

'Did I hear someone say you have two sons, Meredith?'

'Yes,' Meredith says, pleasantly. 'That's right.'

'Are they both in London?'

'Only my younger son, Charlie. The other is here in Spain. We're not in touch.'

I sense Moira and Humphrey exchanging looks at this and catch my breath in anticipation.

'Is Charlie the one you were talking about earlier?' Caro asks. 'The one at college? Whereabouts in London does he live?' It strikes me as wholly unnatural that she should seize on the detail about Charlie rather than the far more intriguing one about Max, but luckily the consensus around the table is relief rather than disbelief.

'In Dulwich, with me,' Meredith says.

'Really? How old is he?'

'What is this, the Spanish Inquisition?' I joke, laughing too brightly.

'He's almost thirty.' Meredith looks totally unfazed by Caro's bludgeoning; you'd almost believe she has nothing to hide.

'And he still lives at home?' Caro exclaims. I hold my breath. 'Can't you chuck him out, Meredith? What're they called again, kids who won't leave home? Something to do with breakfast?'

'Breakfast?' the others repeat, puzzled.

'KIPPERS,' I mutter.

'Kippers?' Again the word seems to echo from person to person like some sort of absurdist parlour game.

'That's right!' Caro says. 'Kids in Parents' Pockets Eroding Retirement Savings.'

'How amusing,' Humphrey says. Seated between Caro and Meredith, he looks mightily pleased with himself this evening.

'Well, I think I'll let Charlie decide for himself,' Meredith smiles. It looks as though she's going to leave it at that but, unexpectedly, she adds, 'It seems wrong, somehow, in London, to have so much space and keep it to yourself. I know how young people struggle to find accommodation these days.' So that's how she's decided to pitch it: as a moral issue. *Charity.*

Then she adds, 'So when Charlie suggested it, I didn't object.'

She didn't object! You forced him into it, I want to protest. It is frankly bizarre hearing this discussed, as I remember very clearly the 'accommodation' dilemma. Charlie had moved back in with Meredith in the weeks following his father's death to help handle the practicalities and keep Meredith company. Of course, once she got her claws into him he never moved out again. He continued to pay his share of the rent to Rich until their lease came up for renewal, at which point Rich moved in with his girlfriend down the road.

'Why not keep the flat on your own?' I asked, but Charlie said that now he was back at college he couldn't afford the rent. I always found it slightly preposterous that he pleaded poverty when his family was clearly so wealthy, but I played along. 'You could move in with me,' I suggested. 'Then you'd be close enough to cycle to college. That would save you money.'

'I can't. You've only got one bedroom.'

Such were the conversations I'd become accustomed to having. What other boyfriend would object to his girlfriend having just one bedroom? But I knew instantly what the issue was. 'Tell Meredith it's just a flat share and that one of us uses the living room as a bedroom. Even she must realise unmarried men and women sometimes share a bathroom.'

'She'd want to visit,' he said. 'All the time. It would be ridiculous to have to stage an extra bedroom.'

'It would be ridiculous, I agree,' I said and he conceded defeat with a little nod. He'd walked straight into that one. 'I'm not trying to trap you,' I said, for I was also feeling defeated. 'I'm trying to help.'

'I know, I know, but seriously, where would I work at yours?' he asked. 'I'm going to need a lot of space.'

He was right: there is no space in my flat for his drawing board and tools and set squares and bits of Lego. And Charlie is a big guy; when he stays over we're forever colliding in doorways and tripping over outstretched legs.

'One day we can get a flat together,' he said, pulling me towards him. 'A bigger one with room for everything.'

*One day.* The flat and the dog called Smudge and everything else normal couples share. It makes me want to scream.

I tune back in just in the nick of time, it seems, for Meredith is still in the spotlight and Moira has now joined Question Time: 'Do you know if Charlie's seen anything of Gemma since you've been back from San Francisco?'

*Gemma?* Who the hell is Gemma? I go cold.

Caro actually gasps. 'What's this?' she says, so plainly knocked off course that Angus is moved to give her a protective look. 'A new romance for your son, Meredith?'

'I'm sure I'll be the last to know,' Meredith says, for all the world like a typical mother exasperated by her lack of access to her child's busy life.

'Meredith's keen to see Charlie settled,' Angus

286

says, drily, to Caro and me. 'Aren't you, Meredith? She believes men need anchoring by the time they're thirty or we start to — what was it again? — 'get beyond the point of being able to compromise enough for marriage'. You won't believe the matchmaking these two have attempted for me!' He chunters away as though it's all just the biggest joke.

I laugh along, jaw clenched, insides churning beneath the sackcloth. I repeat, Who the hell is Gemma?

'You've met her, haven't you, Angus?' Moira says.

'When we were about five,' he says. 'Isn't she Charlie's cousin or something?' Great, an old friend *and* a cousin; might have known Meredith would be a fan of in-breeding.

'They're not cousins, no,' Meredith says, 'but he did call her mother 'aunt', so I can see why you'd get that idea. Julia and I were very close friends. We worked in London together after university.'

'What's Gemma like now?' Angus asks.

'Apparently quite a beauty,' Moira tells him.

'Blonde or dark?' Caro asks.

'Fair, if I remember.'

Caro just nods as though that explains everything.

'She has a very interesting look,' Meredith concedes. 'Very natural. She's really blossomed, I must say.'

Is she going to fill us in on the history or not? I think, impatiently. Though she hasn't touched her wine for a while, I am swilling mine like nobody's business.

'So what's she doing in San Francisco?' I ask. 'Is she on a student placement as well?'

'Oh no. She's the daughter of old friends of ours who moved to California when Gemma was, goodness, a toddler, I suppose. She has quite an American accent now.' That can't be in her favour, I think, wretchedly, but I have a feeling I'm going to need more than that to overpower this eleventh-hour rival. It's as if someone has slipped something in Meredith's drink, so willingly is she opening up on a personal level. 'We all got together when I was over there,' she says, 'but they'd already been in touch with each other.'

'So you *are* matchmaking.' Angus says, grinning.

Meredith twinkles back at him. 'I must admit I was intrigued when she told us she'd just parted company with someone.'

'She's divorced?' Moira asks, disapprovingly.

'No, nothing like that. But they were living together, for a year or so, I think. Flats seem to be inordinately difficult to come by in that city.'

'They divorce at the drop of a hat, Americans,' Humphrey says, but no one is looking for a digression and he is ignored.

'Are they the same age?' Caro asks Meredith.

'She's a bit younger than Charlie. That's right, they're two years apart. It used to make a difference when they were small, but not now.'

'It's about right, I'd say,' Moira nods. 'I always think the man should be a little older.'

'Funny, I always think the man should be a little younger,' Caro retorts, wickedly. 'Oh, and maybe a little stupider, too.'

They all chuckle away at this while I wonder whether I should boil my own head or choose one of theirs instead. This is unbearable. Far from keeping Charlie to herself, Meredith is busy arranging a wife for him! It's all so obvious now I know: she's not taking any chances after the loss of Max; this time she's going to hand-select her successor. Quite a beauty. They'd already been in touch. The magical setting only makes it more painful; what crueller backdrop for disappointment than soft night air and a ceiling of stars? For a moment I feel like I really might not be able to hold it together.

I scramble to my feet. 'Caro, can I borrow you for a bit?'

'Sure.' She's up already. 'I need the loo, anyway.'

We hurry inside and find the ladies' room.

'What are you going to do?' Caro asks. The rose has wilted behind her ear and she drops it in the bin.

'I don't know. I can't believe this is happening.' I look at my stricken face in the mirror. At least if I cry, the damage to nude make-up is less devastating than it would be to full warpaint.

She takes my arm. 'This could be a good thing, Anna. If she's on the lookout for suitable young 'gels', then, hey, isn't that exactly what you are? How does she think Charlie's going to have a relationship with someone who lives halfway round the world? He's only there for another couple of weeks, anyway. Let her get used to the idea with this Gemma character and by the time he's back she'll be psychologically prepared for him to be in a relationship with you. Perfect!'

'Unless . . . ' I can't bear to voice what I'm thinking now. What if all this work, all this winning, is not going to benefit me but someone else? And if not Gemma, then the next girl? I groom Charlie to stand up to Meredith, I groom her to stand down from him, and I groom myself in her image — only to be dumped in the bin like a dead rose. It's a classic scenario; after all, you often hear of women busting a gut to re-educate their men, only to be replaced by the real beneficiary. One girl I know at work was even sought out by her ex's new girlfriend and thanked for training him up so well. How luckless is that? And then there are all those women desperate for children but with partners who refuse to try, who claim still to be children themselves. No sooner has the relationship ended over the issue than, lo and behold, he's off impregnating the very next girl he meets. No one is safe, however loved they think they are. All this time I've been congratulating myself on identifying the perfect man for me, but can I be sure I'm still the perfect woman for him?

'Darling, I really don't think you should worry,' Caro says. 'You can imagine all kinds of terrible things, but the important thing is that you trust him. And you do, don't you?'

'Yes, of course.' But why 'of course'? Didn't I

imagine, less than a month ago, that he hadn't gone to San Francisco at all? I practically blacked out in the middle of a marquee with the confusion and guilt of it all. But that was just one insane moment born of a lookalike-led delusion and I was obviously wrong about it. I need to get a grip on myself. This is how relationships *do* sour. Elvis knew: suspicious minds.

'Well then,' Caro says. 'He's in New York now, anyway, isn't he? Nowhere near the girl.'

She's right. It's highly likely that he's thinking fondly of me at this very moment. Rich is a fan of mine, he'll attest to my new fresh-faced vitality and remind Charlie that he's got a good 'un waiting for him back home. Besides, *I'm* the one choosing not to contact my partner this weekend; *I'm* the one who's been vetting my own communications like a Soviet censor; he's been nothing but the same old Charlie all along.

'She did only say 'interesting-looking',' I concede. 'Though Charlie doesn't care about looks.'

Caro snorts. 'I think with all this restyling you've forgotten how gorgeous you are. He cares, believe me.'

I sniff. 'I might just borrow your lipstick.'

We both do our lips. Looking at myself in the mirror, pale and haunted with a neat crimson mouth, I look like a geisha; how strange that after fifteen years of not being seen in public without make-up, it's suddenly the lipsticked me who feels like the fake.

'God, we've been ages,' I say. 'I hope they

291

don't think we're doing drugs.'

'They're the ones doing drugs,' Caro says. 'Did you see those pills Humphrey took with dinner? He practically needs a vanity case to carry them all.'

I laugh.

'That's better,' she says, taking my arm and propelling me through the door and down the steps as though guiding the blind. 'Now stay calm. Nothing has changed, OK?'

'OK.'

Moments later we are back at our table, main courses in front of us, wine replenished, and Caro is informing the others of how it is that her minted brother allows her to live with him rent-free in a fuck-off flat on the river.

'Property prices are truly scandalous,' Moira tuts. 'It's terrible that you young people are being priced out of the market.'

'It's not that,' Caro says. 'I've got my own buy-to-let. I just like living somewhere where someone else pays for a fantastic cleaner to do all my washing and ironing.'

'Not so different from your KIPPERS,' Humphrey points out and Caro fixes him with a long, smouldering glare.

'Humphers, has anyone ever told you you look like Paul Newman? You could almost have been separated at birth!'

I roll my eyes. Humphrey has the physique of Pooh Bear and his own wife refers to him as an egg. How can he be anything like Paul Newman?

'Once or twice, as it happens,' he says, modestly.

It is only afterwards, during a bout of insomnia, that I reach the end of 'The Legend of the Rose of the Alhambra'. After nabbing her rose, the dashing page leaves our heroine to pine for years and years until the two are finally reunited and married. The reason for his long neglect: the interference of a parent.

# 21

Jojo let slip in one of her less tactful confidences that a psychologist friend of hers had told Dad I'd never had closure because I didn't see Mum's body in the hospital. Apparently Dad got annoyed with him and said, 'You don't show a four-year-old child her mother's body all bashed up after a car crash. Now that *would* have fucked her up.'

'They think I'm fucked up?' I asked Jojo, surprised.

'No, of course not,' she said, voice velvety. 'I think they were just wondering why you're not married yet.'

I rolled my eyes at her, genuinely believing I was the superior of the two of us. 'Maybe because this is the twenty-first century and I'm concentrating on my career?' How to explain this to a woman who gave up her career before even settling on what it might be? She was temping in Dad's office when they met; later he joked that she was tempting in his office. 'I want to make my decisions for myself,' I added, maybe a bit self-importantly.

'Oh, it's not so different making them for two as for one,' she said, only half joking. 'And then, of course, for three.'

We both lowered our eyes to her neat little six-month bump, where, incredibly, a human lodged.

She added, 'You'll see, one day.'

'Don't be so sure,' I said, and she just gave me a look. One day: they all keep saying this, as though I'm still a child waiting to see what I'll be when I grow up.

Let's get one thing straight. This whole thing has never been about body clocks and a need to go shopping in the newborn section of Baby Gap. I haven't been going to these lengths with Meredith because I've identified Charlie as prime daddy DNA, not that I expect anyone to believe that. I know it's me who's the odd one out.

'Whatever women say, they all want children,' Charlie said once — Il Bordello, porcini ravioli, fruit salad, Sicilian red.

'I don't,' I said, and wondered why it was that so many of his observations about women began with 'they all' or 'you all'. How could he generalise in that way when his own mother was like no other woman on earth?

'How can you be sure? Isn't it a hormonal thing?' At least, unlike Jojo, he didn't just dismiss my denial with a single look; he really wanted to know. My stand intrigued him, though that's all it was to him, a stand. But it's quite true: I don't want children, not even with *him*, and I want him . . . well, we know how much I want him.

Dad tells a story about Mum that I can't ever forget. When I was about eighteen months she came into my room one morning to get me up; normally my parents had a policy of waiting until at least seven o'clock, but Mum came early that day because she'd arrived home late the night before and hadn't seen me for a few days. She'd been away because Grandma was ill in hospital and Grandpa needed meals cooked for him. (How a grown man could be deemed more helpless than a one-year-old child I don't know, but evidently he couldn't open a tin or toast a bit of bread without assistance.) Mum couldn't wait to see me again but, apparently, as I stood in my cot, the expression on my face stopped her in her tracks. It was one of pure, frozen incomprehension, as though I'd seen a ghost. Later she told Dad it had unnerved her, made her feel that no sin could be greater than that of the mother who deserts her children. Amazement turned to shy joy when she lifted me up and cuddled me, and it took thirty seconds before I dared look at her face again, as if I feared she'd disappeared again. She promised herself she would never leave me again, not even for a night, not until I could talk and listen and understand, understand that she'd always be coming back again. Later, when trips to Father Christmas in Lapland stretched the truth somewhat, at least I was confident of her return.

Which is partly why I'm convinced I can't be a mother myself; I just don't think I can give that much to someone so dependent on me and then remove it again. Unless someone can guarantee I'll outlive my child's childhood, I don't want to risk it.

★　★　★

For the second night I find it hard to sleep in our little room, and not only for the full-on debating society that has taken hostage of my head, replaying every conversation of the evening and imbuing it with fresh doubts. There is also the early morning business of the Alhambra itself. No sooner have the tourists shuffled back to their hotels from the entertainment at the Charles V Palace (an Andalusian dance extravaganza eschewed by Meredith as inauthentic) than it seems they're back again for first admittance to the Alcazabar. The sliver of time in between is filled with the armies of the site cleaners and their apparently jet-sized machinery.

I'm up while it's still early enough to admire the dusting of cloud on the horizon, soft as icing sugar, and the tender glaze that dawn light brings to the terraces of green beyond the walls. It's such a calming sight that I feel close to surrender — surrender to the strange intoxicating grip of the Alhambra, to *Meredith*. What on earth is going to happen next? Am I still naïve enough to imagine that I can influence events in a place where both history and legend are crowded with acts of unyielding will?

I'm still sitting in the armchair staring at the sky when Caro wakes. 'Jesus, Anna, you gave me a fright.'

'Sorry, there's just nowhere else to sit. I was just about to go down for breakfast. D'you want some water?'

I pass the tumbler to her and she sits up, back propped against a pillow. You can almost hear her brain engaging fully within seconds of awakening. 'I've been thinking about last night and maybe I *dreamt* this, but you know what?'

'What?'

She bites down on her lip as though uncertain whether to go through with the announcement after all, then decides she will. 'I reckon old Meredith knows who you are.'

'What?' I jump about a foot in the air at this. 'Are you *joking*?'

'Hang on, chum, I need the loo.'

She swivels out of bed and I wait in agony for the sound of the flush, for hands to be towelled dry, hair straighteners to be plugged in.

'Think about it,' she says, re-emerging and standing, hands on hips, in the doorway. 'All these revelations she's making, the stuff about the girl in San Francisco . . . '

'What about it?'

'Well, don't you think she might be saying it deliberately, I mean, for *your* benefit? To make you realise she's on to you, that she knows more about Charlie than you do . . . '

'That's ridiculous!' Utterly preposterous. Poppycock, as Eric and Jill would say. In all my hours of brooding since last night this theory hasn't once occurred to me. *Meredith* toying with *me*? A double bluff? Would she have the temperament for such subterfuge?

It doesn't seem to be at all consistent with reports of her previous interaction with Charlie's girls. Even before Charlie made that fateful suggestion that he might move in with Jessica, she was known to be confrontational in style, often surprising them together and ringing endlessly at Charlie's doorbell once when they were upstairs in bed.

'I'm surprised she didn't have a key,' I said to him when he told me about the incident.

'Do you take me for a complete fool?' he responded.

Three months later, when he and Meredith were sharing keys all right, living under the same roof, folly was the least of it as far as I could see.

Caro pulls open the shutters and peers out. 'Another scorcher. I must find something strapless to wear today or I'm going to have horrendous lines on my shoulders.' She pulls off her camisole.

'You do know the tourists will be able to see your boobs,' I tell her. 'No wonder they're always standing there with their cameras.'

'God, you're right.' She wraps her arms around herself. 'Who *are* these eager beavers? Why are they here so early? It's just a bunch of tiles and plaster.'

'What do you mean about Meredith?' I ask, impatiently. 'Wasn't it Moira who asked her about the girl? It's not like she brought the subject up herself.'

'Even so, she didn't have to discuss it quite so openly with us. You said she hardly talked about herself at all the night before.'

'She's getting more comfortable with us,' I say. 'And you and Moira were asking direct questions. I didn't think what she said sounded staged at all.'

Caro tilts her head to one side and begins

straightening the ends of her hair. 'Nothing you've said this weekend sounds at all staged, but it is, isn't it?'

'Not all of it,' I protest. The truth is I've started losing track of whether remarks I've been making this weekend have been spoken by the real me or the fake one. And then there was that weird sensation when I looked at myself in the mirror last night and couldn't recognise the face that looked back. Leading a double life is very disorientating. 'Anyway, I thought you said you liked Meredith?'

'Oh, I do.'

As she sets about the rhythmic squeeze and pull of her hair straightening she finally spots my stricken face and says, 'It's only an idea, babe, don't take it as gospel.'

'It's a totally mad idea!' I want to get up and pace the room but there isn't the space. I'm caged with a co-conspirator turned conspiracy theorist.

'Look, maybe Angus might know something useful about all of this?'

I consider. 'OK, d'you want to pump him a bit today?'

She cackles.

'For *information*,' I cry. 'He *must* know more about Charlie's life than he's told me so far. Their families are close, he and Charlie went to school together. He probably still lives at home as well . . . '

'Of course he doesn't,' Caro says. 'He's thirty years old, for God's sake. Oops, sorry, chum. I forget sometimes.'

I close my eyes. 'And don't give the game away, whatever you do. This is getting really risky, Caro.'

'Of course, don't worry, I know what I'm doing. I'm meeting him this morning if you want to join us? He's blown out the oldies so it'll just be us?'

'Thanks for the offer,' I say, 'but I think I need a bit of time to myself.'

★ ★ ★

It was always going to happen that I'd plunge into a gloom at some point over the weekend. I can only thank the Lord that it occurs when Angus's itinerary states 'Free time to explore Granada or relax' and not during group detail. Quite apart from Caro's madcap new theory, how can I fail to be unaffected by her easy new attachment to Angus? How could I not compare it with my own situation with Charlie? 'It's not the same at all,' she said, and she's absolutely right. It's not the same on any level, not least the parental one. Despite the occasional defensive twinge, which isn't so different from her behaviour over competitive cake baking, Moira has coped with Caro's arrival with admirable grace. Surely she must be disappointed to find herself sharing her son with two interlopers this weekend, one of whom thinks it appropriate to wear fancy dress to a quiet family dinner, but she has obviously resolved not to interfere and spoil things for anyone, herself included. Which is how normal mothers of grown-up sons *should* think, *should* react. They may not always like it, but they know the natural order must be respected: mother makes way for girlfriend, girlfriend turns into wife, mother becomes grandmother and, if tenacious enough, *great*-grandmother. It's Meredith who is the exception. But *why*? One assumes she and Moira share a value system developed together from early adulthood; otherwise they couldn't be such close friends. Why, then, is Clara despaired of but Max disinherited? Why is Angus given space but Charlie wrapped in cotton wool? Why is Caro accepted while I must be kept hidden?

I don't like to admit it but part of the reason, of course, must be Angus himself: he 'wouldn't dream' of living at home at his age; he's comfortable enough to flirt openly with Caro in front of his parents; and, as we speak, he has 'blown them out' to be with her. After *two days*. Why won't Charlie do the same for me after a whole year? If, by some bizarre set of circumstances, Meredith *does* know what's been going on, Lord knows she must be as amazed as I am that it's been going on for so long.

I decide to get out of the Alhambra. Being behind this thick fortress wall is making me want to bang my head against it. The constant bounce of the optimistic crowds making their way to the palaces, the pressure of remembering all those names and pretending to understand the concept of painting with tempera — or is that a Japanese snack? — it's all too much.

I march through the Puerta de la Justicia and

cut across the winding roads down a walkway through the elms, so steep I lose my balance a couple of times and break into a run. At the bottom of the hill I look back up at the fortress, as though I've escaped through a tunnel and don't ever intend to return. Directly ahead of me is a large, crowded square: Plaza Nueva. It smells of diesel and fried food and sun-baked tarmac but has that welcoming, inclusive air of all tourist zones. I sip scalding black coffee while I look at the street signs. There's one for the Albaicín — that was the pretty, white-washed quarter we saw from the watchtower — and lacking any better idea, I decide to head there.

There's a tourist bus but I'd rather walk. I stride along, trickle of a river on one side, strip of shops selling Moorish trinkets on the other. The hulk of Sabika Hill is to my right and I can just make out the crowds clogging the roofs of the towers and the gallery of the king's chamber, flailing in all directions like incarcerated ants. The Albaicín Hill is steep, too, and my lungs soon groan inside my ribcage, but I don't stop moving until it levels out. Then I start walking along the white streets, barely distinguishing one nutmeg-coloured roof from the next, one black wrought-iron balcony from another. I reach a market square, where the whitest onion bulbs and smoothest tomatoes are sold alongside padded bras and cheap chandeliers, but I still keep walking and walking. Then, just as desperate heroes do in movies, I reach another square, the *right* square, tranquil and remote, with the kind of silvery cobbles and sensuous breeze that might have been conjured with a wand. Only then does my body register the relief of escape.

I choose the café in the far corner for its green-and-white checked paper tablecloths and swaying umbrellas. There's a family or two about, some language students, but no British accents, no Merediths or Moiras. With nothing else to do, I leaf through *Tales of the Alhambra*, finally settling on the story of a novice nun who makes her irrevocable vow and removes herself from the world. Old Irving believes her to be another victim of a tyrannical father, forced to her 'living tomb' against her will while her lover tears his heart out from the sidelines. But, as it turns out, she is perfectly willing to give up the outside world for God. Right here, right now, with my own cast of characters beating their tiny fists against the inside of my skull, I can understand quite readily her retreat from matters of the flesh. Better that than to be stalking the streets crazed with passion, blood bubbling.

I close the book, trying — though not quite succeeding — to laugh at myself. How have I reached the point at which daft romantic legends are my truest point of reference? I really must be losing it. Then the wind lifts a leaf or two and I notice a handwritten passage in faded royal-blue ink right at the back, in the section after the index that I'd assumed had been glued stuck with thirty-year-old coffee spills. But only the corners were stuck and they can, I find, be separated easily. It's my mother's writing and on closer inspection I see that it is just a few lines of jottings, beginning with what looks like a list of train times. I've always wished she'd left diaries, something fuller than the snapshot captions in her albums, something that shared her real feelings, and it takes a while for me to accept that this material has been in my possession since Jojo gave me the book on Wednesday. It's been sitting in my bag, on my pillow, like forgotten treasure right under your feet.

And the treasure is to do with me. *Feeling like a bad mother,* I read. *Very frustrated and tired. I needed to run away* ... The next bit is lost in scribble but the meaning resurfaces again a line or two later: *sometimes I feel I can't breathe, when she wants me all the time, all of me. Then when I need her, she pulls away or twists my nose. She doesn't sleep! There's no end and Clive doesn't listen.* There's a line break after that and then: '*The water of the fountains is like music*' (in inverted commas, so perhaps courtesy of Irving?). And that's it. Maybe she was interrupted. Maybe that was when the waiter nudged her elbow and the pages were soaked in coffee.

There's no end?

I have to have a cigarette, look anxiously around for a waiter. My eye falls on an open pack of Marlboro Lights on the next table, white filters, American. I catch the customer's eye. 'Could I be a pain and steal a cigarette?'

'Sure.'

'You're from the States?'

He is from Colorado. He is studying marketing. He is in Spain with friends, travelling around and 'doing' the famed triangle of Seville, Cordoba and Granada. The others are up in the Alhambra now for a second visit but he wanted to shake off the crowds today and see something of The City Itself. He is good-looking in a fine-boned, long-fingered way and his voice is soft and dry. Something about him reminds me of Charlie, though he's leaner, more languid, with legs that stretch under the table and out the other side, a tripping hazard if the place weren't so deserted. He has thin lips that curve upwards and pale eyes that narrow with curiosity. He looks clever. And I don't know what makes me do it but when he offers to buy me a beer I sit down at his table, accept another cigarette and tell him everything I can think of about the Meredith situation. He is kind enough to let me go on for some time.

'That's some campaign,' he says, finally. 'Pretty intense.'

'I know,' I say, hoarse from the talking and smoking. 'It's a big, full-on charm offensive. I feel like a secret agent, a total imposter.'

'Wow. You know what you need?'

'What?'

'A bit of perspective.'

As pick-up lines go, it isn't the worst I've heard, not by a long shot. Two years ago I'd be paying the bill by now and allowing myself to be grappled into the back of a cab. Then I'd go wherever he suggested and do whatever he wanted, whatever *I* wanted, too. And I can't say I dismiss the idea out of hand, though it might have to be the back of the tourist hopper as I haven't seen many cabs about. No one would know, he probably has condoms in his wallet, I'll never see him again. If I showered immediately afterwards I could convince myself it hadn't happened at all, was just a hallucinatory product of the insane heat and too many old stories of unrequited passion.

But two years ago I wouldn't have been in Granada, I wouldn't have known Charlie. I stand up, lean forward and kiss him on the lips. The contact is more solid than I intended and his upper lip sits between mine long enough for me to want to keep it there. Encouraged, he cups the back of my head with his hand and starts to move his lips properly. I pull away.

'Thank you,' I say, 'but I think I ought to stay on-message.'

As I scurry away I just hear him mutter, 'Hey, lucky guy.'

★ ★ ★

As I walk back I start crying. It's as though I've wanted to for days, for weeks, for years, but never got around to scheduling it in. What I'm weeping for I can't be sure: it's not just my mother and the fact that, out of the blue, I know she saw no end; it's also Charlie and the fact that he is in New York with Rich and not me; the fact that my father has a new son, a proper heir; it's Meredith, of course, for all the tumult she's brought to my life, but also Caro and the powder puff that tickled; it's even the American, who may or may not have been a figment of my

307

imagination. Whatever it is, the tears aren't going to get it out of my system; that would be too easy. I can only hope that they at least clear my vision for a few hours. I *have* to hold it together for a little longer: tonight is probably going to be my last chance.

As I re-enter the Alhambra it is with a different pull, something fiercer than my own will, not magical of course but somehow sort of predestined. I know that I'm not going to be leaving again without having my answer.

# 22

As soon as I get back to the room I call my father.

'He's in the pool with Felix,' says Jojo. 'Did you know it's the hottest day of the year here? Hotter than Bombay! How many degrees there?'

'I don't know,' I say. 'A lot.'

'How are you getting on with the wicked stepmother?'

'Wicked mother-in-law,' I correct her. 'You're the wicked stepmother, Jojo, remember?'

She laughs. 'Oh yeah, I keep forgetting. Hang on, sweetie, I'll get Clive for you.'

'Anna? Is anything wrong?' I'm reminded of something Moira said the other night: if Clara calls her, she assumes something must be wrong. How awful must that feel?

'I'm reading Mum's copy of *Tales of the Alhambra*,' I say to him straight away.

'*Tales of the* . . . ?'

'The book you're supposed to read when you come to Granada.'

'Oh, OK.'

'Anyway, it's not about that, it's about the notes. She's written stuff in the back.'

'Oh?' he says again, but more warily now. 'What kind of stuff?'

I don't want to crucify him with this but I have to know. 'Just thoughts about, y'know, how hard motherhood was.'

'No harder than for any other mother,' he says and I catch a distinctly pre-emptive tone to his voice.

'She says she can't breathe.'

'She had a dramatic streak.' Where do you think you got yours from? — that's what he wants to add, but he knows I'm too upset for teasing.

'I twisted her nose.'

He laughs. 'You used to do that. For *years*. You had a sly little two-handed technique. *And* you poked things in our ears — we thought it was cute until my mother couldn't get a bead out of hers and had to be taken to casualty.' I hear him relaxing; this isn't the hard conversation he feared.

'Dad, she says there was no end.'

Silence.

'She means to *me*, no end to my demands.'

He sighs and there's such love and regret in that sigh I feel tears bubbling again. 'That's how parenthood feels, sometimes,' he says, carefully. The line is so clear he could be in the armchair opposite. 'I'm afraid until you do it yourself you're going to have to take my word for it.'

'I was just wondering, do you think she was planning on — '

He interrupts, so quick to guess my thoughts the only explanation can be that he's had the same ones himself. 'She wasn't planning on doing anything, Anna. That trip to Spain was at least a year before she died. She was visiting a friend who'd married a Spaniard and had just had a baby.'

'Why didn't she take me with her? She said she wouldn't leave me after . . . ' It occurs to me it's so long since he told me about the ghost story he may not remember it; he may not hoard such snippets, precious as heirloom jewels, as I do.

He's sighing again. 'I don't remember, to be honest. That might have been the time you went to the caravan with Don and Pauline. You were asked which you preferred.' Grandma and Grandpa. I remember now; the squidgy seat in the window that they said was made of foam, the funny steps with no backs, the trampoline that I was allowed to bounce on every night before dinner; no bathtub but washes with a flannel by the sink, Grandma's fingers bony but warm. I was asked which I preferred and I chose that! Had I known our time together was finite, I would never have made the choice I did. And suddenly I remember something else: the flamenco doll brought back from Spain, sitting in its box behind a plastic window; Mum's cheek pressed against mine as we looked at the doll together. Her hair was different, but this time I knew it was her.

'Your mother was probably away from you half a dozen times in four years,' Dad says, 'and every time you were with me or your grandparents. You were always her first priority, always.'

'OK,' I say, voice small, but eyes dry again.

'All that stuff, you'll feel that yourself if you have small kids, exactly the same. Jojo feels it now, keeps telling me she's suffocating, and she gets plenty of time away from Felix. Imagine if

311

they *didn't* want to keep a part of themselves, they'd be like Charlie's mother, clinging on for bloody ever. It would be unhealthy. You know what? Reading someone else's diary should be made illegal.'

I feel better; it takes so little. He's right: if I sometimes wrote down my thoughts and fears and let everyone read them I'd be sectioned. The Meredith book, for instance, God forbid! 'So everything was OK, then?'

'Of course it was. Just remember the moo,' he says.

I didn't know he knew about the moo. I thought that was my own secret memory. When I was very tiny Mum used to come and play on the rug with me beside my big wicker chest of toys. She'd get down on all fours and pretend to be an animal and she'd say, 'If I love you a lot I'll do a meow, if I love you very much I'll do a woof, but if I love you more than anyone else in the whole wide world I'll do a moo.' I would wait, confident but watchful. And it was always a moo.

★   ★   ★

The hotel bar is empty. Seven-thirty is no man's hour here, too late for the end-of-day beer but too early for a pre-dinner one, and you hear the pipes groaning as all the guests take their showers at once. With my glass of cava the waiter brings a note from Caro saying she'll meet me at the parador before dinner as she and Angus are taking a walk. I wonder if that might be a

Harding euphemism and if they are in fact ensconced upstairs in bed.

At eight o'clock there's the sound of cannon fire. Without Angus here to explain, I can only wonder why. Then, to my surprise, Meredith drops by. She's already dressed for dinner in a moss-green dress with a nipped-in waist and full skirt; more girlish than anything I've seen her in before but she carries it off well. Her wedged sandals must have rubber soles as they're quite silent on the cobbles.

She says she's here to deliver some messages left at the parador for me, which is a perfectly reasonable errand, but I can't help thinking nervously of Caro's suspicion — 'she knows who you are' — when I read the notes. Maggie and Viv have both called for news of my progress: Viv's *call me at any time if the going gets rough* is discreet enough, but Maggie's *How are you getting on with Mrs G?* is a little close for comfort given that the messages have been handwritten by reception staff on squares of notepaper and folded loosely into quarters. Thank God Meredith is too well bred to have thought of peeking.

'I think the parador manager has the idea that we're related,' she says with a chuckle. 'I do hope they're not expecting a review from me. I'd be happy to provide one, of course, but I'm no travel writer.'

My instinct is to leap in with a compliment — 'Oh, but I would have imagined you to have a wonderful turn of phrase, Meredith!' — but I'm still a little thrown and so just nod blankly.

She looks around the courtyard. 'This is very pretty.'

'Would you like a drink?' I ask, remembering my manners.

'Yes, why not. Is that cava? Maybe I'll have a glass of the same.'

The same. Nervous or not, I get a thrill from the words, along with a sudden, powerful glimpse of the significance of the moment. This could be the final entrance exam to the life I long for; if I can just impress her now! What on earth would Charlie say to see the two of us together, on our own, drinking the same drink, the two women he has worked so hard to separate? My phone is lying on the table by my glass; all it would take is a quick click and an image could be captured and sent across the world. Would Rich have to pick him up from the floor?

I don't get much further with this frightening fantasy because as soon as Meredith's drink arrives she says, straight away, with no small talk or anything, '*My* mother died when I was very young, you know. I never really knew her.'

I look up, surprised. She must have sensed that I lack my usual teacher's pet devotion, perhaps thinks I'm sad to have been abandoned by my friend in favour of a man, or maybe she just sees a quality to my solitude that I don't even recognise myself. Whatever she is thinking it is clear that she doesn't know who I really am at all. Meredith is simply intuitive and kind.

'I always think it makes you a different kind of person,' she goes on. 'I mean for your whole life.'

'What do you mean? What kind of person?'

'Oh, you're independent, of course, colder in a way, but somehow more reliant on there being, oh I don't know, grand passion in your life.'

I feel knocked for six. Is Meredith talking about sex? 'Aren't all women?' I ask, with no idea where this is leading.

She widens those large, unsettling eyes. 'I suppose what I mean is that a casual *affaire*' — she somehow adds an extra 'e' to the word — 'is not intense enough because everything has to measure up to what it is that you think you've missed out on. Maternal devotion.'

I mull this over. Am I being counselled or are these pronouncements just more self-contained homilies for me to take or leave as I please? Either way, I'm not convinced. 'But aren't people who've lost someone close to them more reluctant to trust — in case they lose all over again?'

'I don't know what the psychologists say, but I haven't found that,' says Meredith. 'I think we're more likely to seize on what's not appropriate and try to make it what we want.'

Her use of the plural gives me that shiver again and for the first time I am able to forget my agenda and feel curious about her in her own right. Is she expressing regrets about her own choice of husband? Is that what lies at the heart of her own parenting style? 'Protecting children from making terrible errors when they're too young to realise that's what they are', that's how she described it a couple of nights ago. Does she believe that there was no one there to protect her? Was she, like my own mother, too young when she married? But *she*'d been to university and worked in a job before being subsumed by the needs of her husband and children.

'It must be strange for you to travel without your husband?' I say, tentatively. I'd like to touch her arm but I don't dare.

'Yes, in a way. You think you won't enjoy things as much if you don't share them. But you can; it's amazing how selfish you can be about beautiful things.'

'I've never travelled on my own,' I say. 'I know it's probably shallow, but it's sort of as if, I don't know, just if there's no one to hear you say how much you're enjoying yourself, then you're not really enjoying yourself.'

'Precisely.' When she agrees with me it feels like praise from the headmistress known for never giving it.

'How long were you married for?'

'Thirty-seven years.'

'God!' I can't help exclaiming at this and she smiles, amused.

'And do you have a partner, Anna? That's what we're supposed to call them these days, isn't it?'

'No, I'm on my own.'

'Oh yes, I remember you saying at the cake stall that day.'

She remembers *now*, but does that mean she hasn't heard any of my strategic little hints over the last couple of days? What about the conversation by the bell? Did she, like Angus, simply tune herself out of my charming little plea for a soulmate?

'Dulwich seems so far away . . . ' I say. It also, oddly, feels like home.

'Oh yes, perspective is a great thing.'

Perspective, it keeps on coming up.

We've finished our drinks. 'Goodness,' Meredith says, 'the air feels exactly the same as body temperature, doesn't it? Do you think it is?'

'Maybe,' I say. 'This dress certainly feels too hot and it's paper thin.' I'm wearing Caro's daisy print, too casual for the gala dinner, but I couldn't go another moment without colour, not here, where black is for mourning and beige is for the woodwork.

I'm pleased when she suggests we head over to the parador together. We walk with final-night deliberation, memorising the red-tinged walls, the rich green trees, the postcard-perfect Sierra Nevada.

'Is this what you imagined,' Meredith asks, 'when you dreamed of coming to the Alhambra?'

She'll never know how much it is, but not at all in the way she means. 'Yes,' I say, 'though I must admit there are more . . . ' — I break off as we're passed by a pair of taxis filled with elderly tourists — ' . . . well, fewer young people about.'

She laughs. 'It probably seems impossible to you to imagine what it's like to be sixty.'

'But you're not sixty yet,' I protest, remembering too late that there's been no overt reference to her age, just comments about a forthcoming celebration. 'Are you?' I add, lamely.

But it's fine, of course, she just assumes I'm

paying her a compliment. 'I will be in . . . goodness . . . ' — she checks her watch — ' . . . two weeks or so. But what I mean, Anna, is that I can remember exactly what it is to be your age — what, about Charlie's age, thirty?'

I don't correct her.

'Well, it doesn't seem long ago at all. I would have had both my sons by then. That's right, Leo and I had just moved to Dulwich. There was so much to do domestically, people wanting to come to stay and so forth, I don't think I set eyes on a newspaper for months. It was chaos.'

She's pointing out the differences between us just as I hope for her to fall upon the similarities. I think of my pristine capsule by the river where newspapers sit in piles awaiting professional scrutiny, the sort of childless space people choose to inhabit so they needn't rub shoulders with suburban dullards.

'You could never entertain here,' Jojo said when she first visited.

'It depends on what you call entertainment,' I told her, not quite winking, but certainly intending her to note the sexual innuendo and compare my own freedom with her position as the married partner of an 'old' man.

She didn't seem to get it, though, adding, as if in concession, 'Well, maybe drinks for eight, I suppose.'

Meredith is still reminiscing. 'It was hard enough to get time to catch my breath, much less catch up on a career.'

I can't breathe, that's what Mum wrote, that's what Mum *felt*. 'It's not so different now,' I say.

'Things just get more delayed. Careers come first for a while, but not for ever, not for everyone.'

'Yes, I can see your jobs are important to you and Caro, very important.' Why does the idea of her viewing me as the same as Caro ignite a sudden spark of protest in me?

'It's the industry we're in,' I say, 'it's very intense, all-consuming. It's not like real life, you know, conventional life.' If she even knew the half of it! I'm glad we've reached the hotel entrance. I don't want to talk about work; I want to quit while I'm the girl who dreamed of the Alhambra, not the one who's chosen a second-rate tabloid newspaper over bouncing babies.

But she doesn't walk through the doors; there's more she wants to know. 'Tell me, Anna, a place like this, where people are treating themselves to dinner . . . ' She motions to the other arrivals, groups from the city busy with their cameras, already snapping memories of their special night at the famous Alhambra parador. 'Does this feel at all like a treat to you after your London media life?'

She's wondering if I know the value of anything, that's what this is, even though I've worked hard all weekend not to mention the price of everything.

'Of course,' I say. 'I'm just an ordinary office girl, you know, dreaming of a way out.'

Meredith lets out that lovely musical peal of laughter and then looks at me abruptly. 'You don't fool me for a minute.'

I actually stop dead. It all freezes, everything:

the paper rattle of the leaves on the trees, the cries of the guests as they pose for their portraits, even the whoosh of the door.

'No,' she goes on, 'you don't strike me as ordinary at all. You must know you have extraordinary freedom. And Caro too.'

So that's what's on her mind, thank God. Widowhood has made her reassess what it was she gave up for marriage in the first place. Jojo may not want my life, but Meredith does, at least she wants it for her younger self. What on earth would she say if she knew I considered *her* the only threat to that extraordinary freedom?

She turns to look at me, dispassionately now, as though appraising the workmanship of a piece of furniture at auction. 'In a funny kind of way, you remind me of myself.'

The leaves rattle again, the tourists chatter, the doors whoosh, and I smile. 'That's a lovely compliment.' And my chest actually puffs, my heart really quickens, as though in response to a first declaration of love. Yes, this is exactly what I dreamed of when I allowed myself to indulge in best-case-scenario Granada fantasies: Meredith and me. The two of us talking, the two of us bonding, the two of us Moving Forward. Dare I suspect that my scheme might just have succeeded? She may not yet have hit on the idea of Charlie and me together, but isn't it only a matter of time? What better match for her son than someone who reminds her of herself?

My handbag vibrates. 'Is that your telephone?' she asks with a disapproving roll of the eyes.

'Sorry, yes, I'll just . . . ' But when I see

Charlie's name on the screen I click him on to
voicemail and slip the thing back into my bag.

★  ★  ★

Meredith goes to freshen up in her room, so
after a chat with the assistant manager, who is
anxious for me to confirm plans for our tour in
the morning, I go in search of Caro. I find her in
the hotel's private gardens, sitting on the swing
for two with a jug of sangria for four. Not having
a room here has clearly done nothing to deter
her from availing herself of the superior facilities.

She makes room on the swing and passes me
the glass to share. 'How was your day?'

I fill her in on the man in the café ('Hey,
you're human, after all!') and the conversation
with Meredith.

'It's in the bag,' she assures me. 'I really don't
think this could have gone any better. Just you
wait, if she doesn't mention the party tonight,
there'll be an invitation in the post when you get
back.' Conspiracy theories are all forgotten now.
'I'm so happy for you,' she adds, putting her
arms round my waist and her head on my
shoulder, and we swing together for a minute or
two.

'How about you?' I ask, loving her for saying
the right thing when I've spent too much time
this weekend worrying about her saying the
wrong.

She straightens up to light a cigarette. 'Well,
we went to the Summer Palace in the morning
and I heard all about how young men used to

321

shimmy up the tree to have their wicked way with the sultana. That reminds me: no opportunity to interrogate Angus, I'm afraid. We bumped into the oldsters after about ten minutes.'

'Not to worry. What did you do after that?'

'I ended up having lunch with Moira and Humphrey. Angus got a call from some curator and was off being earnest somewhere so I got stuck with them. God forbid a sit-down meal be missed!'

Lunch alone with the in-laws already! 'What did you talk about?'

'Lord only knows. The weather in nineteen sixty-eight? Correction: the weather in Dulwich in nineteen sixty-eight. I was dying of boredom. I'm sick of them, aren't you?' She lowers her voice and swivels her eyes left and right as if fearing the Pooles might be eavesdropping in the shrubs. 'I mean, all the fussing and stuff.'

'It is getting a bit wearing, I have to admit.' Nothing is too wearing after that breakthrough one-to-one with Meredith, but I'm keen to show willing.

'Their obsession with filtered water,' Caro says. 'It's as if raw sewage flows from the taps.'

'The medication,' I add. There are blood-pressure tablets for Moira and something to do with diabetes for Humphrey; even Meredith can't resist the incessant chat about health and all things sanitary.

'The drill over the toilets,' sighs Caro, and adopts a comically poor Scots accent: ' "Down the corridor, past the flowering oleander, and third on your left.' I swear, Moira even reported back on the water pressure today!'

'It could be worse,' I say. 'At least they're not at the walking-stick and hearing-aid phase. They're relatively youthful, you know.'

'I never want to be that old,' she says, vehemently. Caro's parents, long divorced, have retreated to opposite ends of the British Isles with new older spouses, her father to Cornwall and her mother to the Scottish Highlands. She says the only thing they have in common is allowing themselves to grow old before their time.

'Where's Angus?' I ask.

'He's having a shower. I was tempted to jump in with him but you've seen the size of our showers! Tell you what, though, I've decided tonight is the night. I'm not going to let a couple of cottonheads put me off my stroke.'

'Glad to hear it,' I giggle.

'Anyway, they leave first thing in the morning, don't they? So I won't have to face a Poole family debrief.'

First thing in the morning, I think; it's almost over, I'm so close. 'But, Caro, I thought you said true love waits?'

'It does.' She looks at her watch. 'About another five hours.'

# 23

At dinner, the dynamic has changed both in the restaurant and at our regular table. The usual romantic purr has been replaced by festive chatter and the terrace bar is filling up far earlier than usual (the flamenco guitarist due to play is, we're told, no mere waiter required to double up for the tourists but a musician of some local renown). There are tall ruby-coloured cocktails and a special menu to supersede the à la carte; I decide not to worry about this and just take my chances tonight — if I must eat goat's gonads then it's a small price to pay for a spoonful of Meredith's approval.

At our table, Caro and Angus are decidedly together. They've ignored the protocol established by the previous night's seating plan and are sitting side by side, an official couple, which means Moira must now switch to Caro's other side. This she takes in her stride.

'That's a pretty scarf,' she compliments her usurper, pleasantly.

'Free with *Elle*,' Caro replies. 'I love the summer issues, don't you, Moira? Such fantastic giveaways!'

I, thankfully, am still next to Meredith, who tells me how much she enjoyed our 'little talk'. I beam at her, close to a high in this celebratory atmosphere. It's in the bag, that's what Caro said.

'What did you do today, Anna?' Angus asks me as Caro insists Moira try the scarf herself. From my vantage point it looks as though she is trying to strangle her.

'Not much, really. I had a look around the Albaicín.'

'I haven't been there yet; what's it like?'

'Very local. Sometimes it's nice to just wander and not feel like you ought to be cooing over something historical.' I surprise myself with the honesty of this remark. Somehow I am feeling less guarded this evening; it's as if now Meredith has validated the new me I can begin to reintroduce certain elements of the old one without feeling overwhelmed with identity crisis. I must be careful, though; since this is, I hope, only the beginning of a long-term relationship with Meredith, then I'll always need to keep the bits she likes in ready view. I find that I don't mind the idea of that at all; sackcloth notwithstanding, Dulwich Anna is growing on me.

'I know what you mean,' Angus says. 'You can be a slave to the guidebook, can't you?' He looks and sounds like a different person, he's so relaxed. Forty-eight hours with Caro and the crustiness has been dusted right off him; even his curls look springier.

We all look around as volume levels rise sharply with the arrival at a nearby table of a large Spanish family, complete with grandparents (and possibly one of the greater variety) and more children than you'd see after dark in a whole year in central London. All are dressed up to the nines, one even costumed in full flamenco, and look full of glee to be included in such an adult occasion. As iced cocktails are presented to us by immaculate staff, I remember Meredith's question, 'Does this feel at all like a treat to you . . . ?' Yes, it does, but if I choose to put a name to that mysterious prodding somewhere inside my ribcage then it feels rather like a trick, too.

'Good to see a few more youngsters in the house,' Caro says, scanning the crowd in the bar area with a practised eye. 'Oh, no offence, chums.'

'None taken,' says Humphrey, who I suspect has never been addressed as 'chum' in his life.

'I love the way the Spanish are about family, don't you?' she goes on. 'I mean, look at all these little kids still up. So cute and well behaved. You'd never see that in Britain, would you?'

'Not these days,' Moira says. 'Children are allowed to run riot, if you ask me.'

'What I find interesting,' says Meredith, 'is how involved fathers are in caring for young children these days. It was so different when I had my boys. I don't think Leo knew what a nappy was. He wasn't at all interested and if I tried to explain he would look at me as if I was speaking some obscure dialect he couldn't understand.'

'You did have Elaine, though,' Moira points out, bravely.

'I think we all know mothers-in-law can be as much of a hindrance as a help,' Meredith says wryly.

As I ponder the profound irony of that statement, Moira reminds her friend of the boys' nanny and the various other staff members at her disposal during their childhood. Meredith concedes defeat with good humour. They are a funny pair.

'I always think being a mother-in-law must be incredibly difficult,' I say, barely believing my luck at such an opening, 'because by definition you have to let go a bit, don't you?'

They both open their mouths to answer but, to my irritation, are distracted by the sound of Caro singing 'If You're Happy and You Know It, Clap Your Hands' with two of the Spanish kids, one of whom has climbed on to her lap and responds to the cry of the song with an energetic clatter of the castanets.

'They look so alike, don't they?' Moira says, and it is true that Caro could be the girl's mother, so similar is their colouring.

But something about this image leaves me cold with fear, fear that Caro and Angus will go back to London, marry, have beautiful, noisy children and leave me alone and stuck in my Charlie situation for ever. What was I thinking, it's in the bag? All Meredith said was that she enjoyed our talk.

'So will you be celebrating your birthday, Meredith?' I ask her over the squealing. If I can just secure that invitation, *then* I can sit back and congratulate myself.

'Yes,' she says, obviously surprised by the abrupt change of subject. 'I never thought I would, but I'd like to thank a lot of people for being so kind to me since . . . well, in the last year or so, so I'm holding a party.'

'What a lovely idea. At your house?'

'Yes. We considered hiring the gallery — it's such a terrific space for functions — but Charlie suggested doing it at home. The whole thing was his idea, actually, though he's conveniently out of reach now it's come to the practical arrangements. Doesn't stop him inviting all his friends, of course, but I'm sure you'd do the same. It's a child's prerogative. Oh, how sweet, Caro's given that little girl her bracelet.'

We all look, but I'm the only one who is frowning. Charlie's idea? All his friends? I hear my own voice, irritatingly whiny, saying to him, 'This birthday party would be the perfect opportunity! You could invite me . . . ' and his reply, 'I'm just not in a position to invite anyone.' What on earth's going on? This must be a glimpse of Meredith the fantasist, the famous emotional trickster of Charlie's complaints. In any case, two people often give differing accounts of the same events, the same conversations; Lord knows my father and I would never tell the same anecdote the same way. No, agreeable though Meredith is this evening, her moods are known to be changeable and her version of reality considerably less reliable than Charlie's. She thinks he's invited his friends to the party but in fact they're all her guests, children of friends, young people like Angus and Clara, certainly no one like Rich or David.

'God, they're exhausting,' Caro breaks in,

shooing the last child away and lighting herself a cigarette. I sit on my hands to avoid reaching for one, too. Then the guitarist tunes up, first courses are served, and I gratefully abandon further thoughts of mothers-in-law and birthday parties.

Slowly, I relax, even close my eyes for a moment, and it's a while before I realise that the music is the reason why; it licks itself around me, simultaneously soothing the mind and stirring the body. I think of Charlie, just Charlie, Charlie when I first knew him, before the complications set in.

With which a large serving implement is waved over my plate and Moira's voice asks, '*Revoltillos* for you, Anna?'

★   ★   ★

It is only when the guitarist takes a break and Caro screams out, 'That was fucking amazing!' that it strikes me she is rather drunker than anyone else in the group. 'Wow,' she adds, with a shudder of abandonment that makes her cleavage wobble, 'I could listen to flamenco *all night long.*' She draws out the last three words with unmistakable sexual innuendo.

'Let's go on somewhere after dinner?' Angus suggests, and he has the good grace to sweep his eyes inclusively around the whole table. 'I know, what about the Sacramonte caves where the gypsies live? There might be more music.'

'Is that safe at this time of night?' Moira asks.

'Of course it is. Obviously we'll have to cross

their palms with silver. That's where the term 'flamenco' came from, you know?'

'From the gypsies?' Caro asks.

'Yes, it means 'Flemish'. It referred to the courtiers of Charles V. They used it as a derogatory term.'

'You know *everything*,' Caro smoulders at him. And with her next blink the eyelids are noticeably lazier in reopening. 'I had a jug of sangria earlier,' she tells me, as if reading my mind.

'I know,' I remind her. 'I had some with you.'

'They were a bit funny about it when I ordered.' Her voice rises with indignation. 'Suggested I couldn't possibly manage *quattro* glasses myself. Yeah, right.'

'I've never noticed the Spanish deprive themselves,' Humphrey says.

'Oh, but they do if it's not with dinner,' Meredith says. 'They're like the French. They'll nurse a glass of wine or a beer for hours. What on *earth* . . . ?' She breaks off at the sudden squeal of feedback from the amplifier across the terrace, followed by the sound of a male voice too close to the microphone. It seems someone has taken advantage of the guitarist's break to hijack the mic.

'Sorry, everybody, we're pretty loaded, but . . . ' Then the voice starts to sing 'I've Been Waiting for a Girl Like You' in the most excruciating falsetto you could imagine. I suppress a giggle.

'Where's the maître d'? They look like students,' Meredith grumbles, clearly displeased that frat-house jinks should be allowed to disturb her Andalusian idyll.

But the mood in the restaurant is high-spirited and hers is the only dissenting voice as adults and children alike applaud the arrival of a bit of unscheduled fun. These nights are a regular fixture in high season; doubtless this is the part of the evening for public marriage proposals and other painful acts of devotion. I can only hope Angus isn't going to step up next with his take on 'Sweet Caroline'.

'I've been waiting . . . I know this one,' says Humphrey, straining to hear the lyrics. 'Talented fellows as I remember. Years ago.'

I can't see the singer but I catch sight of a pair of what look like British blokes whooping him on from the sidelines.

'Is she here, the girl I've been waiting for?' The voice is familiar, what *is* that accent, Yorkshire perhaps? I hold my breath and squeeze shut my eyes. No, it's surely, surely not *Sammy Duncan*? Dad's little idiot sent to 'help me out'. Would either of them really be so bonkers, so absurdly out of step with the spirit of my campaign? I'll kill my father, I think grimly. The last thing I need just as I've finally established my credentials is to be associated with some travelling buffoon.

Some of the crowd are clapping along now and the guitarist has returned to improvise a flamenco-style accompaniment. Sammy knows all the words, I'll give him that — no doubt a nauseating cover version is in the pipeline — and except for the strain of the chorus line he holds the melody decently enough.

'Isn't this an adorable serenade?' Caro exclaims, standing up for a better view. 'Who *is* that guy? I haven't seen him at either of our hotels.'

Strange that she wouldn't recognise him, I think to myself. She was quite a fan of his old band. 'Isn't it Sammy?' I hiss sideways.

'Sammy Davis Jr?' Humphrey says, perking up. 'I think you've got the wrong chap, Anne. Now he *was* a proper entertainer . . . '

Then the disembodied voice asks us all, 'Where is she, the girl from the Albaicín?'

'He's looking over here,' Caro yelps in excitement. 'He's American, I think.'

'Another admirer?' Angus asks her, with a look that would liquefy granite.

'I don't think I know him,' she says, puzzled.

But I think I do. Oh sweet Jesus, oh, please, no. Sammy Duncan is suddenly forgotten as I slink to my feet and then sit straight back down again. I seriously consider a scissor jump over the terrace railings and into oblivion, but can't remember how far the drop is to the gardens below (this is *almost* worth dying for, but not quite).

Sozzled or not, Caro gets it in a flash. 'Oh my God, Anna, is he the one you snogged?'

'We didn't snog,' I mutter.

'You didn't tell me he was a *septic*?' she cackles.

'A septic?' Humphrey queries, leaning in to hear her better.

'Yeah, y'know, septic tank, Yank.'

Wild clapping denotes the end of the song, but

not the torture. Colorado café boy, for it is he, is bundling over towards us with pals in tow, walking into chairs and ignoring the waiters' protests as he goes. One of his posse makes a ham flamenco pirouette while chanting 'cha-cha-cha!'; another falls about as though in the presence of Groucho Marx. It seems to me that the whole restaurant is watching, as though collectively sensing the unfolding of a modern-day Alhambra legend before its very eyes. Again, I keep mine very tightly shut.

'Hola!' says my courtly suitor. 'Hey, which one's the mother, then?'

I can smell the *cervezas* on his breath. 'Hi, there!' I say, brightly, as though his arrival is nothing more than sociable table-hopping. 'This is Caro and Angus,' I say quickly, 'and his father, Humphrey, and *mother*, Moira . . . ' Horrendously ill-mannered though it is, I have no choice but to miss out Meredith's name, which, foolishly, I used unstintingly during my afternoon rant. 'Everyone, this is . . . '

'Doug,' he supplies, after a giveaway pause.

Caro crows delightedly. 'You sucked face and didn't know his name?' She's practically bouncing up and down in her seat; we could be having a drink on our own after work so completely does she seem to have forgotten where we are and *who we're with*.

I scowl at her, nodding crossly in Meredith's direction, but she just winks back at me like this is all some huge joke and we're in it together. Thankfully, by this stage the maître d' prevails and the invaders allow themselves to be ushered back to the bar area where they belong.

'Come and join us,' Doug calls to me, like a man being carted off to jail and crying out his final requests. Briefly I think of the upside-down funnel dungeon and wish him there.

'Aged rather well, hasn't he?' Humphrey says, but I'm far too busy freezing my smile to roll my eyes.

Finally, peace is restored, the guitarist has resumed his set, and providing Meredith doesn't know what 'suck face' means or, better still, didn't catch that remark at all through the hysteria of Caro's laughter, I might just be out of the woods.

'Hey, Anna,' Caro calls across the table, excitedly. 'Anna! I was just thinking . . . '

'*What?*'

'Maybe *Doug* will be your next husband, not Ch — '

'Shut up, Caro,' I say, sharply.

She does, at once, clamping her hand over her gaping mouth with a melodramatic sucking noise. I sense the collective still. Even the neighbouring children have suspended their prattle in favour of dessert; it's too much to pray that Meredith didn't hear this time.

'*Next?*' Angus repeats, finally. 'What d'you mean? Is Anna married already, then?'

Too late, Caro hides her face in his shoulder.

'Divorced,' I say, quietly.

'Really?' says Moira, making the word the length of three. It's not quite as if she's discovered I've got a criminal record but, equally, it's not the response I'd expect if I'd just let on I'd won the Nobel Prize.

My instinct, honed over the course of a decade in ad sales, is to gloss over the gaffe. 'Yes, well, don't we all look back on things we've done and wonder what we could possibly have been thinking at the time?'

'Yeah,' Caro nods energetically, obviously looking to make amends. '*Totally*. When I slept with our old sales director, in the morning I took one look at his big paunchy body and thought, What the fuck was I smoking?'

Angus laughs, Humphrey frowns, Moira glowers, but I don't know what Meredith does because I don't dare look.

'Do you mean marijuana?' Humphrey asks, pronouncing it 'mari-ji-hoo-ah-na'.

'Sorry,' Caro says. 'Did I overshare?'

'Oversharing is not the word,' I mutter. I am immobilised with shock. Given the chance, I would erase this whole summer from history in a heartbeat.

'*You* were married!' Angus says. 'I had no idea! Sorry, I don't know why I'm so surprised, it's hardly a crime.'

'Yeah,' Caro jokes, artificially jolly. 'Are you insulting my friend? Who wouldn't want to marry her, she's gorgeous?'

This couldn't get any worse if Doug came back and gave Moira a lap dance.

'They call it 'spliff' now,' Humphrey tells his wife, but she's too gripped by the drama to acknowledge his tip.

'So, a glamorous divorcee,' Angus says, but there's something about the phrase that seems to cause a further shift in the air with everyone. A new danger.

I can't avoid Meredith's face a moment longer; I *have* to know her reaction. All my senses have melded together and I'm not sure if I can even see through my eyes any more, but I turn anyway. Her head is bowed and she is looking at her dessert plate, fork playing with a sliver of cake, apparently shuttered from the unseemliness of the free-for-all taking place in front of her. And instinctively I know it's over. My charm offensive has been shattered with one single vulgarism that no compliment can smooth over, no gentility overcome. The truth is out: this *is* Edward and Mrs Simpson, after all.

Just then, from the depths of the bar terrace, comes the unmistakable heckle, 'Anna! Come and have a beer! I've got cigarettes!'

'Yep, it's official, if *Doug* has his way, you'll be going to the chapel all over again,' Caro smirks. She's given up on rescuing the victim now, but leans right back in her seat better to survey the scene of the crash. And, stunned with music and melodrama, we all just sit there and watch as she tilts further and further back in her chair before tumbling out of sight — taking Angus with her. Only when they are on their backs on the cobbles, legs in the air like puppies looking for a tickle, is it revealed that he has his hand stuck in her knickers.

# 24

The answer is yes. I was married. To Paul. The venue was the Green Mango Hotel, Barbados. The reason: we were both three sheets to the wind and egged on by people only marginally less foolish than we were. Bear in mind that this is an island where you decide for yourself if you're fit to drive; no one's going to stop you doing something stupid in Barbados, which is why to this day I'm still not sure how it was that we were able to take the place of the cancelled couple. He was discovered to have made another woman pregnant; she would have forgiven him if she hadn't had a new offer from his best man. But, thanks to some administrative trickery beyond the ken of a band of drunks, it seemed that anyone in possession of a passport could have got married on the beach that afternoon. Paul and I just happened to be the clowns who stepped up.

Caro, my maid of honour in a Burberry bikini (super-hip at the time), crooned 'We've Only Just Begun' as we drank our umpteenth bottle of champagne in the shallows. But rather than being the beginning, the marriage was the end. It was the wake-up call I needed that Paul was not the man for me. We'd agreed on an uncontested divorce almost before the hangover lifted and by the time we flew home I'd also sworn him to secrecy (I had work dirt on him that knocked this little misadventure into a cocked hat). Yourquickiedivorce.com handled the rest (its slogan: 'Painless, no. Quick, yes!'), and I'd be lying if I said it wasn't a magnificent relief when he later took a job overseas. Contact between us has since been limited to occasional emails and Christmas cards. Caro's companion on the trip was a client of her brother's based in the north-west, and as far as we're aware, he has also remained tight-lipped.

No one else knew: not my father, not Maggie, not a single solitary dickie bird in the office. And, a couple of years later, when he'd arrived in my life and been identified as the one I really *did* want to marry, not Charlie either.

It should never have happened. I'd almost forgotten it had.

★ ★ ★

Caro didn't come back last night; I presume she spent the night in Angus's room. Thankfully, he's in a different part of the building and so I didn't have to hear the poor boy being put through his paces, on top of everything else. It's probably just as well she didn't return, I'd probably have said some things I'd regret.

But it's morning now and I'm not blaming Caro for this. It's not her fault that I have dirty little secrets she's expected to keep. I've lost. I've lost the challenge, I've lost Meredith and, worst of all, I've lost Charlie and me, at least Charlie and me as I really want us, out in the open, legitimate, *normal*. If Meredith won't accept a

Spaniard for her eldest son then she certainly won't accept a divorcee for her favourite. A slightly older woman with a suspect job and a bawdy best friend might just have had a shot — should perfect Gemma have chosen to pass him over — but this? Not likely.

I lean out of the window and take long breaths. They feel like my last. The walkway is quiet below, the weekend tour groups long gone. How glad I am now that I'm in a different hotel from Meredith. Turning, I notice a scrap of paper pushed under the door. It's a note from Caro.

*Sorry, sorry, sorry. I will take any punishment, just don't hate me. C x*

(I could use the same words in a note to Meredith from me.) Underneath, in a less spidery hand, is a PS: **She really is sorry. Angus**.

I must speak to Meredith. Though technically we said goodbye at the end of the evening (when I looked back at the table from the bar, having fended off Doug and the frat boys as efficiently as possible, I could see Meredith and Moira in rapt conversation), I'll go on the pretext of checking for messages, try to apologise, say goodbye, claw *something* back, if not for the Charlie situation then for me.

But when I pitch up at the parador reception I find the manager has been expecting me and I am in fact twenty minutes late.

'Signorina Anna, you are here for your tour, I think?'

I'd forgotten all about it, of course, but I can't refuse now. 'Of course, just let me run back and grab my camera and notebook.'

Returning, I have a new idea. 'Could I possibly have a look at the room my friend took instead of me? I'm sure she won't mind us dropping in.'

The manager consults the ledger. 'I will show you, of course, but the maid is there, I think. Signora Grainger has checked out.'

Too late. 'OK, no problem. Let's go.'

The private courtyard is as beautiful as they've all been saying, with tinkling fountain, ancient-looking trees and antique rocking chairs. Upstairs, the room where Meredith stayed is simplicity itself, with terracotta floor tiles, an octagonal mirror, a couple of watercolours of the fort. The dark-wood furniture is austere but good quality; I imagine her walking in just days ago, her eye charmed by its unfussy lines. I wonder if I will ever see her again.

Then, as we come back down, I have my answer. She is sitting in an armchair in the far corner of the courtyard, framed by an arch and shaded by a tree, looking very Empire in stiff white linen. The expression on her face is easier to read than usual: it is one of optimism.

'I'll join you in reception, if I may,' I say to my guide.

'Of course. I shall send you in a cup of tea,' he promises.

Meredith sees me and stands, hands out in greeting. 'Anna. Good morning.'

'Hello,' I say. 'I was just taking my tour for the article. This is such a beautiful courtyard, isn't it?' Something Charlie always says occurs to me

340

now. 'Who was it who described great architecture as 'frozen music'?'

'Goethe, I think,' Meredith frowns. 'I could be wrong.'

'May I join you for a second?' I ask.

'Of course.'

I notice that there are jackets and travel bags on a third chair — Moira and Humphrey must still be about too. I imagine them on the garden swing together, bantering, bickering, discussing their children, sharing their thoughts on the trip.

'Sorry about all that craziness last night,' I say, and make an effort to look her directly in the eye. Skirting around the subject is far more excruciating than tackling it. In any case, I don't have time for skirting.

'Caro is rather high-spirited,' she says, as if in agreement.

I hold her gaze. 'No, I mean about my being married before. It was just a silly mistake. We shouldn't have done it. I was very young.' Not *that* young, I think to myself.

'It's none of my business,' Meredith says, surprised. Is that distaste in her face, or am I looking too hard to find it there?

'I know, I just wanted . . . ' I trail off, lost for an answer.

She notices the daybook in my hand. 'Did you get any drawing done in the end?' She thinks it's my sketchbook; if she only knew. That would be just about the only thing that could make matters worse.

I grip it tightly shut. 'A few little studies, but they're not very good.'

341

'Can I see?'

'Oh, do you mind if I say no? I'd like to work on them at home before I show anyone.'

'Of course, I quite understand.' There's a pause. 'You should follow your dream about the painting, you know, I can see it's in you.' So she's not even a good judge of character, can't tell a fake from the real thing. Then she says the most curious thing: 'I'm a great believer in heart over hand.'

'Heart over hand?'

'Yes, by hand I mean technical perfection. So few people have both, but if I had to choose I'd go for heart.'

Does that apply to people as well as paintings? I wonder.

'Perfectionism is a tyranny,' she declares, leaning towards me in soothsayer mode. 'Take it from me.'

'OK.' I turn to tuck the book under my legs but a waitress has appeared at my side and I don't notice her until my elbow has collided with her tray. The tea and the book fall to the ground. Shocked, I react too late and Meredith has already swooped forwards to rescue the book as the waitress, in a flurry of apologies, takes care of the broken china. To my horror, the book has landed open and face down and as Meredith turns it she glances down at the pages.

'Moira was right,' she says, looking from the page to my face.

'What?' I whisper.

What is it to be? 'Lies to Remember'? 'The Countdown Calendar'? 'Things I Know About

342

Meredith'? I know the list by heart, right down to my silly little comments in brackets: *brought up in Surrey (traditional, snobby)*; *went to university at Edinburgh: history of art (blue-stocking, dull)*; *spent a year in Vienna and likes pastries a lot (any weight issues?)* ... Or perhaps the book fell open on one of the downloaded documents about Dulwich and its various societies? Or on the printout of Angus's Art Explorers' itinerary? There are even receipts from clothes shopping expeditions and taxis stuffed deep in there.

Finally, she speaks. 'Yes, you girls are extraordinary how you're able to juggle all these things.'

She hands the book back to me and as my eyes settle on the top lines of text the befuddlement that takes hold is exactly how I imagine it must feel to emerge from a ten-year coma: *BT→ Starcom→ Ds + Ss 25×4/20×3, all adults, offer £56pscc*? It's my daybook from work. I must have brought the wrong book. Elated, I allow the clichés to rush in: this is a sign, a sign as clear as day! I'm back from the dead, salvation is mine! It's not too late for me to seize victory from the jaws of . . .

'Are you all right?' Meredith asks. 'You weren't cut?'

'No, no, I'm fine, thank you.'

The waitress mops up the spilled tea and promises a replacement without delay. Meredith and I sit back down.

'So, are you looking forward to getting back home?' I ask her, beaming.

'Actually, I'm hoping to change my flight at the airport and make an impromptu visit to Valencia.'

'To see . . . ?'

'Max,' she supplies, simply. 'My other son. I think it's time to make things up.'

'That's *wonderful*,' I say, meaning it. 'How long has it been since you've seen him?'

'Oh, years.' She can't bring herself to say how many. 'Max and I always fought, you know; we were too similar. We've always locked horns, which is natural for the child but it shouldn't be for the mother.'

To my surprise — and pride — she's using the same confiding tone as last night; could it be that that tawdry revelation of my own transgression has made me *more* accessible a confidante? For a second I almost allow myself to believe that the divorce thing is not a big deal to her, after all, that she might still consider me for Charlie . . . but, no, that's not possible. It may be no impediment to our remaining on friendly terms but a holiday cohort and a daughter-in-law are two very different beasts.

'What changed your mind?' I ask.

'I've been thinking about it for a while, I suppose, but it was Charlie who persuaded me,' Meredith says.

'Charlie?' I squeak.

'Yes, I discovered he'd been seeing Max and not telling me. He's been visiting Valencia secretly over the years. I suppose it's been more obvious to me since he's been living with me again.'

344

'It has?' I try to think. Has Charlie been to Valencia and not told me either, or has he used Valencia as an alibi for weekends spent with me? Which of us has he judged to be the more wicked in Meredith's eyes, banished brother or illicit girlfriend?

She sighs. 'I don't want to put him in a position where he has to lie to me. That's not right.'

We look at each other for a long moment.

'Of course not,' I say. 'So what made you decide . . . ?'

'Well, I spoke to him last night and he told me Max and Sara are expecting a baby. He'd just found out himself and wasn't prepared to keep it a secret. He thinks it's wonderful news and he's right.'

'Congratulations. It *is* wonderful news,' I repeat.

She spoke to him last night? Was that before or after the flamenco fiasco? And, if the latter, did she report the drama at the table? Did she mention the offending guest by name? Or did all of that pale into insignificance next to big family news like this? Of course it did. But why has Charlie not told *me*? Then I remember the call I diverted last night and my phone charging in the room; there's probably a message waiting for me with exactly this news.

'A baby changes everything, doesn't it?' I say. Jojo was never real to me without Felix, any more than Sara was to Meredith without Max's child.

'It does rather.' She looks at me. 'It's kind of

you to take such an interest.'

'It sounds as though you have an interesting family,' is all I can think of to say.

'Ah, Angus, ready for the off?'

He has appeared at my shoulder, freshly showered and obviously having held back an outfit for return travel. For some reason this causes a pang of yearning; it's the sort of sensible thing Charlie would do too. He stoops to pick up a last shard of china. 'That could hurt somebody. Meredith, the car is here for the airport.'

Meredith turns to me. 'Goodbye, Anna, and thank you again for your kindness over the rooms.'

'My pleasure.' There are no kisses exchanged, but a handshake, during which she places her left hand over the top of my right one and holds it there.

'See you in London,' Angus says to me.

It's been discussed then; he and Caro will be meeting again on home turf. I'm pleased.

'Are you OK?' he asks me when Meredith is out of earshot. 'Last night got a bit out of hand, didn't it?'

'I'm fine, yes, don't worry. We'll have to go out for dinner in London soon, that's if you don't mind me being a gooseberry.'

'Not at all. They're my favourite fruit, especially in a crumble.'

'Bye, then.'

'Bye, Anna.'

Gooseberry crumble. How did it come to this?

★ ★ ★

They've barely been gone five minutes when Caro comes flying over from our hotel, last night's make-up smudged under her eyes.

'Oh my God, oh my God, *there* you are!'

'Hi, Caro.' I brace myself for the inevitable grovelling.

'Have you not checked your messages?'

I shake my head. 'My phone's in the room charging.'

'You don't know, then?'

'Know *what*?'

She throws herself into the chair vacated by Meredith with a force that rocks it back and forth. 'I've just spoken to Steve. Nigel has gone.'

'*Nigel*? What? Gone where?'

'Left! Resigned or been sacked, we don't know. It all happened late Friday night when everyone had already left for the weekend. Then Simon was in the office this morning catching up . . . '

I roll my eyes. 'On a bank holiday Monday?'

'I know, what a sap. Anyway, he saw Nigel clearing out his office and went in to ask what was up. Apparently all he said was he was out of there. For good.' And Simon told Steve, who called Ronnie, who texted Pippa . . . Caro and I will certainly be the last to know.

'Bloody hell!' I breathe.

She looks back at me, exhilarated. 'This is it, Anna, this is your chance!'

# PART 3:
# LONDON

# 25

Only ever give an ultimatum if you have the nerve to act on it. An ultimatum is by definition a final word and if you renege on it you can't expect anyone to be listening to you the next time. You are no better than the boy who cried wolf. Did I cry wolf to Charlie, after all, that day I gave in and agreed not to tell Meredith? Just give me the summer, he pleaded, and so I have, if not quite in the way he meant.

The last time I applied for the ad director's job and didn't get it I told myself that if I failed a third time I would not try again. (I can never remember exactly who Robert the Bruce was — Angus could supply a full biography — but he certainly wasn't a woman working in the sales department of a tabloid newspaper.) I intend to hold myself to *that* promise, at least, and the first person to step forward and help me on my way is Simon. I've been in the office less than a minute when I'm told that he has already applied for the job himself, apparently staking his claim 'personally' within hours of Nigel's departure. That means he must know the home phone number of our MD, Jeremy, or — worse — Jeremy was also in the office yesterday and Simon was able to make his pitch face to face. Either way, he already has a tactical advantage.

I am not at all surprised, then, to find him ingratiating himself with my team, hands in his trouser pockets as he chortles away, jiggling his bits as if in preparation to mark his territory the more traditional way. He is charged, anyone can see that. Like me, he thought Nigel was here for a good few years and that any promotional prospects of his own would have involved the tedium of looking On The Outside. Now it's so close he can smell it.

Having spent the entire return journey from Granada in intense speculation, I find that the truth about Nigel's departure is eye-rollingly familiar: he has gone back to his comfort zone, the *Sun*. (This is a dynamic we're all too familiar with at this paper, in terms of readers as well as staff.) His secret was out when he was spotted on Friday having lunch with our great rival's MD. On his return, he was immediately called up to explain himself to his own. He then got in the lift and whizzed straight past our floor back to ground level, counting the storeys as he went. Such is the detail in Simon's account anyone would think he had already staged some sort of police reconstruction.

'It was just like Mary, Mungo and Midge,' he adds, to blank faces all round, which allows him to make a joke of the fact that he's a few years older than we are. Another point in his favour: ad directors should be closer to forty than thirty. If they are male, that is; we don't yet know if the rule applies to the female as there has yet to be one in the job, but Maggie has a theory that it is only when her age exceeds her bra size that a woman can be taken seriously in this company. (I have a horrible feeling that the opposite may be true in my particular department.)

Officially no one knew about Nigel's departure until this morning, but there are few who haven't had a weekend's head start on the gossip. By the time he came back to collect his belongings IT had wiped his hard drive and collected up any disks, but the big question is, was anything sensitive taken in advance? Like the contract file? This precious disk contains details of all the department's contracts and rates, and it would be considered a grave blow indeed if it were to find its way into the hands of the enemy.

As Nigel's PA, Rosie is best placed to cite evidence of malice aforethought but she is no sleuth at the best of times. In any case, she had a very heavy bank holiday weekend. The skin around her eyes is intensive-care blue and she has the look of someone who hasn't ingested a vitamin for a decade. When pressed, she doesn't even rule out the possibility that Nigel asked her to make a copy of the file on the very morning of his defection.

'They already know most of the stuff that's on there,' Steve says, spinning his chair from side to side. He hasn't been able to sit still all morning, none of us has.

'If he was planning to go he'd have printed it off weeks ago,' Ronnie agrees, as he himself would undoubtedly do in the same position.

'What about RingMe?' someone asks.

'Yeah, has he even rung you?' Pippa asks Rosie, misunderstanding.

She shakes her head.

'Rude bastard.'

'Least I never had to organise a collection.'

'Oh yeah, they're a right pain.'

I withdraw, sighing. Caro was right, this *is* my big chance, but after a weekend like the one I've just had, I'm not convinced I have the spirit to seize it. I force myself through the motions: I try to make an appointment to see Jeremy, but am told he's busy all morning. He will, however, be coming down presently to address the troops and has said he'd like a quick word with me then. As the most senior remaining member of the sales team, I know where the bodies are buried — all of them — so he'll want to make it clear my application is very welcome if he's to avoid a full-scale Night of the Living Dead. Even so, I should get something to him in writing first.

I stick my head round the door of my office: 'We'll do the morning meeting after Jeremy's talk, everyone.'

'Yep, Simon already said,' Pippa replies.

I bet he did. Back at my desk I compose my bid and my fingers are just hovering over the 'Send' key when I get the 'All Staff' email from HR inviting applications. The wording is exactly the same as it was last time and, if memory serves, the time before that too. 'Internal and external applications welcomed . . . Swift appointment . . . Apply promptly for a presentation brief.'

I find Simon in his business development command centre, a cramped internal office that replicates my own in its lack of size and status, and let it be known that I will be joining him as an internal applicant. He tells me that Bob, the Shire horse who runs Classified, will make it three. We agree the old duffer doesn't stand a chance.

In the days to come Simon and I will seek each other out repeatedly, pooling information about external threats to our challenge and dissecting every development as though we're running mates in a general election. We'll be the only ones who'll understand how the other feels, we'll be yin and yang (Coe and Ovett, as Simon sees it) and then, when it's all over, one of us will envy the other bitterly and the other will be too powerful to care.

'Hear anything new?' he asks, checking over my shoulder for spies.

I tell him that Nigel's predecessor at the *Sun*, Eddie, is rumoured to be relocating to Manchester for personal reasons.

'Yeah, makes sense, he's got a northern wife. Better schools, as well, d'you think?'

One can only imagine Nigel's satisfaction with the situation. For years he'd been in waiting at the *Sun*; it seemed as though he would always be the bridesmaid to Eddie's bride, which was why he allowed himself to be wooed by us in the first place. Now he's where he wanted to be all along without having had to lift a finger to make it happen; Moving Forward, his sojourn here must seem, in retrospect, little more than a bonus bit of espionage.

'At least we know Eddie won't be going for the job here,' Simon says. He's right: that would be considered an industry demotion for nothing surpasses the top slot at the *Sun*. But that still leaves all the ad managers of the other papers looking, as we are, for that first director's job, not to mention the myriad wildcard possibilities peculiar to our own MD — friends in old places, as Paul used to call them.

'Shall we get this underway, people?' We both jump at the sonic boom of Jeremy's voice from outside the doorway. Seeing him now, I realise it is a while since I've had any face-to-face contact with him. He is no looker — not enough hair, too much chin, and either vanity or dizziness causes him to remove his reading glasses every time he looks up from his notes — but that foghorn voice, combined with the silencing frown of an authoritarian parent, serves him well in situations where excitable staff must be calmed. Even the likes of Ronnie regard him with reverence as he trots out the standard spiel: 'Don't read anything ominous into this. We just need to pull together, we've got a paper to put out' and so on. I stifle a yawn.

Afterwards, as expected, he shepherds Simon and me into Nigel's office — Nigel's *old* office — and growls at us, 'I'm counting on you two to hold this together.'

I make the mistake of allowing my eye to wander covetously around the empty office and before I know it Simon is out of the starting blocks before I've even tied my shoelaces. 'I'll run the meetings till then, shall I, boss?'

'I know the day-to-day business better,' I snap back. 'You're BD, Simon.'

'I could do it standing on my head.'

'OK, well, why don't you go ahead and do the yoga while I run the meetings?'

356

Simon concedes a grin but shoots Jeremy a look that says, 'Women, what are they like?'

For his part, Jeremy regards the two of us as he might a pair of obstinate toddlers he's been tasked with separating. 'I think it makes sense for Anna to run the morning meetings for now.'

Yes! If I were six I'd shout, 'Ace!' and run and cuddle his legs. Naturally I don't, but add briskly, 'And attend the editor's meeting.' He nods. They're the ones that count; whoever does those will be acting ad director, though that title will not be used. Nor will there be very many of the meetings in question for it's rare that a national newspaper would go as long as two weeks without an ad director in place.

'I'll focus on keeping both teams motivated,' Simon says to Jeremy, agreeably. 'And give you the heads-up if there are any rumblings of note.'

'Good.'

'And what about the RingMe business?' Simon asks. 'I'll make that my priority, shall I?'

'Yep, I take it it'll be solus pop?'

'Yes,' I say, quickly. 'All or nothing.'

'Fuck. When will we know who's got it?'

There's a pause. I know what Simon's thinking because it's the same thing I am: Nigel pitched for us *against* the Sun — magnificently as it happened — and if there is any chance that he was perceived to be the difference between us then won't that now be in their favour and not ours?

'This week,' I say, at last. 'Next at the latest.'

'I'll chase it up,' Simon says. 'The marketing director is a mate.'

I grind my teeth with impatience. There can't be a man left in Christendom who hasn't heard that Simon is bosom buddies with Mike at RingMe.

'Good,' Jeremy nods. 'Right, well, the two of you need to get everyone together this morning and make sure they're all aware that we won't be losing revenue over this.'

'On to it,' Simon says.

'We're meeting now,' I add, unnecessarily.

But as we assemble for the morning meeting I find Simon already sitting in Nigel's spot at the head of the table. He's even flicking through a copy of the *Mirror*, lingering over the latest shots of Britney's booty like an old timer. He allows me to run the meeting, but the damage is done. It's an image thing: the reps' eyes are straying back to him at the end of every discussion. There's no way the team will view me as queen if someone else is in my throne. Bloody male heirs.

As the day wears on, it becomes increasingly clear there's nothing to be done with the staff by either of us. The term 'fever pitch' no longer does justice to the atmosphere here; I don't remember a buzz like this since a band of Rat Pack lookalikes were booked to play last year's summer party. I find myself torn: my instinct is to share in the demob spirit of an unexpected departure, to taste that tantalising limbo where you could do your worst and get away with it, but I'm also aware that I'm being tested, watched to see if I'm capable of *stopping* the worst from happening.

'There's no paper in the ladies' again,' Pippa

announces, coming back from the loo and scowling at Steve.

'What, like I'm the janitor now?' he grins.

'So you had to shake your lettuce,' Ronnie adds. 'Big deal.'

'I'll shake your head for you if you don't look out,' Pippa retorts, bewilderingly. 'Wanker.'

Steve gives a shout of laughter. 'Just be glad you didn't have to crimp one out, eh, Pip?'

'You're disgustin'. Anna, *tell* them!'

I hold my hands up in despair. Was it really only a day or two ago that I was standing amid the splendours of an eighth wonder? 'I have tissues in my bag . . . '

'Caro's looking for you, Anna,' someone calls.

'Oh good.' That means she must have scheduled her debrief — sorry, date — with Angus and we can discuss the best line of questioning for her to take.

Steve's eyes flicker wickedly in my direction. 'So, what *did* you and Miss Spinney get up to in Spain?'

'Tour rules,' I smile, automatically. What goes on tour stays on tour, a little rock 'n' roll code we adopted long ago for sales conferences, the real-life shenanigans of which would make Meredith and Moira choose novels over non-fiction for the rest of their days.

'Is it true that Nigel was with you?' Ronnie asks. 'Caught a plane from City straight after getting his marching orders?'

I look at him wearily. 'Why would he do that, exactly, Ronnie? Getting specialist Spanish dental care, was he?'

'Or tennis lessons, I heard . . . ' Ronnie mutters.

I can feel myself losing my rag, never a good idea with these bulls. 'Really, guys, is the truth not interesting enough for you? I would have thought there was ample to talk about already.'

''Ample', what the fuck kind of word is that?' Steve snickers.

'What the fuck kind of moron hasn't heard the word 'ample' before?'

'Alerting all staff! Sense of humour failure!' Steve crows with delight. 'Keep your 'air on, missy.'

'You're lucky this ad director thing isn't being put to the popular vote,' Ronnie says, grinning insolently.

'Yeah, a plebiscite,' Pippa pipes up.

Now all hell breaks loose. Ronnie spins a full revolution in his chair and Nick, visiting from Martin's team, even snorts coffee over the desk.

'What the fuck was that she said?'

'How's she know a word like that, then?'

'What's a 'plebiscite' when it's at home, eh? A club in Bromley?'

'It's a bar,' Pippa says, standing firm. 'In Croydon, actually. My dad told me what it meant.'

Even I have to laugh at that.

Towards the end of business I get a text message from Nigel: **You must be very surprised?**

I text back, **Nothing surprises me.**

If only that were true.

His next missive reads, **You know I put a word in for you before I left**.

If only *that* were true, too.

360

I send a long, excited email to Charlie outlining the job situation and neatly sidestepping any mention of how I chose to spend my long weekend. It's a relief to have something substantial to write about after weeks of avoiding the topic that has really consumed me. His reply, a day later, is equally thorough, including details of which museums he and Rich visited in New York, which bars they drank in, even an account of shopping at the flea market, where Rich dithered over false eyes for a dollar fifty apiece. Stopping just short of reporting air temperature and humidity levels, he signs off with the news that the project he was assigned to has been postponed and so his final two weeks with Endo will be quiet. This will allow him to explore San Francisco better and maybe even take a weekend trip to Lake Tahoe. Of Max, Meredith or the famous Gemma there is not a word, which could set all sorts of alarm bells ringing in my head, or, if I manage to be rational for the briefest of interludes, it could indicate that in the twenty minutes or so it took him to pen this mail not one key figure of *my* obsession occurred to *him*.

I am guessing that Meredith must still be in Valencia, though she is expected in Cornwall on Friday and so will presumably be back in the UK in time to prepare for the weekend. She returns to London from the coast, I believe, next Monday (even I wouldn't follow her to Cornwall, at least not when everything's kicking off at work as it is). This gives me a little breathing space, a good thing, I decide. I have a lot to consider.

A full post-mortem of the Granada expedition must wait until Caro has had a chance to quiz Angus. Of the three of us only he will know whether the damage done by Caro's revelation is irrevocable. I don't imagine for a moment that the subject didn't come up during the three-hour transfer from Granada to Malaga. Not that that stops me indulging in speculation as to my status — which I've started to think of as 'Meredith's Final View' — a truly painful ping-pong game between the euphoria I felt that early Sunday evening (and once again the next morning when I realised the books had been switched and my skin saved) and the misery of having been exposed as a scarlet woman to the only person in England who still believes such a classification exists.

One conclusion I *have* drawn is that I must finally give up on my Cinderella dream of going to the ball. It's far too late for an invitation now; Meredith would surely do such things by the book and our PR girl tells me that tradition dictates invitations be sent out at least three to four weeks before the event. Meredith wouldn't flout etiquette, I'm sure of it.

I even go back to my original mission statement and read it over and over, reliving with a little thrill that surge of purpose I felt as the words were set down:

*My aim: To become the type of woman Meredith Grainger likes (and to charm her*

*into inviting me to her sixtieth birthday party,*
*where she will 'introduce' me to Charlie).*

I'm tempted to put a line through the bracketed clause, but that would be no better than going back on an ultimatum and I don't intend ever doing that again.

# 26

It is Saturday morning and I am walking across Tower Bridge towards Caro's place. I was glad to leave the flat this morning; it has felt wrong all this week, empty and isolated, as though no one but me has set foot in it since Charlie left. I've surprised myself with a yearning to strip away the layers of neutrals and slosh a bit of colour about the place. I've even experimented with putting Yvonne's American quilt on the bed — it looked like my twin sister the virgin had just moved in.

Just as I step over the line that marks the meeting point of the two halves of the bridge ('those magnificent arms', Charlie calls them), my mobile rings and I scramble to get to it in time. If it is him it is surely a sign that everything is going to be all right. It isn't him and I berate myself for falling back on such superstitious nonsense when everyone knows you have to create your own destiny. What do I think I've been doing all summer?

'Hi, Anna, is now a good time?' It's Jill from the Dulwich Dogooders', calling to ask if I can make it to the duck ceremony next week. At first I think she means some sort of feasting club, but then I remember that the charity auction I helped with was in aid of something to do with pondlife.

I enquire as to the guestlist, eventually having

to get specific and say, 'What about my new friends from Spain, the Pooles and Meredith Grainger?'

'No, all busy, I'm afraid.' Jill adds that Meredith, though the generous donor of Edwardian egg cups at the auction, isn't in fact especially keen on the duck world, being more of a 'tit and thrush sort' who enjoys birds from the comfort of a garden chair. So now I know.

'It's hard for me to take time off during the week,' I tell her, 'but I'll do my damnedest.'

'Okey-dokey. Toodle pip!' she says. (She really does.)

*　★　*

The first thing Caro says when she sees me is: 'You're not going to like this.'

'What?' I say.

'Hang on.' She motions for me to sit on a circular rug big enough for a helicopter to land on in the middle of her living room, before disappearing off to fetch coffee. This turns out to be a lengthy process as their new machine has more controls than a flight deck and by the time she returns she's taking a phone call.

More restless than I realised, I get up again and wander around the room. The flat is a stunning split-level space with three bedrooms, two bathrooms and a proximity to Tower Bridge of the kind Americans think all Londoners enjoy. We are so close that the succession of iron balconies along the façade of the building feels like splinters from the ribs of the great giant.

Even though clouds cover the city today in a dense, oppressive husk, it feels sunlit in here and I wonder, romantically, if it's because this is where I met Charlie; I'm standing on the very spot where our first conversation took place. David Harding, who has as much sense as money, has added quite a bit of furniture since then, mostly costly design classics familiar even to the uneducated eye (or at least to those who, like me, have been dragged by partners to the Design Museum next door).

David is currently in bed, alone, sleeping off the effects of a four-figure client dinner, and won't be seen before noon. Caro is prepared to receive me this morning only because she got it into her head to despatch Angus to his own flat last night after a kissing-only close to the date — 'like the opposite of prostitution,' she explained sweetly — and have a once-in-a-blue-moon early night.

'Jesus, do they have to ring this early?' she grumbles to herself, off the phone now. 'The delivery's not till this afternoon. David's bought *another* chair. The new lamps look good, don't they?' She gently pats what looks like a paper palm tree. 'He found some designer in Leeds to make them.'

'Lovely. So what am I not going to like?' I remind her, sitting down next to her.

'Oh yes. Brace yourself.'

'What?'

'Angus thinks Charlie is gay.'

'What?'

'And he reckons Meredith thinks the same.'

'*What?*'

'Stop saying 'what?'.'

'Why?' I can't help raising my voice. 'For God's sake, Caro, Charlie's the least gay man I know.'

'Hardly,' she says, amused. 'What about the pack of alpha males we work with?'

'Well, apart from them.'

She separates a chocolate muffin top from its base and bites at the edge. 'Think about it. He's very artistic and sensitive. He left management consultancy to become an architect.'

I interrupt: 'Architecture is not a gay profession. They stomp around building sites in hard hats half the time.'

'There you go! It's the Village People factor!'

I roll my eyes. I hope she's got something more sensible than this to report.

'And think about it, babe, he's desperately shielding his real self from his family. Angus says Meredith definitely knows he's hiding something and not just the Valencia trips.'

I spoon cappuccino foam into my mouth with the little sugar swizzle stick Caro has provided for sweetener. 'He's hiding *me*, you noodle. If he was so busy pretending not to be gay, wouldn't he be flaunting me to his family, not keeping me a secret? I'd be his cover, wouldn't I, his beard?'

She giggles.

'And he's always had girlfriends, Meredith has *met* them. What about Jessica, the one he almost lived with?'

Now it's her turn to roll her eyes. 'The world is full of gay men who've almost lived with girlfriends.'

367

'Well, what about the sex? The sex is great.'

'Gay men have sex with women all the time, they're always fathering children,' she says, decisively. 'If you read the papers a gay man is practically more likely to conceive than half the women in this country over thirty-five.'

'The papers lie,' I remind her.

'True.'

We sit for a moment in distracted silence. 'You forgot the key evidence,' I point out sarcastically. 'He's currently in San Francisco, so he *must* be gay. Hey, how do you think he gave Meredith the slip when she was out there and he felt the need to satisfy his carnal urges with some neighbourhood ass?'

Caro laughs, abandons the muffin and lights herself a cigarette. I recognise the ashtray as having been nicked from the restaurant downstairs.

'OK, chum, it's just a theory. Besides, it's hard for me to argue the case properly, isn't it, when Angus thinks I only know what he's told me? I can't tell him I know Charlie's great in bed, can I? That he's definitely got a girlfriend? He thinks I've never met the guy.'

I nod uncertainly. I never expected to have to deal with the additional complication of Caro and Angus and if I wasn't losing sleep over the ad director's job I'd be losing it over these two all right, in particular over the prospect of her getting drunk again and blurting out the truth about my secret scheming to a roomful of Dulwich doyennes. At the very least she is going to crack and confide in Angus and Lord only knows where that will lead. As a pre-emptive strike, just this morning I dropped a reference into an email to Charlie: **Bit of gossip: Caro has got together with someone who says he knows you from school. Angus Poole. Do you remember him?**

It was not a move I made without serious thought, for Charlie will not like this development one little bit — from total segregation to two degrees of separation in one fell swoop — and the last thing I need is him running scared at this stage in the game. Will he accept the small world theory I'm hoping to get away with peddling, or will he suspect meddling straight away?

I drain my coffee, feeling grumpy. Now David's impeccably eclectic chair collection annoys me, as does the witty lighting and the fact that his coffee machine is too complicated for me to bother asking for a refill. *He*'s the one who's gay, not Charlie.

'So did Angus say if they mentioned me on the way to the airport? They *must* have discussed what happened on Sunday night.'

'I don't know. He concentrated mainly on the gay theory,' Caro says, newly contrite. 'Anyway, I don't think old people are salacious gossips like us.'

'I don't think they consider sixty to be old,' I say, 'and I can assure you they are gossips all right. Just think how they discussed everyone who's ever set foot in Dulwich Picture Gallery.'

'OK.' She looks at me through the cigarette smoke. 'I'll talk to him today and find out if they mentioned you being married.'

'Divorced,' I say, stonily. I can't decide whether I should have a cigarette myself or just get up and go. 'Nothing else, then?'

'Well . . . ' She looks sheepish, a sight so rare I'm immediately on my guard. 'He did mention the party.'

I'm left gasping at the ease of the manoeuvre. Apparently Meredith suggested to Angus that he bring a guest to her party, Angus duly asked Caro, and she's in. Only now do I consider that this might have been a better approach for me: the Trojan horse. Should I have flirted with Angus and got in that way? Would he have fallen for me as categorically as he did Caro? Perhaps not.

'She's putting a formal invitation in the post,' Caro says. 'Angus says she doesn't recognise the concept of 'plus one' and likes to send separate invitations to unmarried couples.'

So she *is* issuing late invitations. Well, at least I'll be able to see one of these elusive prizes, *touch* it.

'Don't worry,' Caro says, 'you'll get your invitation too. She *loved* you.'

'I don't think so,' I say, but without self-pity, for I can't think of anything else I could have done for this campaign; I simply couldn't have worked harder.

'You could come with us to the party,' Caro adds. 'No one would mind.'

'Thanks, but this is not something I want to blag. It's not one of your perfume launches.'

'Fragrance,' she corrects me. 'Anyway, maybe

370

Angus will see Meredith this weekend and get more feedback for us?'

'She's out of town,' I say. 'Visiting her sister-in-law on the Cornish coast.'

'What, did you put a chip in her neck?' Caro laughs.

'That's my *next* evening class. Surveillance for Beginners.'

'Oh, you're no beginner,' she says. And she doesn't appear to have realised I was joking.

★   ★   ★

**I know Angus**, Charlie replies, later that day. **How on earth did those two meet? Would have thought they were chalk and cheese.**

I ignore the first question and answer the second. **People are never as different as you think. She says they've really hit it off.**

He responds in the form of a cryptic crossword clue: **Some cheese does taste like chalk, I suppose.** What's that supposed mean? Or is he just thinking about bland American dairy products? He certainly doesn't seem worried, which is odd. Wouldn't it occur to him Angus might tell Moira that he and Caro have friends in common and that she might then mention it to Meredith? What's more, shouldn't he be worrying that the same chain of communication might bring news of his friendship with Gemma back to me? He knows I trust him, of course, but given the circumstances of our parting, isn't he the least bit keen to protest his innocence?

It's almost as though he's tracking my

371

thoughts in real time, because the next message that pops up says, **Have you met him yet?**

I think carefully before replying to this, still clinging as I am to the idea that omission is nobler than outright fibbing. **Yes,** I type. **He seems like a decent guy. I didn't mention I know you, of course, but I gather that his parents are friends with your mother? Small world — maybe we don't need all your new bridges after all!**

His final reply is unambiguous enough: **Tread carefully.**

**I always do.**

I log off with the distinct feeling that warnings have been exchanged.

★ ★ ★

Caro is right, I do receive an invitation: a phone message from Moira inviting me for coffee chez Poole the following Tuesday. She and Meredith are meeting to look at their Granada photographs and they'd love to see some of my photos and sketches if I happen to be free to bring them.

I have no compunction in inventing a doctor's appointment and taking the morning off work. It's been hell trying to keep things together in the office. Without proper direction (for 'proper' read 'male'), the boys are taking liberties. Only yesterday Nick called in sick with tales of food poisoning and an agonising A&E stomach pump. Thursday's ropey lunch at the local pizzeria was blamed and a complaint put in to the manager. Not long after, however, one of Simon's team,

Beth, called in with exactly the same story. His and hers stomach pumps: nice. Except Beth wasn't at the lunch, but out of the office all day with a client. What's more she and Nick were spotted in the evening with their tongues entwined at First Edition.

Leaky alibis: the constant mopping-up is getting to me.

# 27

Dulwich suits the end of summer. The leaves are yellowing but not yet falling and the effect is of a canopy of fluorescent green as you walk through the parks and streets. I gather from snippets of pavement conversation that the new school term has recently begun and that this has created 'pandemonium' about the place, but it still strikes me as miraculously tranquil. None of my father's grumbles about the traffic in Hampstead and Highgate apply here, at least not on this particular Tuesday mid-morning in September.

Moira's house is just off the high street in a narrow lane that has about it the kind of hush that would point to a body of residents if not absent then certainly ageing. Her front door has none of the grandeur of Meredith's entrance, with its winding pathway and well-stocked garden to shield her from passers-by, but opens directly on to the pavement. Even so, it doesn't feel vulnerable: all is safe in Dulwich, and were someone daft enough to attempt a burglary, he'd soon be seen off by a neighbour with a seven iron.

Moira welcomes me with a smile of real warmth; you would almost believe we were old friends and, with a start, I realise that that is something I would quite like. As I follow her into the house I can smell baking and hear the tumbling of laundry, am momentarily overcome with gratitude that she would choose to invite me here. It's homely in that old-fashioned family style that Jojo — or I for that matter — seems to have no interest in cultivating. And to think that not so long ago I sneered at her marmalade loaf.

'Your house is lovely,' I say, noticing how well lit and fresh the rooms are, the carpet pile as well tended as a prize lawn. Somehow I would have imagined Moira and Humphrey to be living amid tartan wallpaper and faux-Victorian oil lamps, but it is all surprisingly contemporary. There are lots of framed travel shots in the living room and some paintings that defy the classifications I've learned in my evening class. Abstract or figurative? Kind of both. Pastel or chalks, I'm afraid I can't tell either way.

'It's a bit crowded,' Moira says, apologetically. 'We used to have a bigger house on Burbage Road, just a few streets down.'

'I know it,' I say. 'It's near the tennis club, isn't it?'

'That's right. We moved when Angus and Clara left home. Downsizing, they call it now, don't they?'

'Do you miss the space?' I ask, peering through French doors at a compact patio crammed with stone pots.

'Only the garden,' she says. 'And we looked on to cricket fields, that was very nice. It wasn't like being in London at all.'

There it is again, the area slogan: London without letting on. It strikes me that the only way this neighbourhood has managed to retain its air of being a best-kept secret is through the efforts of its residents. They are, to a man, what the papers call 'tireless busybodies', a type, now I come to think of it, that's not so far removed from my own.

I can tell which is Humphrey's customary chair by the ancient indentation in the seat cushion. There are newspapers stacked in a wicker rack nearby and I don't need to go through them to know there are no copies of my own breathless organ.

'Is Humphrey well?'

'Yes, thank you, a touch of sinusitis, but nothing serious. He's playing golf. He has a regular Tuesday round at the club.'

'Nothing gets in the way of the golf,' I smile. 'I like your hair, by the way, Moira. It really suits you.' She's had it feathered around the ears and neck, exposing quite a bit of skin. It probably feels quite daring to have shorn off some of that protective bowl just as the warm weather is fading and I wonder what made her do it. Does she pat at it in that mahogany mirror in the hallway and remember the styles of her youth? What does it feel like to be married for this long — thirty-seven years, Meredith said, and I can't imagine that the Pooles are too far behind — and to find yourself with all this time on your hands, rediscovering yourself right down to the little bit of pink skin behind your earlobes you haven't seen for fifteen years? Does she feel attractive? Does she care whether Humphrey notices her in that way any more?

'How are you finding being back at work after that lovely Spanish break?' she asks me.

I don't point out that of the four days spent in Granada just one had to be taken as official leave, for people who live their lives outside of offices rarely have the same sense of passing time. Mondays, Fridays, one o'clocks and five-thirties: all approach and slip by with none of the same brouhaha.

'There's a bit of a crisis going on, as it happens,' I say, 'but you don't want to know, Moira, believe me.' And she doesn't, it would be beyond her. I try to imagine her fielding the quips as she emerges from the under-the-stairs cloakroom: 'Remember to shake your lettuce, Moira?' It's unthinkable.

She goes to check on the coffee and I take the opportunity to look at framed photos on the mantelpiece and the shelves of a nearby cabinet. Almost all depict one, other or both of the Poole children. It's funny but part of what I've yearned for during my bid for Meredith's approval is access to material like this, to be invited to laugh and coo over pictures of Charlie and Max as swaddled babies, uniformed schoolboys, sulking adolescents. Angus was a very cute child in the curly-haired chorister mode; Caro will enjoy giggling over these if she hasn't done already. The sister, on the other hand, seems to have started out as the classic duckling, and her slow transformation into swan is painstakingly chronicled (no wonder she doesn't bring the Shepherd's Bush boyfriend home too often).

'How old were you when you had Angus?' I ask Moira as she comes in with the coffee cups. 'If you don't mind me asking.' She must have been older than Meredith was when she had her first baby if the two women are a similar age and Max several years older than Angus.

'Twenty-nine,' she says, 'which was considered rather elderly then. We had some trouble . . . Let's just say we felt very blessed when Angus came along. And Clara was nothing short of a miracle!'

Blessings, miracles, this is how these women describe their offspring, even the more well balanced among them. Do grown-up children have any idea how adored they once were? And still are? Charlie, I suspect, may be one of the few who does.

'You worked before then?'

'Yes, and afterwards for a time. I was a music teacher. I still do a few private lessons here and there.'

'I didn't realise.' How little I know of her, or how little I've listened. I wonder rather shamefully if she sensed my greater interest in Meredith during those mealtime conversations at the parador. Was I too dismissive in my haste to get past her, and, worse, did I encourage Caro to be the same? *I prefer Meredith to Moira*, that's what she said. *Moira shouldn't go bare-legged . . . her calves are like sausages.* The mother of these two children deserves better from us than that.

And then I see it, on the mantelpiece, propped against the wall behind an ebony photo frame, in exactly the stiff, gold-edged card you'd expect Meredith to choose. The invitation. Mesmerised, I peer at the words: *Mrs Meredith Grainger requests the pleasure of your company* . . .

The doorbell rings and I jump out of my skin. As Moira goes to greet Meredith, all feelings of cosy security desert me: I'm back in the taxi winding towards the Puerto del Justicía; I'm walking down the path to the Dulwich Picture Gallery wearing shapeless clothes and carrying that awful straw bag (actually I *am* carrying that awful straw bag); my secret is out and they're all staring at me in horror . . .

'Anna, how lovely to see you again.'

'You too, Meredith!' I don't bob forward with a kiss on her cheek as I did instinctively with Moira, but hold out my hand and keep a more formal distance.

Her hair looks longer and fuller, as though months have passed, and her wide-set eyes are defined with brown powdery pencil. Navy cotton jeans and T-shirt look casual but are both minutely pressed. She looks refreshed, happy.

'How was Cornwall?' I ask as we sit.

'Oh, very blustery. But the food was magnificent.' She eyes the cakes Moira has arranged on the coffee table. 'Moira, is that a cherry sponge? How *perfect*. I'm going to have a piece straight away.'

Moira fusses with the cake slice and, misgivings forgotten for now, I focus on Meredith. 'Did you say it was your sister who lives there?'

'My sister-in-law. Her house is beautifully situated, right on the edge of a headland overlooking the sea. It's art deco, with curves and lots of windows, and when the weather is

379

wild like that it feels as though, goodness, as though you're being whisked in a glass bowl.' This is a very Charlie kind of description, the rhythm of their voices is the same, the narrowing of the eyes as they make one of those comments about how a place or an object or building moves them.

'Does she live there with her husband?'

'She's widowed,' Meredith says, adding 'as well' in a smaller voice, as though she's still getting used to the label and applies it to herself only with a sense of wonder, as though there must be some mistake.

'I'm sorry.'

'That's kind of you, but I think she does very well, generally.'

Moira's cherry cake has a photogenic cracked crust and lovely crumbly consistency. She tells us of the organic unsalted butter she has discovered for her baking that you can order over the phone, much easier than the Internet, which she finds rather baffling. I relax again and listen to her updating Meredith on local news. Then they discuss the new exhibition at the gallery. (Meredith likes it, finds the pictures 'comforting'; Moira isn't convinced, she got through the whole thing in five minutes.)

I finish my cake and take a breath. 'And how did you get on in Valencia, Meredith?'

Moira looks surprised at the sudden change of subject and rattles her sugar spoon on her coffee cup just a fraction too long, but Meredith just smiles, her shoulders sinking in satisfaction.

'That went very well, thank you. I was just

380

telling Moira yesterday that I think Max and I may have reached some sort of *rapprochement*.'

I'm not a hundred per cent sure what this means, but it's obviously good. 'That's wonderful. Do you think he'll visit London soon?'

'I'm very much hoping he will, after the baby comes.'

I want her to say he will be in town for her birthday and that I must drop by and meet him, meet *both* her boys, make myself a part of such a special occasion. I can't believe I'm still thinking about the party; it must be because I can just see a corner of gold behind Moira's photo frames and knick-knacks.

'You know, there are congratulations cards for grandparents these days,' Moira tells Meredith. 'I noticed some in the gift shop yesterday. It's quite an industry, apparently.'

'I'm starting to realise,' Meredith says. 'And thank goodness they haven't invented some ghastly euphemism for grandma. I'm perfectly happy with the original.'

'You're so lucky to be expecting a wee baby,' Moira says. 'And Charlie will be a wonderful uncle.'

'Yes, he'll be building bridges out of Lego, won't he, and lecturing the poor thing on spatial experience and God knows what else?'

For a terrifying, dislocated moment I wonder if it were I who made this last remark, and, if so, whether or not it betrayed a level of knowledge that really couldn't be laughed off. But it is Meredith who laughs, Meredith who spoke, Meredith who has that public right.

There has still been no mention from Charlie of the extraordinary Grainger family break-through. Surely its enormous significance can't have passed him by? He *has* to see it as a sign that Meredith is mellowing. Or perhaps it merely confirms for him that since she's compromised so irrevocably with one son there is now less hope than ever for the other? With a sudden ache in the stomach that makes me put my cake aside, I want Charlie back. I want him whichever way it has to be, back to how it was, Charlie on his terms, Charlie on any terms. Granada was one thing (and, I admit, one immense thing), but the intimacy of a shared cake in Moira's sitting room while future generations of Graingers are discussed seems suddenly a step too far. *Charlie will be a wonderful uncle.* Will he? I absolutely cannot imagine it. It seems to me that the more I get to know of his family and his life here in Dulwich, the stranger he becomes to me.

Moira's voice breaks my reverie. 'Let's have a look at some pictures, shall we? I spent all of last night sorting out my best ones.'

It's jolting to see images of the Alhambra. I show them some of the digital shots on my laptop and they are fascinated as much by the technology as the images, which are not spectacular but decent enough to have passed muster with Maggie ('Not bad at all, must have been beginner's luck'). Their own prints, all well-composed vistas and thoughtful close-ups, remind me of those concertinaed strips of postcards you tear off one by one along the serrated folds. Maybe it's the printing but the colours are hardly as vivid as those I've just seen during my walk from West Dulwich station. Was Granada really so special, or did we just imagine it? And those *Tales of the Alhambra* that I scanned so eagerly for parallels with my own plight, weren't they just ridiculous fantasies?

'The paradox of travel,' says Meredith, reading my thoughts. 'You feel a place so deeply when you're there, its history, its uniqueness, its *smell*, it's as if nowhere else exists. But when you leave it's like you were never there, just something you read in a fairytale.'

'That's it,' I agree, staring at her. 'That's *exactly* what I was just thinking.'

She looks back at me and that connection passes between us again, that closeness I felt in Granada. There is something so persuasive about her, so beguiling, she doesn't so much speak to me as cast out and draw me in. Is it charisma, *charm*, pure and simple, the very same human magic I've been trying to use on her? Whatever it is, it is the same thing Charlie has and it seems to inspire in me something near to . . . hero-worship. Not quite my original plan, admittedly.

The two women admire my mother's pen-and-ink sketches, which I pass off as my own with a modesty I don't have to fake. Meredith uses the word 'fine' a great deal and I can tell she and Moira are surprised by 'my' talent.

'What inks have you used here? The shading already looks so beautifully faded.'

'It's a grey-brown rather than a black,' I improvise, half-buoyed and half-shamed by their praise.

What would my mother have said if she'd known her private work would be studied in this way? I have a feeling she wouldn't have minded. 'She'd do anything for you,' Dad said to me years ago, 'anything at all.' I wish he'd said it more.

'The medium suits the subject so well,' Meredith says. 'I always think that's the key to that feeling of true satisfaction you get when you see something very good.'

'Thank you,' I say, 'but I'm really just a beginner.'

'What about art school, Anna?' Moira asks. 'Are you still thinking of applying?'

Now I do call on a prepared response. 'I've decided not to, actually, Moira. I don't see how I can give up working; it won't be possible financially. And in a funny way I always think that when your hobby becomes your work you lose your passion for it.'

They nod sympathetically.

'Has your son found that?' I ask Meredith, daringly. 'I assume architecture was a passion of his before he took it up?'

'It was a family passion, really,' Meredith replies, turning the page. 'My uncle was an architect, a rather successful one, as it happens. But, no, Charlie is working far too hard to have any regrets.'

'He's not a quitter,' Moira chips in, as though she's read the word in the newspaper and wants to hear how it sounds aloud.

Meredith nods. 'The San Francisco placement has really opened his eyes and he was very lucky to get a place at the Bartlett, I think he realises that now.'

'It was very last minute,' Moira says lightly.

Meredith sends her friend a look of mild exasperation. 'He originally declined the place,' she explains to me, 'and was lucky enough to be given a second chance when he changed his mind again.'

I nod, knowing the history already. Charlie changed his mind when his father died, taking with him the last opposition to the scheme. I make a mental note to check the school's website for Friends or whatever they call them there; perhaps Meredith made a sizeable donation to ease the path of her favourite son? Then I cancel the thought. Why am I still asking questions? Shouldn't the investigation be closed by now?

I gather up the sketches and return them to their folder.

'You're so talented,' Meredith says, 'perhaps you could do some sort of advanced painting course part time?'

'Perhaps.' If they could see me sitting in that semicircle with the other philistines enrolled on the Looking at Pictures course, being shown the difference between the marks made with a brush and with a knife (Session 4: Techniques), or playing that game where we had to look at a reproduction of a famous picture and remember all the objects in it (Session 7: Symbols), they wouldn't believe their eyes.

'You can always go back to it later in life,' Moira says. 'You'll have plenty of time when you're our age.'

'The important thing is to keep painting,' Meredith says. 'You'll find a balance.' Before she leaves she turns to Moira and says, 'We must talk to Angus about organising Seville.'

'Oh yes,' Moira says, excited. 'He's already been researching hotels.'

Meredith is far too well mannered to make a joke, as I would, about avoiding mix-ups with hotel rooms this time. 'We must try to go during Semana Santa if we can.'

The photos and the sketches are tucked away, the laptop clicked shut. Granada really is forgotten. They've moved on to Seville, but where am I going next?

★   ★   ★

On my way back to the station I decide to visit the picture gallery. The exhibition is called 'Undiscovered Victorians' and I'm soon wondering if there wasn't a good reason for them to have been languishing unsung for so long. I have to agree with Moira on this one; there's nothing comforting about crusty portraits of middle-aged men who look as though they're deciding who to give a damn good whipping the second the sitting is over. Fiddling in my bag to turn my mobile back on (I didn't dare risk it ringing in Meredith's presence), I find the old glasses I wore for that first meeting with her. I prop them on the end of my nose and peer over the top, amusing myself by pretending to be Marilyn Monroe in *How to Marry a Millionaire*.

'You don't like?' a voice asks me from a couple of portraits away.

I look past the two sour faces that separate us and see a slight man with hair like the bristles of a broom. 'Personally I love this sort of austerity,' I say, pompously. 'I find it comforting. But you can understand why people would wet their knickers when Monet came along.'

'That's one way of looking at it.' He looks at me with a rather sorrowful smile. He's not hapless, exactly, but he has an air of having been unexpectedly stood up, abandoned even. Or maybe I need to stop being so melodramatic and consider that he might, like me, just be killing time.

'Do you work here?' I ask, noticing he is not wearing a jacket or carrying anything in his hands.

'No, but I live nearby. I've just moved to the area, actually.'

'Oh, I'm looking for a place around here, too,' I say, then take off the silly glasses and slide them in the nearest bin. If he finds anything odd about this he doesn't say so. 'What I mean is I was thinking of looking around here, but I wasn't really serious. I live in St Katharine's Dock. By the river.'

'It would be, I suppose.' In the same spirit of random exchange, he adds, 'I'm divorced.' There is definitely an experimental air about this pronouncement, as though he's testing its newness. Perhaps he's just considering getting divorced and wonders what it will feel like to say it to a new person. Only a stranger will do. Then, when he gauges his own response, he'll make his decision. Either way, I sense my heart sinking and am amazed by my own hypocrisy.

'Me too,' I say, firmly. 'I'm divorced, as well.'

'I wanted to stay close to the kids,' he says. So that's where the sorrow comes in. 'It won't be long before they're leaving home and then, well, then that will be it.'

'Leaving home?'

He watches me with amusement. 'Do you realise you just gasped?'

I laugh, embarrassed. 'Sorry, it's just that you seem too young to have children old enough to be leaving home soon.'

'Teenagers,' he confirms. 'I suppose I started too young, hence the irretrievable breakdown.'

I nod. 'Do you know anyone else around here?'

'One or two.'

'Meredith Grainger?' I have an idea that I'm saying her name just to hear myself say it, to boast aloud that I know her, legitimately, that we can be mentioned in the same breath because we are friends and have just had coffee and cake together.

'No,' he says.

'What about the Pooles? Or Eric and Jill? I've forgotten their surname.'

He chuckles. 'Sorry, I don't know any Graingers or Pooles or Forgotten-their-Surnames. I'm really not part of the scene, I'm afraid.'

There's something about this encounter, possibly the stirring of desire behind my waistband, that reminds me of the student in the

Albaicín, my karaoke suitor, Doug.

'What's your name?' I ask, suspiciously. 'I mean, I'm Anna Day, pleased to meet you.'

'Daniel. Pleased to meet you, too.' He obviously thinks I'm deranged, but gives me his card anyway.

Not knowing what else to do, I turn to go.

He calls after me, 'I don't suppose they can afford the Impressionists, but I'll keep my fingers crossed for you.'

And when I look back he is holding out his hands to show me.

# 28

Caro once asked Charlie, 'So she's minted, your mum, is she?' and he just shrugged and looked unimpressed. Of all the accusations levelled at him over the Meredith situation the one he most dislikes is the (true) one that he is funded by her.

'Comfortable, I suppose,' he muttered, when he saw she was expecting an answer. 'It's not like she's the Queen or anything.'

'I think we know that, more like Maggie Thatcher,' Caro said, winking at me because the two of us had only recently coined the nickname The Iron Mother for my *bête noire*.

For my part, I've never tried to discuss money with him. Considering I sell for a living and work in an environment where it's perfectly natural to ask how much a gift cost straight after you've opened it, I've always felt peculiarly uneasy about it. Maybe it's precisely because I *can* put a price to everything that I don't want to know what sum it is that I might not be worth to him — a sum that doubled overnight when Max voted with his feet. I wonder if Meredith has now returned it to its original size.

Just once, Charlie brought the subject up himself. We'd just had dinner at Dad's and a recent delivery of antique furniture had lent the Day residence a new lavishness.

'Your friends are so curious about my mother being comfortably off,' he said, as the taxi pulled away (he would never use the word 'rich' or even 'wealthy'), 'but what about your father? You're set to inherit a bit, as well, aren't you?'

I laughed. 'Quite apart from the fact that my father is still breeding, he's also completely self-made.'

'So?'

'So self-made men always think their offspring should understand how it feels to earn their own crust. They don't believe in handouts.'

'I don't find that,' Charlie said. 'It's all the same.' He looked out of his window at the latest street to be dubbed a millionaire's row (now 'two a penny' in this part of London, according to the *Sun*), and turned back to me. 'There's really no difference between us, you know.'

'If there was really no difference,' I said, 'we'd have just spent the evening with Meredith, wouldn't we?'

I wondered why he insisted on defending his corner when he was so easily knocked out. But he surprised me with the ferocity of his next remark. 'You think I don't want that too? Rather than another evening with that . . . that *trophy* wife?'

'Jojo isn't all bad,' I said. 'And she speaks very highly of you.'

But it was too late for jokes. We lapsed into silence, each of us considering the evening we'd spent and the parents from whom we could never imagine breaking free.

I needn't add who paid for the cab.

★　★　★

Meredith isn't the only one throwing a party this month. My father and Jojo are having a get-together to celebrate their fifth wedding anniversary and I've been summoned for Sunday lunch at their house to discuss arrangements. As often occurs when their au pair and their nanny share a day off, I must talk to the parents in turn while the other handles the baby — if you can still call Felix a baby now he's tottering around all over the place like some sort of intoxicated hobbit.

'You and Charlie will be able to make it, of course?' Dad asks.

'I will,' I reply, lightly, trying not to put too much emphasis on the 'I'.

'What about Charlie? He's back by then, isn't he?'

'Yes, next week. I'll need to check his diary but I'm sure it will be fine.'

Dad waits impatiently for me to meet his eye. 'You're still being very mysterious about what happened down in Granada. You know, Jojo's so curious she's on the verge of hunting down this woman herself?'

Now there's an idea that makes me very nervous indeed. 'Nothing happened,' I say quickly. 'It was a success, I think. We got to know each other and I guess we're friends now.'

'Well, if it was such a success I suppose we'll be meeting her at some point,' he says.

I imagine Jojo planning a meeting of the in-laws, she the young cross-generational star of the production, and treating Meredith to one of her brisk all-mothers-are-equals nods. 'So *you're* the famous mother. Anna's been in such a tizzy about you.'

'In my own time,' I say, trying not to shudder. I'm starting to understand how Charlie might have come about his compartmentalisation solution.

'In your own time,' Dad repeats. This was a founding tenet of his parenting philosophy. As a child I was allowed to apologise in my own time, eat in my own time, tidy my room in my own time. In a way it worked, for when he did say 'now' I jumped.

Jojo returns, counting steps with Felix. ' . . . three, four, five, clever boy! Anna, I was just saying to Clive this morning how nice it will be to see Charlie again.'

Cold-blooded though I sometimes consider her, Jojo has enough of a woman's pulse to be very keen on Charlie. She wasn't the first to admire my taste in ravishing bone structure and come-to-bed vocals, but she was the first to make me slightly protective of it. The last thing I needed was her setting her cap on my dream man, just as she once had my father. But as it turned out, Charlie's bereavement brought out something maternal in her and whenever they meet she fusses rather than flirts.

'What a shame you weren't together for our wedding,' she says. 'He would have looked lovely in the photos.'

'Jojo, he's my third boyfriend since then! I've only known him a year and a bit!'

'I know, but it seems like he's been around for ever.'

I went to their wedding on my own, the groom's dateless daughter who was older than the bride. Technically, Paul should have been by my side but the happy couple had specified low key and Paul was genetically incapable of low key. While others content themselves with throwing confetti in the general direction of the bride and groom, he's the sort to rugby-tackle them to the ground and shave off their eyebrows. One wedding we attended together ended sourly when Paul was among those to keep the groom up all night doing tequila shots while the bride wept in the four-poster upstairs. She refused to speak to either of us again.

'Look, here's my favourite photo from the big day.' Jojo hands me a framed picture of Dad and her on the steps of Marylebone Register Office.

It's impossible to look at it without thinking of the corresponding shot of Mum and him from 1971 — and not just because he hasn't changed that much in the interim. It's how Jojo did her hair that day, full on top and straight over her shoulders, the way she sculpted the contours of her eyelids with dark shadow while leaving her lips quite pale, it gave her such an authentic look of the earlier era. I wondered if Dad's older friends noticed, too, or if it was just me. The union was celebrated with a wedding breakfast at Jojo's favourite restaurant in Primrose Hill. Photos were black-and-white reportage style, the photographer skulking around and sneaking shots from unexpected angles, which caused one guest to trip and almost fall into a potted plant. It felt like the wedding of someone famous.

Maybe Jojo wanted to feel like one of Dad's celebrities that day. Maybe she was looking to outshine a ghost.

In any case, I didn't tell Paul the wedding had taken place until after the event, brushing it off as a surprise thing. Recovering from a weekend that had included some sort of fifteen-pint challenge with his mates, he didn't appear to register the slight.

'Now I've tried everything,' Jojo says to me, when Dad has been sent to replenish Felix's juice, 'I think I know what ranks above everything else in terms of the female experience.'

'What's that?' Tried everything, honestly, I think, mentally rolling my eyes. Try poverty, Jojo, try prison, try proper *work*.

She holds my eye for a charged moment like some sort of veteran TV interviewer lining up the killer question, then says, 'Your first pregnancy. It's like nothing else. The connection I felt with Felix was so different from any other relationship I've had before or since. There's nothing like a mother's love for her first child, even before it's born.'

I'm struck as usual by her sureness that it's all about her, something quite different from the arrogance you see when other mothers elect themselves spokeswomen for the fertile masses. It's purer than that; she speaks with the wonder of the pioneer, as though she really is the first to discover a woman may have an emotional bond with her foetus. But, as usual with Jojo, what she says does interest me. If it's true, that must be what my mother felt about me — *like nothing else*. I like that.

I must be thinking slowly today, for it is only when I get home that I realise that what Jojo was really doing during that conversation was dropping an almighty hint. She only knows the first pregnancy is so different because she has another one to compare it with. Felix and I are getting a sibling.

★ ★ ★

Anyone would think current affairs have been suspended the way the race for ad director now consumes our department to the exclusion of all else. Frank Sinatra could be posthumously elected president of the United States — with Elvis as his gay lover — and it would be less interesting than the fact that Danny from the *Star* was seen entering the building at one-thirty and leaving two hours later looking a bit cheeky. As far as I'm aware, the job has now been offered and declined at least twice: first to Danny, of course, and then to Rod, an old-timer at the *Mirror*. Simon asked Jeremy outright about the latter and was told that the rumour was 'categorically wrong'. We then spent some time discussing the implications of this tricksy denial: did he mean categorically wrong as in factually incorrect, or categorically wrong as in anyone found to be perpetuating such an untruth was behaving immorally? Would our MD even bother to pay us the compliment of enigmatic wordplay? Wouldn't he simply lie through his teeth? Such are the debates that engage us at the moment;

it's a miracle the paper's going out with ads in it and not page after page of blank boxes.

The internal interviews are on Thursday morning, the brief strikingly similar to the last one: 'If you were ad director how would you protect and grow ad revenue for the next three years? Describe your vision.'

'I'd like to see his fucking vision,' I grumble to Pippa as I prepare to go up to Jeremy's office.

She hoots. 'With or without his glasses on, eh?'

'Very good,' I laugh, trying not to sound surprised.

Encouraged, she adds, 'With or without his shoes on?'

There is no answer to that so I leave her chuckling to herself and head two floors up for my interview. Jeremy and the HR director, Andrew (a faceless suit type), are sitting in leather club chairs in front of the City skyline like a pair of regional news presenters. The way the light falls makes their seated figures look as permanent as the landmarks lined up behind them, but I refuse to be intimidated by the illusion. Instead, I fix on my mental picture of Hillary Clinton addressing Congress and launch straight into My Vision: streamline the magazines and papers into one integrated team; get rid of dead wood; hire specialists at controller level for beauty, motors, airlines and so on. The key words are 'streamline' and 'progress' (used as a verb) and Jeremy nods his approval each time I say one of them. It's going well. They're not doodling on their pads and they're not using their coffee cups to hide yawns.

Only once (briefly and when Andrew is talking and therefore not in any way calamitously) do I make that dangerous move of stepping outside of myself and thinking about whether or not I *mean* any of this. Or, for that matter, *need* it. Do I have the energy for all this streamlining? If I do get the job, then certain others within the department will quickly devote themselves to streamlining *me*; do I want to deal with that? Fragments of faces start to lick at the edges of my vision — my mother, Jojo, Caro, Maggie, Meredith — and I can't help wondering if a single one of those women would choose to switch places with me.

It is time for my questions and I have just one: 'How quickly will you be making your decision?'

'Very quickly,' Jeremy says, then Andrew snaps shut his file and it's over.

★ ★ ★

Over coffee Simon and I enjoy what will be one of our last moments of solidarity as we pool notes about our respective interviews and speculate once more as to the significance of X returning from a three-hour lunch yesterday at exactly the moment Y was seen boarding the Jubilee Line back into town. Still raking over every last detail, we share a cab to Soho for a twelve o'clock at the agency that represents, among other clients, RingMe. Though slow in making their choice, RingMe has given us no reason to believe there'll be any news today (personally, I've already written off the rest of this week and am mentally preparing myself for a Monday morning fallout); if there were anything to know, we'd already have been leaked it by Simon's friend, Mike. However, we're just finishing a routine briefing for another client when we run into the account director on RingMe coming out of the lift and he grins at us, a big ear-to-ear grin that can only mean . . .

'You didn't hear this from me,' he says.

'What, mate?'

'Yep, just spoken to Mike, you goddit.'

We goddit. Simon and I almost kiss each other, but not quite; after all, we'll be enemies again once one of us gets the top slot — for there's no doubt about it now: with Nigel not around to take the glory, this win will put both of us ahead of the Rods and Dannys of the outside world.

Simon puts in a call to Mike and I can see he's itching to follow it up with one to Jeremy. 'Are you going straight back?' he asks me. 'Why don't we go up and tell Jeremy the news together?' Like we're Andy Pandy and Looby Lou. I know exactly why he's suggesting it, though: it's because he's got a client lunch in Hammersmith and won't be back in the office for hours. A phone call is one thing but it's the victor's email that everyone is going to remember, that Jeremy is going to remember.

I make a show of checking my texts. 'Actually, I've got a lunch in town after all, a friend's birthday. Why don't we meet back at base at three-thirtyish and do it then? Then we can go straight out for celebration drinks with the team?'

'Cool.'

The words 'taste of your own medicine' spring to mind but not to my lips as we climb into separate cabs and wave goodbye.

I'm on the Strand heading east for the office when Caro calls. 'What now?' I say, happily. 'You've decided Charlie's really a woman?'

'You sound cheerful,' she says.

'We got RingMe,' I say. 'But keep it to yourself, I want to tell Jeremy in person. I'm on my way back now.'

'Congratulations, that's fantastic. And how was the interview?'

'I think it went quite well, but, you know, I thought that last time, didn't I?'

'This is different: I really think you've got it this time, chum,' she says. 'Listen, I was actually just calling to say that my invitation came this morning. Y'know, from Meredith. Did you get one, as well?'

I can feel goose bumps rising under my clothes. 'I very much doubt it, but my post doesn't come till after I leave.'

'OK, well, I'll show you mine as soon as you get back to base.'

How has this woman done this to us? I wonder, as I hang up. Caro, who can take her pick of members-only drinking holes and guestlist parties and PR junkets where you can't move for the champagne and goodie bags, is apparently more excited about an invitation to a sixtieth birthday party than to anything else she's been to in the last five years. And, despite the best business news I've had this year, I'm doing my level best to hide the fact that I'm as desolate as a teenager dumped by her first boyfriend *not* to be invited!

I can't resist the detour, of course, partly because Simon will be ages, and partly because good luck really does come in threes: great interview, even better RingMe news; only one thing could top those two.

'I just need you to stop off in St Katharine's Dock,' I tell the cabbie. 'Just off Thomas More Street, please.'

'Right you are.'

Right you are. I haven't heard that for a while and it brings on a twinge so raw it means my mother probably used to say it. Then I remember it wasn't her at all but our neighbour, June.

'I'll be back in a tick,' I hear Mum's voice say, clear as a bell. 'Don't let her have another one or she'll be sick.'

Then June calls back, 'Right you are, love.'

My hands fly to my face. Am I remembering Mum's final words? Was 'another one' a reference to my ice cream, the long-lasting treat from June's freezer that was widely cited as having saved me from joining my mother in the morgue that day? Or could that exchange have occurred any time? Mum and June were in and out of each other's kitchens and gardens every day for tea and cigarettes. Later, when the policewoman had arrived, my father close on her tail, June couldn't look at me without breaking into sobs. Right we were not.

401

The cab pulls up outside my building and I hurry into the lobby and turn the key in my pigeon-hole. There's a whole pile of mail today — Inland Revenue brown, direct-marketing orange, bank-statement white — and I file through them one by one until my fingers fall on the stiff creamy stationery of a formal invitation. The envelope is handwritten (1950s-era italic, dare I believe?) and, like a fan preserving her idol's autograph, I take care not to tear across the ink before I pull out the precious gold-edged card:

*Mrs Meredith Grainger requests the pleasure of your company*
*At a celebration of her birthday*
*on Saturday the eighteenth of September*
*at seven o'clock*
*At Three Park Crescent, Dulwich*
*RSVP*

And if that isn't sweet enough, there is also the most perfectly piped icing any cake could wish for — in the form of a handwritten message on the back:

*Anna, I know this is rather eleventh hour but we are such new friends. I do hope you can come — I'm so looking forward to introducing you to my son Charlie. Meredith.*

It can't be true. It's like exam results with a string of As, the doctor's letter putting you in the clear, the confirmation in writing of the life-changing lottery win. It's the result of a summer's endeavours but it feels like a life's work. I sit down on the sofa in the lobby and examine the card properly. If I had a magnifying glass upstairs in my flat I'd go and get it. The brisk pen stroke of that dash: was what follows a spontaneous afterthought or was it a carefully constructed statement of intent? Either way, it is there. My name and Charlie's have been joined by Meredith's hand.

Back in the cab I look at the lunchtime crowds with new eyes, that elite workforce leaving its steel workhouses to stretch legs and refuel. Whatever these people have achieved today I have bettered it. I've done *exactly* what I set out to do. This is what triumph feels like. I want to spray champagne into the sky.

Why then, by the time we pull up at One Canada Square, do I get an uneasy feeling?

★　★　★

Of course, Simon has already announced the RingMe win and taken full credit for it. Whether or not he lied about that Hammersmith lunch or just had a lucky cancellation I'll never know, but I wouldn't put it past him to have rehearsed the route in advance. Did he dip his head, fists clenched, as his cab streaked past mine on Shaftesbury Avenue? Certainly he'd have outstripped me even if I hadn't stopped off at my flat: it's the advantage of being the only one who knows it's a race.

I have no choice but to get to Jeremy for a

helping of sloppy seconds. I find him in reception on his way to a meeting.

'Great news about RingMe,' he says and goes to move past me as though he has no time to chat. It is just as I'd feared: already he no longer associates me with the business.

I change direction to walk with him. 'Yes, I'm just about to firm up the details,' I say with as much self-importance as I can muster. 'They're asking sixteen K a page, though, which I'm not happy about.' It's a risky lie, because a higher rate is already agreed.

He frowns. 'That's way too low.'

'I'll get them up to seventeen,' I say, confidently. 'No problem, just leave it with me, Jeremy.'

'Good, make sure you squeeze their balls on this. We want *at least* seventeen.'

His voice reverberates around the marbled reception like a town crier's. I imagine Meredith wincing at the vulgarity. I almost wince myself.

# 29

It is with less surprise than you might suppose that I realise I haven't spoken to Charlie since before leaving for Granada. This is by the far the longest period we've spent without speaking and, since he's left two messages for me this week and I haven't responded to either, the silence is entirely my own.

My reasons are complicated. A part of me is just too damn scared to speak to him; now I've put it out there that our camps are linked in the form of Caro and Angus, this whole enterprise has started to feel distinctly more dangerous than before, more *real*. How could Charlie *not* want to quiz me about it? Will it not become obvious, even to someone in another continent, that there is more to this little coincidence than is being divulged? If I could postpone for ever the moment when keeping the man I love in blissful ignorance must be replaced by lying to him, I would; instead, I'll just put it off for a few more days.

And then there's the small matter of perfectionism, a characteristic so vaunted in job interviews but so deadly in reality. The moment I opened Meredith's invitation I knew I wanted to preserve the exquisite potential of the fantasy ending, of Meredith being the one to bring Charlie and me together again in the surprise of his life and the making of mine. It will be *perfect*. I can't possibly risk the premature blurting of my triumph in the disconnected form of an international phone call.

But it's hard. I'm a communicator. Nights are worse than days as I've usually had a few drinks and the time difference means I'll easily be able to get hold of him at his desk at the Endo practice. It is torture to know that I could, at any time I choose, just dial that number and break my silence, change in a matter of seconds the way he feels about the two most important women in his life, remove the complications, *liberate* him. Lord knows he must by now be anticipating the resumption of hostilities left behind at that lunch table in Il Bordello. I could save *him* five extra days of torture if I told him now. But I want to be there to see his face, I want to be there to kiss his lips, I should also be there to answer face to face any queries he might have . . .

And so I remember Viv. I invite her to lunch and she drops by the office beforehand to say hello to her former colleagues. This is always an event loaded with paranoia on the part of those still in situ: will the former inmate be doing better than those left behind, or, worse, will she be struggling, hoping to return and upset the newly established order of things? For Viv's part, the appeal is in reassuring herself that she made the right decision to go in the first place. I strain to imagine the detachment she feels as she kisses the cheeks of Steve and Pippa and co., fingers skimming their waists, but I just can't. My workmates feel like family, they infuriate me for a million reasons (not least because they remind me of myself), but I'm with them for life.

Perhaps because her dress is more appropriate for a pilgrimage to Mecca than a visit to Canary Wharf, word of a VIP visit spreads around the office and Viv is fallen upon like some sort of prophet. I almost expect people to start stroking her clothes and prodding her skin to see if she's real. Only Ronnie, who joined the team in her place and so doesn't know her, keeps his distance, going all still and alert like a snake sensing an imminent earthquake.

'I'm getting sooo sick of my horoscope,' Pippa moans to her. 'Maybe *you* could do it for me, Viv?'

Viv smiles. She's perfected that expression of fake sympathy to the point where her face looks numb. 'I'm not actually an astrologer, Pippa, more of a problem-solver.'

'Can't you solve the problem of my rubbish stars? They're always so rude about Gemini and it's not like I can switch.'

'Viv, tell us about the losers you're 'helping',' Steve teases, drawing inverted commas in the air with his fingers.

At this Viv, to her credit, resists a glance in my direction. 'They are not losers, Steve, they are tomorrow's winners.'

'Do you have to speak in that lingo, then?' he says. 'Y'know, like saying, 'I'm not comfortable with that' when you really want to say, 'Fuck off, you sad bastard!'?'

'Generally I wouldn't tell a client to fuck off,'

Viv twinkles at him, 'but I'm sure I could make an exception if I were ever approached by you, Steve.'

My lips twitch. They slept together for a while, Steve and Viv, in spite of their respective partners. I have a feeling she scores well on the spreadsheet.

Even Simon drops by to pay his disrespects. 'Hey, Viv, I've got a job for you: help Anna realise there's more to life than making ad director!'

Viv smiles at him. 'Maybe I will.'

'Maybe she already has,' I say, and his blue eyes dart hungrily at the thought. Am I like that, I wonder, *nakedly* greedy for the extra power, the swollen salary, the upgraded trappings? I must be; after all, I was prepared to double-cross him in exactly the way he double-crossed me, which is why we are still on perfectly amicable terms. I'd probably ask him to join us for lunch if I didn't have something more private to discuss with Viv.

'That was a bit strange,' she says when we're alone in the lift. 'Why are they all so wired?'

'Oh, it's the whole director job thing; they smell blood.'

'Whose?'

'Mine, Simon's, anyone's.'

She shakes her head. 'It's amazing you don't ever get upset by that atmosphere, Anna.'

'Oh, I'm used to it.'

'You probably think you couldn't live without it,' she guesses, correctly as it happens. 'But you could, you know. You'd be fine.'

408

I can't help thinking she's not just talking about work.

In the restaurant I update her on the Granada trip and show her Meredith's invitation. She handles it with due reverence, stopping just short of genuflexion.

'This message on the back, Anna! You've pulled it off, I don't believe it! I mean, I knew you would,' she adds, smoothly.

She wants to know all about Meredith, says she's been thinking about her, wondering how charismatic someone would need to be to exert this kind of fascination over those who've never even met her.

'She actually seems like quite a reasonable woman,' I say. 'She obviously likes to get her way and she's a horrible snob all right, but all of that stuff Charlie told me just doesn't seem possible.'

'Are you sure what he said was true?'

'What?' But her timing is deft and the query gets quickly forgotten in the sudden barrage of options — Sparkling or still? Red or white? Salted or unsalted? — delivered by a slightly jumpy waiter as though conducting a multiple-choice test. Perhaps our IQ results will be delivered with dessert.

'Actually, Viv, I wanted to run an idea by you.'

She nods. 'Of course. Charlie's reaction. I've been thinking about it myself.'

I pause for the reappearance of the waiter and the subsequent cascading of mineral water into our glasses from a great height. Amazingly, not a drop is spilled. I take a sip.

'What do you think of the idea of telling

Charlie *before* Saturday?'

'What? On the phone?'

'No, in the flesh, but before the party.'

The thought came to me as I walked to work this morning, inspired perhaps by the brilliant crystalline quality of the light. It was like nothing I've seen in this city all my life, so magically soft and fresh. Enough of the murkiness of subterfuge, I thought, skipping a step or two, enough of double lives. It's time for honesty, his *and* mine.

'He's due back home on Friday,' I explain, 'so I could meet him that night or the next morning and, well, come clean. I mean tell him *everything*. Then *he* can advise *me* on how to play the party.' I don't mention that initial confession fantasies include his coming straight from the airport to the flat to see me and, after a spot of breathless lovemaking, noticing Meredith's invitation on the mantelpiece and teasing the story out of me as one might the tale of something really quite innocent and harmless.

Viv laughs, not taking me seriously, but I notice a flicker across that serene mask of hers, a flicker of horror. 'Don't worry, sweetie, you're just feeling a bit guilty.' She breaks off a piece of bread and rolls it into a dough ball.

'No, I mean it. He can't be anything but delighted, can he?' *Can he?* 'Besides, I need to tell him some other stuff and maybe it's better to get it all out at once.'

'What other stuff?'

I shrug. 'Nothing serious, just about old boyfriends, you know ... ' Just about having

410

been married to a buffoon and needing to tell him before someone else does. 'But I'm definitely leaning in the direction of full disclosure.'

She puts down her bread ball and brings her palms together as though in prayer. 'I'm not sure confessing at *any* time is the right strategy, Anna,' she says, voice throaty with concern.

'That's just it! I don't care about strategy any more,' I say. 'I feel like strategy is *strangling* me.'

'Well, you should care. Come on, you're almost there! It's incredible what you've achieved! But I really wouldn't come out in the open with this. People generally don't like to feel they've been deceived.'

'That's exactly why I want to be open about it.'

'Think about it,' she says. 'If everything could be handled openly, then you wouldn't have consulted me in the first place, would you? You'd have cooked it up with Charlie himself months ago. Have you still got that book you showed me? The Meredith file?'

'Yes.'

'Well, just imagine how you would feel if he got hold of that book. If you tell him everything, that's how exposing it will feel. He'd be horrified. It would look as though you've approached the relationship like a piece of business.'

Remembering that end-of-the-world roar of panic when I saw my daybook in Meredith's hands, I suppress a shudder. 'But if he could see it was all in a good cause? Like a surprise party

411

or something? That's not so bad, is it?'

'Not quite the same.'

God, nothing is ever quite the same as this situation. But she's right, of course: I'm just getting twitchy with the combination of guilt and stage fright; it would be insanity to switch tactics now. In any case, back at my desk I find that Charlie has emailed to say he won't be back until the Saturday evening owing to a last-minute change of flight, and he'll travel straight home. He doesn't add 'in time for the party', probably hoping I've forgotten all about that. The young innocent! Nor does he give a reason for the schedule alteration, which strikes me as odd; if anything, I imagined he might come home earlier than planned since his work has petered out early. **I'll call you on my way from the airport or the next morning. Speak then, Charlie**. No 'love', no kisses. Is it me or does that sound a bit short? Is he punishing me because he's feeling neglected? I haven't visited him while he's been away, I haven't met him in the middle in New York, and, recently, I haven't even returned his calls. Surely he can't think I've lost interest? My will-power crumbling, I turn to my calendar. I *have* to hang on. True love has waited this long: it can probably wait another five days. I tap out an email: **The Endo is nigh! See you on Saturday, can't wait! Anna xxx** It is only as the cursor hovers over 'Send' that I spot my mistake and replace 'Saturday' with 'Sunday'.

And, with that, everything is finally in order: Viv has kept a lid on my eleventh-hour crisis, Charlie is just too distracted by homecoming arrangements to be constructing soppy messages of love, even my colleagues have their heads down for once, thanks to the new RingMe business.

But I'm restless. I keep getting up for no other reason than to hop about and ponder. However hard I try to ignore it, one phrase keeps coming back: *are you sure what he said was true?* It's the one spoilsport in an otherwise harmonious game, a game in which the final whistle is just minutes away. Finally, I give in and address it. Has Charlie been telling the truth about Meredith? Has she ever really been the she-devil he portrayed? Where is the *evidence?*

As I think, I automatically jot down a list as I go. Granada: yes, Moira and the others deferred to her preferences but there were no tantrums, not even any unduly sharp words, more the amicable falling-in-line of a long-established pecking order among friends.

The village bookshop: OK, the assistant reported an argument, but no name was given and Meredith can't be the only person in south London after a book about West Coast architecture. In any case, it probably wasn't a row, just impatience with poor service. The girl was plainly no Employee of the Month.

Next? Well, there's Charlie's stories, like the one about strong words being exchanged when the power tools of a neighbouring DIY enthusiast threatened to drown cocktail hour on the Grainger terrace, but, again, isn't that understandable? DIY *can* be antisocial, the papers are full of vendettas over illegal hot tubs,

413

and our own is engaged this very week in naming and shaming the nation's noisiest neighbours.

And then there are Meredith's crimes against her own family. As I doodle a simple family tree, I struggle for a moment to remember what Charlie's personal grievances have been. Oh yes, what about that business of her screaming and throwing a wooden spoon at him when he announced his desire to move in with Jessica? That does sound demonic. But then again maybe Jessica really *wasn't* right for him, maybe she was already married or a single mother, maybe she was twice his age or the daughter of a convicted murderess? There could easily be some detail Charlie has neglected to tell me. And let's remember that he is still in his twenties; it's not inconceivable that he *hasn't* ever hooked up with the 'right' kind of girl.

Next, Charlie's father: well, there've been implications from all sides that Leo endured his fair share of ear-bashing, but which spouse doesn't in a marriage of that length? His obstructive attitude over Charlie's application to architecture school could have been typical of a general killjoy tendency that *any* woman would find exasperating.

Which brings us to the Max situation. That has always been Charlie's chief demonstration of Meredith's ability to make her sons miserable, and not only did Angus corroborate the story but Meredith confirmed it herself, admitting her fault to me that morning in the parador: 'we've always locked horns, which is natural for the child but it shouldn't be for the mother.' So Max

414

is the evidence that Charlie *can't* have been lying and, like his brother, really has been subjected to a side of Meredith that is genuinely intimidating. His reservations have been reasonable all along. I've done the right thing, the right thing for both of us, and there is no good reason why everything shouldn't still be on track for my perfect happy ending.

Exhausted, I put down my pen and sit back. No good reason. Why then, two minutes later, do I find myself picking up the phone and dialling directory enquiries? 'Selfridges, please.'

★ ★ ★

Such has been my fixation with the mother that I've never given the ex-girlfriend the focus she traditionally receives in a new romance. I certainly haven't tracked Jessica down to thank her for doing such a good job training up my man. Frankly, I think she did a lousy job, since at the end of their relationship he returned to Meredith and has resisted all subsequent attempts to lure him away again. If I've considered her at all it has been only to pity her for her weakness, for running away from battle. She was a deserter, in my view; they both were. But she's still a stone unturned and — who knows? — there may be something she can tell me that will subdue these last-minute doubts.

She no longer works for Selfridges, I'm told, but for a new Japanese clothing franchise with office headquarters on Regent Street. She has agreed to meet me in her lunch hour but is so

415

'up to her neck in it' our rendezvous must be in her own office café high above the bus lanes and shoppers. Quite unlike my own work canteen, hers has been done out with plasma screens and rows of single lilies arching elegantly towards the light from elongated slate pots. Everything is slender, even the people, who are mostly British girls in their twenties and Japanese men in their forties. Green tea is served as an alternative to cappuccino.

'Are you Anna?'

Her clothes are so snug that at first I think she might be wearing a catsuit (Meredith wouldn't approve of that, for starters), but it turns out to be jodhpurs and a long-sleeved top in exactly the same shade of chocolate. A belt buckled low across the hips is her only accessory. There remains something very feline about her, partly because she moves in a kind of prowl on the balls of her feet, partly because the highlights in her brown hair give it a tortoiseshell effect. She is pretty, of course, with green eyes and freckles, but I knew that from having seen her photograph (courtesy of Rich, not Charlie). Glances from neighbouring tables suggest she might be something of a company babe.

She is all smiles, as you might expect of someone in communications liaison, and the business card she hands me announces that she is no less than director of this mysterious art.

'Funny you should do this,' she says, in a low neutral tone, somehow disappointing for not being a purr, 'because I always wanted to track down the one before *me*. What was she called

416

again, Sophie or something?'

The one before me. Straightaway I don't like her, don't like the implication that we are merely two of a whole conveyor belt-load of girls who Charlie selects like plates of sushi as and when his appetite requires.

'Why did you want to track Sophie down?'

'Maybe you should tell me why you wanted to track *me* down first.'

'OK.' It feels even more humiliating than I expected to have to explain to her what is clearly so predictable. 'He doesn't know I've been in touch with you, but the thing is I'm getting confused about the relationship between Meredith and him and I just thought it might be good to talk to someone who's been through it too.'

She leans right forward, propping her chin on a balled fist like a patient getting into position for a glaucoma test. 'Ah, Meredith. Now how did I guess her name might come up?'

She's so knowing, so pleased with herself; she's hardly covering up the fact that this is entertainment for her.

'He's never introduced me to her . . . ' I begin.

'Think yourself lucky.'

'OK.' I don't think myself lucky, I want to snap, I think myself a hardworking romantic strategist in danger of losing everything with one last slip of confidence. How melodramatic this episode has become within two minutes, how desperate, as I sit amid this sleek and glamorous workforce waiting for Catwoman to toss me some scraps.

'To be honest,' Jessica says, sitting up normally again, 'I always thought Charlie used Meredith as a bit of an excuse so he didn't have to get too serious.'

I stare. I wasn't expecting a proper insight, not after that dismissive start. 'But . . . but he says he wanted to move in with you?'

'Well, that was my idea.' She pulls a fond face as though remembering the act of an ingénue. 'Maybe I'm wrong, but I felt that when it started looking like something long term he used her to get out of it. I don't think he had any intention of getting a place with me, not really, he knew Meredith would block it. It just brought things to a head.'

I take this in. 'He told me she hounded you out of town.'

'Well, I'm still here, aren't I?'

'So she didn't break you up?'

She shrugs. 'Look, she was a bit of a pain, that's for sure. To be honest, I thought she was a rude old cow. She was obsessed with getting him to see more of his old school friends — I guess they were more socially acceptable to her than someone who worked in a shop.' She throws up her hands in indignation. 'A *shop*.'

For the first time I'm in total agreement with her: 'Selfridges is more than a shop.'

'Thank you! But, anyway, she wasn't the only issue. Charlie just didn't want to take things further, it was as simple as that. What he likes is the *beginning* of a relationship, the first year.'

Our moment of sororial bonding is gone as quickly as it came.

As I simmer over that use of the present tense, she adds insult to injury: 'How long have you guys been together now?'

'A year and a bit.'

She's back in the glaucoma position, staring ahead at me with intense, unblinking concentration. 'Look, I know how hard it is when you're in the middle of it to see how things really are.'

This is insufferable; I have no choice but to argue. 'Well, in my situation, Meredith *is* the only issue. Everything else is perfect. But she obviously needs special handling, especially after her husband died, and I just wondered if you had any tips . . . ' I trail off.

Jessica pouts. 'Tips? I don't know, change your name to one of the oldest families in Dulwich? Donate a fortune to that bloody gallery? Wear less make-up? God, I can hardly remember — it was yonks ago.'

*Yonks?* What kind of a word is that? The kind my *father* might use. This girl is out of touch. And she calls those tips? I'd worked all that out by the end of day one. And then for the first time I notice her playing with a ring, a rather large figure-of-eight diamond ring. So that's why she's so magnanimous: she's made the great psychological leap of getting hitched, for nothing helps a girl rewrite the history of past relationships quite like the success of a present one. Goodness, Charlie should thank his mother for warning him off this creature; he'd be married with a squadron of kiddies by now if she'd had her way.

'Do men ever do this kind of thing?' Jessica

asks. 'I mean meet up with their girlfriends' exes to try to understand them better. I don't think so. Why do we do it?'

Smiling is a major feat of endurance now. 'I suppose we can't help forcing the issue.'

'It's a shame when love has to be forced.' She's thinking how wonderful it is to not have to contend with skirmishes like this any more. She's thinking that if I'm lucky I might be able to follow in her footsteps and replace Charlie with The Real Thing. The ring shuttles repeatedly over her knuckle and back into place again. 'I'd better get back,' she says, tiring of old news like mine.

But I still need more. 'Wait — what was the father like?'

'Leo? Oh, outvoted.' She gets up. 'Everyone is eventually.'

The worst thing is that I sense that somewhere under the cosy down of that self-satisfaction she feels genuinely sorry for me.

# 30

The venue is the same, the orders for skinny lattes the same, we're even outdoors once more, for the fine weather has held and half of those passing through with their little blue beakers of coffee are wearing sunglasses with their suits.

'We must stop meeting like this,' Maggie says from under a wide-brimmed hat. 'I'm starting to feel like a plain-clothes detective.'

'I have that effect on people,' I giggle. 'How are you? Not at all disfigured, I'm glad to say.'

'Much better. You should have seen me when it really struck. It was hell. And Ian treated me like some sort of leper. He even slept in the spare room! But they won't care about a few facial flaws in Cheltenham, will they?'

The pox gave Maggie time to consult with Viv and re-evaluate Her Life, and the upshot is that she is leaving her job and going to work full time on *The Painter's Brush*. There were several hundred applications for the job and I like to think my Alhambra material helped sway the vote in her favour. She hasn't looked this happy since her wedding day. I expect babies will soon follow.

'When will you know about *your* job?' she asks.

'Any day now. That's why I suggested meeting here: I'm getting cabin fever in the office. You know when you feel you're going to spontaneously combust?'

'I've felt that for years,' Maggie says. 'And then I did!'

Now I notice a dent or two in the skin around her nose. In an odd way the effect softens her face; once they've abandoned their quest for physical perfection, women often look considerably better. I'll miss Maggie. We both know my ventures west will be few and far between, just as we know that people who leave London never come back 'all the time' for the theatre and museums. For a moment I wonder if my situation would be any different if Maggie had made it to Granada after all — certainly no one would have come away knowing about Paul. I'd probably be in exactly the same position as now but with an almighty secret to defend.

'You said you had something to tell me?' I remind her. 'Have you sold your house yet?'

'No, no, nothing like that. I just thought I ought to tell you that I had a phone call yesterday from your woman.'

*My* woman. 'You mean *Meredith*?'

'Yes.'

I frown. 'I don't understand. What did she want?'

'Well, this is it. She made out it was part of some drive, doing her bit for the Dulwich Picture Gallery: you know they have a certain number of friends or donors they like to recruit every year?'

'But you're a journalist!'

'Exactly, like I'm going to give them money!

422

But that was just an excuse. She really rang to talk about you.'

My stomach flips. 'Oh my God, do you think she's on to me?'

Maggie looks around with the air of a fugitive scenting the approach of the authorities; she's enjoying being a part of the intrigue again, I can tell. 'No, not at all, don't worry. It was more like she wanted a *reference*. I gave you a glowing one, obviously.'

'Obviously.'

She tells me the details: how Meredith had begun by saying how much she enjoyed meeting me again in Spain, how we'd had some interesting talks. But it was mostly Maggie who spoke in this conversation, it seems, despite their respective professions, Maggie who was drawn out on the matter of my parentage, my moral fibre, my art.

'I had to improvise a bit on that one,' she says, laughing. 'Since when have you been the new Frida Kahlo?'

'Who?'

'Anna, please tell me you're joking!'

Sitting here listening to her feels rather like having your parent report back to you after a particularly triumphant parents' evening, or in my case grandparents', as Dad rarely put in an appearance at such events. I feel pleased, grateful, proud to have made them proud. Then I have a horrible thought.

'She didn't say anything about Paul, did she?'

Maggie looks surprised. 'Paul, no, why should she?'

'Oh, no reason, I just wondered if she asked any questions about my romantic history.'

'No, but if she had, don't you think I'd have thought twice about bringing up that fool!'

I chuckle. 'I thought you said he was right for me?'

'I said he wouldn't have let his mother push him around like Charlie, that's all.' She takes a moment to stir and sip. 'I don't mind telling you, Anna, I thought this whole thing was a bit ambitious. That night at the gallery party, it seemed pretty damn impossible. But I think you might have pulled it off, you know.'

'I think I'd better wait till the fat lady sings,' I say.

'So you're into opera now, as well?'

I laugh. 'How did Meredith get your number, anyway?'

'From Virginia at the gallery, though she could just as easily have got it from Angus, I suppose.'

'He's seeing Caro now,' I say, 'so she may have thought the Virginia route more discreet.' Thank God.

Maggie puts her spoon down with a loud clink. 'Did you say Caro and Angus? Goodness, this *has* got complicated, hasn't it?'

That's one way of putting it.

★　★　★

I'm in the ladies' at work, just about to flush, when I hear the latest rumour.

'Isn't he American or something?'

'No, Irish.'

'Irish? Another pisshead, then. You weren't here when we had James, were you?'

'Was he the one who peed himself that Christmas lunch? Steve told me about that.'

There are loud squeals of delight and revulsion.

'Hope the new guy's better-looking than Nigel, don't you?'

'Not if he's Simon he won't be. Slaphead.'

More giggles. 'I reckon he'd be all right, though, don't you?'

'Yeah, he's OK.'

They are juniors in the sales and promotions teams, women of course; it's a shame they so readily assume the new director will be a man.

When I get back to my office Simon is sitting in the chair in the corner of the room in the shadows, not moving a muscle, like a jealous spouse observing the body language of his partner for signs of guilt.

'Are you all right, Simon? What's up?'

His mouth moves. 'You seen the email?'

'No.'

'We've got our slots.'

'This afternoon?'

'Yep.'

He means the appointments with Jeremy that will tell us who has got the job. We both know the form: the slots will be fifteen minutes apart and whoever gets the first slot will get the job.

'I'm three-fifteen,' he says, watching. 'Bill's three-thirty.'

'OK.' I log straight into my email and find Andrew's last unopened message. My eyes scan the text for the figures: will it say 3 p.m. or 3.45 p.m.? Breathing is suspended in the room as I pray for the former and Simon the latter. It takes an age to locate it in those brief three lines. 'Hey, I'm three o'clock,' I say, trying not to smile.

'Right.'

'It doesn't mean anything, Simon.' How strange that my instinct is to comfort him even though I know he'd be gloating openly were our positions reversed.

'Congratulations,' he says and leaves.

I sit for a moment swallowing the euphoria that's coming in big gulps. Finally, finally, despite the hitches and the hair-raising, it's coming together: the job I want, the man I want, the *life* I want, and all through sheer hard work. I'd be crazy to apologise to anyone for this, because I deserve it, I really deserve it.

It's hard not to beam as Andrew opens the door at three on the dot and leads me back to those expensive chairs in front of that expensive skyline. It feels like admittance to a club, the power office club. Maybe I'll ask Moira and Meredith to help me choose some prints for my new walls, something striking but not so eye-catching that it distracts from the view. Some framed photographs of historic Dulwich, perhaps, or a couple of my mother's drawings.

Jeremy takes a noisy sip of coffee and when he speaks it is in as near to an undertone as his larynx can deliver. 'Anna, thank you for coming up. We just wanted to let you know as soon as we could that we've made an appointment for the

426

ad director's position.'

'Oh yes?' The phrasing isn't quite what I would have expected and my nose registers for the first time a faint trace of cigar smoke. I look around. One Canada Square is a non-smoking building; I must be imagining it.

Another amplified swallow of liquid. 'We've offered the job to Paul Brunton and I'm pleased to say he has accepted.'

I go still. 'Paul Brunton?'

'Yes, he's been in the *Mail*'s Dublin office for a couple of years and is ready for the move back to London. Actually, you may know him from his days at the *Mirror*?'

Paul. *My* Paul. 'Yes, I know him.'

Jeremy slips his spectacles on and looks across at Andrew, who nods his support, eyes glacial. They're both on their guard now, chests tense as if in preparation for the barrage of blows they expect to come raining down on them. Violence they can handle, along with the girlie tears and general snorting hysteria one expects from the more hormonal sex; what they don't want is any mention of employment lawyers or discrimination suits.

Autocue-perfect, Jeremy continues, 'Of course I very much hope you'll continue to be a valuable part of the department. We'll be relying on you to . . . '

To make sure we don't lose revenue over this. Yeah, yeah, yeah.

'Thank you for letting me know,' I say, when he has finished, and I stand up.

'We wanted to let you know first,' Jeremy says,

as though it's a consolation prize worth having. He also rises, but Andrew stays in his seat and I see him peel off the top sheet of his A4 pad and tuck it away at the bottom of the pile. Next?

I look into the space between them at the view. The light bouncing off those shiny, buffed towers is perfect; it looks alpine pure, as if there's not a single car down there chuffing out exhaust fumes, no cigarette smoke from office doorways, no evaporating particles of blood, urine, vomit, sweat, spittle. But it's there, we all know that.

The meeting has been so brief Simon hasn't even appeared yet for his three-fifteen. I call him from my mobile as I wait for the lift, and by the time I get back downstairs there are commiserating faces everywhere I turn. Caro is the first to make human contact.

'Bloody hell, chum, *Paul?*'

'I know.'

Quite apart from our personal history there is the fact that Paul was my opposite at the *Mirror* and generally considered the meteor crashing to earth next to my rising star. 'Twinkle, twinkle little star,' he used to say to me, not without admiration. So how is he now my senior? It is illogical, intolerable, unfair. I feel like the pupil whose exam papers have been deliberately marked down or, worse, switched with those of a poorer student. I would cry if my brain weren't numb with the inevitability of it all.

'I'm just so tired of being shafted,' I say to Caro.

Her sigh is long and sympathetic. 'I know. It's just so much harder to be the shafter when you haven't got a penis.'

I realise I am gathering up my personal possessions from around the room and putting them together in my cupboard. As I assemble them, Caro quietly returns them, one by one, to their original places.

Simon is soon back by my side, cheerier than when he thought I'd got it but a loser nonetheless and no one is going to be happy about that. 'From now on, we need to look out for each other,' he says.

Until the next time. 'Yeah, sure,' I say. I call through the open door, 'Pippa? Can you take messages, please? I'm leaving early today.'

'Don't blame ya,' she says, not raising her head from the text message on her mobile phone.

★ ★ ★

They couldn't have asked for better weather for the duck ceremony, assuming ducks like crisp September air and dazzling sunlight. The park is quieter than usual; other than the occasional cyclist we have the luxury of all this shimmering green to ourselves.

'The recumbent bicycles have been a great hit,' Jill tells me as we walk from the main gate to the central lake. She also tells me about the veteran oaks, the bats, the kingfishers, and about Queen Mary and her rhododendrons. I feel like a guest of honour and, indeed, am introduced to new faces as a 'key fund-raiser.' Thank God Jojo didn't know how much people would pay for

Dad's old celebrity junk: she'd be livid to see it rerouted to a good cause.

'Are you the one who donated Michael Caine's underpants?' I'm asked by a woman dressed as if for a Victorian mountain hike. She looks faintly familiar — that's right, she was the one who bought Meredith's egg cups at the auction.

'Handkerchief,' I correct her, laughing. 'I'm not sure I'd be able to get my hands on his smalls.'

'That's rather a shame. A most charming man, wouldn't you say?'

'Oh yes.'

A group has gathered by the pond and word gets round the other side of the fence until there are as many birds on the bank watching us as there are us watching them.

I notice a new sign that refers to the Friends of the Park. 'Is that us?' I ask Jill.

'Oh no, dear, they're quite different. We're Friends of the Lake.'

'There must be some overlap, since the lake is in the park?'

She winks. 'Let's put it this way: all Friends of the Lake are Friends of the Park, but not all Friends of the Park are Friends of the Lake.'

'Right.' This is so kooky I wonder if it might be some secret Mossad code or something. 'So our auction raised money for the lake?'

'That's it. Not everything we wanted; there are still plans for a new boathouse and boardwalk if we only had the lolly.'

Lolly. So much nicer a word than the ones we

use at work: 'grand', 'K', 'thou' and, Jeremy's favourite, 'revenue'.

I wonder what is going to happen next. Nothing would surprise me: skinny-dipping (though there are 'No Swimming' signs everywhere and this lot are nothing if not law-abiding); the ritual throttling of Canada geese, for I've learned that they are the enemy in this little enterprise. Sure enough, they boldly patrol the edges of the pond, waiting to see if anyone's hard enough to take them on. They are like Steve and Ronnie and Nigel and Paul, they probably have a spreadsheet for grading the passing heron.

'Do the geese kill the others, then?' I ask a man who has silver hair growing over his ears in shaggy sporrans.

'No, nothing like that, not directly. But their droppings cause nutrient enrichment and that helps kill the fish. They're such tramplers, as well, heavy-handed little buggers.'

'Heavy-footed,' someone corrects him, laughing.

'And they monopolise as well: they eat all the vegetation on the banks.'

'Shame they don't make themselves useful and eat the bloody pigeons,' mutters Eric. More laughter.

'Wouldn't it be easier to just get rid of them?' I ask. 'Or give them a pond to themselves?'

'It's not that simple,' says the silver-haired man. 'Lake ecology is a finely balanced science.'

'It's all in the mix,' Eric agrees.

It is then that a van drives up and a man

dressed in waterproof clothing, presumably a lake ecologist, starts lowering ducks on to the water one by one. I don't know if they are mallards or shovellers or whatever else, but he handles them with real tenderness and we all watch as though witnessing the first wails of a newborn.

'Excess bread encourages rats!' shouts a nearby sign, a warning that would hardly be out of place in the building I've just come from. *It's all in the mix.* These lovely duck-petting, egg-cup-buying citizens occupy the same city as Jeremy and Andrew, breathe the same air as Ronnie. Some may even be neighbours of Nigel. And standing here now, I don't know which species it is that I belong to: stampeding goose or gently paddling tufted duck? I have an arm dislocated in either direction.

'We've proposed you for membership at the club,' Eric says to me. 'Should come through in time for the annual supper buffet.'

'Don't forget to drop by and see the pictures from the open,' Jill adds. 'They're an absolute hoot!'

'You must come to the gallery's Halloween masked ball,' says Virginia, who has popped out of her office for ten minutes ('Just 'ducking out', good eh?'). 'I'll reserve tickets for you and Maggie. You know Meredith was asking for her number the other day? I do hope she managed to track her down: we always need more media folk on our side.'

'Are you coming back for tea and cakes?' the Victorian hiker asks, apparently recording cake orders in a reporter's pad. 'There are cheese scones, if you like those?'

'I love them.'

As we walk back I think what delightful parents these people must have been, and still are, of course. No wonder the kids don't always want to leave home.

# 31

Meredith and I are both in green.

'You look wonderful!'

'And so do you, Anna. My goodness me, your hair! I wouldn't have recognised you!'

'It was time for a change,' I say. 'But how funny that we've chosen the same colour.'

'Not funny at all,' Meredith says, taking my arm and leading me into a large room filled with smiling people. The full skirt of her dress swishes gently between us as we go. 'We obviously have very similar tastes.'

Though a part of me feels exactly like the mistress making an illicit visit to her lover's marital home — a choking blend of shame and exhilaration — another part is astonishingly calm, enabling me to wish my hostess happy birthday and exchange opening niceties with new faces just like any normal guest. As Meredith slips away to greet more arrivals I notice how the pure leaf-green of her dress makes vivid, fluent strokes against the canvas of whites and pinks that so many of the other women have chosen to wear this evening. Around the room tall glass vases of summer flowers continue the theme, beautiful umbrellas of hot orange and pink amid fronds of that same perfect green.

'Meredith has a very good eye for colour,' says a woman standing nearby who introduces herself as Kay, president of the local horticultural society.

'She has a very good eye for everything,' I agree.

For once Charlie's reporting skills are not in question: the Grainger house is exactly as he described. Huge dividing doors have been pulled back to link the two principal downstairs rooms, creating a space that could have been designed specifically for pictures. They are everywhere, a seemingly disordered collection of styles and periods, drawings in freshly limed frames alongside oils in crumbly old ones, but I know at once that Meredith will have personally hand-picked and positioned every last one of them.

At the rear, open French doors lure guests out on to the sundrenched terrace and the tumbling gardens beyond. Despite its size, the terrace feels intimate and shaded, the garden an English hide-and-seek paradise with shrubs and bowers and curving beds of wild herbs. And it smells lovely: by turns sweet and earthy.

'This is one of the finest gardens in Dulwich,' says the horticulturalist. 'It's the rolling quality, with the park beyond. You almost expect to see the South Downs in the distance.'

'It feels so . . . relaxed,' I say, which is more than I can say for myself. It is only now that the audience are taking their seats that I appreciate the scale of the performance required of me this evening. Everything around me seems exaggerated, not only the colours and the fragrances but also the sound of my own blood pulsing through my veins, the stickiness of my saliva as I clear my throat. And try as I might to concentrate on the information Kay gives me about her forthcoming lecture series on suburban wonderlands, I can't get my mind off the extraordinary fact that I'm here, *in Charlie's house*. This is where he grew up, where he became him. I'm itching to sneak upstairs and try all the doors until I find his bedroom, his bathroom, his studio up in the eaves, but as there's just one staircase to the upper floors and it's directly behind the hallway where Meredith was last seen welcoming her guests, I'll do nothing of the sort.

I am satisfied, at least, with how I look. I shopped, without Caro's help, buying purely on instinct a stiff white skirt with appliquéd flowers and a fitted satin shirt in that same lovely green as Meredith's dress. It's not what I'd choose if I were welcoming Charlie home to dinner for two (though I have taken renewed care with my underwear just in case), nor is it for Meredith's benefit entirely, bordering as it does on the outré, but it is just right for meeting the two of them halfway. Best of all is my hair. It would break any mother's heart (it will certainly break Caro's) but the silky handfuls I loved so much have been swept into a hole in the floor of Toni & Guy. I'm as shorn as those sheep at the Dulwich Country Fair. The funny thing is that in exposing me so completely it provides the nearest to a disguise I've had this summer and face after familiar face glides by without its owner recognising mine. I have to call out names to say hello and identify myself: Friends of the Lake, the gallery folk, the tennis circle, all are here in force.

'There she is!'

'Where?'

'Oh my God, I can't believe it's you, Anna. Your hair!'

I turn with a smile. Caro and Angus have arrived with Moira and Humphrey, having enjoyed a cocktail at the Pooles' before strolling over. It's the first time I've seen Humphrey and Angus since Granada and I'm surprised to feel my nerves displaced for a moment by real affection. Humphrey, portly in a light suit, has his hand on his wife's arm to steer her through the throng, and they greet friends and neighbours with a togetherness I long to be able to emulate one day with Charlie. Angus, meanwhile, is as happy as Larry with the woman on *his* arm. He and Caro are by far the most glamorous couple of the gathering. She's in a white trouser suit so gorgeous Bianca Jagger would scratch her eyes out for it, and that signature mane bounces down her back with so much shine I feel the first pang for my own. Somehow she has managed to get Angus into a white jacket, too, and I, for one, find myself doing a double take, so handsome does he look in it.

'You both look . . . dazzling!'

'Thanks, babe. Nice skirt. We'll talk about your hair later.' Caro, smelling of bluebells, pulls me away from the Pooles and back into the corner of the room. 'Listen, I've got some *very* interesting gossip.'

'Oh?'

'Moira just told me that Meredith is *medicated*. To counteract mood swings. They've adjusted the dosage once or twice after she's totally lost it. That woman you heard about in the bookshop, that was her, all right. Apparently she went straight to her doctor and told him she'd lashed out, she was mortified. Oh, and she used to drink, as well. I mean seriously drink. She's supposed to have stopped completely but — '

'I don't think that's any of our business,' I interrupt in a whisper.

'Yeah, right,' she laughs, withdrawing an inch or two to treat me to a wink.

'I mean it,' I say, gripping her hand. 'Sorry, Caro, I know it's hypocritical but I feel bad about what I've done and now we're friends with Meredith I don't want to know anything else about her unless *she* tells us.'

'All right,' Caro says, carefully. I know what she thinks; she thinks that I'm traumatised about what's happened at work, that I'm reinventing myself yet again, not only in appearance this time, but in moral outlook. She thinks this must be some textbook reaction to my promotional knock-back and that it will, more likely than not, be temporary. The sacrificial hair is a classic symbol of change, but at least she knows that will grow back. Less certain is whether or not I'll withdraw my resignation, tendered on Thursday, and be back again on Monday just in time for the morning meeting. She thinks I just need time to recover from the shock reappearance of Paul

— after all, no reformed bad girl likes to be reminded of exactly how bad she once was.

As it turns out, Paul is something of a reformed character himself these days, married now and very concerned about what's happened to house prices in London since he left. I won't deny that it was strange meeting him again. I had no idea which feelings would resurface and which remain buried when we were reunited for a one-to-one soon after the announcement of his appointment. He didn't strike me as being any of the figures I'd imagined: lover, friend, industry contact, boss. Instead, he was just the son of a woman I used to have cups of tea and cigarettes with. I asked him straight away how Yvonne was and he looked both wrong-footed and relieved by the early diversion.

'Given up smoking,' he said, finally. 'Otherwise pretty much the same box of frogs as ever.'

After that he filled pauses with his own news. He's glad to be back in the London tabloid fray: he missed it because Dublin felt so much smaller and there was nowhere to hide (like there is in Canary Wharf!); his Irish wife is excited to be here and is settling in well; and if the great house-selling public of Hackney think he's shelling out half a million for a poxy terrace they're very much mistaken. He thought I was looking good and sounding cheery but he was still happy to negotiate the terms of my release: three months' salary and permission to leave that very day. Nothing like a proper redundancy pay-off but there we are; the position isn't redundant, in fact, it's now Steve's.

Now, just two days later, the only discomfort that remains is in the parallel my mind insists on drawing between my professional and private lives. Three months ago I had a job at the top of my field and a boyfriend who made women fall off their barstools for a better view. Neither were enough for me, evidently, at least not in their original form, and I applied for an upgrade on both counts. Now I have no job . . .

'What time is he due?' Caro asks, and I realise I'm staring over her shoulder at the door.

'Meredith thinks about eight-thirty.' I hug her. 'I'm so happy you're here. I'm really nervous.'

'Me too, this is so dramatic! Do you think he'll react on instinct and greet you with a passionate snog? He might not recognise you, of course. Did you warn him about the hair?'

'No, we haven't actually spoken for a while.'

'Have you decided how much you're going to tell him?'

'Yes, as little as I can get away with.'

Viv was right, of course, the less I let on the better, so I will be sticking to the basic half-truths: Maggie's connection with Angus meant that I met Meredith by pure chance; she had a press trip lined up and I ended up stepping in when she fell ill; Meredith and I hit it off well enough and now a relationship between Angus and Caro has brought our social groups closer together. I'm hoping that Charlie will be too busy concentrating on the relief he feels at no longer having to break the news himself to be able to dwell for too long on the heap of coincidences being served up — not to mention the joy of seeing me again. And then there is the diversion, a lively one by any standards, of my having been married before. However well this evening goes, I'll need to tell him about that at some point during its course; otherwise I risk Meredith doing it for me. I can just imagine them discussing the evening's guests over breakfast tomorrow. 'Anna? Yes, we met over the summer. Such a nice girl, divorced, you know, but interesting.' Yes, her knowing about me is one thing but her knowing more about me than he does is quite another.

I'm just rehearsing my lines in my head when Caro says suddenly, 'Isn't that Charlie's mate over there, what's his name, Rich?'

I follow her gaze across the room to a squat young man smiling up at a lady in a long, plum-coloured dress. 'So it is.'

How did he wangle an invitation? Didn't Charlie say he hadn't been allowed to invite any of his friends? But, then, didn't Meredith complain that he *had*? Either way, I consider avoiding Rich altogether. The last thing I need is an interrogation in front of her guests, in front of *her*. But it's too late, Caro is waving to him and his eyes leap in the eager way of a man looking to escape a bore. Then he stares. His face is suddenly closer in shade to his companion's dress than to its usual pink-grey. He's seen me.

'Anna, is it you? What happened to your hair? I mean, it looks great . . . '

'Hi, Rich, how are you? You remember Caro, don't you?'

He's still eyeing my hair with puzzlement and

441

I can only imagine the scenarios pulsing through his mind: I've altered my appearance to resemble that of a bona fide guest and have sneaked in without Meredith knowing; I've got a TV crew outside on standby to film a Showdown in the Suburbs . . . It's almost comical: how can he possibly be effective in disciplining teenagers when his every fear is telegraphed across his face? At least mine are kept hidden beneath the surface.

'Er, I didn't realise you knew Meredith, Anna.'

'Oh, I didn't, not until recently. And you?'

'We've met a couple of times.'

'You must be looking forward to seeing Charlie,' I say, confusing him even more. 'He didn't tell me you'd be here.'

'So he knows you are, then?' he asks, trying to sound jovial as he looks from Caro to me in confusion.

'Actually he doesn't.' I see the fingers of his right hand wiggle, no doubt in anticipation of the keypad on his mobile phone. 'It would be great if you didn't tip him off, Rich,' I add, playfully. 'I was hoping to surprise him.'

Now the fingers actually pat his trouser pocket. Drat, I've given him the idea, he was probably too shell-shocked to have thought of it himself.

'Are you here with Susan?' I ask, hoping to distract him.

'Oh yes, your girlfriend, how is she?' Caro asks.

The hand is back by his side. 'She's away on a girls' weekend. Payback for my trip to New York.'

And he looks away a little guiltily, as though he's said too much. Of course. New York. They must have discussed the Meredith situation then; no wonder it's fresh in his mind.

'Anna, there you are!'

We both turn at the sound of Meredith's voice and I see, out of the corner of my eye, Rich's hand finally cup the phone in his pocket.

'Meredith,' Caro cries, 'this is such a lovely party. We were just chatting to a very charming friend of your son's.'

As Meredith turns to acknowledge Rich, I see with horror that he has the phone out now, is fidgeting with the keys, all thumbs in his haste.

Meredith sighs. 'Do switch that off, Richard, I can't bear the things. We have an informal house rule here, you know, in fact . . . ' And, right in front of us all, she actually confiscates the mobile from him, like a mother snatching a forbidden lollipop from her child, and then she hands it to a minion passing by with fresh drinks. 'You can pick it up from the cloakroom later.'

As I beam, Rich is contrite. 'Of course. Sorry, Meredith.'

'Now, Anna, come out on to the terrace with me a moment, will you? I wanted to have a little talk. Do you need a new drink?'

'Thank you.' As I'm led away I see Rich reclaimed by the lady in plum while Caro sends me a thumbs-up sign over his shoulder. I can only hope Charlie arrives before his friend relocates that mobile.

At least half of the guests have gravitated to the terrace, sipping drinks and enjoying the evening sun. Most break off to smile at or greet their hostess, who fields the attention with magnificent ease, and I get a powerful sense of what Meredith's life has involved beyond her children: being the good wife of a senior civil servant, maintaining the Graingers' position among the area's finest, socialising, circulating, *charming*.

We perch together on heavy wrought-iron chairs.

'What a perfect garden for entertaining,' I say. 'I can imagine sitting out here for hours.'

'We're very lucky with the weather this evening,' she says. 'It's not nearly so perfect when the heavens open, I can tell you.'

Then, unexpectedly, she says she wants to thank me.

'But why?' I ask.

She meets my eye with such keenness I'm quite taken aback, but her voice is almost tender. 'You helped me see that family feuds are a terrible waste of time for all of us.'

'I don't remember saying — '

She interrupts me. 'Please don't be offended, Anna, but it's not anything specific that you said, it's more . . . well, you have a very *independent* quality that made me see that real loss is something that is quite out of our control, as it has been for you, not something we should be creating for ourselves.'

'You mean like my . . . like the loss of someone in the family?'

'Yes, that's exactly what I mean. It just seems to me that accidents and illnesses are terrible enough; we certainly shouldn't be adding to our anguish when we have all the means to do the exact opposite.'

I nod, understanding exactly what she is saying. 'Independent' is her tactful alternative for lonely, for motherless. My motherlessness makes her want to gather up her remaining family and hold them close to her for the rest of her life. She can no longer bear to be the one who pushed them away. As far as Max is concerned, this is good news, but what about Charlie? The last thing we need is her tightening her maternal grip.

'I agree,' I say quietly. 'If things aren't right and we have the power to do something about it, we should act, of course we should.' Without meaning to I'm once again mimicking her speech patterns. 'I always think it's nice when good things come together at the same time. This lovely party, your reunion with Max . . . '

Now her eyes gleam with a new playfulness. 'As it happens, my dear, I may have *another* pleasant surprise in store for me soon.'

'Oh?'

'Between you and me, *Charlie* tells me that he has someone special for me to meet.'

I gulp. 'Wh . . . who?'

'I'm not exactly sure yet, but he said just as soon as can be arranged.'

'Do you think he means . . . ' — I affect an air of vague recollection — ' . . . that family friend, Gemma, was it?'

She shakes her head decisively. 'I don't think so. There'd be no need for the secrecy if he meant her. He didn't give a name, though of course he means a girl.'

So the gay theory wasn't just Angus's fabrication then, it was a very real fear. 'How very exciting.' Almost stammering, I add, 'Are his girlfriends usually nice?'

She pulls a face. 'The last one was dreadful, everyone said so, like a scruffy little tabby. And, how can I put it . . . not what you'd call a deep thinker, if you understand. But we'll see about the new one when we meet her. And *you'll* meet *him*, of course, any minute now if he's on schedule.' She checks her watch. 'Excuse me, I must pop back in case I've had any late arrivals. We're not quite a full house yet.'

'Of course.' I am glad to have my buttocks planted squarely on the heaviest garden chair in the western hemisphere because I am knocked for six by this pronouncement. *Someone special.* A girlfriend. *Me.* This is the last thing I would have predicted: Charlie has come up with the goods, after all. He finally wants to introduce me to Meredith. He's spent the whole summer clearing his head and he's set actions in motion before he's even landed on British soil. *Just give me the summer*, he pleaded back in June. Who would have thought he *meant* it?

My instinct is to run, to let him proceed exactly as he wants to and at his own pace. But, quite apart from the fact that Rich has identified me, the fact remains that I need to get to him before Meredith does. She and I are becoming closer, surely close enough for there to be a risk that she'll mention me to him, if not tonight or over breakfast tomorrow then certainly some time soon. After all, she's just reiterated her wish for us to meet. Panic floods my lungs and rises into my throat. There is no way I can leave now: I must carry on as I intended, and once I've been able to make Charlie understand the situation he'll just have to withdraw that promise of producing someone new for her to meet, make up some story about it not having worked out. Oh, the irony.

I find Caro at once, barely caring that Angus is nearby and within earshot of my whispered update. Her eyes go as round as is humanly possible without actually popping out of their sockets.

'My God, you know what this means?'

'What?'

'You needn't have done any of this after all! You could have just chilled out the whole summer and not given Meredith a single thought.'

She's right. My personal reinvention, the Dulwich infiltration, Granada, the art, the tennis, the haircut, the *ducks*: I didn't need to do any of it. I'm like a property developer who has spilled blood renovating a house only to find that the market has risen and I'd have made my millions without lifting a finger.

'I'm glad you did, though,' Caro adds, 'or I wouldn't have met Angus.' He looks over at the sound of his name and they exchange charged glances.

'You would have done eventually.'

'Oh, I don't know,' she says. 'I get the

impression he and Charlie are not exactly great mates.'

'We'll have to change that,' I say. 'We'll go on double dates in Dulwich.' If I can just survive this extra complication, if I can just convince Charlie that I trusted him all along, that my appearance here is nothing but happy coincidence.

Caro is sniggering. 'Double dates in Dulwich. Well, how the mighty have fallen.' Then she says, 'I have a confession to make.'

'What?' I brace myself for the worst: Angus now knows everything, for the same garrulous exchange over G&Ts that yielded Meredith's medical history also threw up a secret or two of mine . . .

But she surprises me completely when she says, 'I *was* waiting, you know.'

'Waiting? Waiting for what?' It takes me a while to catch on. She means that conversation we had when all of this first started, about my having been waiting for Charlie, waiting for him to come along in the first place. 'Ah, you mean you were waiting for Angus.'

She sends another blade of desire deep into the body of her lover. 'Yes. And he came.'

# 32

He is the guest of honour, of course, the returning hero, the crowd-pleasing favourite. Clusters of guests break apart to allow Meredith to lead him by the hand into the centre of the room and it reminds me of nothing more than the bride and groom arriving at their own reception. I almost expect a burst of 'Wedding March' to accompany the thrilled murmurs. Tucked away by the wall, I don't get a clear view of him until he is feet away, just the other side of Virginia and the gallery colleague to whom she has just introduced me.

Then I ogle unobstructed. His hair is longer, streaked a little by the sun, and his skin more golden. The freckles are more defined, as though they've been dotted on to his nose with an eye pencil, and the teeth look whiter. And he seems younger, less the big male bear, more the soft-eyed cub — my first instinct is to run to him like a child at a petting zoo and stroke his nose. My second, however, is to step back and wonder if this might not be an actor sent to impersonate my lover. He has so possessed me these last months that I've come full circle and made him feel like a stranger again. I'm the little girl whose face was wreathed in bewilderment as her mother reappeared at her cot-side. It feels like a haunting, as though I never really expected to see him alive again.

I'm amazed I don't cry out as I watch Caro, just as she and I have planned, place herself among the first to greet him.

'Hi, Charlie, how are you?'

I sense the rush of surprise through his body as keenly as if it were my own, but he is rattled, not rocked; this much he might have expected — after all, I had warned him about Caro and Angus.

Meanwhile Meredith oversees her son's exchange of greetings first with an older couple I don't recognise and then with Caro with exactly the same tender pride Moira did when Angus talked to us of the Moors. Charlie may be the returning party but it seems to me that it is she who has come home.

Craning, I hear her ask Caro, 'Do you two already know each other?'

'Charlie used to work with my brother,' Caro replies, perfectly naturally. 'I haven't seen him for ages. I can't believe this is the same Charlie you talked about in Granada, Meredith!'

'I can,' Meredith says, agreeably, eyes moving over her son's face. 'I'm starting to learn that the older you get, the smaller the world becomes.'

There is laughter at this remark but none of it from Charlie's lips. As the news registers that Caro has been in Granada *with his mother*, the expression on his face mutates from wary to aghast and I long to rush in and rescue him, reassure him that everything is going to be fine.

'I've been away for a while,' he mumbles, struggling to play along. I notice his hand reach for his mother's waist as if for protection and they stand side by side, facing Caro together. 'How is David these days? Is he well?'

'Thriving,' Caro beams, 'you know he's senior partner now?'

'That's great. So you and Angus . . . ?'

'Now,' Meredith says at the same time, eyes scanning the immediate circle around them. 'Where's Anna gone? I saw her just a minute ago . . . '

Over her shoulder I see the figure of Rich silhouetted against the dying light; he is alone and advancing, just moments from taking aim. I breathe in through my nose, my mouth, my every pore, before stepping forward myself.

'Hello, everyone!'

'*There* you are, my dear!' Meredith cries. 'Oh, do come and meet my son . . . '

Perhaps he missed my name, perhaps he is thrown by the hair-dressing wizardry, but you can actually count the seconds before Charlie realises who it is standing in front of him. He takes a step back, bumping into a girl who hovers just behind him; she, in turn, retreats and collides with Rich, who begins bumbling and apologising, though not before sending Charlie a glare of urgent warning. Then Charlie turns back to see if I am still here. I am. I smile with as much tenderness as I dare while Meredith watches, but the look in his eyes tells me that of all the fears that keep him awake at night this is beyond his worst and I feel my confidence start to ebb. It occurs to me that with Meredith standing guard and the rest of the room waiting its turn to welcome our hero, it may not be as easy as I thought to pull him aside and explain my little coup.

'Oh,' Meredith continues, lightly, 'and I mustn't forget Charlie's new friend, Ashley, of course.'

And now it is I who needs the long seconds to see what is in front of her eyes: Charlie is with someone, he's with the girl whose foot he just stepped on, and the way her hand cups his elbow as she moves into position for introductions tells me that she is not just *someone*: this Ashley, she is Charlie's special someone. She is the one he wanted Meredith to meet.

'Hi, guys!' The girlish wave that accompanies the carefree North American tones suggests that whoever she is she is unaware of the quicksand she's just stepped into.

We all stare at her. She is tall and bony with short dark hair, beautiful hooded eyes, an upturned nose and full lips, and she dresses in that Parisian gamine way: short-sleeved cashmere cardigan with coloured glass buttons, a cute mismatching scarf, vintage denim skirt (denim at a cocktail party? Meredith won't like that), ballet pumps. Later, I'll consider that there's something too self-conscious about it all, as though someone once told her she looks a bit like Audrey Hepburn and she rented a few movies to get her frame of reference. But for now her mere presence is enough. Meredith is no longer the only woman in my way, and suddenly Charlie won't meet my eye.

'Ashley has come over with Charlie for a

holiday,' Meredith explains. 'She hasn't visited Britain before.'

Cold comfort it may be, but Meredith doesn't like Ashley. It's all there in the tone. Minutes ago, out on the terrace, she was visibly excited by the prospect of meeting Charlie's new friend, but she is displeased to have had the event sprung on her without proper warning, tonight of all nights, when all she wanted to do was bask in the sunlight of her official return to local society and his to her. I know precisely why she has allowed a faint emphasis to separate the word 'holiday' from the rest of the sentence: it's to let Charlie know that this is no permanent arrangement, not if she has anything to do with it. Resistance has settled over her eyes like a skin. I envy her that skin. I envy her the superior grade of her claim.

'Anna and I met in Granada,' Meredith goes on, ostensibly to the two of them, but already Ashley is losing her share of eye contact. 'Well, that's where we met *properly*. She draws beautifully, Charlie, you two must show each other your work.'

We look at each other then, Charlie and I. From the sliver of incredulity about his lips, I know he must have read the implication as clearly as I did: Anna is better for you than this Ashley creature, that's what Meredith means. Anna is *her* choice.

He clears his throat. 'Yes, yes, good to meet you, Anna.'

'I'd love to see your work,' I say, surprised by the silkiness of my voice considering my heart feels like it is being sandpapered to shreds.

Meanwhile Caro turns to Ashley. 'Do you live in San Francisco, then?' she asks, sweet as apple pie.

'New York. That's where we met,' Ashley says, still oblivious to the heightened watchfulness of those around her. 'But I grew up in Rhode Island. This is actually my first time in Europe.'

'Well, from what I know of Charlie here, you have an excellent guide.' There's an edge to Caro's voice now, discernible only to those who know her well. Meredith seems to miss it, Ashley certainly does, but Charlie and I get it all right. And in the few seconds his eyes hold mine I see that fear has been eclipsed by fury. It is as Maggie suspected: he thinks this is an ambush. As for me, all other sensibilities have been swamped by sadness. If I disappear any deeper into it I won't be able to breathe.

It is then that Jill bowls up, heaving with party spirit, and thrusts a plate of food under my nose: 'How about this, Anna, foie gras canapés! I told you Meredith doesn't care about our feathered friends, didn't I?'

'Oh, gross,' Ashley says, presumably without thinking, and Meredith turns away from her with a feather-light sigh of finality, as though she has seen and heard quite enough of this particular young lady for one evening.

'Darling,' she protests to Jill in the wickedest of tones, 'you make it sound as though I took my shotgun to the lake and killed the poor bird myself.'

★ ★ ★

He finds me, of course, minutes later, in the breakfast room, where I've allowed myself to get lost among an ant farm of caterers.

'Come upstairs,' he commands, sharply enough to make a couple of ants lift their eyes in surprise.

He doesn't speak a word as he guides me into the hallway and up the patterned runner with its shiny steel rods, past the stained-glass window and the continuing jigsaw of artworks. He shadows my footsteps closely, as though he has a revolver pressed between my shoulder blades, and for a moment all I can think of is how this mirrors my original fantasy: we'd escape the party crowd, sneak upstairs and find an empty room, fall on each other . . . but he's breathing hard not with desire but anger, and instead of triumph I feel only loss.

Reaching a closed door off the main landing, Charlie opens it, nudges me in first and then shuts it behind us. My eyes are immediately drawn to two symmetrical rectangles of sky, the windows overlooking the garden and the park beyond. Adjusting to the light, I look around the room. There are twin beds, dark-wood drawers and a pile of green towels folded on a wicker chair. The walls are relatively unadorned for this house, just a single prim line of framed architectural drawings. There is a small bookcase and I recognise on its shelves titles that have been pressed on me over the past year by my better-read partner. It is Charlie's room.

He backs me against the nearest wall and for

the first time in our history I truly dislike his closeness to me.

'What are you doing here?' Already his voice cracks and gives way: he knows he has nothing to threaten me with, he knows this situation can only deteriorate unless I can be persuaded to sneak down to the side door and get the hell out of his house. He's furious with himself for focusing on Ashley, on how to pull *her* off; he thought he'd try the very safety-in-numbers ploy I had pitched to him myself before he left; he never considered that the loose cannon he left behind might have rolled in with the crowd.

I make him wait, half-praying for salvation, half-itching to slap that pretty face of his. 'Your mother invited me, believe it or not, and here I am. I know a few of the guests as it happens . . . '

'As it happens? What the fuck has been going on since I left?' His tone is so violent the words feel like physical jabs.

'You tell *me*, Charlie.' I pause. 'And why don't you start by explaining who the hell Holly Golightly is down there?'

He backs off a step. 'I was going to tell you on Monday.'

Christ, not even tomorrow, the day after he gets back, but the one after that. A month ago he was begging me to come to San Francisco; now he's putting me back, a day at a time, fitting me in between the Tower of London and the Changing of the Guard.

'Tell me what?' I say, coldly. 'That you've made me redundant? That I'm surplus to requirements?' That you don't want to lose revenue over this . . . Jojo would throw her hands up in despair at the business-speak but it's quite applicable, all of it, and I suddenly want to weep as I add, almost in a whisper, my real question: 'That you love someone else?'

He closes his eyes. 'No, it's not like that, she's just a friend.'

'Oh, come on.'

'Nothing has happened between us. We just met in New York and . . . ' He trails off, seeing the pain in my face, and grimaces. How to explain the thunderbolt to the burns victim? Then he remembers that he has as much right to play plaintiff as I do and is back on the offensive: 'I want to know exactly how you met my mother.'

I move away from him and sit on the edge of the nearest bed. Which one does he sleep in? I wonder. Or does he alternate between the two like a child with his first bunk beds? Then I see the corner of a folded pyjama shirt tucked under the cover of the farther one. It looks so chaste it makes me feel sordid to the bone.

'We met through Maggie,' I say, flatly. 'At the gallery. Then we bumped into each other in Granada.'

'You 'bumped into each other'? You expect me to believe that?'

'You can believe what you like, but it is absolutely true. Maggie has been doing more arts reviews; in fact, she's about to leave London to edit an art title. She had a press trip to Spain but she got chickenpox and I went instead with Caro. We weren't in the same hotel as Meredith or anything, you can ask her yourself.'

He stares. 'If it was all such an innocent little coincidence then why the hell didn't you tell me? All those emails, you never once mentioned it.'

'I wanted it to be a surprise,' I say, but seeing now that he will never accept an answer so naïve from one so cunning, I add, 'I thought it might be difficult to explain over the phone so I decided to keep it a secret until you were back. This was supposed to be a *nice* surprise, believe it or not.'

He just snorts and looks as though he'd like nothing better than for a trapdoor to open up beneath my feet and remove me permanently from his line of vision. This isn't going well and I sense it wouldn't be much better if Ashley weren't standing abandoned in the room below us.

'You've been keeping a few secrets yourself,' I say, finally, and I see his eyes dart to the door. 'Not just *her*. What about the fact that your mother has made up with Max? Or that you've been seeing Gemma in San Francisco?'

'What?' He's actually wringing his hands now, flexing the thumbs together as though preparing to throttle a chicken. 'I didn't think news of what one member of my family says to another was worth a transatlantic telegram. And what do *you* know or care about Gemma? She's a childhood friend. Do I need permission now?'

I fold my arms. 'Apparently not.'

There are footsteps on the landing outside.

'Ssh!' Charlie gestures with his finger to his lip, like we're infants playing out of bounds.

'I will not shush.' I stand up. I've had enough of this. He didn't expect me here and he clearly doesn't want me here, but I don't deserve this kind of hostility, not from the man I thought loved me better than I love myself.

'Are you in there, mate?' It's Rich, just inches behind the closed door.

I look at Charlie. 'Come to my flat tomorrow,' I say, quietly. 'We'll finish this conversation then. In the meantime I suggest we avoid each other for the rest of this evening.'

He throws up his hands. 'You can't be thinking of *staying*?'

For a second I enjoy his anguish, really enjoy it, because for that same second it overrides my own. 'I'll leave as soon as it's decent. Right now you have a special guest to entertain. I'll see you tomorrow. Shall we say twelve?'

'I don't think . . . '

'Then or never,' I say, turning the door handle. 'I mean it.'

I don't stay much longer, only until one or two others say their farewells and it doesn't look too odd for me to add mine. Meredith promises to be in touch and, a little tipsy now, despatches me with a fond kiss on the cheek. In the taxi on the way home I feel like an ice sculpture brought out from the deep-freeze into a well-heated room. It doesn't take long before I start to weep.

# 33

So I'm back where I started, sitting in my flat, looking at that slender funnel of river water and thinking about Charlie. In my hand I grip Meredith's invitation like a souvenir from a destination I can never revisit. There's no longer any dilemma, of course. I'm furious. It's just that I am still in so many pieces the furies haven't yet connected with one another. Even now, after a night of sleepless agony, I still can't believe my dream has dissolved, my special love curdled in front of my eyes — and partly by my own hand. Did my commitment to our cause turn out to be a form of neglect? Charlie met Ashley in New York, the very weekend jaunt I turned down in favour of following Meredith to Granada. Was I too busy moving our relationship on to remember to maintain it? Had I met him in New York instead, had I flown to meet him *anywhere* over the summer, this might never have happened, Ashley might never have happened.

But I forget one thing: it is Charlie's faith that failed, not mine; that's if it ever existed in the first place. What was it Viv said that Sunday morning in June when we first discussed the Meredith situation? 'Essentially the issue is that you're not good enough for her son.' Then she saw my face and added, 'In her eyes.' Maybe what she should have said was 'In *his* eyes.' Later, when I couldn't reconcile the Meredith

I'd met with the protagonist of Charlie's tales, there came that smothered query, 'Are you sure what he said was true?' And wasn't this, in turn, just an echo of Maggie's sentiment that night after the Friends' drinks party? 'If you're sure he's worth it.' Or a dozen doubts voiced over the past year by my own father? They all saw what I wasn't ready to see. Charlie is weak. This is his flaw. Even so, it's hard for a heart to process the shift from present tense to past in less than a day. The overnight break was wise, however; at least my crying is done.

I turn to him, where he sits in silence at the far end of the sofa, waiting to hear my verdict and to deliver his own, unsure of which will come first. He is subdued now, knows his wrong is greater than mine; that anger of last night was born of shock.

'I loved you,' I say, with a strange blankness, as though I'm interpreting the message for a third party who doesn't speak English. 'I thought you loved me.'

'I do, Anna, but . . . '

'But you rather like someone else, too?' I'm looking at him with a kind of fascination; the concept of 'us' seems so very abstract now. We will never again lie together naked, he will never take my wrists and press them into the pillow above my head as I squirm in delighted submission. Our intimacy is gone for ever, and though I am certain it is right to be gone, its absence doesn't yet feel real.

Charlie clears his throat. 'You know, I haven't lied to you any more than you've lied to me.'

461

I give a short laugh. 'I may have lied to you, Charlie, but I haven't *betrayed* you.'

'No.'

I wait for the follow-up deflection, the next slippery denial, for there will be one; it's second nature to him. But instead, for once, he stays silent, just stares at his shoes, and I know in that moment that he's not going to fight for me. A part of me is relieved — even if Ashley were to be sent home on the next plane to JFK we could never have continued, could never have got over this — but a part of me is knocked right off my feet with the pain.

'I need you to tell me about Ashley. Are you in love with her?'

There's a pause. 'No.'

'What's she doing here, then?'

I've been over this all night long. Meredith said Charlie had mentioned someone special, and for him to use that word about another woman to his mother she would have to be pretty damn *super*-special. He *must* think that he's in love with her. It must feel different from everything — everyone — that has gone before. Either he's trying to spare my feelings by denying the strength of his own or he's playing some sort of game with both of us. Nothing is made clearer by the snippets of their three-week history he now shares with me: Gemma asked her old college friend back East to show him around the art museums in New York and that friend was Ashley (I *knew* Gemma wasn't to be trusted); they felt an 'odd connection' and didn't know what to do about it (ignore it, dear, what do you think fidelity *means*?); Ashley is a graduate student who would like to start her own fashion business and is famous among her friends for her customised denim (*everyone* is famous among her *friends*); when he invited her to London he thought her decision to accept or decline would help him make up his own mind, but she's here (of course she is, Charlie, it's *you*, one of the most attractive men in the British Isles) and he feels no less confused. Or so he says. He doesn't know what will happen next but he realises that it's too much to expect me to wait around while he finds out.

'Thoughtful of you,' I say, icily.

At this point his eyes brim with tears and plead with mine. I cannot believe he is doing that male thing of killing you and then asking for your comfort because murder feels so much lousier than he expected. And I can't believe a nerve ending somewhere unidentifiable actually twinges in his direction. How I wish I could locate it and snap it off, right there in front of him.

'You're a bastard, Charlie, don't pretend to be anything better.'

Again, he nods in meek acceptance. My grip on Meredith's invitation tightens still. It's funny, but I always had an idea that my plans would rework themselves somehow, take on a life of their own. Trying to be two different people, there was always a chance I might split the vote. But throughout it all I never once doubted my intentions, never once doubted that I acted for

Charlie as well as for myself, spoke for him, *deceived* for him.

'Tell me something, Charlie. If you hadn't met Ashley and brought her home with you, how would you have reacted when you saw me last night?' I watch those brown eyes closely; I want the truth.

'I don't know,' he says, finally. 'It's not just her, it really isn't. I've been thinking, Anna, and . . . Well, we just don't want the same things, do we? We never have.'

I frown. 'We want each other, don't we? At least, that's what I thought until last night.'

He shakes his head. 'No, I mean long term.'

'I haven't been allowed to *think* long term,' I protest, hating that my argument echoes Jessica's and that he's probably had this conversation before. In the end, they split quite suddenly, Charlie and Jessica. Before me, months before me; I couldn't bear to have been the Ashley. 'Give me an example,' I demand.

He shrugs. 'Well, for one thing, you don't want children.'

I stare. 'Nor do you.'

'Yes, I do,' Charlie says.

'You do?'

'Yes, of course I do. Not *now*, but at some point. I want a family life and a family house and a family car and a family to go in them.' He gets up and joins me at the window, looking down at the deserted street below. 'Not this . . . this *sterility*.'

I have no idea what to say to this. This is certainly no reprise of any conversation with

464

Jessica. So my flat, my life, my body, we're *sterile*, are we?

'Well,' I say, edging closer, my face inches from his, the snarl on my lips meeting a tremble of distress. 'Not that it's anything to do with you any more, but I haven't ruled all that stuff out totally either.'

He looks straight at me. 'You have, Anna. You know you have.' Then he turns and goes to sit back down and when he next speaks it is theatrically, into the space in front of him, as though facing me again will blind him. 'You think I've caused all this . . . ' His voice ruptures but he continues, hoarse, 'That I've made things more difficult than they should have been, but you're not that simple yourself, you know.'

'Go on,' I say, stonily.

'Your work for one thing. You're *obsessed*, Anna.'

'We all are. Name someone our age who isn't. Go on?'

'But with you it's not in a healthy way. It's under your skin like, I don't know, like ringworm.'

'For your information,' I say, quietly, 'I've resigned. I left on Thursday. Thanks for the ringworm analogy, though. Very nice.'

Now he looks up, face pinched in amazement. 'That's incredible. What happened?'

I start to tell him but tales of Simon and Nigel and Paul seem meaningless now and neither of us wants to prolong this with a discussion of my career prospects, especially as he won't be around to share them, so I don't protest when he interrupts.

'There, you see, I have no idea what's going on with you. We've become strangers.'

I feel my temper flaring at the triumph in his tone and it's remarkable I don't leap forward and punch him. 'You've been out of the country, Charlie! That's hardly my fault. God, to think I've spent this whole summer . . . '

He blinks, eyes rather drier now. 'This whole summer what?'

I catch myself. I wouldn't give him the satisfaction of knowing. 'Thinking about you, thinking of ways we can be together without all those complications. I must have been mad! When I met Meredith and she seemed to like me I thought you'd be so pleased . . . It seemed like the dream solution.'

He shuffles forward in his seat and I stand, arms folded, right in front of him, forcing him to look steeply up at me. 'Anna, listen to me. Whatever you think you know about her, however friendly you've become, I can assure you it would be totally different if you were presented to her as my girlfriend. You obviously won't take my word for it, but I really do know what I'm talking about. With Jessica — '

'But this is different from you and Jessica,' I break in. 'It's different from us before. Don't you get it? She thinks *she's* bringing us together!' It seems important to defend Meredith, as well as myself, but in reverting to the present tense, I sense the balance of power shifting away from me and I find I can't stop it. 'If it's her idea, how

466

could she possibly disapprove? You heard her say we should meet up — '

He cuts in. 'Only as a decoy for Ashley.'

'What?' I clutch the invitation so hard it dog-ears in my hand. 'Don't be ridiculous.'

He's shaking his head as though he'll never get through to me. Then, spotting the card, he grabs it from me and says, 'Tell me, when did you get this stupid thing? When, exactly?'

*Stupid thing!* Reeling, I try to think. 'Last week.'

'OK, last week. Which day?'

'Tuesday, I think.'

He leaps up, almost overbalancing with the force. 'Well, if I told you it was Monday when I spoke to my mother and mentioned I had someone I wanted her to meet, would you start to see what's going on here? You got the invite on Tuesday — I bet she sent it first class.' He reads aloud the note on the back, ' 'I am so looking forward to introducing you to my son Charlie',' and adds a nasty little 'pah' of contempt. 'It's so obvious, Anna! She was lining you up as kind of a spoiler.'

'So what?' I cry. 'It doesn't matter what her motives were, or anyone's. If we got together and she didn't oppose it, then that's all we want . . . wanted. Wasn't it?'

Charlie looks down. 'It's too late.'

'I think you'll find I'm the one entitled to make that call.'

'Whatever.'

I loathe him, loathe his smugness, his self-conscious tear-blinking. It's as though he's

467

heard that this sort of experience is normally quite distressing and is acting the part required of it. I step right forward until our bodies are almost touching. 'You know what I think, Charlie? I think you were *never* worried Meredith wouldn't like me, you just weren't serious enough about me to bother trying.' And again I hear Jessica: *I know how hard it is when you're in the middle of it to see how things really are . . .*

'That's rubbish,' Charlie says. 'I *was* worried, of course I was.'

And the easiness of that past tense is like a fist in my side.

'What I don't understand is why you were ever going out with me if you didn't want to give me . . . *everything*? Why not end it sooner?'

'I did give you everything,' he says. 'Everything I can . . . ' He trails off and there's a long silence as I digest this half-admission, possibly the most profound expression of self-awareness the man has ever uttered. He *was* giving everything, everything he was able to give. The problem is he doesn't possess the full human quota of 'everything'. Viv would have some cod-psychological label for his emotional inadequacies, but I know exactly what it is in layman's terms: not good enough.

I glare at him. 'Who would have thought I'd be good enough for Meredith, just not good enough for *you*.'

His eyes are pleading again. 'Of course you're good enough for me. Too good.'

Now I really have heard enough. 'You know what, Charlie? You're right. It *is* too late. Ashley is welcome to you; you can tell her that from me.'

He closes his eyes. 'Don't do this, Anna.'

'Do what? Break up with you? I think you've done that for me.'

'I mean don't hate me.'

'I wouldn't waste my energy.' I march to the front door and pull it open, waiting, but he's still standing there by the sofa, won't stop shaking his head. He's not distraught, he's not torn in two; he just doesn't want to be the bad guy in this. I thought he was so complete, that those passions for buildings and bridges and lidos and roof gardens represented a passion for the people who used them. But they didn't; they merely filled the empty space. And in the end Meredith didn't stop me getting to the real Charlie; no, she made the real Charlie more interesting than he actually was.

'Are you going to keep in touch with my mother?' he asks me, in the hallway now.

'That's none of your business.'

'I really think . . . '

Now it's my turn to 'pah' with contempt. 'I'm afraid I don't care what you *really* think.'

He lingers, floundering, confused.

'Go, Charlie. *Please.*'

He stands there for a moment, arms just hanging; then he leaves.

★  ★  ★

My father has come to meet me for a river walk. He says he needs to escape from the chaos of preparations for next weekend's anniversary party, now a full-scale Indian summer extravaganza with jazz band, a lifeguard for the pool (weather permitting, there's to be drunken swimming) and an actor from some hit CBeebies show to entertain the kiddies. I haven't yet told him that I'm on garden leave, as it will only lead to protracted discussions about my joining him in his business, which is the last thing I want to do. When you only have one parent you don't need him to be your employer as well. In any case, I have an instinct about what's next for me. Dulwich needs someone to run its new lottery bid. Humphrey has been approached, but he doesn't have the time, what with his golf commitments. I, on the other hand, have no plans to take up golf.

Dad tells me that the new baby is going to be a boy.

'That's wonderful,' I say, ashamed to be relieved by the news. I reach out to touch him, but he's moved his arm to check his watch and my hand makes contact with his jacket pocket instead.

He turns back. 'You're still my girl, you know, Annie.'

I can tell he's not looking at me so it doesn't matter that I'm not looking at him either. 'I know.'

'And Charlie is a fool.' Always was, he's itching to add.

'I know,' I repeat. Always will be.

470

He picks up his car at the end of Wapping High Street and I start to walk the rest of the way home on my own. I pull the envelope out of my pocket as I've been itching to do since leaving the flat two hours ago. The postmark is the same as it was when I retrieved it from the daybook the moment Charlie left: 11 September. Meredith posted my invitation on the Saturday before I received it, two days before Charlie hinted to her of new romance. She invited me to her party and introduced me to her son for no other reason than that she wanted to. I was her sort of person.

Caro calls and I confirm that Charlie and I are no longer Charlie and I. She is sorry but not surprised. She tells me that when I was upstairs with him at the party she took the opportunity to grill the girl (well practised by now, she even slipped into the loo afterwards to make notes). Having not been fully briefed by her man (now there's a surprise), Ashley didn't have a clue who Caro was and spoke to her quite freely. Much of her account matches Charlie's, but there is a telling difference in tone. She is crazy in love and has no reason to hide the fact. She never expected to fall for an Englishman, knew it was a mad, impossible thing, like something out of the movies, but when Charlie bought her a ticket at the last minute she had a once-in-a-lifetime hunch to go for it. (A year and three months I waited for the invitation; she gets it after three weeks!) She didn't know much about Meredith before she arrived but her first impression was that her hostess seemed 'very British'. She and

Charlie are planning a weekend in Valencia before she flies back to New York; he says he wants her to meet 'everyone'.

'He probably didn't mean us, though,' Caro chuckles.

'Do you think she even knew about me?' I ask.

'Well, I said I'd heard he was seeing someone in London and she said yes, he was, but it had fizzled out before he left.'

'Before he left? He is unbelievable.'

'She's very New Age spiritual,' Caro reports, disapprovingly. 'She told me she isn't going to have any expectations; she's just going to let the relationship grow organically.'

I pull a face into my phone. *Organically?* That's exactly the word Jojo used to trot out when giving me the benefit of her wisdom on winning Charlie.

'D'you think that's where I went wrong?' I ask.

'What?'

'Using too many pesticides, wanting to make it too perfect?'

'Men need pesticides,' Caro says. 'You just wanted to make the whole thing normal. This isn't your fault at all, babe, it's his and *hers*. He's a bastard and she's . . . '

'She was perfectly sweet,' I say, truthfully. 'You know, in another situation we'd probably quite like her, buy a pair of her jeans or something.'

'I would *never* wear customised jeans,' Caro says. 'I made that decision a long time ago.'

I laugh and laugh and find I can't stop. At the other end of the line Caro waits patiently.

'Drop by later if you like. We've got a new

cocktail-shaker thingy that you don't actually have to shake and Angus is coming over.'

'Thanks, I might.'

'This will be OK, you know.'

'I know. Actually, I feel good, like I'm accidentally on holiday.'

She knows exactly what I mean. 'It has all been a bit labour-intensive, hasn't it? But there's nothing more you can do. You'll have to start a charm *defensive*.'

'Now there's a good idea.'

We hang up. Before I turn away from the river for my building, I glance at the water and find myself doing a double take. A moment ago it was that shade of sludge you get when a whole palette of pigments are mixed together and lost in each other. Now, just for a moment, I can see the individual colours.

We do hope that you have enjoyed reading this large print book.

Did you know that all of our titles are available for purchase?

We publish a wide range of high quality large print books including:

**Romances, Mysteries, Classics**
**General Fiction**
**Non Fiction and Westerns**

Special interest titles available in large print are:

**The Little Oxford Dictionary**
**Music Book**
**Song Book**
**Hymn Book**
**Service Book**

Also available from us courtesy of Oxford University Press:

**Young Readers' Dictionary**
**(large print edition)**
**Young Readers' Thesaurus**
**(large print edition)**

For further information or a free brochure, please contact us at:

**Ulverscroft Large Print Books Ltd.,**
**The Green, Bradgate Road, Anstey,**
**Leicester, LE7 7FU, England.**
**Tel:** (00 44) 0116 236 4325
**Fax:** (00 44) 0116 234 0205

*Other titles published by*
*The House of Ulverscroft:*

## SEEDS OF GREATNESS

### Jon Canter

Two friends grow up in a North London Jewish suburb. Whilst wayward Jack gets expelled from school, David, the bright one, is destined for great things. But it's Jack who gets rich and famous as a TV chat-show host, while David works in a bookshop. When Jack dies, his widow and publisher commission David to write Jack's authorised biography, confident it will be nice and bland. But David writes Seeds of Greatness instead . . . The story of his friendship with Jack, it's got sex, drugs, blackmail, and jealousy. David knows it can never be published — he thinks that writing the truth will get Jack out of his system. But he'll never be free of Jack. Jack will be with him for as long as he lives . . .

# DIVIDED LOYALTIES

## Patricia Scanlan

Shauna and Greg's marriage is under pressure. She also has to endure her obnoxious in-laws, Della and Eddie, and their spoilt daughter. They arrive at her home, stay as long as they like, and eat and drink everything. Shauna's glad to be moving abroad to be free of them . . . Meanwhile, Carrie, Shauna's sister, bears the burden of looking after their elderly father Noel — and she's fed up. Will Carrie stand up for herself at long last . . . ? Noel has always blamed Bobby, Shauna and Carrie's younger brother, for the premature death of their mother. Can they ever settle their differences? The last Christmas the family got together was a disaster. But can they finally put the past behind them as they prepare for another family gathering?

# THE ABORTIONIST'S DAUGHTER

## Elisabeth Hyde

Living in a small town in Colorado, nineteen-year-old university student Megan Thompson is beautiful, cool, and sexy — the kind of girl boys fall in love with. She's steered clear of family life since the death of her younger brother . . . until the day she hears her mother, Diana, has been found floating face down in their swimming pool. Diana, as Director of the Center for Reproductive Choice, was a national figure who inspired passions — and made enemies. Detective Huck Berlin is brought in to investigate when it becomes clear that Diana was murdered. Several people had quarrelled with Diana on that fateful day, including her husband Frank, and her wayward child. Now father and daughter are thrown together in an unexpected twist of family life.

# ANYBODY OUT THERE?

## Marian Keyes

Anna Walsh is a wreck. Physically broken and emotionally shattered, she lies on her parents' Dublin sofa with only one thing on her mind: getting back to New York. New York means her best friends, The Best Job In The World™ and, above all, it means her husband, Aidan. But nothing in Anna's life is that simple any more: not only is her return to Manhattan complicated by her physical and emotional scars, but Aidan seems to have vanished. Is it time for Anna to move on? Is it even possible for her to move on? A motley group of misfits, an earth-shattering revelation, two births and one very weird wedding might help Anna find some answers — and change her life for ever.